The Dialogue of
PYAASA

The Dialogue of

PYAASA

Guru Dutt's Immortal Classic

Dialogue: Abrar Alvi
Lyrics/poetry: Sahir Ludhianvi

Original dialogue transcribed in Urdu & Roman scripts: Suhail Akhtar
Original dialogue transcribed in Hindi: Vijay Jani

Concept, introduction, translation & commentary: Nasreen Munni Kabir

OM
Om Books International

hyphen
f i l m s

Published by

Om Books International

Corporate & Editorial Office
A-12, Sector 64, Noida 201 301, Uttar Pradesh, India
Phone: +91 120 477 4100

Sales Office
4379/4B, Prakash House, Ansari Road, Darya Ganj, New Delhi 110 002, India
Phone: +91 11 2326 3363, 2326 5303   Fax: +91 11 2327 8091
Email: sales@ombooks.com
Website: www.ombooks.com

Screenplay, Dialogue & Songs © GDF Enterprise
All visual materials from the film *Pyaasa* © GDF Enterprise
Introduction and commentary © Nasreen Munni Kabir
English Translation of Dialogue/Songs © Nasreen Munni Kabir

Editor: Dipa Chaudhuri
Introduction/commentary editors: Shameem Kabir & Dipa Chaudhuri
Design: Vijay Jani

ISBN: 978-93-80070-53-7

Year of Publication: 2011

Printed in India by Gopsons Papers Ltd., Noida

CONTENTS

Pyaasa: A meeting of minds and hearts: Nasreen Munni Kabir   vi

The Dialogue of *Pyaasa:* Guru Dutt's Immortal Classic   I
By Abrar Alvi
Songs/poems by Sahir Ludhianvi

Film Credits   194

Commentary   196

Bibliography   213

Guru Dutt as the poet Vijay on the banks of the Hooghly River, Calcutta.

Pyaasa

A meeting of hearts and minds

The talent and tragedy of Guru Dutt continue to fascinate people since the day he committed suicide on 10 October 1964, at the age of thirty-nine. In a brief career spanning thirteen years, starting with *Baazi* in 1951, he made many wonderful films, including crime thrillers, comedies and melodramas. But it is *Pyaasa,* a deeply personal film that is regarded as his most significant work. Sophisticated cinematic language, fine dialogue, stunning songs, social edge and a melancholic tone characterise it. Ranked among *Time* magazine's top 100 films of all time, audiences the world over who have seen *Pyaasa* are drawn to learning more because it is a film on par with the great classics of world cinema.

Unlike many of his contemporaries, Guru Dutt is among the most documented director of Hindi popular cinema. Essays, articles and several books (including the biography I wrote, first published in 1996), speak of his tragically short life and the enduring impact of his work. Given France's love for cinema, it is not surprising that one of the early seminal pieces on Guru Dutt is by French critic Henri Micciollo, who recognised his unique talent in 1976, years before his film legacy returned to the limelight. Micciollo adored the film and also had special praise for the director's acting skills: "Today it is difficult to imagine *Pyaasa* without Guru Dutt. His acting has none of the mannerisms of well-known professional actors. He is at all times discreet, sensitive, underplaying the role. In the context of Hindi cinema, he is an actor way ahead of his time." (Micciollo, "Guru Dutt," *Anthologie du Cinéma, L'Avant-Scène,* Tome IX, Paris, 1976.)

Variously translated as "The Thirsty One" and "The Thirsting," *Pyaasa* is the story of Vijay (Guru Dutt), a poet in Calcutta whose Urdu poetry is rejected by all. His college sweetheart Meena (Mala Sinha) decides to abandon her impoverished lover in favour of a marriage of convenience to the well-off publisher Ghosh (Rehman). When Vijay's mother (Leela Misra) dies, his money-grabbing brothers (Radheshyam and Mehmood) close the family door on him. An old college friend Shyam (Shyam Kapoor) is also happy to betray the poet when it suits him. The only redeeming examples of humanity are his friend Abdul Sattar (Johnny Walker) the masseur, and Gulaab (Waheeda Rehman), a young prostitute.

Frustrated by the constant rebuttal of the world and driven to despair, Vijay contemplates suicide. He makes his way to the railway tracks but changes his mind at the last minute. An aged beggar, who has followed him, gets caught in the track switch and falls under the oncoming train. The beggar's mutilated body is mistaken for Vijay and everyone believes the poet has committed suicide. Distraught, Gulaab persuades Ghosh to have Vijay's poetry published and his book of poems becomes the talk of the town.

(l) Waheeda Rehman as Gulaab and Mala Sinha as Meena.

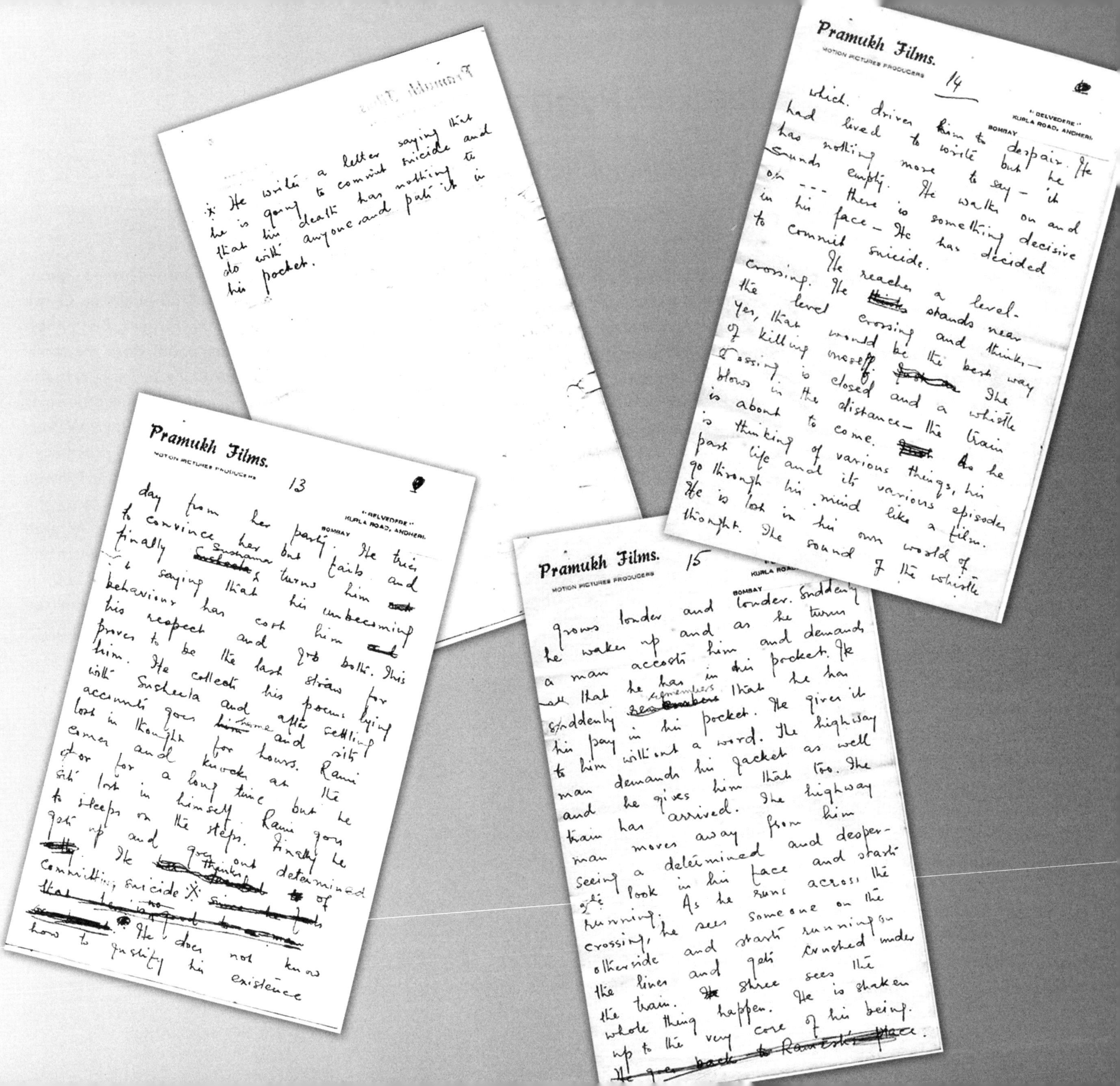

Pramukh Films.
MOTION PICTURES PRODUCERS
13
"BELVEDERE" KURLA ROAD, ANDHERI, BOMBAY

day from her party. He tries to convince her but fails and finally ~~Susheela~~ Sushama turns him out saying that his unbecoming behaviour has cost him his respect and job both. This proves to be the last straw for him. He collects his poems lying with Susheela and after settling accounts goes home and sits lost in thought for hours. Rani comes and knocks at the door for a long time but he sits lost in himself. Rani goes to sleep on the steps. Finally he gets up and goes out determined of committing suicide X. He does not know how to justify his existence

X He writes a letter saying that he is going to commit suicide and that his death has nothing to do with anyone and puts it in his pocket.

Pramukh Films.
MOTION PICTURES PRODUCERS
14
"BELVEDERE" KURLA ROAD, ANDHERI, BOMBAY

which drives him to despair. He had lived to write but he has nothing more to say – it sounds empty. He walks on and on --- there is something decisive in his face – He has decided to commit suicide.

He reaches a level-crossing. He ~~thinks~~ stands near the level crossing and thinks – Yes, that would be the best way of killing oneself. The crossing is closed and a whistle blows in the distance – the train is about to come. As he is thinking of various things, his past life and its various episodes go through his mind like a film. He is lost in his own world of thought. The sound of the whistle

Pramukh Films.
MOTION PICTURES PRODUCERS
15
KURLA ROAD, ANDHERI, BOMBAY

grows louder and louder. Suddenly he wakes up and as he turns a man accosts him and demands all that he has in his pocket. He suddenly ~~Remembers~~ remembers that he has his pay in his pocket. He gives it to him without a word. The highway man demands his jacket as well and he gives him that too. The train has arrived. The highway man moves away from him seeing a determined and desperate look in his face and starts running. As he runs across the crossing, he sees someone on the other side and starts running on the lines and gets crushed under the train. ~~He~~ Shree sees the whole thing happen. He is shaken up to the very core of his being. ~~He goes back to Ramesh's place.~~

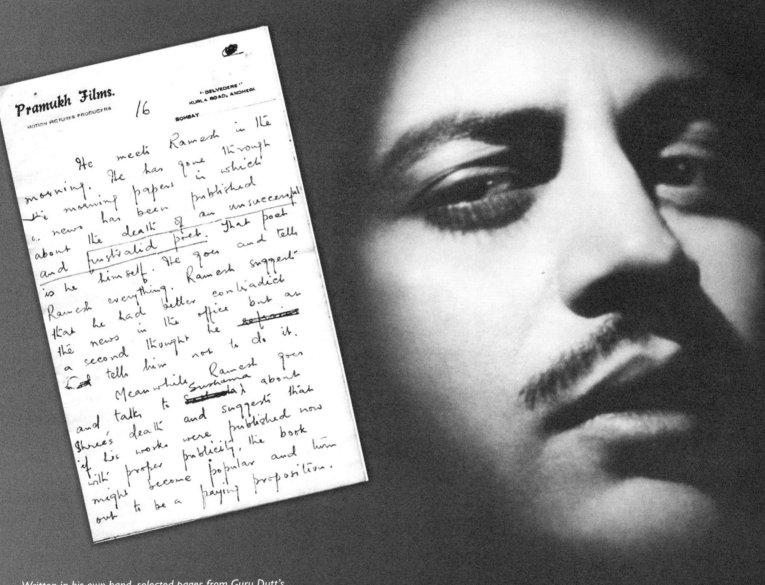

Pramukh Films.

MOTION PICTURES PRODUCERS

16

"BELVEDERE"
KURLA ROAD, ANDHERI

BOMBAY

He meets Ramesh in the
morning. He has gone through
the morning papers in which
a news has been published
about the death of an unsuccessful
and ~~frustrated poet~~. That poet
is he himself. He goes and tells
Ramesh everything. Ramesh suggests
that he had better contradict
the news in the office but on
a second thought he ~~refuses~~
~~and~~ tells him not to do it.
Meanwhile Ramesh goes
and talks to ~~Sushama~~ about
Shree's death and suggests that
if his works were published now
with proper publicity, the book
might become popular and him
out to be a paying proposition.

Written in his own hand, selected pages from Guru Dutt's
original story "Kash-ma-kash" on which Pyaasa is loosely based.
Documents preseved by his son Arun Dutt.

A rare still of Johnny Walker originally cast as the treacherous Shyam.

Rehman and Mala Sinha in a still from a deleted scene.

A publicity still of Johnny Walker and Kum Kum.

Meanwhile recovering in hospital, Vijay discovers his poetry has finally been published to much acclaim. But the greedy Ghosh and Shyam do not want to share the spoils and so disown him. They have him incarcerated in a mental asylum as an imposter.

At a gathering held to commemorate the poet's first death anniversary, Vijay resurfaces, having managed to escape from the mental asylum with the help of Abdul Sattar. Vijay sings a moving song decrying the world's hypocrisy. Ghosh attempts to get rid of Vijay once again but it is too late. Another grand event is held to celebrate the return of the dead poet and much to the amazement of his phony well-wishers, Vijay announces that he is not the Vijay they seek. Affectionate again, Meena tries to persuade him to take the riches on offer but he refuses. *Pyaasa* ends with a shot of Vijay and Gulaab walking away hand in hand to a place from where, in Vijay's words, he "shall not need to go further."

Gurudutt Padukone was born into a Saraswat family in Bangalore on 9 July 1925. He later dropped his surname and became known only as Guru Dutt. As Dutt is a common Bengali surname, many assumed he was from Bengal. Bengali culture was indeed an integral aspect of his personality as he had spent much of his childhood in Calcutta, living there from the ages of five to seventeen. Guru Dutt was initially drawn to choreography and photography, and thanks to his maternal uncle, B.B. Benegal, he won a scholarship to train as a dancer under Uday Shankar. But soon his interest in choreography was replaced by his passion for cinema.

Guru Dutt worked as an assistant director and choreographer before he finally managed to direct his first film *Baazi*, produced by his friend Dev Anand in 1951, and written by Balraj Sahni. This enjoyable crime thriller showed the many skills (dance, photography, direction) he had learned along the way. The film was hugely important to Guru Dutt for personal reasons too, as it brought Geeta Roy, a gifted playback singer, into his life. During the

Geeta Dutt (1961). Photograph: Wolf Suschitzky.

recording of the *Baazi* song "Tadbeer se bigdi hui taqdeer bana le," he met and fell in love with her and two years later, in 1953, they were married.

Geeta Dutt passed away eight years after her husband, at the tragically young age of forty-two. Her contribution to her husband's films was enormous. She added melancholy and atmosphere to his work through her remarkable singing. Though they were said to have had a stormy marriage, they were deeply attached to one other. Their eldest son Tarun passed away on 1 January 1989, aged thirty-four. Their second son Arun Dutt (born in 1956) is soon opening an acting academy in Pune in his father's name. Their daughter Nina (born in 1963) has now settled in Mumbai with her family.

Following *Baazi* (1951), Guru Dutt gradually developed a masterly touch on how to tell stories through cinema. He started his own film company by 1954 with *Aar Paar* and was producing, directing and now acting. Guru Dutt's first lead role was in his 1953 *Baaz*. It was not unusual for directors to also act, as Indian cinema has other early examples of actor-director-producer combinations in V. Shantaram and Raj Kapoor. When his fifth film as director, *Mr & Mrs 55* (1955), did well at the box-office, Guru Dutt was ready to make the film he had previously discussed with many colleagues who initially persuaded him to wait till the time was right. The idea of the film was based on a story he had written sometime in 1948/49 when struggling to find work. Guru Dutt's mother, the

Kannada writer, Vasanthi Padukone, remembers their life in their modest two-room flat in Matunga, Bombay: "Gurudutt knocked at many studio doors to get a chance by meeting several well-known producers. He even went to Madras to Gemini Studios and others. During this period of struggle and stress he wrote his experiences. Its original name was 'Kash-ma-kash' [Struggle], which was changed later to *Pyaasa*." (Padukone, *Imprint*, April 1979, Bombay.)

Despite the link between his story and *Pyaasa*, Guru Dutt does not have a story or screenplay credit in the film — possibly because the plot lines had changed and new characters had been added by the time the film went into production. But what remains at the heart of both works are the frustrations and torment of unrecognised artists. Guru Dutt's sister, the well-known painter, Lalitha Lajmi, believes their father's ordeals are echoed in *Pyaasa*: "My father was a poet. Amma [Mother] told me when I was born in Calcutta, he was editing a poetry journal and some of his work was published. But one could not live on poetry so he worked at Burma Shell as an accounts clerk and never rose to be an officer. My father was not an ambitious man and was unaware of success. And I am sure the poet in *Pyaasa* must have been written with my father in mind. The youngest of ten brothers and three sisters, my father was from a large, intellectual and artistic family. Among his brothers were a sculptor, a well-known photographer and painter, and an actor. Another of his brothers was Swami Ramdas, who had an *ashram* in a small place called Kanhangad near Mangalore. During World War II, when the Japanese were set to invade Calcutta, father decided to send us to my uncle's *ashram* for eight months. My father was then later transferred to Bombay. At that time, my brother Gurudutt received a scholarship to join Uday Shankar's Dance Academy in Almora. And so our family came to Bombay in 1942 during the Quit India movement. It was the time of the freedom struggle and Amma, being very patriotic, inspired us to learn how to spin a Gandhian *charkha* [spinning wheel]. We used to live in Matunga and

(l to r) Tarun, Arun, Guru Dutt and Geeta Dutt (1961). Photograph: Wolf Suschitzky.

those were days of great struggle for all the family." (Lajmi, interview by NMK, October 2010.)

From the start, Guru Dutt knew that creative work comes from a creative team. In directing *Baazi,* his connection was made with composer S.D. Burman, poet/lyricist Sahir Ludhianvi, Johnny Walker, Raj Khosla, editor Y.G. Chawhan, and production-in-charge S. Guruswamy. He also met cinematographer V.K. Murthy who was an assistant cameraman on *Baazi,* and recognised Murthy's talent and desire to push the boundaries of film photography: "Guru Dutt had a jeweller's eye. He knew how to pick the diamonds." (Murthy, interview by NMK, 1987.)

The songs by Sahir Ludhianvi and Majrooh Sultanpuri in the early Guru Dutt films are superb, but the screenplay and dialogue of the movies are not remarkable. Guru Dutt still needed to find a good writer. It was in 1952 that he met young Abrar Alvi who was visiting his cousin, actor Jaywant, on the sets of *Baaz.* A friend of Raj Khosla, Alvi was asked to rewrite a few scenes, as the original dialogue did not satisfy Guru Dutt. Though un-credited, Alvi's reworked lines ended up in *Baaz* (1953).

Though Abrar Alvi's father had wanted his son to study law, he had initially come to Bombay from Nagpur with dreams of becoming an actor. He appeared in a few minor roles, but soon abandoned acting. He credits Guru Dutt entirely for making him a screenplay writer. From his next film, *Aar Paar* (1954), Alvi, then twenty-seven, became Guru Dutt's regular writer, associate and close friend.

Despite the fact that many films by Guru Dutt are now over fifty years old, Abrar Alvi's dialogue shows no sign of sounding old and musty. Full of emotion, charm and wit, his language feels lived-in. Far removed from the stilted and somewhat theatrical language frequently used in films made till the early 1950s, he had a natural voice, adding the colloquial and regional when required. So, from the way Kalu (the hero of *Aar Paar*) speaks, we know he is

Writer/director Abrar Alvi (Bombay, 1988). Photograph: Peter Chappell.

from Madhya Pradesh, while Johnny Walker as Rustom is identified as a Parsee, not only by the character's name, but also by his witty turn of phrase.

Although Hindi cinema goes by the name of the language in which the films are made, it must be noted that the dialogue by Abrar Alvi (and the language of the majority of films, especially in the 1950s) was in fact Hindustani, a mix of the sister languages, Hindi and Urdu.

A literary movement starting in the 19th century strove to separate the two languages, and Hindi became Sanskritised and Urdu more Persianised. At India's Independence in 1947, the division grew further and Hindi became the official language, entering the school curriculum and used in state propaganda and on the radio. The well-known historian Ramachandra Guha writes: "Notably, the content of the movies also reflected their [Muslims] presence and contribution. Because so many scriptwriters and lyricists were Muslims, the language of the Bombay film — spoken or sung — was quite dissimilar to the stiff, formal, Sanskritised Hindi promoted by the state in independent India. Rather, it was closer to the colloquial Hindustani that these writers spoke, a language suffused with Urdu words and widely understood across the Indian heartland." (Guha, *India After Gandhi*, Picador, 2007, p. 729.)

Alvi gave his screen characters personality and flair. Perhaps it was the actor in him that helped him understand the difference between the written and the spoken. Johnny Walker's hilarious conversations, and the moving exchanges between Vijay and Gulaab bear this out. Abrar Alvi was subtle too. A marvellous example is when Pushpa meets Vijay, after some years have passed: she introduces her sons as Gullu and Fullu, adding that her husband's name is similar to theirs. When Vijay asks what she means, she does not reply. Alvi leaves the audience to

figure out that Pushpa probably means her husband is known as "Ullu" (fool), the obvious rhyme to her sons' names.

Guru Dutt and Abrar Alvi remain one of the great director-writer teams in Indian cinema. They shared a deep passion for work and got to know one another closely. "Guru Dutt was essentially a loner. In fact loneliness was an obsession with him. So much so that at times even his best of friends became intruders. Then he'd withdraw into himself and refuse to meet anybody…I had remarked a peculiar trait of his — he needed different friends for different moods. Take Johnny Walker for instance, he used to go hunting with him, for *gupshup* [chit-chat] he had Rehman, and others for merry-making…when he was disturbed, he sought me out. We used to spend hours together, sitting and drinking, and later, he would take me along everywhere — we even went to Europe together." (Alvi, *Memories* as told to Sushama Shelly, *Filmfare*, 16–31 December 1987.)

Abrar Alvi passed away in Mumbai on 18 November 2009. He will always be remembered for his modern, idiomatic use of Urdu. A sharp wit and smart puns are also evident in his work. This repartee between the publisher Shaikh and Vijay is a fine example:

Shaikh:
"Agar aap shaayer hain toh main gadha hoon."
If you're a poet, I'm a donkey.

Vijay:
"Ji. Agar aap apni taareef na bhi karte toh bhi main pehchaan jaata."
Obviously, but it's nice to hear you admit it.

The idea behind *The Dialogue of Pyaasa, Guru Dutt's Immortal Classic* is to preserve in book form the wonderful dialogue by

Abrar Alvi. But the dialogue is half the story, as *Pyaasa* benefits immeasurably from the poetic soul and political edge that come from the work of Sahir Ludhianvi.

Although Guru Dutt knew Sahir's talent in song writing from *Baazi* and *Jaal*, it was Raj Khosla, once dreaming of becoming a singer, who introduced Sahir's poetry to Guru Dutt: "Actually I was an admirer of Sahir saaheb right from college. I had noted a poem that he had written during his college days called 'Chakle,' and I sang it at college functions. The poem was 'Sana khwaan-e-taqdees-e-mashriq kahaan hain' [Where are they who sing praise of the East?]. This was the poem that Guru Dutt later picturised as 'Jinhen naaz hai Hind par vo kahaan hain' [Where are they who claim to be proud of India?]. The language of the refrain was simplified for the film because no one would understand the difficult Urdu of the original. I first came to Bombay wanting to become a singer. When I sang that song to Guru Dutt, he said: 'Raj, this is it! This is *Pyaasa*.' In the form of art, Sahir and he were very close, but they were not close personally." (Kabir, *Guru Dutt: A Life in Cinema*, Oxford, Delhi, 2005, p.128, new edition.)

Guru Dutt used some of Sahir's poems written years before *Pyaasa* was made, and in addition asked the poet to write new songs for the film. Sahir's pen name means "magician." He was born as Abdul Hai on 8 March 1921 into a rich Punjabi land-owning family of Ludhiana. Following the various marriages of his father, Fazaluddin Mohammed, his parents divorced. A long and acrimonious battle over the custody of their only son followed. His father eventually turned vindictive and threatened to have his son murdered rather than let him live with his estranged wife.

In an article, well-known scriptwriter Suraj Sanim gives an insight into the poet's early life: "Sahir, who was only a child, took his mother's side. His father couldn't bear this and threatened to either have him kidnapped or killed. His mother had to

employ security guards to protect him…he grew up suspicious of everyone…he could never trust anyone." (*Filmfare*, 16–31 August 1985.)

In his childhood Sahir lived in Ludhiana with his two young sisters and mother Sardar Begum in a maternal uncle's modest home near the railway tracks. Young Sahir is said to have spent hours at his window watching coal pickers working all day under the hot sun. Even as a young boy, he empathised with labourers and peasants and grew up loathing the feudal system, personified by his cruel father. He also came to understand and admire the strength of women, as he witnessed his mother challenge her powerful husband, and then face the resulting struggle to get by.

In an early interview, Sahir commented: "I never loved my father and lived with my maternal uncle. He was responsible for my education. My father was a grand landlord and from the start I hated the feudal system. What was engraved in my heart at that point was the terrible treatment that peasants continued to suffer at the hands of landlords." (Sahir, interview by writer Balwant Singh, Allahabad.)

Marxist ideology and a disenchantment with society and love is present in many of Sahir's songs and poems in *Pyaasa*, including the duet "Hum aap ki aankhon mein," written in question and answer form. Guru Dutt cleverly disguises this song as a gushy romantic number while Meena's lyrics point to a cold indifference to love. Childhood traumas and strong feelings about social inequality and injustice run through much of Sahir's work. An important song in *Pyaasa* is also replete with Sahir's sense of betrayal and distrust of human nature.

Ye duniya jahaan aadmi kuchh nahin hai
Wafa kuchh nahin dosti kuchh nahin hai

These drawings were featured in the original 1957 publicity booklet.

جانے کیا تونے کہی، جانے کیا میں نے سنی
بات کچھ بن ہی گئی، جانے کیا تونے کہی

سنتا ہاہٹ سی ہوئی، تھرتھراہٹ سی ہوئی
جاگ اٹھے خواب کئی، بات کچھ بن ہی گئی
جانے کیا تونے کہی . . . . . .

نین جھک جھک کے اٹھے، پاؤں رک رک کے اٹھے
آ گئی چال نئی، بات کچھ بن ہی گئی
جانے کیا تونے کہی . . . . . .

زلف شانے پہ گری، ایک خوشبو سی اڑی
کھل گئے راز کئی، بات کچھ بن ہی گئی
جانے کیا تونے کہی . . . . . .

گیتا دت

مالش . . . . تیل مالش . . . . چمپی . . . .

دکھے تیرا چکرائے یا دل ڈولا جائے
اچا پیارے پاس ہمارے، کاہے گھبرائے کاہے گھبرائے

تیل میرا ہے مشکی، گنجے رہے نہ خشکی
جس کے سر پہ ہاتھ پھرا دوں، چمکے قسمت اسکی
سن سن ارے بے پیاس، اس چمپی میں بڑے گن
لاکھ دکھوں کی ایک دوا ہے، کیوں نذ آزمائے
کاہے گھبرائے . . . . . .

پیار کا ہو جھگڑا یا بزنس کا ہو رگڑا! !
سب جھگڑوں کا بوجھ بنے جب ہاتھ پڑے اک نگوڑا
سن سن ارے بے ہوس، اس چمپی میں بڑے بڑے گن
لاکھ دکھوں کی ایک دوا ہے، کیوں نہ آزمائے
کاہے گھبرائے . . . . . .

نوکر ہو یا مالک، لیڈر ہو یا پبلک
اپنے آگے سبھی چھکے ہیں کیا راجا کیا سینک
سن سن ارے راجا سن، اس چمپی میں بڑے بڑے گن
لاکھ دکھوں کی ایک دوا ہے، کیوں نہ آزمائے
کاہے گھبرائے . . . . . .

محمد رفیع

جلنے والے جلتے جائیں
ہم نے تو جب کلیاں مانگیں، کانٹوں کا ہار ملا

خوشیوں کی منزل ڈھونڈی تو غم کی گرد ملی
چاہت کے نغمے چاہے تو آہ سرد ملی
دل کو بجھ کے دونا کر گیا، جو غم خوار ملا
پھر گیا ساحل پہ جتنا دے کے کرپی دو پل کا ساتھ
کس کو فرصت ہے جو تھکے دیوانوں کا ساتھ
ہم کو اپنا سایہ بھی اکثر بیزار ملا
جلنے والے جلتے جائیں . . .

اس کو ہی جینا کہتے ہیں اگر یوں ہی بیتے
اف نہ کریں گے، لب سی لیں گے، آنسو پی لیں گے
غم سے اب گھبرانا کیا، غم سو بار ملا
ہم نے تو جب کلیاں مانگیں، کانٹوں کا یار ملا
جلنے والے جلتے جائیں . . .

لتا منگیشکر

لڑکا: ہم آپ کی آنکھوں میں اس دل کو بسا دیں تو
لڑکی: ہم موند کے پلکوں کو، اس دل کو سزا دیں تو

لڑکا: ان زلفوں میں گوندھیں گے ہم پھول محبت کا
لڑکی: زلفوں کو جھٹک کر ہم یہ پھول گرا دیں تو
لڑکا: ہم آپ کی آنکھوں میں اس دل کو بسا دیں تو

لڑکا: ہم آپ کو خوابوں میں، لا لا کے ستائیں گے
لڑکی: ہم آپ کی آنکھوں سے نیندیں ہی اڑا دیں تو
لڑکا: ہم آپ کی آنکھوں میں اس دل کو بسا دیں تو

لڑکا: ہم آپ کے قدموں پر گر جائیں گے غش کھا کر
لڑکی: اس پہ بھی نہ ہم اپنے آنچل کی ہوا دیں تو
لڑکا: ہم آپ کی آنکھوں میں اس دل کو بسا دیں تو

گیتا دت اور محمد رفیع

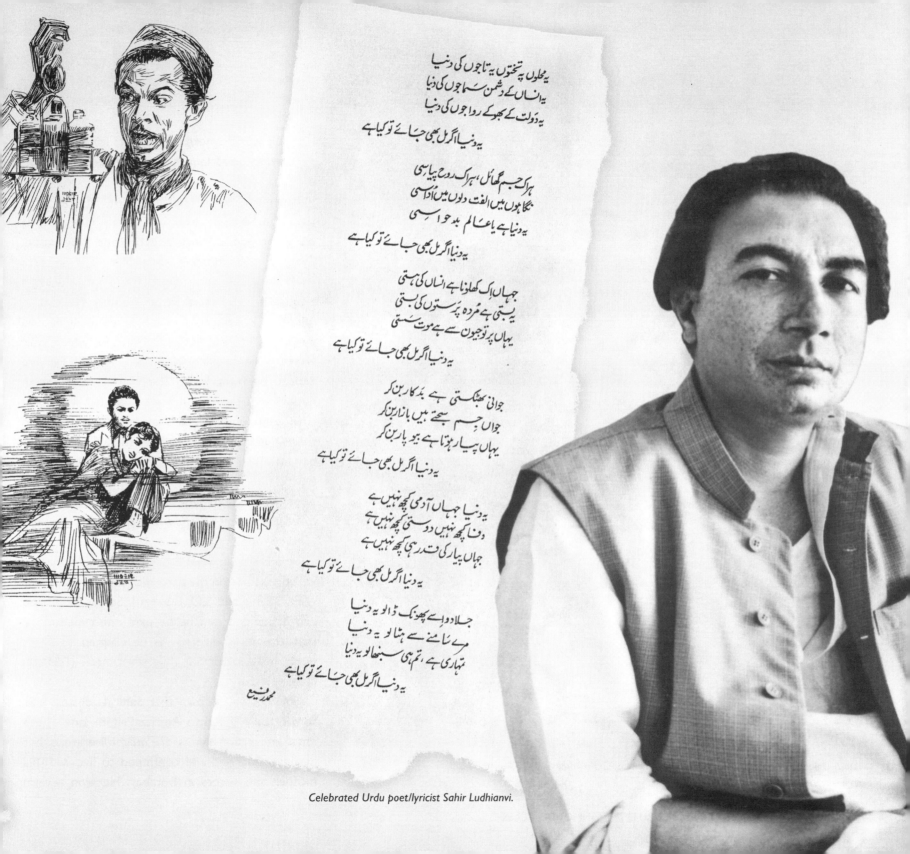

یہ محلوں پہ تختوں، یہ تاجوں کی دنیا
یہ انساں کے دشمن سماجوں کی دنیا
یہ دولت کے بھوکے رواجوں کی دنیا
یہ دنیا اگر مل بھی جائے تو کیا ہے

ہر اک جسم گھائل، ہر اک روح پیاسی
نگاہوں میں الفت، دلوں میں اداسی
یہ دنیا ہے یا عالم بدحواسی
یہ دنیا اگر مل بھی جائے تو کیا ہے

جہاں اِک کھلونا ہے انساں کی ہستی
یہ بستی ہے مردہ پرستوں کی بستی
یہاں پر تو جیون سے ہے موت سستی
یہ دنیا اگر مل بھی جائے تو کیا ہے

جوانی بھٹکتی ہے بدکار بن کر
جواں جسم سجتے ہیں بازار بن کر
یہاں پیار ہوتا ہے بیوپار بن کر
یہ دنیا اگر مل بھی جائے تو کیا ہے

یہ دنیا جہاں آدمی کچھ نہیں ہے
وفا کچھ نہیں دوستی کچھ نہیں ہے
جہاں پیار کی قدر ہی کچھ نہیں ہے
یہ دنیا اگر مل بھی جائے تو کیا ہے

جلا دو اسے پھونک ڈالو یہ دنیا
مرے سامنے سے ہٹا لو یہ دنیا
تمہاری ہے، تم ہی سنبھالو یہ دنیا
یہ دنیا اگر مل بھی جائے تو کیا ہے

محمد رفیع

Celebrated Urdu poet/lyricist Sahir Ludhianvi.

(l to r) Unidentified technician, boatman, Guru Dutt, S. Guruswamy and V.K. Murthy on a recce in Bengal.

This world where man counts for nothing
Loyalty and friendship count for nothing.

What made Sahir Ludhianvi one of the most significant lyricist ever of Indian cinema was his great poetic range and brilliant imagination. Even in a humorous song like "Sar jo tera chakraaye," he adds depth while introducing a political touch. Abdul Sattar (Johnny Walker), in full flight, is wonderful in this scene brought alive by Guru Dutt. But not all the films for which Sahir wrote were on par with *Pyaasa*, and in a *Filmfare* article, he remarked: "The trouble with Indian films is that they are more concerned with form than content. Producers lay great emphasis and lavish much expense on 'how to say' a thing, but pay little attention to 'what to say.' It was Guru Dutt's film, which gave adequate scope to my poetic talent, and following the success of the film, it led producers to show a willingness to accept literary songs." (*Filmfare*, 26 January 1962.)

Ironically it was *Pyaasa*, says Suraj Sanim, which "resulted in the parting of ways of these two giants [Sahir and S.D. Burman]. Sahir's king-sized ego demanded that he be paid one rupee more than the music director as he claimed his lyrics were more important than the tunes." (*Filmfare, op.cit.,* 1985.)

It was well known that Sahir Ludhianvi was romantically linked to Amrita Pritam, one of the most important names of Punjabi literature, but he never married and continued to live with his mother and sisters in Bombay. He won several

Several scenes of Pyaasa *were filmed on location in Calcutta during May and June 1956.*

sway. Burman approaches "Ye duniya agar…" in much the same way, ending the song with a dramatic crescendo that mirrors the rage the poet directs at a corrupt and ruthless society.

Unusual for the time, Guru Dutt had S.D. Burman compose recurring tunes (leitmotivs) for the film's main characters. The simple mouth organ tune (played by his son R.D. Burman) is Meena's musical theme, and underscoring Gulaab's key scenes, Burman uses an instrumental version of "Aaj sajan mohe ang laga lo." Besides the outstanding songs of the film, S.D. Burman's background score is one of the finest in Indian cinema.

Pyaasa is the result of the meeting of open hearts and gifted minds. From the set design (the excellent Biren Naug), the sound recording (S.V. Raman), to the extraordinary contribution of its actors — all excel. Who can ever forget the ethereal

awards, including the Padma Shri in 1971. He died of a heart attack in Bombay on 25 October 1980, at the age of sixty-one, while playing cards with his friend, Dr. R.P. Kapoor.

Aside from the film's extraordinary spoken and sung texts is Guru Dutt's sublime talent in creating many wordless scenes. Shots of the lonely Vijay wandering near the waterfront, or Gulaab trying to catch the windswept papers on which Vijay's poems are written, are there to create ambience. Guru Dutt is a master of suggestion. And S.D. Burman, a most exceptional and restrained composer, matched Guru Dutt's natural lightness of touch and depth of meaning.

S.D. Burman had an intuitive understanding of when music should dominate a scene and when not — a case in point is "Jinhen naaz hai Hind par." With minimal musical accompaniment, this compelling song/poem has the quiet ambience of a *mushaira* (poetry symposium). Mohammed Rafi's great agility and purity of voice foreground the words and allow their meanings to hold

(l to r) Film extra Hira, Johnny Walker and Guru Dutt.

M.R. Achrekar's portrait of Guru Dutt.

Waheeda Rehman who brilliantly underplays the most dramatic scenes, the sparkle of Johnny Walker, the quiet contempt of Rehman, the complexities of the flawed Meena so well brought out by Mala Sinha, and the restrained intensity of Guru Dutt?

Cinematographer V.K. Murthy's work is an equally active force in *Pyaasa*'s achievements. In India, and particularly in Guru Dutt's movies, Murthy's work can be compared to that of the great Chinese American cinematographer James Wong Howe. Howe was affectionately called "Low Key" thanks to his dramatic lighting and deep shadows, techniques that came to define the *film noir*. He was the first to use deep focus cinematography, in which foreground and distant planes remain in focus — and did this ten years before Gregg Toland *(Citizen Kane)*. An ace at framing close-ups, Murthy too is a recognised master of low-key lighting, producing depth and shadow. His lighting selectively illuminates the prominent features of a face, allowing us at once to enter the interiority of the characters.

In 1983, V.K. Murthy discussed the prevalent filming styles: "The style of shot-taking in early Indian cinema was similar to Hollywood action films. Most directors believed in mid-shots and long shots. Guru Dutt was the first to use the establishing or master shot followed by close-ups. Thereby the expression of the artist is highlighted and the story becomes immediately intimate, more like cinema, less like theatre. He was also the first person to use long focal length lens such as the 75mm and 100mm. These lenses are useful for close-ups and have the effect of creating movement. He was willing to take risks, to introduce new styles." (Kabir, *op.cit.*, p. 130.)

There are many truths and premonitions in *Pyaasa* that make it still relevant. Guru Dutt was right in the belief that some artists are fated to achieve posthumous glory — and this has been poignantly true of the admiration that Guru Dutt has won some forty-six years since he passed away in 1964, in a flat in

Ark Royal on Peddar Road in Bombay where he had lived alone for the last year of his life. But how many directors are there in the world who have achieved immortality through cinema? The poignancy and impact of *Pyaasa*'s evocative black and white images of billowing curtains, doors blown open by a gust of wind, and melancholic faces sculpted in light and shade will never diminish. Equally pertinent is his understanding of human failings. The world he descried, half a century ago, is not far removed from the one in which we live today — a world that largely rates materialism and monetary success above values and virtues. The search for a lost moral purity is at the heart of *Pyaasa*. On reflection perhaps the film's title could be translated as "The Seeker" rather than the literal "The Thirsty." Guru Dutt's eternal search was indeed for the impossible.

Mala Sinha as Meena on the set of the song "Hum aap ki aankhon mein."

Great film classics come from great writing and the aim of this book is to preserve the dialogue and poetry of Guru Dutt's compelling and perfect film. Suhail Akhtar has faithfully transcribed the entire dialogue and song lyrics from the original soundtrack and reproduced these in Urdu and Romanised Urdu. He has also helped in researching and identifying the source of Sahir's poems used in the film. The English translation attempts to give a flavour of the original dialogue and particular attention has been paid to the translation of the songs. The elegant and uncluttered layout and design are by Vijay Jani who is also responsible for carefully transcribing the texts in Hindi.

Drawing from the original 1957 publicity booklet of the film.

The intention here is to bring together in a single publication the complete dialogue and songs, so as to fully appreciate their extraordinary depth; and in the commentary and introduction, to provide a fresh in-depth look at *Pyaasa* by pulling together detailed reference material, personal views, anecdotal insights, film analysis and history, which would otherwise be lost. Researchers and historians know of the joy experienced when a previously overlooked fact is unearthed. This joy of discovery was mine, when curious about whether the *Life* magazine that Meena (Mala Sinha) reads was a genuine copy, or a fabrication for the scene in which she hears about the hero Vijay's suicide, led me to find that *Life* did indeed publish a "Special Issue on Christianity," with the cover image of Christ on the Cross. Interested in all religions, Guru Dutt would have seen this Special Issue dated 26 December 1955, a few months before the start of *Pyaasa*'s filming (see commentary: 46 for further details). It is possible that the magazine set off a chain of ideas resulting in the many allusions that he makes to Christ in *Pyaasa*. There is every reason to believe that Guru Dutt preserved his own copy to use for dramatic effect in the film. Digging up material that could have contributed in some way to the creative process is deeply satisfying. Doubly so when Guru Dutt is no longer with us to provide finer details and information on the way he conceived the film.

Other research establishes links between Sahir's film poetry and his published works. Ultimately the proof of a great work like *Pyaasa* lies in the way it reveals itself to every examining eye.

This book would not exist without the support of Arun Dutt. I am most indebted to each member of Guru Dutt's team who provided insight and anecdotal information. I am grateful to his family, especially his sister Lalitha Lajmi and brother Devi Dutt, who so generously shared their memories and experiences. Special thanks to Dipa Chaudhuri, my sister Shameem Kabir, Suhail Akhtar and Vijay Jani for their meticulous efforts in the production of this book. I am grateful to Gopal Gandhi, who fine-tuned the English translation of the songs, "Jinhen naaz hai..." and "Ye duniya agar..."

For help and encouragement, many thanks to Peter Chappell, John Minchinton, Ramachandra Guha, Ajay Mago, Hazel Morgan, Iqbal and Saeeda Khan, Shaukat and Sue Khan, Anju Rodrigues, Alaknanda Samarth, Barbara Meyer, Leo Mirani and my sister Priya Kumar.

This book is dedicated to the memory of Tarun Dutt, whose smile so resembled his father's.

Nasreen Munni Kabir
London
January 2011

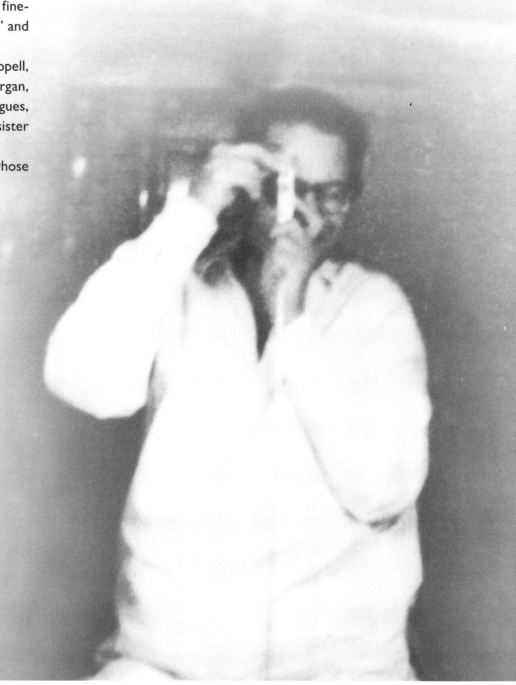

Self-portrait taken in a mirror at his Ark Royal apartment, some days before Guru Dutt commited suicide on 10 October 1964, Bombay.

The Dialogue of

PYAASA

Guru Dutt's Immortal Classic

Fade in. A photograph of director Gyan Mukherjee is super-imposed on a freeze frame shot of a pond covered with lotus. The title reads: "In the fond memory of Late Shri Gyan Mukherjee."[1]

The opening credits[2] follow this dedication until the last credit: "Produced and Directed by Guru Dutt." The still frame unfreezes into a panning shot over the pond, finally tilting up to reveal a man in the distance. He is the poet Vijay (played by Guru Dutt).[3]

Lying on the grass in a small park in Calcutta,[4] Vijay is looking at the trees and flowers and the birds circling in the sky. A voice-over recitation of a poem is heard in the style of a khudkalaami (or a form of soliloquy).

Recitation in Mohammed Rafi's voice:[5]

"These smiling flowers, this fragrant garden
These paths dipped in colour and light *(2)*
(the next line is on a shot of a bee hovering around a flower and then settling on the grass)
"Drinking the nectar of the flowers, the bees sway *(2)*
(a passer-by steps on the bee, crushing it. Seeing this, Vijay walks away from the garden. He stops, looks back)
"What can I give to you, O splendid Nature?
All that I have is a few tears, a few sighs."

Dissolve to the next scene. Vijay enters a small and noisy office belonging to the publisher Shaikh (played by Rajendar). Shaikh is also referred to as "Shaikhji" or "Maulana."[6] The office is crammed with manuscripts and papers.

"Ye hanste huwe phool, ye mehka huwa gulshan
Ye rang mein aur noor mein doobi huwi raahen *(2)*

"Ye phoolon ka ras pi ke machalte huwe bhanware *(2)*

"Main doon bhi toh kya doon tumhen ae shokh nazaaro
Le-de ke mere paas kuchh aansu hain, kuchh aahen."

फ़िल्म के आरम्भ में एक तालाब में खिले हुए कमल के फूलों के दृश्य पर निर्देशक ज्ञान मुखर्जी की तसवीर दिखाई देती है। "सद्गत ज्ञान मुखर्जी की याद में" ये शब्द दिखाई देते हैं।

इस क्रेडिट के बाद इसी दृश्य पर दूसरे कलाकारों के नाम दिखाई देते हैं। अंतिम नाम "निर्माता-निर्देशक, गुरुदत्त" का होता है। दृश्य बदलता है और कुछ दूरी पर एक व्यक्ति दिखाई देता है जो एक शायर, विजय (गुरुदत्त) है।

कलकत्ते के एक छोटे से बाग़ में घास पर वह लेटा हुआ है। विजय पेड़, फूलों और आसमान में चिड़ियों की ओर देख रहा है। बैकग्राउंड में उसी की लिखी हुई ग़ज़ल के बोल सुनाई देते हैं।

मोहम्मद रफ़ी की आवाज़

"ये हँसते हुए फूल, ये महका हुआ गुलशन
ये रंग में और नूर में डूबी हुई राहें (२)
(अगली पंक्ति पर एक भँवरा फूल पर से उड़ कर घास पर बैठता दिखाई देता है)
"ये फूलों का रस पी के मचलते हुए भँवरे (२)
(भँवरा एक राहगीर के पैरों तले दब जाता है। विजय बाग़ से उठ कर जाते हुए पलट कर देखता है)
"मैं दूँ भी तो क्या दूँ तुम्हें ऐ शोख़ नज़ारों
ले-दे के मेरे पास कुछ आँसू हैं, कुछ आहें"

दृश्य बदलता है। विजय एक प्रकाशक के छोटे और शोर भरे दफ़्तर में दाख़िल होता है। इस उर्दू प्रकाशक का नाम शेख़ है पर उसे "शेखजी" और "मौलाना" कह कर पुकारते हैं। हर तरफ हस्तलिखित पत्र और काग़ज़ बिखरे हुए हैं।

منظر اُبھرتا ہے۔ایک تالاب میں کھلے ہوئے کنول کے پھولوں پر ڈائرکٹر گیان مکرجی کی تصویر دکھائی دیتی ہے،مرحوم گیان مکرجی کی یاد میں، کے الفاظ نظر آتے ہیں۔

اس پاس نامے کے اِس فریم کے بعد اُسی منظر پر دوسرے کرداروں کے نام اُبھرتے چلے جاتے ہیں۔ آخری نام ''پیشکش اور ہدایتکار'' گرودت سامنے آتا ہے اور منظر بدل کر کچھ فاصلے پر ایک شخص دکھائی دیتا ہے جو کہ ایک شاعر ہے (گرودت)۔

کلکتے کے ایک چھوٹے سے باغ میں گھاس پر لیٹا ہوا وجے درختوں، پھولوں اور آسمان میں اُڑتے پرندوں کو تک رہا ہے۔ پس منظر میں اُسکی خودکلامی کی کیفیت میں ڈوبی آواز سنائی دے رہی ہے۔

محمد رفیع کی آواز:

''یہ ہنستے ہوئے پھول، یہ مہکا ہوا گلشن
یہ رنگ میں اور نور میں ڈوبی ہوئی راہیں (2)
(اگلے مصرعے پر ایک بھونرا پھول پر سے اُڑ کر گھاس پر بیٹھتا دکھائی دیتا ہے)
''یہ پھولوں کا رس پی کے مچلتے ہوئے بھونرے(2)
(بھونرا ایک راہ گیر کے پیروں تلے دب جاتا ہے۔ وجے باغ سے اُٹھ کر جاتے ہوئے پلٹ کر دیکھتا ہے)
''میں دوں بھی تو کیا دوں تمھیں اے شوخ نظارو!
لے دے کے میرے پاس کچھ آنسو ہیں، کچھ آہیں''

منظر بدلتا ہے۔ وجے ایک پبلشر کے ابتر آفس میں داخل ہوتا ہے۔ اُردو پبلشر کا نام شیخ ہے لیکن اُسے شیخ جی اور مولانا بھی کہہ کر پکارتے ہیں۔ دفتر میں ہر طرف مسوّدے اور کاغذات بکھرے ہوئے ہیں۔

Shaikh (flustered):
You silly Khairati, I've told you a thousand time to keep the papers in order. If that manuscript was here, has a ghost whisked it away? Where is it?

Abey Khairati ke bachche, laakh martaba kaha ki kaaghzaat tarteeb se rakkha kar. Agar vo masavvada yahin tha toh phir kya usay bhoot aur jinn uda le gaye? Aakhir kahaan hain vo kaaghzaat?

Khairati (publisher's assistant):
I…

Main…main…main…

Vijay:
Good morning, Maulaana.

Aadaab arz hai, Maulaana.

Shaikh (to Vijay, absent-mindedly):
Morning.
(to assistant)
Did you hear something?

Tasleem.

Abey kuchh suna tu ne?

Khairati:
I did. He wished you "Good Morning."

Ji haan, suna. Unhon ne kaha: "Aadaab arz hai."

Shaikh:
You fool! I mean that manuscript! Where is it?

Aadaab arz ke bachche, main poochh raha hoon kaaghzaat kahaan hain?

Vijay:
Maulaana, have you looked at my things?

Maulaana, vo meri cheezen dekhien aap ne?

Shaikh:
Wings?

Chooze?

Khairati (repeating parrot-like):
Wings?

Chooze?

Shaikh:
God Almighty! Why would I see wings? This is a publishing office, not a birdhouse.

Laahaul-wala-quvvat! Ye akhbaar ka daftar hai ke murghi ka darba jo mujhe chooze nazar aayen?

Vijay:
Not "wings." "Things." I left you some poems to read, have you read them?

"Chooze" nahin, "cheezen." Main aap ke paas kuchh nazmen chhod gaya tha, padhien aap ne?

शेख़ (गुस्से में):
अबे ख़ैराती के बच्चे, लाख मर्तबा कहा कि काग़ज़ात तरतीब से रखा कर। अगर वो मसव्दा यहीं था, तो फिर क्या उसे भूत और जिन्न उड़ा ले गए? आख़िर कहाँ हैं वो काग़ज़ात?

ख़ैराती (प्रकाशक का कर्मचारी):
मैं... मैं... मैं...

विजय:
आदाब अर्ज़ है, मौलाना।

शेख़ (बेध्यान होकर विजय से):
तसलीम।
(अपने कर्मचारी से)
अबे कुछ सुना तूने?

ख़ैराती:
जी हाँ, सुना। उन्होंने कहा: "आदाब अर्ज़ है।"

शेख़:
आदाब अर्ज़ के बच्चे, मैं पूछ रहा हूँ काग़ज़ात कहाँ हैं?

विजय:
मौलाना, वो मेरी चीज़ें देखीं आपने?

शेख़:
चूज़े?

ख़ैराती (तोते की तरह रटता है):
चूज़े?

शेख़:
लाहौल-वला-कुव्वत! ये अख़बार का दफ़्तर है के मुर्ग़ी का दड़बा जो मुझे चूज़े नज़र आएँ?

विजय:
"चूज़े" नहीं, "चीज़ें।" मैं आपके पास कुछ नज़्में छोड़ गया था। पढ़ीं आपने?

شیخ (جھلایا ہوا)
ابے خیراتی کے بچے، لاکھ مرتبہ کہا کہ کاغذات ترتیب سے رکھا کر۔ اگر وہ مسودہ یہیں تھا تو پھر کیا اُسے بھوت اور جن اُڑا لے گئے؟ آخر کہاں ہیں وہ کاغذات؟

خیراتی (پبلشر کا اسسٹنٹ):
میں ۔۔۔ میں ۔۔۔ میں ۔۔۔

وجے:
آداب عرض ہے، مولانا۔

شیخ (بے دھیانی میں وجے سے):
تسلیم۔
(اسسٹنٹ سے)
ابے کچھ سنا تُو نے؟

خیراتی:
جی ہاں، سنا۔ اُنھوں نے کہا، "آداب عرض ہے"۔

شیخ:
آداب عرض کے بچے، میں پوچھ رہا ہوں کاغذات کہاں ہیں؟

وجے:
مولانا، وہ میری چیزیں دیکھیں آپ نے؟

شیخ:
چوزے؟

خیراتی (طوطے کی طرح دہراتا ہے):
چوزے؟

شیخ:
لاحول ولا قوۃ! یہ اخبار کا دفتر ہے کہ مرغی کا ڈربہ جو مجھے چوزے نظر آئیں؟

وجے:
"چوزے" نہیں، "چیزیں"۔ میں آپ کے پاس کچھ نظمیں چھوڑ گیا تھا۔ پڑھیں آپ نے؟

Shaikh:
Yes, I have.

Vijay:
Did you like them? Will you publish them in your magazine?

Shaikh:
Why should I publish them, mister? Have I lost my mind? Call that gibberish poetry? It's a crusade against hunger and unemployment. Sir, poetry deals with fine delicacies: write about flowers and songbirds.

Khairati *(to Shaikh):*
You're incomparable, sir!

Shaikh:
Write about wine and the carafe.

Khairati:
Write about a woman's delicate neck. Or the curve of a woman's eyebrow.

Shaikh *(to Khairati):*
Be quiet!
(turning to Vijay)
Are you a poet or a butcher? Have you studied poets like Mir and Momin?[7]

Khairati:
Well? Have you?

Vijay:[8]
Yes. Josh and Faiz, too — who are beyond your comprehension. Give me my poems.

Shaikh:
They're around somewhere. We'll look for them when we have the time.
(the publisher is appalled to see Vijay rummaging through his papers)

Ji haan, padhien.

Pasand aayin aap ko? Unhen apne risaale mein chhaapiye na?

Kyun chhaapun, saaheb? Mera dimaagh kharaab huwa hai kya? Aap ki bakwaas koi shaayeri hai? Padd gaye bhook aur be-rozgaari ke peechhe lath le ke. Janaab, shaayeri naam hai nazaakat ka. Gul-o-bulbul pe sher kahiye.

Jawaab nahin hai aap ka.

Jaam-o-suraahi pe sher kahiye.

Suraahi-daar gardan par sher kahiye. Kisi baanki chitvan par sher kahiye.

Chup bey.

Aap shaayeri karte hain ya hajaamat? Mir-o-Momin ko padha hai aap ne?

Padha hai aap ne?

Ji, unhen bhi padha hai aur Josh-o-Faiz ko bhi — jo aap ki samajh se baahar hain. Laayiye meri nazmen.

Hongi yahin-kahin. Le jaana fursat ke waqt.

शेख़:
जी हाँ, पढ़ीं।

विजय:
पसंद आईं आपको? उन्हें अपने रिसाले में छापिए ना।

शेख़:
क्यूँ छापूँ, साहब। मेरा दिमाग़ ख़राब हुआ है क्या? आपकी बकवास कोई शायरी है? पड़ गए भूख और बेरोज़गारी के पीछे लठ ले के। जनाब, शायरी नाम है नज़ाकत का। गुल-ओ-बुलबुल पे शेर कहिए।

ख़ैराती *(शेख़ से):*
जवाब नहीं है आपका।

शेख़:
जाम-ओ-सुराही पे शेर कहिए।

ख़ैराती:
सुराही-दार गरदन पर शेर कहिए। किसी बाँकी चितवन पर शेर कहिए।

शेख़ *(ख़ैराती से):*
चुप बे।
(मुड़ कर विजय से)
आप शायरी करते हैं या हजामत? मीर-ओ-मोमिन को पढ़ा है आपने?

ख़ैराती:
पढ़ा है आपने?

विजय:
जी, उन्हें भी पढ़ा है और जोश-ओ-फ़ैज़ को भी – जो आपकी समझ से बाहर हैं। लाईए मेरी नज़्में।

शेख़:
होंगी यहीं-कहीं। ले जाना फ़ुरसत के वक़्त।
(विजय को काग़ज़ात उलट-पलट करते देख शेख़ दंग रह जाता है)

God Almighty! What's this misbehaviour? You're making a mess of my papers. Have you lost your mind? Some nerve.

Vijay (finding his papers in a wastepaper basket):
So that's where you've kept my poems? Who are you to throw them away?

Shaikh:
Should I make a paper hat of your nonsense?

Vijay:
Don't insult my poems by wearing them on a hollow head.

Shaikh:
So my head is hollow?

Vijay:
That's right.

Shaikh:
If you're a poet, I'm a donkey!

Vijay:
Obviously. But it's nice to hear you admit it.

Wipe to a crowded narrow market lane. Vijay is walking by a vegetable seller and overhears his mother (played by Leela Misra) talking to the vendor. A young boy sits near her.[9]

Laahaul-wala-quvvat! Ye kaisi be-takallufi? Dhunay daal rahe hain aap mere kaaghzaat. Dhuniye ka asar toh nahin hai aap pe? Ye kya? Hadd ho gayi.

Toh aap ne meri nazmen yahaan rakh chhodi hain? Inhen wahaan phenkne waale aap kaun hote hain?

Is khuraafaat ko main is mein na phenkta toh kya apne sar par rakhta?

Meri nazmen kisi khokhle sar par rakkhi jaayen ye bhi unki be-izzati hai.

Ein? Mera sar khokhla?

Ji.

Khokhli aap ki khopdi hai. Agar aap shaayer hain toh main gadha hoon.

Ji. Agar aap apni taareef na bhi karte toh bhi main pehchaan jaata.

लाहौल-वला-कुव्वत! ये कैसी बे-तकल्लुफ़ी? धुने डाल रहे हैं आप मेरे काग़ज़ात। धुनिये का असर तो नहीं है आप पे? ये क्या? हद हो गई।

विजय (*कचरे की टोकरी में अपने काग़ज़ात पड़े देख कर*):
तो आपने मेरी नज़्में यहाँ रख छोड़ी है? इन्हें वहाँ फेंकने वाले आप कौन होते हैं?

शेख़:
इस ख़ुराफ़ात को मैं इसमें ना फेंकता तो क्या अपने सर पर रखता?

विजय:
मेरी नज़्में किसी खोखले सर पर रक्खी जाएँ ये भी उनकी बेईज़्ज़ती है।

शेख़:
ऐं ! मेरा सर खोखला?

विजय:
जी।

शेख़:
खोखली आपकी खोपड़ी है। अगर आप शायर हैं तो मैं गधा हूँ।

विजय:
जी। अगर आप अपनी तारीफ़ ना भी करते तो भी मैं पहचान जाता।

वाईप। एक छोटे से बाज़ार में विजय एक सब्ज़ीवाले के पास से गुज़रता है तब उस सब्ज़ीवाले से बात कर रही अपनी माँ (लीला मिश्रा) की आवाज़ सुनता है। एक छोटा लड़का उसकी माँ के पास बैठा है।

لاحول ولاقوة! یہ کیسی بے تکلفی؟ دھنے ڈال رہے ہیں آپ میرے کاغذات ۔ دھنیے کا اثر تو نہیں ہے آپ پہ؟ یہ کیا؟ حد ہوگئی۔

وجے (کچرے کی ٹوکری میں اپنے کاغذات دیکھ کر):
تو آپ نے میری نظمیں یہاں رکھ چھوڑی ہیں؟ انہیں وہاں پھینکنے والے آپ کون ہوتے ہیں؟

شیخ:
اِس خرافات کو میں اِس میں نہ پھینکتا تو کیا اپنے سر پر رکھتا؟

وجے:
میری نظمیں کسی کھوکھلے سر پر رکھی جائیں یہ بھی اُن کی بے عزتی ہے۔

شیخ:
ایں؟ میرا سر کھوکھلا؟

وجے:
جی۔

شیخ:
کھوکھلی آپ کی کھوپڑی ہے۔ اگر آپ شاعر ہیں تو میں گدھا ہوں۔

وجے:
جی۔ اگر آپ اپنی تعریف نہ بھی کرتے تو بھی میں پہچان جاتا۔

اگلا منظر۔ ایک چھوٹا سا بازار۔ وجے ایک سبزی والے کی دکان کے پاس سے گزر رہا ہے۔ اُس کی ماں (لیلامشرا) سبزی خرید رہی ہے۔ ایک چھوٹا لڑکا اُس کی ماں کے پاس بیٹھا ہوا ہے۔

Vijay's mother (to vendor):
Are you weighing vegetables or gold, brother? Add another eggplant. Go on.

Young boy (spotting Vijay and running after him through the market):
Grandma, there's Uncle Vijay.

Vijay's mother (overjoyed to see her youngest son):
Vijay!
(to the vendor as he tries to return some change)
Never mind.

Young boy (and Vijay's mother call out to him many times but he tries to avoid them):
Uncle.

Vijay's mother:
Vijay!

Young boy (holding on to Vijay):
Grandma! I've caught Uncle.

Vijay's mother:
What is it, son? I'm not your enemy. Why are you running from your mother?

Vijay:
Ma, I…

Vijay's mother:
Son, where have you been all these days? I am an old widow. I can't bear to see you suffer like this.

Vijay:
I'm fine, ma.

Vijay's mother:
Of course! Just look at the state you're in. Come home with me. I've hidden away some food for you. Come, son.

Bhayyaji, bhaaji tol rahe ho ya sona? Ek baigan aur daalo. Eh, chalo.

Daadi, daadi. Kaaka.

Vijay!

Arey jaane do.

Kaaka.

Vijay!

Daadi, daadi. Maine pakad liya kaaka ko.

Kyun, beta? Ma toh teri dushman nahin. Is tarah kyun bhaaga ja raha tha?

Ma, main…

Kahaan tha itne dinon tak? Beta, mujh vidhwa se tera dukh aur nahin dekha jaata.

Main achha tha, ma.

Haan, kyun nahin? Jabhi toh apni aisi haalat bana rakkhi hai. Chal ghar chal. Maine tere liye kuchh, kuchh pakwaan chhupa rakkhe hain. Chal beta, chal.

विजय की माँ *(सब्ज़ीवाले से)*:
भैयाजी, भाजी तोल रहे हो या सोना? एक बैंगन और डालो। ए, चलो।

छोटा बच्चा *(विजय को देखकर उसके पीछे दौड़ते हुए)*:
दादी, दादी। काका।

विजय की माँ *(अपने बेटे विजय को देख कर ख़ुशी से फूली नहीं समाती)*:
विजय!
(सब्ज़ीवाला पैसा देना चाहता है तब उससे)
अरे जाने दो।

छोटा बच्चा *(और विजय की माँ कई बार उसे आवाज़ देते हैं पर वो नज़र बचाकर चला जाता है)*:
काका।

विजय की माँ:
विजय!

छोटा बच्चा *(विजय को पकड़ते हुए)*:
दादी, दादी। मैंने पकड़ लिया चाचा को।

विजय की माँ:
क्यूँ, बेटा? माँ तो तेरी दुश्मन नहीं। इस तरह क्यूँ भागा जा रहा था?

विजय:
माँ, मैं…

विजय की माँ:
कहाँ था इतने दिनों तक? बेटा, मुझ विधवा से तेरा दु:ख और नहीं देखा जाता।

विजय:
मैं अच्छा था, माँ।

विजय की माँ:
हाँ, क्यूँ नहीं? जभी तो अपनी ऐसी हालत बना रखी है। चल, घर चल। मैंने तेरे लिए कुछ, कुछ पकवान छुपा रखे हैं। चल बेटा, चल।

Female neighbour (witnessing the encounter):
So you've found your son?

Vijay's mother:
Yes, I've found him.
(turning to Vijay)
Come, son.

Vijay and his mother leave. The next shot (the neighbour talking to a friend) is missing in some versions of the released film.

Neighbour:
Vijay was such a talented boy. Now look at the state he's in. I hear he's obsessed by poetry.

Wipe to the next scene. Vijay's modest home where his mother lives with Vijay's two elder brothers. She brings him some food.[10]

Vijay's mother:
Here, son. Eat it.

Middle brother (actor Mehmood):[11]
Well, ma? So your poet has come home? Every literate donkey takes himself for a poet. Brother!

Elder brother (actor Radheshyam):
Where will he go? Where else can the parasite eat for free?

Vijay's mother (to Vijay):
Take no notice of them. Here. Eat something.

Middle brother:
See that, brother? We make the money while mother feeds delicacies to her darling son.

Elder brother:
I praise the man who eats so shamelessly. If he had any self-respect, he'd prefer eating dirt off the street rather than coming here to eat.

Kyun Vijay ki ma, mil gaya beta?

Haan, Vishu ki ma, mil gaya.

Chal, beta.

Kitna honhaar ladka tha Vijay. Aur kya haalat bana li hai is ne apni. Suna hai kavita ke peechhe diwaana hai.

Le, beta. Kha, kha.

Hmm. Kyun, ma? Aa gaya tumhaara Kalidas? Ha! Shaayeri kheti samajh kar sab gadhe charne lagay. *Borda! (Bangla)*

Aur kahaan jaayega? Paraayi rotiyaan todne ko isay aur kaun sa ghar milay?

Tu unki kuch na sunn, beta. Le, chup-chaap kha le. Khao.

Dekha, *borda?* Kamaayi-dhamaayi hum donon ki aur ma pakwaan khila rahi hai apne uss laadle ko.

Main toh khaane waale ki be-sharmi ki daad deta hoon. Koi ghairat-waala hota toh is ghar ke pakwaan khaane ki bajaaye sadak ki dhool phaankna kahin behtar samajhta.

पड़ोस की महिला (*यह सब कुछ देखते हुए*):
क्यूँ विजय की माँ, मिल गया बेटा?

विजय की माँ:
हाँ, विष्णु की माँ, मिल गया।
(*मुड़ कर विजय से*)
चल, बेटा।

*विजय और उसकी माँ चले जाते हैं। दूसरा दृश्य जो फ़िल्म के कुछ वर्ज़न में नहीं है।
पड़ोसन एक औरत से कहते हुए।*

पड़ोसन: (*दूसरी औरत से*)
कितना होनहार लड़का था, विजय। और क्या हालत बना ली है इसने अपनी। सुना है कविता के पीछे दीवाना है।

अगला दृश्य। विजय का छोटा-सा घर जहाँ उसकी माँ दो बड़े बेटों के साथ रहती है। विजय की माँ उसे खाना लाकर देती है।

विजय की माँ:
ले, बेटा। खा, खा।

मंझला भाई (*मेहमूद*):
क्यूँ, माँ? आ गया तुम्हारा कालिदास? हँ? शायरी खेती समझ कर सब गधे चरने लगे। *बोरदा!* (*बांग्ला में बड़े भाई को कहते हैं*)

बड़ा भाई (*राधेश्याम*):
और कहाँ जाएगा? पराई रोटियाँ तोड़ने को इसे और कौन सा घर मिले?

विजय की माँ (*विजय से*):
तू उनकी कुछ ना सुन, बेटा। ले, चुप-चाप खा ले। खाओ।

मंझला भैया:
देखा, बोर्डा? कमाई-धमाई हम दोनों की और माँ पकवान खिला रही है अपने उस लाडले को।

बड़ा भैया:
मैं तो खाने वाले की बेशर्मी की दाद देता हूँ। कोई ग़ैरतवाला होता तो इस घर के पकवान खाने के बजाए सड़क की धूल फाँकना कहीं बेहतर समझता।

پڑوس (یہ سب کچھ دیکھتے ہوئے):
کیوں وجے کی ماں، مل گیا بیٹا؟

وجے کی ماں:
ہاں، وشنو کی ماں، مل گیا۔
(مڑ کر وجے سے)
چل، بیٹا۔

وجے اور اُس کی ماں چلے جاتے ہیں۔ اگلا منظر جو دوسرے پرنٹس میں نہیں ہے۔

پڑوس (دوسری عورت سے):
کتنا ہونہار لڑکا تھا وجے اور کیا حالت بنا لی ہے اس نے اپنی۔ سنا ہے کویتا کے پیچھے دیوانہ ہے۔

اگلا منظر۔ وجے کا چھوٹا سا گھر جہاں اُس کی ماں دو بڑے بیٹوں کے ساتھ رہتی ہے۔ وجے کی ماں اُسے کھانا لا کر دیتی ہے۔

وجے کی ماں:
لے، بیٹا۔ کھا، کھا۔

منجھلا بھائی (اداکار، محمود):
کیوں، ماں؟ آ گیا تمھارا کالیداس؟ ہوں؟ شاعری کھیتی سمجھ کے سب گدھے چرنے لگے۔ بورڈا!!(بنگلہ میں بڑے بھائی کو کہتے ہیں)

بڑا بھائی (اداکار، رادھے شیام):
اور کہاں جائے گا؟ پرائی روٹیاں توڑنے کو اُسے اور کون سا گھر ملے؟

وجے کی ماں (وجے سے):
تو اُن کی کچھ نہ سن، بیٹا۔ لے، چپ چاپ کھا لے، کھاؤ۔

منجھلا بھائی:
دیکھا، بورڈا؟ کمائی دھمائی ہم دونوں کی اور ماں پکوان کھلا رہی ہے اپنے اُس لاڈلے کو۔

بڑا بھائی:
میں تو کھانے والے کی بے شرمی کی داد دیتا ہوں۔ کوئی غیرت والا ہوتا تو اِس گھر کے پکوان کھانے کی بجائے سڑک کی دھول پھانکنا کہیں بہتر سمجھتا۔

Vijay's mother:
Shut up, you two! If you say another word against him, I'll fix you both. My son has come home after so long, thirsty and hungry. And you begrudge him.

Chup raho tum donon. Ab uske liye ek akshar bhi moonh se nikaala toh moonh noch loongi tum donon ka. Itne dinon baad mera beta bhooka pyaasa ghar lauta hai toh uska chain se do-kaur khaana bhi tumhen khatakta hai.

Elder brother:
Why shouldn't we? He's hale and hearty. Let him earn his keep. Why depend on our crumbs?

Kyun na khatke? Haath-pair waala hai, khud kama-dhama ke khaaye. Hamaare tukdon par kyun pada huwa hai?

Vijay's mother:
Have you no shame? He's your blood brother. You should take responsibility of him since his father died.

Be-sharmo! Tumhaara saga bhai hai vo. Baap ke marne ke baad tum uske baap ki jageh ho.

Middle brother:
The responsibility of a father ended with father's death. It wasn't our wish that our parents should produce such a good-for-nothing.

Mataji, baap ki jagah baap ke dum ke saath gayi. Ma-baap se hum ne toh nahin kaha tha ki aisi nikhattu aulaad paida karen.

Vijay's mother (mortified):
That I should hear my sons speak like this. It was my misfortune that I gave birth to you. I'm not even allowed to wash dishes for the neighbours because of your "prestige."
(on a shot of Vijay overhearing his mother)
Or else I would have happily done that to feed my son.

Kya? Aaj beton se mujhe ye bhi sunna tha? Mere naseeb phoote thay jo tum donon meri aulaad ho. Tumhaari izzat ke liye main padosiyon ke bartan bhi nahin maanjh sakti.

Warna main vo bhi kar ke apne bachche ka pait bhar sakti thi.

Vijay (addressing a sister-in-law, off-screen):
Sister-in-law, where are my poems?

Bhaabhi, meri nazmon ki file kahaan hai?

विजय की माँ:

चुप रहो तुम दोनों। अब उसके लिए एक अक्षर भी मुँह से निकाला, तो मुँह नोंच लूँगी तुम दोनों का। इतने दिनों बाद मेरा बेटा भूखा-प्यासा घर लौटा है तो उसका चैन से दो-कौर खाना भी तुम्हें खटकता है।

बड़ा भैया:

क्यूँ न खटके? हाथ-पैर वाला है, खुद कमा-धमा के खाए, हमारे टुकड़ों पर क्यूँ पड़ा हुआ है?

विजय की माँ:

बेशरमों! तुम्हारा सगा भाई है वो। बाप के मरने के बाद तुम उसके बाप की जगह हो।

मँझला भैया:

माताजी, बाप की जगह बाप के दम के साथ गई। माँ-बाप से हमने तो नहीं कहा था कि ऐसी निखट्टू औलाद पैदा करें।

विजय की माँ (सदमे से):

क्या? आज बेटों से मुझे ये भी सुनना था? मेरे नसीब फूटे थे जो तुम दोनों मेरी औलाद हो। तुम्हारी इज़्ज़त के लिए मैं पड़ोसियों के बर्तन भी नहीं माँज सकती।
(विजय अपनी माँ की बातें सुन रहा है)
वरना मैं वो भी कर के अपने बच्चे का पेट भर सकती थी।

विजय (अपनी भाभी से कहता है, जो नज़र नहीं आती):

भाभी, मेरी नज़्मों की फ़ाइल कहाँ है?

وجے کی ماں:

چپ رہو تم دونوں۔ اب اُس کے لیے ایک اکشر بھی منہ سے نکالا تو منہ نوچ لوں گی تم دونوں کا۔ اتنے دنوں بعد میرا بیٹا بھوکا پیاسا گھر لوٹا ہے تو اُس کا چین سے دو کور کھانا بھی تمہیں کھٹکتا ہے۔

بڑا بھائی:

کیوں نہ کھٹکے؟ ہاتھ پیر والا ہے، خود کما دھما کے کھائے۔ ہمارے ٹکڑوں پر کیوں پڑا ہوا ہے؟

وجے کی ماں:

بے شرمو! تمہارا سگا بھائی ہے وہ۔ باپ کے مرنے کے بعد تم اُس کے باپ کی جگہ ہو۔

منجھلا بھائی:

ماتا جی، باپ کی جگہ باپ کے دم کے ساتھ گئی۔ ماں باپ سے ہم نے تو نہیں کہا تھا کہ ایسی نکھٹو اولاد پیدا کریں۔

وجے کی ماں (صدمے سے):

کیا؟ آج بیٹوں سے مجھے یہ بھی سننا تھا؟ میرے نصیب پھوٹے تھے جو تم دونوں میری اولاد ہو۔ تمہاری عزت کے لیے میں پڑوسیوں کے برتن بھی نہیں مانجھ سکتی۔
(وجے ماں کی باتیں سن لیتا ہے)
ورنہ میں وہ بھی کر کے اپنے بچے کا پیٹ بھر سکتی تھی۔

وجے (بھابھی سے کہتا ہے جو ہمیں نظر نہیں آتی):

بھابھی میری نظموں کی فائل کہاں ہے؟

Middle brother (*interrupting*):
Don't scowl at the women. Ask me. I sold that file to the paper merchant for ten annas, for waste paper.

Vijay (*shocked, but speaking softly at first*):
Ten annas? You sold my poems for waste paper?
(*continuing in an angry tone*)
Uncouth fools like you would think they were waste paper.

Middle brother:
What did you say? You call me uncouth?
(*to his elder brother, off-screen*)
Did you hear that, brother?
(*grabbing Vijay by the collar*)
How dare you call me uncouth? I got rid of your trash, now I'll get rid of you. Get out! You rascal.

Reel Two

Standing behind the door of the house, Vijay's mother stops her son from leaving.

Vijay's mother:
Son. Where will you go on an empty stomach? Who will look after you, my sweet child? Take me with you. I won't stay in this house a minute longer. Not a minute longer, my son.

Vijay:
Don't worry, ma. I'll try my best and take you away from here as soon as I can.

Auraton ko kya deede dikhaate ho? Mujh se baat karo, mujh se. Maine vo raddi das aane mein baniye ko bech di.

Das aane mein? Meri nazmen raddi mein bech daalein?

Aap jaisa jaahil hi unhen raddi samjhega.

Kya kaha? Jaahil? Main jaahil?

Suna, *borda,* aap ne?

Teri itni himmat ke tu mujhe jaahil kahe? Sabere toh teri raddi utha kar is ghar se phenki thi, ab tujhe is ghar se baahar phenkunga. Nikal ja, badmaash kahin ka. Lafunga.

Beta. Bhooka-pyaasa tu kahaan jaayega? Teri dekh-bhaal kaun karega, mere laal? Mujhe bhi apne saath le chal. Main ab is ghar mein ek pal nahin rahoongi. Ek pal nahin rahoongi, mere bachche.

Tu fikar na kar, ma. Main poori koshish karoonga. Main jaise bhi koi intezaam kar saka — tujhe yahaan se le jaaunga.

मंझला भैया (टोकते हुए):

औरतों को क्या दीदे दिखाते हो? मुझ से बात करो, मुझ से। मैंने वो रद्दी दस आने में बनिए को बेच दी।

विजय (सदमे से बोझल आवाज़ में):

दस आने में? मेरी नज़्में रद्दी में बेच डालीं?

(गुस्से से)

आप जैसा जाहिल ही उन्हें रद्दी समझेगा।

मंझला भैया:

क्या कहा? जाहिल? मैं जाहिल?

(बड़े भाई से, ऑफ स्क्रीन)

सुना, बोरदा, आपने?

(विजय का गिरेबान पकड़ते हुए)

तेरी इतनी हिम्मत कि तू मुझे जाहिल कहे? सबेरे तो तेरी रद्दी उठाकर इस घर से फेंकी थी, अब तुझे इस घर से बाहर फेंकूँगा। निकल जा, बदमाश कहीं का। लफ़ंगा।

रील २

गली में दरवाज़े के पीछे खड़ी हुई विजय की माँ उसे जाने से रोकती है।

विजय की माँ:

बेटा। भूखा-प्यासा तू कहाँ जाएगा? तेरी देख-भाल कौन करेगा, मेरे लाल? मुझे भी अपने साथ ले चल। मैं अब इस घर में एक पल नहीं रहूँगी। एक पल नहीं रहूँगी, मेरे बच्चे।

विजय:

तू फिकर ना कर, माँ। मैं पूरी कोशिश करूँगा। मैं जैसे भी कोई इंतज़ाम कर सका – तुझे यहाँ से ले जाऊँगा।

منجھلا بھائی (ٹوکتے ہوئے):

عورتوں کو کیا دیدے دکھاتے ہو؟ مجھ سے بات کرو، مجھ سے۔ میں نے وہ ردّی دس آنے میں بنیے کو بیچ دی۔

وجے (صدمے سے بوجھل آواز میں):

دس آنے میں؟ میری نظمیں ردّی میں بیچ ڈالیں؟

(غصے سے)

آپ جیسا جاہل ہی اُنھیں ردّی سمجھے گا۔

منجھلا بھائی:

کیا کہا؟ جاہل؟ میں جاہل؟

(بڑے بھائی سے، آف اسکرین)

سنا، بورڈا، آپ نے؟

(وجے کا گریبان پکڑتے ہوئے)

تیری اتنی ہمت کہ تو مجھے جاہل کہے؟ سبیرے تو تیری ردّی اُٹھا کر اس گھر سے پھینکی تھی، اب تجھے اس گھر سے باہر پھینکوں گا۔ نکل جا، بدمعاش کہیں کا۔ لفنگا۔

ریل ۲

گلی میں دروازے کے پیچھے کھڑی ہوئی وجے کی ماں اُسے گھر چھوڑ کر جانے سے روکتی ہے۔

وجے کی ماں:

بیٹا۔ بھوکا پیاسا تو کہاں جائے گا؟ تیری دیکھ بھال کون کرے گا، میرے لال؟ مجھے بھی اپنے ساتھ لے چل۔ میں اب اس گھر میں ایک پل نہیں رہوں گی۔ ایک پل نہیں رہوں گی، میرے بچے۔

وجے:

تو فکر نہ کر، ماں۔ میں پوری کوشش کروں گا۔ میں جیسے بھی کوئی انتظام کر سکا۔۔۔ تجھے یہاں سے لے جاؤں گا۔

Dissolve from his tearful mother to the paper merchant's stall. Vijay is desperately looking through mounds of paper.

Paper-merchant:
Vijay, do you want me to search waste paper or get on with my work?

Vijay bhayya, main subha se shaam tak dhanda karoon ya ye raddi ka hisaab-kitaab karta phiroon?

Vijay:
But there was an important file among that waste paper.

Par bhayya, uss raddi mein do-chaar badi zaroori kaapiyaan thein.

Paper-merchant:
A file? Handwritten papers?

Kaapiyaan? Haath ki likhi huwi?

Vijay:
That's right. Where are they?

Haan, haan. Kahaan hain vo?

Paper-merchant:
A woman bought them.

Unhen toh ek aurat khareed ke le gayi.

Vijay:
A woman bought them?

Khareed kar le gayi?

Paper-merchant:
She came to do some shopping. The file caught her eye. She looked at it carefully, then bought it and took it away.

Haan, haan. Sauda khareedne aayi thi, kaapiyon pe jo nazar padi, ghaur se dekha aur le gayi khareed ke.

Vijay:
Who is she? Where does she live?

Kaun si aurat, bhayya? Kahaan rehti hai vo?

Paper-merchant:
How should I know? She wasn't from this neighbourhood.
(the paper merchant calls out after Vijay)
Vijay! If she comes again, I'll make sure to ask.

Ye main kya jaanun? Kisi doosre mohalle ki thi. Haan.

Vijay bhayya, ab ke vo aayengi toh main khayaal rakkhoonga.

Dissolve. Night. Vijay climbs a flight of stairs and enters the room of his college friend Shyam (played by Guru Dutt's assistant Shyam Kapoor).[12]

विजय की रोती हुई माँ का दृश्य बदलता है और विजय दिखाई देता है जो रद्दीवाले की दुकान पर काग़ज़ात तलाश कर रहा है।

रद्दीवाला:
विजय भय्या, मैं सुबह से शाम तक धंधा करूँ या ये रद्दी का हिसाब-किताब करता फिरूँ?

विजय:
पर भय्या, उस रद्दी में दो-चार बड़ी ज़रुरी कॉपियाँ थीं।

रद्दीवाला:
कॉपियाँ! हाथ की लिखी हुई?

विजय:
हाँ, हाँ। कहाँ है वो?

रद्दीवाला:
उन्हें तो एक औरत ख़रीद के ले गई।

विजय:
ख़रीद के ले गई?

रद्दीवाला:
हाँ, हाँ। सौदा ख़रीदने आयी थी, कॉपियों पे जो नज़र पड़ी, ग़ौर से देखा और ले गई ख़रीद के।

विजय:
कौन सी औरत, भय्या? कहाँ रहती है वो?

रद्दीवाला:
ये मैं क्या जानूँ? किसी दूसरे मोहल्ले की थी। हाँ।
(विजय जाने लगता है तब उसे पुकारते हुए कहता है)
विजय भय्या, अब के वो आएँगी तो मैं ख़याल रखूँगा।

अगला दृश्य। रात। कुछ सीढ़ियाँ चढ़ कर विजय अपने दोस्त श्याम के कमरे में आता है। *(जो गुरुदत्त का सहायक श्याम कपूर है)*

وجے کی آبدیدہ ماں سے منظر بدل کر وجے نظر آتا ہے جو ردّی والے کی دکان پر کاغذات تلاش کر رہا ہے۔

ردّی والا:
وجے بھیا، میں صبح سے شام تک دھندہ دھندہ کروں یا یہ ردّی کا حساب کتاب کرتا پھروں۔

وجے:
پر بھیا، اُس ردّی میں دو چار بڑی ضروری کاپیاں تھیں۔

ردّی والا:
کاپیاں؟ ہاتھ کی لکھی ہوئی؟

وجے:
ہاں، ہاں۔ کہاں ہیں وہ؟

ردّی والا:
اُنھیں تو ایک عورت خرید کے لے گئی۔

وجے:
خرید کے لے گئی؟

ردّی والا:
ہاں، ہاں۔ سودا خریدنے آئی تھی، کاپیوں پہ جو نظر پڑی، غور سے دیکھا اور لے گئی خرید کے۔

وجے:
کون سی عورت، بھیا؟ کہاں رہتی ہے وہ؟

ردّی والا:
یہ میں کیا جانوں؟ کسی دوسرے محلے کی تھی، ہاں۔
(جاتے ہوئے وجے کو ردّی والا پکار کر کہتا ہے)
وجے بھیا، اب کہ وہ آئے گی تو میں خیال رکھوں گا۔

اگلا منظر۔ رات۔ کچھ سیڑھیاں چڑھ کر وجے اپنے دوست شیام (گرودت کا اسسٹنٹ شیام کپور) کے کمرے میں آتا ہے۔

Shyam:
Welcome! So your brothers were as affectionate as ever? Are you hungry? You'll end up starving to death. As for me, I fleeced two hundred rupees off a rich man today.

Aaayiye, aayiye. Aaj bhaaiyon ne phir pyar kiya tumhen? Bhooke ho? Tu hamesha yunhi bhooka marega. Mujhe dekh. Aaj ek sethiye se do sau rupay yun chit kar liye maine.

Vijay:
How?

Kaise?

Shyam:
His car ran over an old woman's leg and broke it, so I gave false witness for him.

Apni car se ek budhiya ki taang tod di thi usnay. Bas jhooti gawaahi de di.

Vijay (as he spreads his bedding on the floor):
Shyam, remember how you found a lamed bird as a kid? You cared for it for a whole week till it was better.

Yaad hai, Shyam, bachpan mein taang tooti ek chidya dekhi thi tum ne? Saat din tak marham-patti kar ke tum ne theek kiya tha usay.

Shyam (a girl enters the room):
I was only a kid then. But you're still the kid.

Abey tab main bachcha tha. Lekin tu toh ab bhi bachcha hai.

Shyam's girlfriend, Chhammo, giggles. Vijay looks at her and Shyam gestures to his friend to leave them alone. As soon as Vijay leaves the room, Chhammo closes the door.

Dissolve. Night. Vijay is sitting on a bench at the Hooghly waterfront. He notices a woman standing at a short distance with her back to him. She is Gulaab, affectionately also called Gulaabo (Waheeda Rehman).[13] Softly, she recites a couplet.

श्याम:
आइए, आइए। आज भाईयों ने फिर प्यार किया तुम्हें? भूखे हो? तू हमेशा यूँही भूखा मरेगा। मुझे देख। आज एक सेठिये से दो सौ रुपये यूँ चित कर लिए मैंने।

विजय:
कैसे?

श्याम:
अपनी कार से एक बुढ़िया की टाँग तोड़ दी थी उसने। बस झूठी गवाही दे दी।

विजय (ज़मीन पर बिस्तर बिछाते हुए):
याद है, श्याम, बचपन में टाँग टूटी एक चिड़िया देखी थी तुमने? सात दिन तक मरहम-पट्टी करके तुमने ठीक किया था उसे।

श्याम (एक लड़की कमरे में दाख़िल होती है):
अबे तब मैं बच्चा था। लेकिन तू तो अब भी बच्चा है।

श्याम की दोस्त छम्मो हँस देती है। विजय उसकी ओर देखता है। श्याम अपने दोस्त को इशारा करता है कि उन्हें अकेला छोड़ दे। जैसे ही वो कमरे से बाहर जाता है छम्मो दरवाज़ा बंद कर देती है।

अगला दृश्य। रात। हुगली के किनारे एक बेंच पर विजय बैठ जाता है। उसकी नज़र एक औरत पर पड़ती है। वो गुलाब है, जिसे प्यार से गुलाबो भी कहते हैं (वहीदा रहमान)। गुनगुनाते हुए वो एक शेर पढ़ रही है।

شیام:
آئیے، آئیے۔ آج بھائیوں نے پھر پیار کیا تمھیں؟ بھوکے ہو؟ تُو ہمیشہ یونہی بھوکا مرے گا۔ مجھے دیکھ۔ آج ایک سیٹھیے سے دو سو روپے یوں چِت کر لیے میں نے۔

وجے:
کیسے؟

شیام:
اپنی کار سے ایک بڑھیا کی ٹانگ تو ڑ دی تھی اُس نے۔ بس جھوٹی گواہی دے دی۔

وجے (فرش پر بستر بچھاتے ہوئے):
یاد ہے، شیام۔ بچپن میں ٹانگ ٹوٹی ایک چڑیا دیکھی تھی تم نے؟ سات دن تک مرہم پٹی کرکے تم نے ٹھیک کیا تھا اُسے۔

شیام (ایک لڑکی کمرے میں داخل ہوتی ہے):
ابے تب میں بچہ تھا۔ لیکن تُو تو اب بھی بچہ ہے۔

شیام کی محبوبہ چھمو ہنس دیتی ہے۔ وجے اُس کی طرف دیکھتا ہے۔ شیام اپنے دوست کو اشارہ کرتا ہے کہ اُنھیں تنہا چھوڑ دے۔ جیسے ہی وہ کمرے سے باہر جاتا ہے شیام کی محبوبہ دروازہ بند کر لیتی ہے۔

اگلا منظر۔ رات۔ ہگلی کے کنارے ایک بینچ پر وجے بیٹھ جاتا ہے۔ اُس کی نظر ایک عورت پر پڑتی ہے۔ وہ گلاب ہے جسے پیار سے گلابو بھی کہتے ہیں۔ (وحیدہ رحمان) وہ گنگناتی ہوئی ایک شعر پڑھ رہی ہے۔

Gulaab (*Geeta Dutt's voice*):
"Do not complain if I look at you with impunity
(Vijay realises at once that the young woman is reciting a poem from the file sold to the paper-merchant)
There! You looked at me again with such longing…"[14]

Vijay (*approaching her*):
Listen…
(the young woman turns and looks seductively)
I say…

Gulaab answers in song.

Singer: Geeta Dutt

Who knows what you said
Who knows what I heard
Something stirred in my heart
Who knows what you said
Who knows what I heard
Something stirred in my heart
Who knows what you said

A ringing sound was heard
A tingling sensation was felt
(both lines repeated)
Slumbering dreams reawakened
Something stirred in my heart

Who knows what you said
Who knows what I heard
Something stirred in my heart
Who knows what you said

My lowered eyes look up again
My stumbling feet no longer falter
(both lines repeated)
New life has come into my step
Something stirred in my heart

"Phir na kijiye meri gustaakh nigaahi ka gila

"Dekhiye aap ne phir pyar se dekha mujh ko
Dekhiye aap ne…"

Suniye…

Maine kaha…

Jaane kya tu ne kahi
Jaane kya maine suni
Baat kuchh bann hi gayi
Jaane kya tu ne kahi
Jaane kya maine suni
Baat kuchh bann hi gayi
Jaane kya tu ne kahi

San-sanaahat si huwi
Thar-tharaahat si huwi
(both lines repeated)
Jaag uthe khwab kayi
Baat kuchh bann hi gayi

Jaane kya tu ne kahi
Jaane kya maine suni
Baat kuchh bann hi gayi
Jaane kya tu ne kahi

Nain jhuk-jhuk ke uthe
Paaon ruk-ruk ke uthe
(both lines repeated)
Aa gayi chaal nayi
Baat kuchh bann hi gayi

गुलाब *(गीता दत्त की आवाज़)*:

"फिर ना कीजे मेरी गुस्ताख़ निगाही का गिला

(विजय को तुरंत एहसास होता है कि यह वही कविता है जो रद्दीवाले को बेची हुई फ़ाइल में थी)

"देखिए आपने फिर प्यार से देखा मुझ को

देखिए आपने..."

विजय *(उसके पास आकर)*:

सुनिए...

(नौजवान औरत उसे लुभानेवाली नज़रों से देखते हुए)

मैंने कहा...

गुलाब उसे गाते हुए जवाब देती है

गायिका: गीता दत्त

जाने क्या तूने कही

जाने क्या मैंने सुनी

बात कुछ बन ही गई

जाने क्या तूने कही

जाने क्या मैंने सुनी

बात कुछ बन ही गई

जाने क्या तूने कही

सन-सनाहट सी हुई

थर-थराहट सी हुई

(दोनों पंक्तियाँ दोहराती है)

जाग उठे ख़्वाब कई

बात कुछ बन ही गई

जाने क्या तूने कही

जाने क्या मैंने सुनी

बात कुछ बन ही गई

जाने क्या तूने कही

नैन झुक-झुक के उठे

पाँव रुक-रुक के उठे

(दोनों पंक्तियाँ दोहराती है)

आ गई चाल नई

बात कुछ बन ही गई

گلاب *(گیتا دت کی آواز)*:

"پھر نہ کیجے مری گستاخ نگاہی کا گلہ

(وجے کو فوراً احساس ہوتا ہے کہ یہ وہی شعر اُس فائل میں تھا جو ردّی والے کو بیچ دی گئی ہے)

دیکھیے آپ نے پھر پیار سے دیکھا مجھ کو

دیکھیے آپ نے...،،

وجے *(اُس کے پاس جاتے ہوئے)*:

سنیے...

(نو جوان عورت اُسے لبھانے والی نظروں سے دیکھتی ہے)

میں نے کہا...

گلاب اُسے گاتے ہوئے جواب دیتی ہے۔

گیتا دت کی آواز۔

جانے کیا تُو نے کہی

جانے کیا میں نے سنی

بات کچھ بن ہی گئی

جانے کیا تُو نے کہی

جانے کیا میں نے سنی

بات کچھ بن ہی گئی

جانے کیا تُو نے کہی

سنسناہٹ سی ہوئی

تھر تھراہٹ سی سی ہوئی

(دونوں لائنیں دوہراتی ہے)

جاگ اُٹھے خواب کئی

بات کچھ بن ہی گئی

جانے کیا تُو نے کہی

جانے کیا میں نے سنی

بات کچھ بن ہی گئی

جانے کیا تُو نے کہی

نین جھک جھک کے اُٹھے

پاؤں رک رک کے اُٹھے

(دونوں لائنیں دوہراتی ہے)

آ گئی چال نئی

بات کچھ بن ہی گئی

Who knows what you said	Jaane kya tu ne kahi
Who knows what I heard	Jaane kya maine suni
Something stirred in my heart	Baat kuchh bann hi gayi
Who knows what you said	Jaane kya tu ne kahi

Gulaab lures Vijay away from the waterfront as she continues to sing. He follows her past imposing pillars and through the empty streets to the house where she lives.

My hair curls about my shoulder	Zulf shaane pe mudi
Filling the air with sweet fragrance	Ek khushboo si udi
(both lines repeated)	*(both lines repeated)*
Secret longings unravel	Khul gaye raaz kayi
Something stirred in my heart	Baat kuchh bann hi gayi
Who knows what you said	Jaane kya tu ne kahi
Who knows what I heard	Jaane kya maine suni
Something stirred in my heart	Baat kuchh bann hi gayi

Who knows what you said	Jaane kya tu ne kahi
Who knows what I heard	Jaane kya maine suni
Something stirred in my heart	Baat kuchh bann hi gayi
Who knows what you said	Jaane kya tu ne kahi

Gulaab starts to climb the many flights of stairs to her room. Vijay follows her.[15]

Vijay:

Listen.	Suniye.

जाने क्या तूने कही
जाने क्या मैंने सुनी
बात कुछ बन ही गई
जाने क्या तूने कही

नदी के किनारे से लुभाते गाते हुए विजय को गुलाब दूर ले जाती है। वो उसके पीछे-पीछे सुनसान गलियों और बड़े-बड़े स्तंभों के बीच से होता हुआ गुलाब के घर तक आ जाता है।

ज़ुल्फ़ शाने पे मुड़ी
एक ख़ुशबू सी उड़ी
(दोनों पंक्तियाँ दोहराती है)
खुल गए राज़ कई
बात कुछ बन ही गई
जाने क्या तूने कही
जाने क्या मैंने सुनी
बात कुछ बन ही गई

जाने क्या तूने कही
जाने क्या मैंने सुनी
बात कुछ बन ही गई
जाने क्या तूने कही

गुलाब अपने कमरे की ओर सीढ़ियाँ चढ़ते हुए। विजय उसके पीछे-पीछे।

विजय:
सुनिए।

جانے کیا تُو نے کہی
جانے کیا میں نے سنی
بات کچھ بن ہی گئی
جانے کیا تُو نے کہی

دریا کنارے سے لبھاتے ہوئے وجے کو گلاب دور لے جاتی ہے۔ وہ اُس کے پیچھے پیچھے سنسان گلیوں اور بڑے بڑے ستونوں کے درمیان سے ہوتا ہوا گلاب کے گھر تک آ جاتا ہے

زلف شانے پہ مڑی
ایک خوشبوسی اُڑی
(دونوں لائنیں دہراتی ہے)
کھل گئے راز کئی
بات کچھ بن ہی گئی
جانے کیا تُو نے کہی
جانے کیا میں نے سنی
بات کچھ بن ہی گئی

جانے کیا تُو نے کہی
جانے کیا میں نے سنی
بات کچھ بن ہی گئی
جانے کیا تُو نے کہی

گلاب اپنے کمرے کی طرف سیڑھیاں چڑھتے ہوئے۔ وہ اُس کے پیچھے پیچھے۔

وجے:
سنیے۔

Gulaab *(coyly):*
I'm listening.

Vijay:
That song you were singing…

Gulaab:
Did you like it?

Vijay:
Where did you get it?

Gulaab *(climbing another flight):*
It's mine.

Vijay:
I know it isn't yours.

Gulaab:
Why ask if you know?

Vijay:
Because I want…

Gulaab *(flirtatiously):*
What do you want?

Vijay *(realising she is a prostitute, his expression changes):*
The file with that song in it.

Gulaab:
Oh! Is that all?

Vijay:
I don't like misplaced humour.

Gulaab:
Do you like me?

Vijay *(sternly):*
No, I don't.

Sunaayiye.

Kuchh der pehle jo aap gunguna rahi thein vo…

Pasand aaya tumhen?

Vo geet aap ko kahaan se mila?

Mera hai.

Main kehta hoon vo geet aap ka nahin hai.

Jaante ho toh phir poochhte kyun ho?

Is liye ki mujhe…

Kya chaahiye?

Vo…vo file jis mein se aap ko vo geet mila.

Oh! Aur kuchh nahin?

Dekhiye, mujhe be-tuka mazaaq pasand nahin.

Main pasand hoon?

Ji nahin.

गुलाब (*एक अदा से*): सुनाइए।	**گلاب** (ایک ادا سے): سنائیے۔
विजय: कुछ देर पहले जो आप गुनगुना रही थीं वो...	**وجے:** کچھ دیر پہلے جو آپ گنگنا رہی ہی تھیں وہ۔۔۔
गुलाब: पसंद आया तुम्हें?	**گلاب:** پسند آیا تمہیں؟
विजय: वो गीत आपको कहाँ से मिला?	**وجے:** وہ گیت آپ کو کہاں سے ملا؟
गुलाब (*सीढ़ियाँ चढ़ते हुए*): मेरा है।	**گلاب** (سیڑھیاں چڑھتے ہوئے): میرا ہے۔
विजय: मैं कहता हूँ वो गीत आपका नहीं है।	**وجے:** میں کہتا ہوں وہ گیت آپ کا نہیں ہے۔
गुलाब: जानते हो तो फिर पूछते क्यूँ हो?	**گلاب:** جانتے ہو تو پھر پوچھتے کیوں ہو؟
विजय: इस लिए कि मुझे...	**وجے:** اس لیے کہ مجھے۔۔۔
गुलाब (*इतराते हुए*): क्या चाहिए?	**گلاب** (اتراتے ہوئے): کیا چاہیے؟
विजय (*उसे एहसास हो जाता है कि वो एक पेशावर औरत है*): वो.. वो फ़ाइल जिसमें से आपको वो गीत मिला।	**وجے** (اُسے احساس ہوتا ہے کہ وہ پیشہ ور عورت ہے): وہ۔۔۔وہ فائل جس میں سے آپ کو وہ گیت ملا۔
गुलाब: बस! और कुछ नहीं?	**گلاب:** اوہ! اور کچھ نہیں؟
विजय: देखिए मुझे बे-तुका मज़ाक पसंद नहीं।	**وجے:** دیکھیے مجھے بے تکا مذاق پسند نہیں۔
गुलाब: मैं पसंद हूँ?	**گلاب:** میں پسند ہوں؟
विजय (*सख्ती से*): जी नहीं।	**وجے** (سختی سے): جی نہیں۔

Gulaab (turning icy):
So why have you been following me?

Vijay:
I just wanted to know if you still have that file. It's very important to me. Whenever I have the money…

Gulaab (angry):
So you've followed me empty-handed? You take this brothel for a family estate? Get out of here!

As Vijay grabs hold of Gulaab, some papers fall from his hand and land on the stairs.

Vijay:
Why don't you understand? I only want that file.

Gulaab:
File, my foot! Get your hands off.

Vijay (pleading, as Gulaab frees herself from his grip):
It's precious to me.

Gulaab:
Get out of here! Are you going? Or must I kick you out?

Taken aback by her aggressive tone, Vijay leaves. Gulaab's friend Juhi (Kum Kum)[16] comes out of the room that they share.

Juhi:
You silly girl, why are you shouting? Your new customer will fly away.

Gulaab:
Just imagine! These paupers never give up. I lured him here only to find that he has no money…

Toh phir abhi tak mere peechhe-peechhe kyun aa rahe ho?

Main sirf itna jaanna chaahta hoon aap ke paas file hai ya nahin. Vo mere liye bahot qeemti hai. Jab bhi mere paas paise huwe main…

Achha! Tu khaali haath aaya hai mere peechhe? Is kothe ko khaalaji ka ghar samjha hai kya? Chal, nikal yahaan se.

Dekho tum samajhti kyun nahin? Mujhe sirf file chaahiye, file…

File ke bachche…hata apna haath.

Mere liye vo bahot qeemti hai.

Aur nikal yahaan se. Tu jaata hai ya utaarun apni jooti?

Ae nigodi, chillaati kyun hai? Naya panchhi hai ghabra ke udd na jaaye.

Dekh toh sahi kahaan ke bhukkad lag jaate hain peechhe. Lubha ke yahaan tak laayi toh pata chala…

गुलाब (बेरुखी से):
तो फिर अभी तक मेरे पीछे-पीछे क्यूँ आ रहे हो?

विजय:
मैं सिर्फ़ इतना जानना चाहता हूँ आपके पास फ़ाइल है या नहीं। वो मेरे लिए बहुत क़ीमती है। जब भी मेरे पास पैसे हुए मैं...

गुलाब (गुस्से से):
अच्छा! तू ख़ाली हाथ आया है मेरे पीछे? इस कोठे को ख़ालाजी का घर समझा है क्या? चल, निकल यहाँ से।

गुलाब को विजय पकड़ लेता है। उसके हाथ से कुछ काग़ज़ात छूट कर सीढ़ियों पर गिर जाते है।

विजय:
देखो तुम समझती क्यूँ नहीं? मुझे सिर्फ़ फ़ाइल चाहिए, फ़ाइल...

गुलाब:
फ़ाइल के बच्चे... हटा अपना हाथ।

विजय (विनती कर रहा है, जबकि गुलाब अपना हाथ छुड़ा लेती है):
मेरे लिए वो बहुत क़ीमती है।

गुलाब:
और निकल यहाँ से। तू जाता है या उतारूँ अपनी जूती?

उसका सख़्त व्यवहार देखकर विजय दंग रह जाता है। वो चला जाता है। गुलाब की सहेली जूही (कुमकुम) कमरे से बाहर आती है।

जूही:
ऐ निगोड़ी, चिल्लाती क्यूँ है? नया पंछी है, घबरा के उड़ ना जाए।

गुलाब:
देख तो सही, कहाँ के भुक्खड़ लग जाते हैं पीछे। लुभा के यहाँ तक लाई तो पता चला...

گلاب (سردمہری سے):
تو پھر ابھی تک میرے پیچھے پیچھے کیوں آ رہے ہو؟

وجے:
میں صرف اتنا جاننا چاہتا ہوں آپ کے پاس فائل ہے یا نہیں۔ وہ میرے لیے بہت قیمتی ہے۔ جب بھی میرے پاس پیسے ہوئے میں۔۔۔

گلاب (غصے سے):
اچھا! تو خالی ہاتھ آیا ہے میرے پیچھے؟ اس کوٹھے کو خالہ جی کا گھر سمجھا ہے کیا؟ چل نکل یہاں سے۔

گلاب کی بانہہ وجے پکڑ لیتا ہے۔ اُس کے ہاتھ سے کچھ کاغذات چھوٹ کر سیڑھیوں پر گر جاتے ہیں۔

وجے:
دیکھو تم سمجھتی کیوں نہیں؟ مجھے صرف فائل چاہیے، فائل۔۔۔

گلاب:
فائل کے بچے۔۔۔ ہٹا اپنا ہاتھ۔

وجے (التجا کرتے ہوئے اور گلاب اپنا ہاتھ چھڑاتے ہوئے):
میرے لیے وہ بہت قیمتی ہے۔

گلاب:
اور نکل یہاں سے۔ تو جاتا ہے یا اُتاروں اپنی جوتی؟

اُس کا سخت رویہ دیکھ کر وجے حیران رہ جاتا ہے۔ وہ چلا جاتا ہے۔ گلاب کی دوست جوہی (کم کم) کمرے سے آتی ہے۔

جوہی:
اے نگوڑی، چلاتی کیوں ہے؟ نیا پنچھی ہے، گھبرا کے اُڑ نہ جائے۔

گلاب:
دیکھ تو سہی، کہاں کے بھکڑ لگ جاتے ہیں پیچھے۔ لبھا کے یہاں تک لائی تو پتا چلا۔۔۔

Vijay's fallen papers catch Gulaab's eye. She looks at them carefully and then rushes into her room to compare the handwriting with the poems she bought from the paper-merchant. She runs down the stairs.

Gulaab:
Juhi, it *was* him.

Juhi, ye vahi tha. Vahi tha ye.

Juhi *(rushing after her)*:
Gulaabo, what's come over you? Where are you running?

Gulaabo, kya ho gaya hai tujhe? Is tarah kahaan udi ja rahi hai?

Gulaab:
I must stop him. I want to apologise to him. I treated him very badly.

Main usay rokne ja rahi hoon. Uss se maafi maangne. Maine bahot bura sulook kiya uske saath.

Dejected, Gulaab realises that Vijay has long gone.

Juhi:
Now stop talking in riddles. Speak in plain language. What's all this about?

Ae bhaai, ye pehliyaan bujhaana chhod aur safa-safa Hindustaani mein baat kar. Ye sab kya gadbad hai?

Gulaab:
The man who followed me is a poet. The poet whose poems I bought as waste paper. Look, the same writing, the same paper. Juhi, I threw him out as a pauper.

Vo jo mere peechhe aaya tha vo shaayer hai, Juhi. Vahi shaayer jis ki nazmen main raddiwaale se laayi thi. Ye dekh. Vahi likhaayi, vaisa hi kaaghaz. Juhi, maine usay bhukkad samajh ke yahaan se nikaal diya.

Juhi:
What? But he *is* a pauper. If you hadn't thrown him out, what would you have done? Hug him? Remember our profession has its standards. Come. Let's go upstairs.

Ein? Bhukkad tha na? Aaye-haaye, tu usay nikaalti nahin toh kya galay lagaati? Arey ustaadon ki saari taaleem par paani pher diya hai tu ne. Chal, chal upar chal.

वजे के काग़ज़ात सीढ़ियों पर पड़े हुए विजय को नज़र आते हैं। बिना उन्हें देखते हुए वह अपने कमरे में रखी उस फ़ाइल से जो वह रद्दीवाले से खरीद कर लायी थी, ख़त मिलाने जाती है। दौड़ते हुए वह सीढ़ियाँ उतरती है।

وجے کے کاغذات سیڑھیوں پر پڑے ہوئے وجے کو نظر آتے ہیں۔ بغور انھیں دیکھتے ہوئے وہ اپنے کمرے میں رکھی اُس فائل سے جو وہ ردّی والے سے خرید کر لائی تھی، خط ملانے جاتی ہے۔ دوڑتے ہوئے وہ سیڑھیاں اُترتی ہے۔

गुलाब:
जूही, ये वही था। वही था ये।

گلاب:
جوہی، یہ وہی تھا۔ وہی تھا یہ۔

जूही (उसके पीछे लपकते हुए):
गुलाबो, क्या हो गया है तुझे? इस तरह कहाँ उड़ी जा रही है?

جوہی (اُس کے پیچھے لپکتے ہوئے):
گلابو، کیا ہو گیا ہے تجھے؟ اِس طرح کہاں اُڑی جا رہی ہے؟

गुलाब:
मैं उसे रोकने जा रही हूँ। उससे माफ़ी माँगने। मैंने बहुत बुरा सुलूक किया उसके साथ।

گلاب:
میں اُسے روکنے جا رہی ہوں۔ اُس سے معافی مانگنے۔ میں نے بہت برا سلوک کیا اُس کے ساتھ۔

विजय जा चुका है, वो निराश हो जाती है।

وجے جا چکا ہے، وہ مایوس ہو جاتی ہے۔

जूही:
ऐ भाई, ये पहेलियाँ बुझाना छोड़ और सफ़ा-सफ़ा हिन्दुस्तानी में बात कर। ये सब क्या गड़बड़ है?

جوہی:
اے بھائی، یہ پہیلیاں بجھانا چھوڑ اور صفا صفا ہندوستانی میں بات کر۔ یہ سب کیا گڑبڑ ہے؟

गुलाब:
वो जो मेरे पीछे आया था, वो शायर है, जूही। वही शायर जिसकी नज़्में मैं रद्दीवाले से लायी थी। ये देख वही लिखाई, वैसा ही काग़ज़। जूही, मैंने उसे भुक्खड़ समझ के यहाँ से निकाल दिया।

گلاب:
وہ جو میرے پیچھے آیا تھا وہ شاعر ہے، جوہی۔ وہی شاعر جس کی نظمیں میں ردّی والے سے لائی تھی۔ یہ دیکھ، وہی لکھائی، ویسا ہی کاغذ۔ جوہی، میں نے اُسے بھکڑ سمجھ کے یہاں سے نکال دیا۔

जूही:
एँ? भुक्खड़ था ना? आए-हाए, तू उसे निकालती नहीं तो क्या गले लगाती? अरे उस्तादों की सारी तालीम पर पानी फेर दिया है तूने। चल, चल ऊपर चल।

جوہی:
ایں؟ بھکڑ تھا نا؟ آئے ہائے، تُو اُسے نکالتی نہیں تو کیا گلے لگاتی؟ ارے اُستادوں کی ساری تعلیم پر پانی پھیر دیا ہے تُو نے۔ چل، چل اوپر چل۔

Reel Three

Fade in. Day. Vijay walks away from the bench at the waterfront where he often spends the night. Dissolve to Vijay walking down Park Street.[17] Vijay sees Meena (Mala Sinha)[18] getting out of a chauffeur-driven convertible. She does not see Vijay. Entering a shop, she talks to a woman (dialogue is unheard). Unseen by Meena, Vijay watches her. A close-up of Vijay slowly dissolves into a flashback.[19]

A college classroom. Three college students: Shyam, Vijay and a friend enter laughing. Shyam notices some girls staring at them.

Shyam:
Hello.

Embarrassed, the girls look away.

Friend:
Well, Vijay? Tell me, have you written any new poems in the holidays?

Arey haan Vijay. In chhuttiyon ke din mein koi nayi ghazal-vazal kahi?

Vijay:
Yes, a few.

Haan, yaar. Kahi hain do-chaar.

Shyam:
Given the time, anyone can write poems. Create something extempore. Then we'll consider you a poet.

Arey soch-bichaar ke toh sabhi keh lete hain. Fil-badih kaho koi cheez. Extempore. Tab maanen hum tumhen shaayer.

Vijay:
Extempore?

Extempore?

अगला दृश्य। सुबह। दरिया किनारे पड़ी बेंच से उठ कर विजय, जहाँ वो अक्सर रातें गुज़ारता है, चलता है। अगला दृश्य। कलकत्ता का पार्क स्ट्रीट। मीना (माला सिन्हा) को विजय एक बड़ी गाड़ी से उतरते देखता है। वो विजय को नहीं देख पाती। एक दुकान में दाख़िल होते हुए मीना एक औरत को कुछ कहती है। विजय उसे देखता हुआ कुछ सोच रहा है। दृश्य बदलकर फ़्लैशबैक सामने आता है।

फ़्लैशबैक में एक कॉलेज का क्लासरूम नज़र आता है। तीन कॉलेज स्टूडेन्ट्स, श्याम, विजय और उनका एक दोस्त हँसते हुए क्लासरूम में दाख़िल होते हैं। श्याम देखता है कि उन्हें कुछ लड़कियाँ घूरे जा रही हैं।

श्याम:
हैलो।

लड़कियाँ नज़रें चुरा लेती हैं।

दोस्त:
अरे हाँ, विजय। इन छुट्टियों के दिन में कोई नई ग़ज़ल-वज़ल कही?

विजय:
हाँ, यार। कही हैं दो-चार।

श्याम:
अरे सोच-बिचार के तो सभी कह लेते हैं। फ़िल-बदीह कहो कोई चीज़। एक्सटेम्पोर। तब माने हम तुम्हें शायर।

विजय:
एक्सटेम्पोर?

اگلا منظر۔صبح۔ دریا کنارے پڑی بینچ سے اُٹھ کر وجے، جہاں وہ اکثر راتیں گزارتا ہے، چلتا ہے۔ اگلا منظر۔ کلکتہ کا متموّل علاقہ پارک اسٹریٹ۔ مینا(اداکارہ، مالا سنہا) کو وجے ایک کنورٹیبل کار سے اُترتے دیکھتا ہے۔ وہ وجے کو نہیں دیکھ پاتی۔ ایک دکان میں داخل ہوتے ہوئے وہ ایک عورت سے کچھ کہتی ہے۔ وجے اُسے دیکھتا ہوا کچھ سوچ رہا ہے۔ منظر بدل کر فلیش بیک سامنے آتا ہے۔

فلیش بیک میں کالج کلاس روم نظر آتا ہے۔ تین کالج اسٹوڈنٹس، شیام، وجے اور اُن کا ایک دوست ہنستے ہوئے کلاس میں داخل ہوتے ہیں۔ شیام دیکھتا ہے کہ اُنھیں کچھ لڑکیاں گھور رہی ہیں۔

شیام:
ہیلو۔

لڑکیاں نظریں چرا لیتی ہیں۔

دوست:
ارے ہاں، وجے۔ اِن چھٹیوں کے دن میں کوئی نئی غزل وزل کہی؟

وجے:
ہاں یار کہی ہیں دو چار۔

شیام:
ارے سوچ بچار کے تو سبھی کہہ لیتے ہیں۔ فی البدیہہ کہو کوئی چیز۔ ایکسٹمپور۔ تب مانیں ہم تمھیں شاعر۔

وجے:
ایکسٹمپور؟

Shyam:
Hmm.

Vijay:
Extempore?

Shyam:
Yes.

Vijay:
Shall I?

Shyam:
Go on.

Vijay:
But on what subject?

Shyam:
Subject?

Vijay sees the lovely Meena Sinha enter the classroom. He is instantly attracted to her.

Vijay:
Hey…

Shyam:
Hmm?

Vijay:
Who is she?

Shyam:
Never mind, my friend. There's your subject: So compose a poem about her.

Meena walks slowly towards a classroom bench.

Hmm.

Fil-badih?

Haan.

Kahoon?

Kaho.

Lekin kahoon kis cheez pe?

Kis cheez pe?

Abey…

Hmm?

Kaun hai ye?

Arey poochhta kya hai, yaar? Misraaye-tarh haazir hai zaalim. Keh daal isi pe kuchh.

श्याम:
हँ।

विजय:
फिल-बदीह?

श्याम:
हाँ।

विजय:
कहूँ?

श्याम:
कहो।

विजय:
लेकिन कहूँ किस चीज़ पे?

श्याम:
किस चीज़ पे?

क्लासरूम में दाख़िल हो रही मीना सिन्हा को विजय देखता है। वह उसकी तरफ़ आकर्षित होता है।

विजय:
अबे...

श्याम:
हँ?

विजय:
कौन है यह?

श्याम:
अरे पूछता क्या है यार? मिसराए-तह हाज़िर है ज़ालिम। कह डाल इसी पे कुछ।

मीना को क्लासरूम में विजय एक बेंच की तरफ जाता देखता है।

شیام:
ہاں۔

وجے:
فی البدیہہ؟

شیام:
ہاں۔

وجے:
کہوں؟

شیام:
کہو۔

وجے:
لیکن کہوں کس چیز پہ؟

شیام:
کس چیز پہ۔۔۔

مینا سنہا کو وجے کلاس روم میں داخل ہوتا دیکھتا ہے۔ اُسے وہ اچھی لگتی ہے۔

وجے:
ابے۔۔۔

شیام:
ہاں۔

وجے:
کون ہے یہ؟

شیام:
ارے پوچھتا کیا ہے یار؟ مصرعہ طرح حاضر ہے ظالم۔ کہہ ڈال اسی پہ کچھ۔

مینا کو کلاس روم میں وجے ایک بینچ کی طرف جاتا دیکھتا ہوئے۔

Vijay:
"When I walk, even my shadow lags behind
(she turns away from him)
"When you walk, the earth and sky keep pace
(she stops)
"When I stop, a lonely evening falls upon me
When you stop, spring and moonlight stand still."

Meena smiles at Vijay. She seems smitten by him. The college professor enters and addresses the students in English.

Professor:
Learning your poetry lessons, Vijay?

Vijay:
Yes, sir. No, sir.

Vijay and his friends hurry to their seats. The professor takes the roll call.

Professor:
Mr. David?

David:
Yes, sir.

Professor:
Miss Shobha?

Shobha:
Yes, sir.

"Jab hum chalen toh saaya bhi apna na saath de

"Jab tum chalo, zameen chale, aasmaan chale

"Jab hum ruken toh saath ruke shaam-e-be-kasi
Jab tum ruko, bahaar ruke, chaandni ruke."

विजय:

"जब हम चलें तो साया भी अपना न साथ दे

(मीना उसकी ओर से पलट कर दूर चली जाती है)

"जब तुम चलो, ज़मीन चले, आसमाँ चले

(वो रुक जाती है)

"जब हम रुके तो साथ रुके शामे-बे-कसी

जब तुम रुको, बहार रुके, चाँदनी रुके।"

मीना मुस्कुरा कर विजय को देखकर उसकी ओर कुछ घायल-सी हो जाती है। तभी प्रोफ़ेसर अंदर आते हैं।

प्रोफ़ेसर *(अंग्रेज़ी में):*
लर्निंग योर पोएट्री लेसन्स, विजय?

विजय:
यस, सर। नो, सर।

विजय और उसके दोस्त भागकर अपनी बेंच पर बैठ जाते हैं। प्रोफ़ेसर उनकी अटेन्डन्स लेते हैं।

प्रोफ़ेसर:
मि. डेविड?

डेविड:
यस, सर।

प्रोफ़ेसर:
मिस शोभा?

शोभा:
यस, सर।

وجے:

’’جب ہم چلیں تو سایہ بھی اپنا نہ ساتھ دے

(مینا کراس کی طرف سے رخ بدل لیتی ہے)

’’جب تم چلو، زمین چلے، آسماں چلے

(وہ رک جاتی ہے)

’’جب ہم رکیں تو ساتھ رکے شامِ بیکسی

جب تم رکو، بہار رکے، چاندنی رکے‘‘

مینا مسکرا کر وجے کو دیکھتی ہے، وہ اُس کی طرف مائل بہ کرم نظر آتی ہے۔ کالج پروفیسر داخل ہوتے ہیں۔

پروفیسر (انگریزی میں):
لرننگ یور پوئٹری لیسنس، وجے؟

وجے:
یس سر۔ نو سر۔

وجے اور اُس کے دوست گڑبڑا کر اپنی سیٹوں پر جاتے ہیں۔ پروفیسر رول کال لیتے ہیں۔

پروفیسر:
مسٹر ڈیوڈ؟

ڈیوڈ:
یس، سر۔

پروفیسر:
مس شوبھا؟

شوبھا:
یس، سر۔

Professor:
Miss Pushpalata? Miss Pushpalata?

Holding an umbrella, Miss Pushpalata, known by her friends as "Pushpa" (comedian Tun Tun), prances into the room.[20]

Pushpa *(partly in English):*
Yes, sir. I'm here, sir. Oh, sorry.   Yes, sir. Main aa gayi. Oh, sorry.

Pushpa is overweight. She squeezes between the benches and sits next to Meena. She notices Meena is trying to attract Vijay's attention by dropping her handkerchief on the ground. Pushpa guesses at once that Meena is attracted to Vijay.

Professor:
Miss Sinha? Miss Sinha?

Meena *(flustered, stands up):*
Yes, sir.

Laughter erupts in the classroom. Dissolve to a montage of Meena and Vijay playing badminton. They become emotionally involved as time passes.

Dissolve to a countryside scene. Day. A group of college students are cycling through the countryside singing a merry song. Meena is riding pillion on Vijay's bicycle.[21]

Singers: Mohammed Rafi, Geeta Dutt & chorus

Vijay:
We may face a thousand trials   Hon laakh musibat raste mein
But we will never be parted   Par saath na apna chhoote

Meena:
We'll never go back on our vows of love   Tooten na muhabbat ki qasmen
Even if the end of the world is upon us   Ab chaahe qayaamat toote

प्रोफ़ेसर:

मिस पुष्पलता? मिस पुष्पलता?

हाथ में एक छाता लिए मिस पुष्पलता (टुन टुन), जिसे 'पुष्पा' कहते हैं, डोलती हुई आती है ।

पुष्पा (कुछ अंग्रेजी में):

यस, सर । मैं आ गई, ओह । सॉरी ।

मोटी-सी पुष्पा बेंचो के बीच फँसती फँसाती मीना की बग़ल में बैठ जाती है । वो देख लेती है कि मीना ने पीछे बैठे विजय को आकर्षित करने के लिए अपना रुमाल नीचे गिरा दिया है । पुष्पा समझ जाती है कि विजय की ओर मीना आकर्षित हुई है ।

प्रोफ़ेसर:

मिस सिन्हा? मिस सिन्हा?

मीना (घबराकर खड़ी होती है):

यस, सर ।

क्लासरूम में खिलखिलाहट-सी हो जाती है । अगला दृश्य एक मोन्ताज का । विजय और मीना बैडमिंटन खेलते हुए । समय के बहते-बहते वो दोनों एक दूसरे के क़रीब आ जाते हैं ।

डिज़ौल्व । शहर से दूर । दिन । कॉलेज के कुछ छात्रों का समूह अपनी अपनी साइकिल पर सवार ख़ुशियों से भरा गीत गाता हुआ चला जा रहा है । विजय के साथ मीना भी साइकिल पर सवार है ।

गायक: मोहम्मद रफ़ी, गीता दत्त और कोरस

विजय:

हों लाख मुसीबत रस्ते में
पर साथ ना अपना छूटे

मीना:

टूटें ना मोहब्बत की क़स्में
अब चाहे क़यामत टूटे

Vijay & Meena (repeat the main verse together):

We may face a thousand trials	Hon laakh musibat raste mein
But we will never be parted	Par saath na apna chhoote
We'll never go back on our vows of love	Tooten na muhabbat ki qasmen
Even if the end of the world is upon us	Ab chaahe qayaamat toote

Chorus:

Leaving the world far behind	Peechhe-peechhe duniya hai aage-aage hum
Advancing step by step	Badhte hi jaate hain qadam har dam
Where are we heading?	Kahaan ka safar hai
No one knows	Kis ko khabar hai
Carefree as we are	Hum ko nahin hai koi gham

Vijay and Meena ride away from the group of students. The flashback ends on a dissolve to the close-up of Vijay, which began on the Calcutta street. He looks into the shop window to find Meena has gone.

Vijay sees a portly man laden with boxes.[22]

Man:
Coolie. Ae coolie.
(Vijay comes forward to the surprise of the man. Vijay does not look like a coolie)
I want a coolie.

Coolie. O coolie!

Mujhe coolie chaahiye.

Vijay:
At your service.

Ji haan. Main haazir hoon.

Man *(with a shocked expression):*
What? Okay, put these in the car.

Ein? Ye saamaan rakh do gaadi mein.

विजय और मीना (मुखड़ा साथ में दोहराते हुए):
हों लाख मुसीबत रस्ते में
पर साथ ना अपना छूटे
टूटें ना मोहब्बत की क़स्में
अब चाहे क़यामत टूटे

कोरस:
पीछे-पीछे दुनिया है आगे-आगे हम
बढ़ते ही जाते हैं क़दम हर दम
कहाँ का सफ़र है
किस को ख़बर है
हम को नहीं है कोई ग़म

विजय और मीना बाक़ी छात्रों के समूह से अलग हो जाते हैं। दृश्य बदलता है और वही दृश्य सामने आता है जिस में विजय कलकत्ता के एक रास्ते पर खड़ा मीना के बारे में सोच रहा था। वो दुकान की खिड़की से अंदर झाँकता है। मीना वहाँ से जा चुकी है।

एक मोटा-सा आदमी कई बक्से उठाए आता हुआ विजय को दिखाई देता है।

एक आदमी:
कुली। ओ कुली।
(विजय को देखकर वह शख़्स हैरान हो जाता है, क्योंकि विजय कहीं से भी कुली नहीं लगता)
मुझे कुली चाहिए।

विजय:
जी हाँ। मैं हाज़िर हूँ।

आदमी (हैरान होकर):
ऐं? ये सामान रख दो गाड़ी में।

وجے اور مینا (مکھڑا ساتھ ساتھ دوہراتے ہیں):

ہوں لاکھ مصیبت رستے میں
پر ساتھ نہ اپنا چھوٹے
ٹوٹیں نہ محبت کی قسمیں
اب چاہے قیامت ٹوٹے

کورس:

پیچھے پیچھے دنیا ہے آگے آگے ہم
بڑھتے ہی جاتے ہیں قدم ہر دم
کہاں کا سفر ہے
کس کو خبر ہے
ہم کو نہیں ہے کوئی غم

وجے اور مینا اسٹوڈنٹس کے گروپ سے الگ ہو جاتے ہیں۔ منظر بدل کر وہی منظر سامنے آتا ہے جس میں وجے کلکتہ کے ایک راستے پر کھڑا مینا کے بارے میں سوچ رہا تھا۔ وہ کھڑکی سے اندر جھانکتا ہے، مینا جا چکی ہے۔

راستے پر چلتے ہوئے وجے کو ایک مالدار شخص کئی بکسے اُٹھائے نظر آتا ہے۔

آدمی:
قلی۔ او، قلی!
(وجے جیسے پڑھے لکھے آدمی کو دیکھ کر وہ شخص حیرت زدہ رہ جاتا ہے جو کہیں سے قلی نہیں لگتا۔)
مجھے قلی چاہیے۔

وجے:
جی ہاں۔ میں حاضر ہوں۔

آدمی (حیرت سے):
ایں؟ یہ سامان رکھ دو گاڑی میں۔

(talking to himself)
Good God! What has the world come to? Educated people are now working as coolies.
(handing Vijay a rupee coin and entering his car)
Here.

The camera tilts down to Vijay's hand. He holds the coin tightly in his fist. Dissolve to the next scene. Night. Vijay is at a table in a modest restaurant. He is eating ravenously. The large-mustached restaurant manager (Om Prakash, known as "Omi") looks at Vijay with scorn.

Restaurant Manager:
Hey mister, have you brought money today? No credit.
(Vijay tosses the rupee coin at the restaurant manager who examines it very carefully)
It's counterfeit.

Vijay *(stops eating)*:
Counterfeit?

Restaurant Manager *(now towering over Vijay)*:
That's right, counterfeit. I suppose you've got nothing else? So that's your game? Paying with a counterfeit rupee. Now who'll pay for the food you've touched? Pay up, or I'll have your shirt. Understand? Waiter, take the plate away.

Unseen by Vijay, Gulaab overhears this exchange. She recognises Vijay from the night she threw him out. She comes to his table.

Gulaab *(tells the waiter, firmly)*:
Put it back.
(the waiter puts the plate back. Gulaab throws a rupee coin at the restaurant manager)
Take your money. Keep the change and go to a barber. He'll make you look more human. Now get lost.
(she sits next to Vijay and says affectionately)
Why don't you eat?

Ram, Ram, Ram, Ram. Kya haalat huwi is duniya ki? Arey padhe-likhe log bhi coolie-giri kar rahe hain.

Ye lo.

Ae babu saaheb. Paise laaye ho aaj? Udhaar nahin milega.

Ye toh khota hai.

Khota?

Haan haan, khota hai. Doosra hai paas ya nahin? Achha, toh ye chaal thi? Jaan-boojh kar khota rupiya laaye thay. Khaana-mangwa kar jo plate jhooti kar di uska daam kaun chukaayega? Daam chukaao, nahin toh coat-kameez utaar loonga. Samjhay? Chhokra, le jaao plate.

Rakkho khaana wahin.

Ye le apne daam. Baaqi ke paise kisi hajjaam ko de dena. Shakal insaanon jaisi kar dega teri. Chal ja yahaan se.

Khaana khaao tum.

(अपने आप से)

राम, राम, राम, राम। क्या हालत हो गई इस दुनिया की? अरे पढ़े-लिखे लोग भी कुली-गीरी कर रहे हैं।

(कार में बैठते हुए वह विजय को एक रुपये का सिक्का देता है)

ये लो।

दृश्य में विजय का हाथ दिखाई देता है। सिक्के को वो मज़बूती से अपनी मुट्ठी में जकड़ लेता है। अगला दृश्य। रात। एक छोटे से होटल में विजय टेबल पर बैठा हुआ है। भूख से बेहाल विजय खाना खा रहा है। बड़ी मूछों वाला होटल का मैनेजर (ओम प्रकाश, उर्फ़ "ओमी") उसे घूरे जा रहा है।

होटल मैनेजर:

ए बाबू साहब। पैसे लाए हो आज? उधार नहीं मिलेगा।

(विजय होटल मैनेजर की ओर सिक्का फेंकता है। वो उसे लपक लेता है और बारीक़ी से उस सिक्के को देखता है)

ये तो खोटा है।

विजय (खाते खाते रुक जाता है):

खोटा?

होटल मैनेजर (विजय के सर पर सवार होकर):

हाँ-हाँ, खोटा है। दूसरा है पास या नहीं? अच्छा, तो ये चाल थी? जान-बूझ कर खोटा रुपया लाए थे। खाना मँगवा कर जो प्लेट झूठी कर दी उसका दाम कौन चुकाएगा? दाम चुकाओ, नहीं तो कोट-कमीज़ उतार लूँगा। समझे? छोकरा, ले जाओ प्लेट।

गुलाबो यह सुन रही है। विजय उसे नहीं देख पाता। गुलाबो पहचान जाती है कि इसी विजय को उसने अपने कोठे से भगा दिया था। वो उसकी टेबल के पास आती है।

गुलाब (सख़्ती से वेटर को):

रक्खो खाना वहीं।

(वेटर थाली वहीं रख देता है। गुलाब एक सिक्का होटल मैनेजर की ओर उछालती है)

ये ले अपने दाम। बाक़ी के पैसे किसी हज्जाम को दे देना। शकल इन्सानों जैसी कर देगा तेरी। चल जा यहाँ से।

(विजय के पास बैठकर बड़े प्यार से)

खाना खाओ तुम।

Vijay:
I'm not hungry.

Gulaab:
Yes, you are. Here, eat.

Vijay (brusquely):
You've no right to pity me.
(in a softer tone)
I'm sorry. Don't mind my anger.

Gulaab:
Of course I won't. You have every right to be angry. I treated you very badly the other day.

Vijay:
I have nothing against you.

Gulaab:
Then please eat…for my sake.

Vijay:
For your sake? But you hardly even know me.

Gulaab:
I know you very well.

Vijay:
How?

Bhook nahin hai mujhe.

Hai kaise nahin. Lo khaao.

Aap ko mujh par taras khaane ka koi haq nahin.

Maaf kijiyega. Meri naaraazgi ka bura na maaniyega.

Bilkul nahin. Tumhen naaraaz hona bhi chaahiye. Uss din maine bahot bura sulook kiya tumhaare saath.

Mujhe aap se koi shikaayat nahin.

Toh phir khaana kha lo. Tumhen meri qasam.

Aap…aap apni qasam kyun deti hain mujhe? Aap mujhe theek tarah jaantein bhi toh nahin.

Khoob jaanti hoon.

Kaise?

विजय:

भूख नहीं है मुझे ।

गुलाब:

है कैसे नहीं । लो खाओ ।

विजय *(नाराज़ होते हुए)*:

आपको मुझ पर तरस खाने का कोई हक़ नहीं ।
(नर्मी से)
माफ़ कीजिएगा । मेरी नाराज़गी का बुरा न मानिएगा ।

गुलाब:

बिलकुल नहीं । तुम्हें नाराज़ होना भी चाहिए । उस दिन मैंने बहुत बुरा सुलूक किया
तुम्हारे साथ ।

विजय:

मुझे आप से कोई शिक़ायत नहीं ।

गुलाब:

तो फिर खाना खा लो । तुम्हें मेरी क़सम ।

विजय:

आप...आप अपनी क़सम क्यूँ देती हैं मुझे? आप मुझे ठीक तरह जानतीं भी
तो नहीं ।

गुलाब:

खूब जानती हूँ ।

विजय:

कैसे?

وجے:

بھوک نہیں ہے مجھے۔

گلاب:

ہے کیسے نہیں۔ لو کھاؤ۔

وجے: (ترشی سے):

آپ کو مجھ پر ترس کھانے کا کوئی حق نہیں۔
(نرمی سے)
معاف کیجیے گا۔ میری ناراضگی کا برا نہ مانیے گا۔

گلاب:

بالکل نہیں۔ تمہیں ناراض ہونا بھی چاہیے۔ اُس دن میں نے بہت برا سلوک کیا تمہارے ساتھ۔

وجے:

مجھے آپ سے کوئی شکایت نہیں۔

گلاب:

تو پھر کھانا کھا لو۔ تمہیں میری قسم۔

وجے:

آپ۔۔۔آپ اپنی قسم کیوں دیتی ہیں مجھے؟ آپ مجھے ٹھیک طرح جانتی بھی تو نہیں۔

گلاب:

خوب جانتی ہوں۔

وجے:

کیسے؟

Gulaab:
Through your poems and songs. If I already know your thoughts and feelings — what more is there to know?

Vijay:
I don't understand, Miss. The other day…

Gulaab:[23]
Why do you address me so politely? It feels strange.

Vijay:
Why?

Gulaab:
Until today I've only heard people insult me. I have heard their crude remarks, their taunts…their abuse and dirty jokes. And you, you show me so much respect.

Gulaab walks to the window and looks out. Vijay leaves the restaurant. Gulaab looks around to find him gone. She wipes away a tear.

Reel Four

The head masseur Abdul Sattar (Johnny Walker) is walking through a park, selling his services to the passers-by.[24]

Sattar:
Massage, oil massage, head massage.
(repeats his cry three times and then sings)

Singer: Mohammed Rafi[25]

If your head is reeling or your heart is sinking
Come to me, my friend
No point fretting (2)
(line spoken)
"Massage. Oil massage."

Tumhaari nazmon aur ghazlon se. Jab tumhaare khayaalaat aur jazbaat ko jaan liya toh ab jaanne ko kya bacha hai?

Main aap ko samajh nahin saka. Uss din toh aap…

Tum baar-baar mujhe "aap" kyun kehte ho? Kuchh ajeeb sa lagta hai mujhe.

Kyun?

Aaj tak logon ke moonh se main sirf tu-tukaar hi sunti rahi hoon apne liye. Unki fiqre-baaziyaan aur taanay sunti rahi hoon, gaaliyaan sunti rahi hoon. Ganda mazaaq sunti rahi hoon. Aur tum itni izzat se pesh aate ho mujh se.

Maalish. Tel maalish. Champi.

Sar jo tera chakraaye ya dil dooba jaaye
Aaja pyare paas hamaare
Kaahe ghabraaye (2)

"Maalish. Tel maalish"

गुलाब:

तुम्हारी नज़्मों और ग़ज़लों से। जब तुम्हारे ख़यालात और जज़्बात को जान लिया, तो अब जानने को क्या बचा है?

विजय:

मैं आपको समझ नहीं सका। उस दिन तो आप...

गुलाब:

तुम बार-बार मुझे "आप" क्यूँ कहते हो? कुछ अजीब सा लगता है मुझे।

विजय:

क्यों?

गुलाब:

आज तक लोगों के मुँह से मैं सिर्फ़ दुत्कार ही सुनती रही हूँ अपने लिए। उनकी फ़िक्रे-बाज़ियाँ और ताने सुनती रही हूँ, गालियाँ सुनती रही हूँ। गंदा मज़ाक सुनती रही हूँ। और तुम इतनी इज़्ज़त से पेश आते हो मुझसे।

गुलाब उठ कर खिड़की की ओर जाती है। विजय उठकर बाहर चला जाता है। वो मुड़ कर देखती है तो विजय जा चुका है। वह अपनी आँखों में आए हुए आँसू पोंछती है।

रील ४

मालिश वाला अब्दुल सत्तार (जॉनी वॉकर) मालिश वाले की आवाज़ लगाता हुआ बाग़ में दाख़िल होता है।

सत्तार:

मालिश। तेल मालिश। चंपी।
(तीन बार दोहराता है और गाता है)

गायक: मोहम्मद रफ़ी

सर जो तेरा चकराए या दिल डूबा जाए
आजा प्यारे पास हमारे
काहे घबराए (२)
(आवाज़ लगाता है)
"मालिश। तेल मालिश"

گلاب:

تمہاری نظموں اور غزلوں سے۔ جب تمہارے خیالات اور جذبات کو جان لیا، تو اب جاننے کو کیا بچا ہے؟

وجے:

میں آپ کو سمجھ نہیں سکا۔ اُس دن تو آپ۔۔۔

گلاب:

تم بار بار مجھے 'آپ' کیوں کہتے ہو؟ کچھ عجیب سا لگتا ہے مجھے۔

وجے:

کیوں؟

گلاب:

آج کی لوگوں کے منہ سے میں صرف تو تکار ہی سنتی رہی ہوں اپنے لیے۔ اُن کی فقرے بازیاں اور طنے سنتی رہی ہوں، گالیاں سنتی رہی ہوں۔ گندہ مذاق سنتی رہی ہوں۔ اور تم اتنی عزت سے پیش آتے ہو مجھ سے۔

ریستوراں کے ٹیبل سے اُٹھ کر گلاب کھڑکی کی طرف کی طرف جاتی ہے۔ اُس کی پشت ہے، اور وجے اُٹھ کر باہر چلا جاتا ہے۔ وہ مڑ کر دیکھتی ہے تو وجے جا چکا ہوتا ہے، انگلیوں سے وہ آنکھوں میں آئے آنسو پونچھ لیتی ہے۔

ریل ۴

مالش والا، عبدالستار (جانی واکر) مالش والی کی صدائیں لگا تا پارک میں داخل ہوتا ہے۔

ستار:

مالش۔ تیل مالش۔ چمپی۔
(تین بار دہراتا ہے اور گاتا ہے)

محمد رفیع کی آواز۔

سر جو تیرا چکرائے یا دل ڈوبا جائے
آجا پیارے پاس ہمارے
کاہے گھبرائے (۲)
(تحت میں)
مالش۔ تیل مالش۔

If your head is reeling or your heart is sinking
Come to me, my friend
No point fretting *(2)*

This oil of mine has perfume, curing baldness and dandruff *(2)*
Once my hands begin to whirl, your fate won't look so rough
(both lines repeated)
Listen to me, my son, listen
This oil has great healing powers
(both lines repeated)
It cures a thousand ailments. Why not give it a try?
No point fretting *(2)*

If your head is reeling or your heart is sinking
Come to me, my friend
No point fretting *(2)*

Suffering a lovers' tiff? Business in the throes?
A touch of this strong hand will dissipate all woes
(both lines repeated)
Listen to me, dear mister, listen
This oil has great healing powers
(both lines repeated)
It cures a thousand ailments. Why not give it a try?
No point fretting *(2)*

Still stinging, Sattar manages to coax an overweight customer
(played by film extra supplier Hira) to have a head massage. Sattar
beats time on the customer's head as though drumming.

If your head is reeling or your heart is sinking
Come to me, my friend
No point fretting *(2)*

Be you a servant, be you a master
Be you a leader, or one of the led
King or soldier, to me all bow their head
(three lines repeated)

Sar jo tera chakraaye ya dil dooba jaaye
Aaja pyare paas hamaare
Kaahe ghabraaye *(2)*

Tel mera hai mushki, ganj rahe na khuski
Jis ke sar par haath phira doon chamke qismat uski
(both lines repeated)
Sunn sunn sunn arey beta sunn
Is champi mein bade-bade gunn
(both lines repeated)
Laakh dukhon ki ek dawa hai kyun na aazmaaye
Kaahe ghabraaye *(2)*

Sar jo tera chakraaye ya dil dooba jaaye
Aaja pyare paas hamaare
Kaahe ghabraaye *(2)*

Pyar ka howe jhadga ya business ka ho ragda
Sab lafdon ka bojh hatay jab pade haath ik tagda
(both lines repeated)
Sunn sunn sunn arey babu sunn
Is champi mein bade-bade gunn
(both lines repeated)
Laakh dukhon ki ek dawa hai kyun na aazmaaye
Kaahe ghabraaye *(2)*

Sar jo tera chakraaye ya dil dooba jaaye
Aaja pyare paas hamaare
Kaahe ghabraaye *(2)*

Naukar ho ya maalik, leader ho ya public

Apne aage sabhi jhuke hain kya raja kya sainik
(both lines repeated)

सर जो तेरा चकराए या दिल डूबा जाए
आजा प्यारे पास हमारे
काहे घबराए (२)

तेल मेरा है मुस्की, गंज रहे ना खुस्की
जिसके सर पर हाथ फिरा दूँ चमके क़िस्मत उसकी
(दोनों पंक्तियाँ दोहराता है)
सुन सुन सुन अरे बेटा सुन
इस चंपी में बड़े-बड़े गुन
(दोनों पंक्तियाँ दोहराता है)
लाख दुखों की एक दवा है क्यूँ ना आजमाए
काहे घबराए (२)

सर जो तेरा चकराए या दिल डूबा जाए
आजा प्यारे पास हमारे
काहे घबराए (२)

प्यार का होवे झगड़ा या बिज़नेस का हो रगड़ा
सब लफ़ड़ों का बोझ हटे जब पड़े हाथ इक तगड़ा
(दोनों पंक्तियाँ दोहराता है)
सुन सुन सुन अरे बाबू सुन
इस चंपी में बड़े-बड़े गुन
(दोनों पंक्तियाँ दोहराता है)
लाख दुखों की एक दवा है क्यूँ ना आजमाए
काहे घबराए (२)

गाते गाते सत्तार आखिर एक मोटे से आदमी (फ़िल्म एक्स्ट्रा हीरा) को तेल मालिश के लिए तैयार कर लेता है।

सर जो तेरा चकराए या दिल डूबा जाए
आजा प्यारे पास हमारे
काहे घबराए (२)

नौकर हो या मालिक, लीडर हो या पब्लिक

अपने आगे सभी झुके हैं क्या राजा क्या सैनिक
(दोनों पंक्तियाँ दोहराता है)

Listen to me, my prince, listen This oil has great healing powers *(both lines repeated)* It cures a thousand ailments. Why not give it a try? No point fretting *(2)*	Sunn sunn sunn arey raja sunn Is champi mein bade-bade gunn *(both lines repeated)* Laakh dukhon ki ek dawa hai kyun na aazmaaye Kaahe ghabraaye *(2)*
If your head is reeling or your heart is sinking Come to me, my friend No point fretting	Sar jo tera chakraaye ya dil dooba jaaye Aaja pyare paas hamaare Kaahe ghabraaye…

Vijay enters the park and is spotted by Sattar. Vijay sits down on a park bench.

Sattar *(elated)*: Mr. Vijay, come! *(to the customer)* That's our Mr. Vijay — a great poet. I was just singing one of his songs. *(to Vijay)* Mr. Vijay, what a song you've written! Business has doubled since I've been singing it.	Ah ha, Vijay babu. Aao, aao. Apne Vijay babu — bahot achhe shaayer hain. Main inhin ke gaane toh ga raha tha. Vijay babu, kya cheez likh ke di hai! Arey jab se gaane laga hoon, apna business double ho gaya hai.
Vijay: Really?	Achha.
Sattar: Yes. Don't go. I'll just finish him off.	Haan. Jaana nahin, haan. Main seth ko khallaas kar ke abhi aaya.
Customer: Come again?	Kya kaha?

सुन सुन सुन अरे राजा सुन
इस चंपी में बड़े-बड़े गुन
(दोनों पंक्तियाँ दोहराता है)
लाख दुखों की एक दवा है क्यूँ ना आजमाए
काहे घबराए (२)

सर जो तेरा चकराए या दिल डूबा जाए
आजा प्यारे पास हमारे
काहे घबराए...

विजय को बाग़ में दाखिल होते हुए सत्तार देख लेता है। विजय बाग़ में आकर एक बेंच पर बैठ जाता है।

सत्तार *(ख़ुशी से)*:
अ हा, विजय बाबू, आओ, आओ।
(अपने ग्राहक से)
अपने विजय बाबू – बहुत अच्छे शायर है। मैं इन्हीं के गाने तो गा रहा था।
(विजय से)
विजय बाबू, क्या चीज़ लिख के दी है! अरे जब से गाने लगा हूँ, अपना बिज़नेस डबल हो गया है।

विजय:
अच्छा।

सत्तार:
हाँ। जाना नहीं, हाँ। मैं सेठ को खल्लास कर के अभी आया।

ग्राहक:
क्या कहा?

Sattar:
Sit still!
(to Vijay)
Mr. Vijay, today Sattar will give you a special massage. And that too — for free.

Vijay:
No, Sattar. The world has battered me quite enough. I don't need any kind of massage.

Sattar:
How amazing! And you still have a smile on your face? Brother, I've seen only two creatures so blissfully oblivious: a donkey in the hot sun and an impoverished poet.

Vijay:
How true, Sattar. The heat may come from melting gold or the sun — only donkeys are entranced by it.

Customer:
What's that? What did you say?

Sattar *(to client):*
Be still! We're discussing donkeys.

Sattar continues massaging. When he sees Juhi (Gulaab's roommate and friend) entering the park, Sattar places his customer's hand on his head. Unconsciously, the businessman starts massaging his own head till he opens his eyes and discovers Sattar's ruse. The masseur has since sped off and is at Juhi's side.[26]

Sattar *(a playful tone):*
Here I am! Juhi, are you waiting for me?

Juhi *(dismissively):*
I'm waiting for a man with a car.

Sattar:
A man with a car? Not a masseur?

Oho, jamay raho, jamay raho.

Vijay babu, aaj Sattar bhai aap ki peshal maalish karenge. Aur vo bhi phokat.

Nahin bey, Sattar. Aaj-kal zamaane ne itna masal daala hai hamen ki ab aur kisi maalish ki zaroorat nahin.

Le, kamaal hai, babuji. Masle jaane ke baad bhi muskuraahat hai chehre par? Bhai, be-waqt do hi cheezon ko magan dekha hai apan ne — ek toh garmi mein gadha aur kadki mein shaayer.

Theek kehte ho, Sattar. Garmi chaahe mausam ki ho ya daulat ki sirf gadhe hi magan rehte hain uss mein.

Ji? Kya kaha hai aap ne?

Aap chamakiye matt. Gadhe ki baat ho rahi hai.

Hum aa gaye. Juhi, tu mera intezaar kar rahi thi na?

Ha! Kisi motor-waale ka.

Motor-waale ka? Maalish-waale ka nahin?

सत्तार:

ओहो, जमे रहो, जमे रहो ।

(विजय से)

विजय बाबू, आज सत्तार भाई आपको पेशल मालिश करेंगे । और वो भी फोकट ।

विजय:

नहीं बे, सत्तार । आज-कल ज़माने ने इतना मसल डाला है हमें कि अब और किसी मालिश की ज़रूरत नहीं ।

सत्तार:

ले, कमाल है, बाबूजी । मसले जाने के बाद भी मुस्कुराहट है चेहरे पर? भाई, बे-वक़्त दो ही चीज़ों को मगन देखा है अपन ने - एक तो गरमी में गधा और सरदी में शायर ।

विजय:

ठीक कहते हो, सत्तार । गरमी चाहे मौसम की हो या दौलत की सिर्फ़ गधे ही मगन रहते हैं उस में ।

ग्राहक:

जी? क्या कहा आपने?

सत्तार *(ग्राहक से)*:

आप चमकिए मत । गधे की बात हो रही है ।

सत्तार मालिश में लगा हुआ है । जूही (गुलाब की सहेली) को बाग़ में दाख़िल होता देख कर, ग्राहक का हाथ उसी के सर पर रखता है । ग्राहक अनजाने में ही अपने सर की मालिश ख़ुद करने लगता है, आँख खुलते ही उसे सत्तार की चालाकी का एहसास होता है । सत्तार तब तक जूही के पास पहुँच चुका है ।

सत्तार *(चहकते हुए)*:

हम आ गए । जूही, तू मेरा इंतज़ार कर रही थी ना?

जूही *(पीछा छुड़ाते हुए)*:

हँ । किसी मोटरवाले का ।

सत्तार:

मोटरवाले का? मालिशवाले का नहीं?

Juhi:
No.

Sattar:
No? May Allah puncture his tyres.

Juhi *(walking away):*
May your head get punctured.

Sattar *(following her):*
My head? Juhi, are you cross with me?

Juhi:
Out with it.

Sattar:
You get upset when I wished the man has punctured tyres, but have no consideration for the heart you've punctured.

Juhi:
For you. Get it patched up.

Sattar:
But how? I have no wife to patch it.

Juhi:
So what am I supposed to do?

Sattar:
Let's go and see the priest.

Juhi:
Get lost, you idiot!

Sattar *(looking up and addressing God):*
Did You hear that? What's the point of giving me the gift of massage? If I had the gift of cheating, I'd be the one driving her around today.

Nahin.

Nahin? Allah kare uski motor hi puncture ho jaaye.

Tera sar puncture ho jaaye.

Mera sar? Juhi. Ae, Juhi, naaraaz ho gayi?

Bak na jo bakna hai.

Maine uski motor puncture hone ki baat ki toh tu ukhad gayi aur tu ne jo mera dil puncture kar rakkha hai uska kuchh khayaal nahin.

Hai. Thigla lagwaale ja ke.

Magar lagwaaun kis se, gharwaali hai kahaan?

Toh main kya karoon?

Qaazi ke yahaan chal.

Chal hatt, mooye!

Suna tum ne? Hunar bhi diya toh tel maalish. Koi chaar-sau-beesi ka dhanda hi sikha dete toh aaj hum motor mein ghumaate usko.

جوہی:
نہیں۔

ستّار:
نہیں؟ اللہ کرے اُس کی موٹر ہی پنکچر ہو جائے۔

جوہی (دور جاتے ہوئے):
تیرا سر پنکچر ہو جائے۔

ستّار (پیچھے پیچھے):
میرا سر؟ جوہی، اے، جوہی، ناراض ہو گئی؟

جوہی:
بک نا جو بکنا ہے۔

ستّار:
میں نے اُس کی موٹر پنکچر ہونے کی بات کی تو تُو اُکھڑ گئی اور تُو نے جو میرا دل پنکچر کر رکھا ہے اُس کا کچھ خیال نہیں۔

جوہی:
ہے۔ تھگلا لگوا جا کے۔

ستّار:
مگر لگواؤں کس سے، گھر والی ہے کہاں؟

جوہی:
تو میں کیا کروں؟

ستّار:
قاضی کے یہاں چل۔

جوہی:
چل ہٹ، موئے۔

ستّار (اوپر والے سے):
سنا تم نے؟ ہنر بھی دیا تو تیل مالش۔ کوئی چار سو بیسی کا دھندا ہی سکھا دیتے تو آج ہم موٹر میں گھماتے اُس کو۔

जूही:
नहीं।

सत्तार:
नहीं? अल्लाह करे उसकी मोटर ही पंक्चर हो जाए।

जूही (दूर जाते हुए):
तेरा सर पंक्चर हो जाए।

सत्तार (पीछे पीछे):
मेरा सर? जूही। ऐ, जूही, नाराज़ हो गई?

जूही:
बक ना जो बकना है।

सत्तार:
मैंने उसकी मोटर पंक्चर होने की बात की तो तू उखड़ गयी और तूने जो मेरा दिल पंक्चर कर रखा है उसका कुछ ख़याल नहीं।

जूही:
है, थिगड़ा लगवा ले जा के।

सत्तार:
मगर लगवाऊँ किस से, घरवाली है कहाँ?

जूही:
तो मैं क्या करूँ?

सत्तार:
क़ाज़ी के यहाँ चल।

जूही:
चल हट, मुँए।

सत्तार (ऊपरवाले से):
सुना तुमने? हुनर भी दिया तो तेल मालिश। कोई चार-सौ-बीसी का धंधा ही सिखा देते तो आज हम मोटर में घुमाते उसको।

(a coconut falls on his head)
I'm done for! What are you? Oh! A coconut? I get it. I won't say another word.

Fade out.

Fade in. Day. Vijay is half-asleep on a park bench. In the distance he sees Pushpa, his old classmate, running behind two young children. He sits up as she cries for help.

Pushpa:
Gullu! Stop! I'm out of breath. Brother, don't let him go. Hold him tight. That naughty boy! Brother, if you let him go, he'll make me run another mile.
(Vijay holds on to Pushpa's son)
Stop! I'm half my size, running after these boys. Well? You naughty boy.

Vijay *(in English)*:
Hello, Pushpa.

Pushpa *(turns to Vijay, and sits on the bench next to him)*:
Vijay? It's you! I didn't recognise you. You used to dress so smartly at college. Whose "love" has reduced you to this dishevelled state?

Vijay:
Someone, who won't let go of me.

Pushpa *(conspiratorially)*:
Who is she?

Oh, mar gaye. Aap ki taareef? Ein? Naariyal. Samajh gaya. Ab nahin boloonga.

Arey Gullu, ruk ja. Mera damm hi phool gaya. Ae bhayya, jaane na paaye, zara pakad lena isay. Arey paaji! Bhayya, aap ke haath se chhoot gaya toh sawa meel ka chakkar lagwaayega.

Thair ja. Bhaga-bhaga ke aadha kar diya mujhe, kyun re paaji? Ein?

Arey Vijay, tum? Main toh pehchaan bhi nahin saki tumhen. College mein kya shaan thi tumhaari. Aur ab ye phate-majnoon bane kis ke liye phir rahe ho?

Hai ek, peechha hi nahin chhodti.

Ein? Kaun hai?

(एक नारियल उसके सर पर गिरता है)

ओह, मर गए। आपकी तारीफ़? एँ? नारियल। समझ गया। अब नहीं बोलूँगा।

दृश्य बदलता है।

अगला दृश्य। दिन। विजय बाग़ में एक बेंच पर लेटा हुआ है। दूर से वो देखता है कि उसके कॉलेज की साथी, मोटी-सी पुष्पा दो छोटे बच्चों के पीछे भाग रही है। वो उठ कर बैठ जाता है, पुष्पा मदद के लिए उसे पुकारती है।

पुष्पा:
अरे गुल्लू। रुक जा। मेरा दम ही फूल गया। ए भय्या, जाने ना पाए, ज़रा पकड़ लेना इसे। अरे पाजी। भय्या, आपके हाथ से छूट गया तो सवा मील का चक्कर लगवाएगा।

(विजय उस भागते हुए बच्चे का हाथ पकड़ लेता है)

ठहर जा। भगा-भगा के आधा कर दिया मुझे, क्यूँ रे पाजी? हैं?

विजय (अंग्रेज़ी में):
हैलो, पुष्पा।

पुष्पा (विजय को देख कर ख़ुश होती है और उसके पास आकर बैठ जाती है):
अरे विजय, तुम? मैं तो पहचान भी नहीं सकी थी तुम्हें। कॉलेज में क्या शान थी तुम्हारी। और अब ये फटे-मजनूँ बने किसके लिए फिर रहे हो?

विजय:
है एक, पीछा ही नहीं छोड़ती।

पुष्पा (आशंक होकर):
हैं? कौन है?

(ایک ناریل اُس کے سر پر گرتا ہے)

اوہ، مر گئے۔ آپ کی تعریف؟ ایں؟ ناریل۔ سمجھ گیا۔ اب نہیں بولوں گا۔

منظر بدلتا ہے۔

اگلا منظر۔ وجے پارک کی بنچ پر غنودگی کے عالم میں پڑا ہے۔ دور سے وہ دیکھتا ہے کہ اُس کی موٹی تازی کالج کی دوست پشپا دو چھوٹے بچوں کے تعاقب میں چلی آرہی ہے۔ وہ اُٹھ کر بیٹھ جاتا ہے، پشپا مدد کے لیے اُسے پکارتی ہے۔

پشپا:
ارے گلو۔ رک جا۔ میرا دم ہی پھول گیا۔ اے بھیا، جانے نہ پائے، ذرا پکڑ لینا اسے۔ ارے پاجی۔ بھیا، آپ کے ہاتھ سے چھوٹ گیا تو سوا میل کا چکر لگوائے گا۔

(قریب سے بھاگتے ہوئے ایک بچے کا ہاتھ وجے پکڑ لیتا ہے)

ٹھہر جا۔ بھاگ بھاگ کر آدھا کر دیا مجھے، کیوں رے پاجی؟ ایں؟

وجے (انگریزی میں):
ہیلو، پشپا۔

پشپا (وجے کو دیکھ کر وہ بہت خوش ہوتی ہے اور اُس کے پہلو میں بیٹھ جاتی ہے):
ارے وجے، تم؟ میں تو پہچان بھی نہیں سکی تھیں تمہیں۔ کالج میں کیا شان تھی تمہاری۔ اور اب یہ پھٹے مجنوں بنے کس کے لیے پھر رہے ہو؟

وجے:
ہے ایک، پیچھا ہی نہیں چھوڑتی۔

پشپا (سازشانہ انداز میں):
ایں؟ کون ہے؟

Vijay:
Unemployment.
(Pushpa does not react)
Are these children yours?

Pushpa:
And their father's. He's Gullu and that's Fullu. Their father's name rhymes with theirs.

Vijay:[27]
Rhymes with theirs?

Pushpa:
That's right. That reminds me — there's a gathering at our old college tonight. All our classmates will be there. You will come, won't you?
(her son runs off)
Gullu, wait. See that? Now we're off for another mile race. I must go. Gullu!
(she comes back to get her second son)
What are you doing here? Come on. Hurry up.
(to Vijay)
Don't forget to come tonight. Come early. Gullu, wait!

Vijay leaves the park. The happy song that Meena and Vijay sang during their college days plays in the background.[28] Dissolve to the old college. Night. Vijay is walking slowly through the corridor, but does not enter the hall.

Singers: Mohammed Rafi & Geeta Dutt

Leaving the world behind
Advancing step by step
Where are we heading?
No one knows
Carefree as we are

Bekaari.

Ye bachche tumhaare hi hain?

Apne baap ke bhi. Ye Gullu. Vo Fullu. Aur baap ka naam bhi kuchh milta-julta hai.

Milta-julta?

Haan. Arey haan, yaad aaya. Aaj shaam ko apne puraane college mein jalsa hai. Jitne apne saath padhte thay vo sab aayenge. Tum bhi aana, hein?

Arey, arey Gullu, thair ja, beta. Dekha? Ab sawa meel ki race phir se chaalu ho gayi. Achha main chaloon. Gullu!

Arey tu kahaan reh gaya? Tu toh chal. Chal chal chal jaldi.

Achha bhayya tum aana matt bhoolna. Jaldi aana, haan. Arey, Gullu, thair ja. Thair ja re.

Peechhe-peechhe duniya hai aage-aage hum
Badhte hi jaate hain qadam har dam
Kahaan ka safar hai
Kis ko khabar hai
Hum ko nahin hai koi gham

विजय:

बेकारी ।

(पुष्पा की समझ में कुछ नहीं आता)

ये बच्चे तुम्हारे ही हैं?

पुष्पा:

अपने बाप के भी। ये गुल्लू। वो फुल्लू। और बाप का नाम भी कुछ मिलता-जुलता है ।

विजय:

मिलता-जुलता?

पुष्पा:

हाँ। अरे हाँ, याद आया। आज शाम को अपने पुराने कॉलेज में जलसा है। जितने अपने साथ पढ़ते थे वो सब आएँगे। तुम भी आना, हैं?

(एक बच्चा भाग खड़ा होता है)

अरे, अरे गुल्लू, ठहर जा, बेटा। देखा? अब सवा-मील की रेस फिर से चालू हो गई। अच्छा मैं चलूँ। गुल्लू!

(लौट कर दूसरे बच्चे को लेने आती है)

अरे तू कहाँ रह गया? तू तो चल। चल-चल-चल जल्दी ।

(विजय से)

अच्छा भय्या तुम आना मत भूलना। जल्दी आना, हाँ। अरे, गुल्लू, ठहर जा। ठहर जा रे।

विजय बाग़ से बाहर आता है। बैकग्राउँड में वो ख़ुशियों भरा गीत सुनाई देता है जो कभी विजय और मीना ने अपने कॉलेज के दिनों में गाया था। अगला दृश्य। कॉलेज। रात। विजय राहदारी से गुज़र रहा है, लेकिन सभागृह के अंदर नहीं जाता ।

गायक: मोहम्मद रफ़ी और गीता दत्त

पीछे-पीछे दुनिया है आगे-आगे हम

बढ़ते ही जाते हैं क़दम हर दम

कहाँ का सफ़र है

किसको ख़बर है

हमको नहीं है कोई ग़म

Leaving the world behind
Advancing step by step…
(the song fades out)

Peechhe-peechhe duniya hai
Aage-aage hum…

Pushpa (inside the crowded hall, talking to herself):
Where is that Bhattacharya loitering? He was going to recite next. Where do I find him?
(she sees Vijay in the corridor and goes to him)
Vijay, why are you standing here? Come inside.

Ye Bhattacharya kahaan charne chala gaya? Abhi uska programme tha. Kahaan dhoondon usay? Haan.

Vijay, ye tum ne kya taak-jhaank laga rakkhi hai yahaan se? Chalo, andar chalo.

Vijay:
No, Pushpa. My clothes…

Nahin, Pushpa. Mere kapde…

Pushpa:
Clothes? What do you mean? You're covered from head to toe. Come on. Let's go in.
(pushing her way through the crowd with Vijay)
Move aside. Come on.

Kapde? Ye kya hain badan par? Sar se paaon tak toh dhake huwe ho. Aao chalo, chalo andar chalo. Aao na. Chalo.

Hato hato hato. Aao na. Aayiye.

Pushpa gets onto the stage and stands at the mike.

Pushpa:
Friends! Girls and boys! Mr. Bhattacharya hasn't turned up. We're delighted…
(laughter)
…we're delighted that Vijay is here. And I request him to recite one of his wonderful poems. Vijay, don't be formal. Come.

Sajjano and sajjaniyo! Bhattacharyaji toh aaye nahin. Khair ye badi khushi ki baat hai…

…khushi ki baat ye hai ki Vijay saaheb tashreef le aaye hain. Aur main unsay darkhwaast karoongi ki vo koi apni achhi si ghazal sunaayen. Aayiye, Vijay saaheb. Aayiye na, Vijay saaheb, kya takalluf kar rahe hain aap? Aayiye.

Vijay reluctantly steps onto the stage. Standing at the mike, he sees Meena in the audience. They look at one another across the crowded room. Pushpa tugs at his jacket sleeve.

Pushpa:
Let's hear you, Vijay.
(more insistent)
Vijay, recite something.

Vijay. Vijay, kuchh sunaao na.

Vijay. Vijay, kuchh sunaao na.

पीछे-पीछे दुनिया है
आगे-आगे हम...
(गाना ख़त्म होता है)

पुष्पा (लोगों से भरे सभागृह में अपने आप से):
ये भट्टाचार्य कहाँ चरने चला गया? अभी उसका प्रोग्राम था। कहाँ ढूँढूँ उसे? हाँ।
(बाहर राहदारी में आती है तब उसकी नज़र विजय पर पड़ती है)
विजय, ये तुमने क्या ताक-झाँक लगा रक्खी है यहाँ से? चलो, अंदर चलो।

विजय:
नहीं, पुष्पा। मेरे कपड़े...

पुष्पा:
कपड़े? ये क्या हैं बदन पर? सर से पाँव तक तो ढके हुए हो। आओ चलो, चलो
अंदर चलो। आओ ना। चलो।
(विजय का हाथ थामे हुए भीड़ में रास्ता बनाती है)
हटो-हटो-हटो। आओ ना। आईए।

पुष्पा स्टेज पर माईक के पास आती है।

पुष्पा:
सज्जनो ऑण्ड सज्जनियों! भट्टाचार्यजी तो आए नहीं। ख़ैर ये बड़ी ख़ुशी की बात है...
(सभी हँस पड़ते हैं)
...ख़ुशी की बात ये है कि विजय साहब तशरीफ़ ले आए हैं। और मैं उनसे दरख़्वास्त
करूँगी की वो कोई अपनी अच्छी-सी ग़ज़ल सुनाएँ। आईए, विजय साहब। आईए
ना, विजय साहब, क्या तकल्लुफ़ कर रहे हैं आप? आईए।

झिझकते हुए विजय आता है और माईक के सामने खड़ा हो जाता है। उसकी नज़र
सामने श्रोताओं में बैठी मीना पर पड़ती है। दोनों एक-दूसरे को देखते हैं। पुष्पा
उसकी जैकेट की बाँहें खींचते हुए।

पुष्पा:
विजय। विजय, कुछ सुनाओ ना।
(फिर से कहती है)
विजय। विजय, कुछ सुनाओ ना।

Reel Five

Recitation in Mohammed Rafi's voice[29]

Vijay:
"I am weary of the struggles of life (2)
The weariness of my heart may spurn the world"

"Tang aa chuke hain kash-ma-kash-e-zindagi se hum (2)
Thukra na den jahaan ko kahin be-dili se hum"

Man in audience:
Why such a sad song on this happy occasion, sir? Recite a happy verse.

Ji janaab, khushi ke mauqe pe kya bedili ka raag chheda huwa hai? Koi khushi ka geet sunaayiye.

Vijay:
"Afflicted by grief, how do I find a song of joy?
How do I find a song of joy?
I can return to this life only what it has given to me (2)

"Hum gham-zada hain laayen kahaan se khushi ke geet
Kahaan se khushi ke geet
Denge vahi jo paayenge is zindagi se hum (2)

Meena looks troubled and guilty.

"Desires of the heart will stir once again
Desires of the heart
I confess that I have been crushed by life's sorrows (2)

"Ubhrenge ek baar abhi dil ke valvalay
Abhi dil ke valvalay
Maana ke dabb gaye hain gham-e-zindagi se hum (2)

A man who is seated behind Meena is intently watching her reacting to Vijay's poem. We later discover it is her husband, the publisher Mr. Ghosh (Rehman).[30]

"There! Today I break...
There! Today I break all ties with hope
All ties with hope
There! Never shall I voice a complaint again."

"Lo aaj hum ne todd diya
Lo aaj hum ne todd diya rishta-e-umeed
Rishta-e-umeed
Lo ab kabhi gila na karenge kisi se hum" (2)

रील ५

मोहम्मद रफ़ी की आवाज़:

विजय:

"तंग आ चुके हैं कश-म-कशे ज़िन्दगी से हम (२)

ठुकरा ना दें जहाँ को कहीं बे-दिली से हम"

एक आदमी:

जी जनाब, ख़ुशी के मौक़े पे क्या बे-दिली का राग छेड़ा हुआ है? कोई ख़ुशी का गीत सुनाइए।

विजय:

"हम ग़म-ज़दा हैं लायें कहाँ से ख़ुशी के गीत

कहाँ से ख़ुशी के गीत

देंगे वही जो पायेंगे इस ज़िन्दगी से हम (२)

मीना को जुर्म का एहसास सता रहा है।

उभरेंगे एक बार अभी दिल के वलवले

अभी दिल के वलवले

माना के दब गए हैं ग़मे ज़िन्दगी से हम (२)

विजय की ग़ज़ल का असर मीना के चेहरे पर होते हुए दिख रहा है। मीना के पीछे बैठा उसका पति पब्लिशर घोष (रहमान) यह देख रहा है।

"लो आज हमने तोड़ दिया

लो आज हमने तोड़ दिया रिश्ता-ए-उम्मीद

रिश्ता-ए-उम्मीद

लो अब कभी गिला ना करेंगे किसी से हम" (२)

محمد رفیع کی آواز:

و جے:

"تنگ آ چکے ہیں کشمکشِ زندگی سے ہم(2)

ٹھکرا نہ دیں جہاں کو کہیں بے دلی سے ہم"

ایک آدمی:

جی جناب، خوشی کے موقع پہ کیا بے دلی کا راگ چھیڑا ہوا ہے؟ کوئی خوشی کا گیت سنائیے۔

و جے:

"ہم غم زدہ ہیں لائیں کہاں سے خوشی کے گیت

کہاں سے خوشی کے گیت

دیں گے وہی جو پائیں گے اس زندگی سے ہم(2)

(مینا کو احساسِ جرم ستا رہا ہے)

اُبھریں گے ایک بار ابھی دل کے ولولے

ابھی دل کے ولولے

مانا کہ دب گئے ہیں غمِ زندگی سے ہم(2)

(و جے کی شاعری کا اثر مینا کے قریب ایک شخص بیٹھا مینا کے چہرے پر دیکھ رہا ہے، پبلشر گھوش)(رحمان)

لو آج ہم نے توڑ دیا

لو آج ہم نے توڑ دیا رشتۂ اُمید

رشتۂ اُمید

لو اب کبھی گلہ نہ کریں گے کسی سے ہم"(2)

ریل ۵

Vijay's poem is followed by an awkward silence. He makes his way out. Ghosh stops him in the college corridor.

Ghosh:
Wait. Are you an ex-student?

Suno! Yahaan ke tum old student ho?

Vijay nods.

Ghosh:
I see. What work do you do these days?

Haan. I see. Tum kuchh kaam-kaaj bhi karte ho?

Vijay:
I look for work.

Kaam ki talaash karta hoon.

Ghosh:
Your poetry is good.

Achhi-khaasi ghazal keh lete ho.

Vijay:
Thank you.

Shukriya.

220

Ghosh:
My card. Come to my office tomorrow morning.

Ye mera card hai. Subha iss daftar pe aa jaana.

Vijay *(reading the visiting card):*
"Modern Publishing House?" Are you…

"Modern Publishing House?" Aap wahaan…

Ghosh:
I am the owner.

Main wahaan ka maalik hoon.

Ghosh leaves. Fade out.

Fade in. Next scene. Day. Ghosh's office. Vijay knocks.

Ghosh *(in English):*
Yes, come in.

Vijay:
Good morning, Mr. Ghosh.

Namaste, Ghosh babu.

विजय की ग़ज़ल सुन कर हॉल में ख़ामोशी छा जाती है। विजय हॉल से बाहर निकल आता है। घोष उसे राहदारी में रोक लेता है।

घोष:
सुनो! यहाँ के तुम ओल्ड स्टूडेन्ट हो?

विजय सर हिलाकर हाँ कहता है।

घोष:
हाँ। आई सी। तुम कुछ काम-काज भी करते हो?

विजय:
काम की तलाश करता हूँ।

घोष:
अच्छी-ख़ासी ग़ज़ल कह लेते हो।

विजय:
शुक्रिया।

घोष:
ये मेरा कार्ड है। सुबह इस दफ़्तर पे आ जाना।

विजय (विज़िटिंग कार्ड देखते हुए):
"मॉडर्न पब्लिशिंग हाउस?" आप वहाँ...

घोष:
मैं वहाँ का मालिक हूँ।

घोष चला जाता है।

अगला दृश्य। दिन। घोष का दफ़्तर। विजय दरवाज़े पर दस्तक देता है।

घोष (अंग्रेज़ी में):
यस। कम इन।

विजय:
नमस्ते, घोष बाबू।

وجے کی غزل سن کر ہال میں خموشی چھا جاتی ہے۔ لوگوں کو اُس کی غزل پسند نہیں آئی۔ وجے ہال سے باہر نکل آتا ہے۔ گھوش اُسے راہداری میں روک لیتا ہے۔

گھوش:
سنو! یہاں کے تم اولڈ اسٹوڈنٹ ہو؟

وجے اثبات میں سر ہلاتا ہے۔

گھوش:
ہاں۔ آئی سی۔ تم کچھ کام کاج بھی کرتے ہو؟

وجے:
کام کی تلاش کرتا ہوں۔

گھوش:
اچھی خاصی غزل کہہ لیتے ہو۔

وجے:
شکریہ۔

گھوش:
یہ میرا کارڈ ہے۔ صبح اِس دفتر پہ آ جانا۔

وجے (وزنگ کارڈ دیکھتے ہوئے):
ماڈرن پبلشنگ ہاؤز؟ آپ وہاں۔۔۔

گھوش:
میں وہاں کا مالک ہوں۔

گھوش چلا جاتا ہے۔

اگلا منظر۔ دن۔ گھوش کا پبلشنگ آفس۔ وجے دروازے پر دستک دیتا ہے۔

گھوش (انگریزی میں):
یس، کم اِن۔

وجے:
نمستے، گھوش بابو۔

Ghosh:
Sit down.

Vijay (hands him a file, smiling):
Here are my poems.

Ghosh:
Oh! When were you at college?

Vijay:
From '48 to '52. Shall I read the poems out loud, or will you read them later?

Ghosh (standing up):
1952? That was the year I got married. Did you study science or arts?

Vijay:
Arts. May I recite the poems?

Ghosh (walking around his desk):
Are you sure you left college in '52? Not before?

Vijay:
No. Mr. Ghosh, I brought my poems to be published…

Ghosh (interrupting):
Will you work in my office?

Vijay:
Work here?

Ghosh:
Hmm.

Vijay:
I thought you called me about publishing my poems.

Baitho.

Ye meri nazmen hain.

Oh! Tum college mein kis saal thay?

Sann adtaalees se le kar sann baavan tak. Main ye nazmen padh ke sunaaun ya aap khud dekh lenge?

Sann baavan? Usi saal toh meri shaadi huwi thi. Tum science student thay ya arts?

Arts. Er…ye nazmen sunaaun?

Tumhen theek yaad hai tum ne college sann baavan mein chhoda, uss se pehle nahin?

Ji haan. Mr. Ghosh, maine ye nazmen chhapwaane…

Mere daftar mein naukri karoge?

Naukri?

Hmm.

Mera khayaal tha aap ne ye meri nazmen chhaapne ke liye bulaaya tha mujhe.

घोष:
बैठो।

विजय (मुस्कराते हुए एक फ़ाइल देता है):
ये मेरी नज़्में हैं।

घोष:
ओह! तुम कॉलेज में किस साल थे?

विजय:
सन अड़तालीस से लेकर सन बावन तक। मैं ये नज़्में पढ़ के सुनाऊँ या आप ख़ुद देख लेंगे?

घोष (खड़े होते हुए):
सन बावन? उसी साल तो मेरी शादी हुई थी। तुम साईन्स स्टूडेन्ट थे या आर्ट्स?

विजय:
आर्ट्स। अरे... ये नज़्में सुनाऊँ?

घोष (टेबल के पास से घूमते हुए):
तुम्हें ठीक याद है तुमने कॉलेज सन बावन में छोड़ा, उससे पहले नहीं?

विजय:
जी हाँ। मि. घोष, मैंने ये नज़्में छपवाने...

घोष (टोकते हुए):
मेरे दफ़्तर में नौकरी करोगे?

विजय:
नौकरी?

घोष:
हूँ।

विजय:
मेरा ख़याल था आपने ये मेरी नज़्में छापने के लिए बुलाया था मुझे।

گھوش:
بیٹھو۔

وجے (مسکراتے ہوئے ایک فائل دکھاتا ہے):
یہ میری نظمیں ہیں۔

گھوش:
اوہ! تم کالج میں کس سال تھے؟

وجے:
سن اڑتالیس سے لے کر سن باون تک۔ میں یہ نظمیں پڑھ کے سناؤں یا آپ خود دیکھ لیں گے؟

گھوش (کھڑے ہوتے ہوئے):
سن باون؟ اسی سال تو میری شادی ہوئی تھی۔ تم سائنس اسٹوڈنٹ تھے یا آرٹس؟

وجے:
آرٹس۔ ارر، یہ نظمیں سناؤں؟

گھوش (میز کے گرد گھومتے ہوئے):
تمہیں ٹھیک یاد ہے تم نے کالج سن باون میں چھوڑا اس سے پہلے نہیں؟

وجے:
جی ہاں۔ مسٹر گھوش، میں نے یہ نظمیں چھپوانے۔۔۔

گھوش (ٹوکتے ہوئے):
میرے دفتر میں نوکری کروگے؟

وجے:
نوکری؟

گھوش:
ہاں۔

وجے:
میرا خیال تھا آپ نے یہ میری نظمیں چھاپنے کے لیے بلایا تھا مجھے۔

Ghosh:
Publishing your poems? There's plenty of time for that. I must first find out more about you.

Chhaapne ke liye? Oh, uske liye abhi bahot waqt hai. Pehle main tumhaare baare mein kuchh jaan toh loon.

Ghosh's employee, Mr. Chatterjee (played by Moni Chatterjee), enters the room.

Vijay:
About me?

Mere baare mein?

Ghosh (*sitting down again*):
Yes. Mr. Chatterjee, this is your new assistant.
(*to Vijay*)
You can start tomorrow.

Haan. Mr. Chatterjee, ye aap ke naye assistant hain.

Tum kal se kaam pe aa sakte ho.

Vijay (*gets up to leave*):
Goodbye.

Namaste.

Ghosh:
Bye.

Namaste.

Cut. Vijay leaves Ghosh's office and heads off to the lift. The lift gates open and Vijay enters. He sees Meena standing there.

Vijay (*in English, with a half-smile*):
Hello, Meena.

Meena is moved to see him. She wants to talk to him but other people enter the lift. Vijay and Meena stand silently in a corner. Dissolve from a reflection of Meena's smiling face to a flashback.

घोष:

छापने के लिए? ओह, उसके लिए अभी बहुत वक़्त है। पहले मैं तुम्हारे बारे में कुछ जान तो लूँ।

घोष का एक कर्मचारी, चैटर्जी (मौनी चैटर्जी) कमरे में दाख़िल होता है।

विजय:

मेरे बारे में?

घोष *(बैठते हुए):*

हाँ। मि. चैटर्जी, ये आपके नए असिस्टेन्ट हैं।
(विजय से)
तुम कल से काम पे आ सकते हो।

विजय *(जाने के लिए उठता है):*

नमस्ते।

घोष:

नमस्ते।

अगला दृश्य। घोष के दफ़तर से निकल कर विजय लिफ़्ट की ओर जाता है। लिफ़्ट का दरवाज़ा खुलता है और विजय लिफ़्ट में दाख़िल होता है तब उसकी नज़र मीना पर पड़ती है।

विजय *(थोड़ा-सा मुस्कुराकर अंग्रेज़ी में):*

हैलो, मीना।

विजय को देख मीना मुस्कुरा देती है। वो उससे कुछ कहना चाहती है लेकिन कुछ और लोग लिफ़्ट में आ जाते हैं। विजय और मीना एक कोने में ख़ामोश खड़े रहते हैं। मीना के मुस्कुराते हुए चेहरे पर से फ़्लैशबैक सामने आता है।

Night. Vijay and Meena are walking hand in hand in a garden. In another part of the garden, young couples dance a waltz. Vijay and Meena sit on a bench. She looks anxiously towards Vijay, but he is lost in the music that drifts from the dance floor.[31]

Dissolve from a close-up of Vijay to an imaginary, dream-like place engulfed in wisps of mist. Meena walks slowly down a large staircase. She finds Vijay waiting for her beyond a gate. They are dressed in elegant European clothes and dance a slow waltz as they sing.

Singers: Mohammed Rafi & Geeta Dutt

Vijay:
What if my heart were to dwell in your eyes?
Meena:
What if I close my eyes and punish your heart?
Vijay:
What if my heart were to dwell in your eyes?
Meena:
What if I close my eyes and punish your heart?
Vijay:
What if my heart were to dwell in your eyes?

Hum aap ki aankhon mein is dil ko basa den toh

Hum moond ke palkon ko is dil ko saza den toh

Hum aap ki aankhon mein is dil ko basa den toh

Hum moond ke palkon ko is dil ko saza den toh

Hum aap ki aankhon mein Is dil ko basa den toh

Vijay:
I will weave flowers of love in your hair
Meena:
What if I were to shake them to the ground?
Vijay:
I will weave flowers of love in your hair

In zulfon mein goondhenge hum phool mohabbat ke

Zulfon ko jhatak kar hum ye phool gira den toh

In zulfon mein goondhenge hum phool mohabbat ke

रात । एक बाग़ में विजय और मीना एक-दूसरे का हाथ थामे दाख़िल हो रहे हैं । बाग़ के दूसरे कोने में कुछ नौजवान जोड़े वॉल्ट्ज़ की धुन पर नाच रहे हैं । विजय और मीना एक बेंच पर बैठ जाते हैं । मीना बेचैनी से विजय को देखती है लेकिन विजय का ध्यान डान्सफ्लोर से आ रहे संगीत की ओर है ।

अगला दृश्य । विजय के चेहरे से होता हुआ, धुंध में लिपटा एक सपनों जैसा दृश्य सामने आता है । एक बड़ी सीढ़ी से उतरकर मीना नीचे आ रही है । दरवाज़े पर इंतज़ार करता हुआ विजय उसे दिखाई देता है । दोनों ख़ूबसूरत यूरोपियन लिबास पहने हुए हैं । वॉल्ट्ज़ की धुन पर नाचते हुए गा रहे हैं ।

गायक: मोहम्मद रफ़ी और गीता दत्त

विजय:
हम आपकी आँखों में इस दिल को बसा दें तो
मीना:
हम मूँद के पलकों को इस दिल को सज़ा दें तो
विजय:
हम आपकी आँखों में इस दिल को बसा दें तो
मीना:
हम मूँद के पलकों को इस दिल को सज़ा दें तो
विजय:
हम आपकी आँखों में इस दिल को बसा दें तो

विजय:
इन ज़ुल्फ़ों में गूँधेंगे हम फूल मोहब्बत के
मीना:
ज़ुल्फ़ों को झटक कर हम ये फूल गिरा दें तो
विजय:
इन ज़ुल्फ़ों में गूँधेंगे हम फूल मोहब्बत के

رات۔ایک باغ میں وجے اور مینا ایک دوسرے کا ہاتھ تھامے داخل ہو رہے ہیں۔ایک گوشے میں کچھ نوجوان جوڑے والٹز کی دھن پر تھرک رہے ہیں۔وجے اور مینا ایک بینچ پر بیٹھ جاتے ہیں۔بے چینی سے وہ وجے کی طرف دیکھتی ہے لیکن وجے ڈانس فلور کی طرف سے آتی ہوئی موسیقی میں کھویا ہوا ہے۔

اگلا منظر۔وجے کے چہرے سے ہوتا ہوا، دھند میں لپٹا ایک خوابناک منظر اُبھرتا ہے۔ایک طویل زینے سے اُتر کر مینا نیچے آ رہی ہے۔ایک گیٹ کے باہر اُسے انتظار کرتا ہوا وجے دکھائی دیتا ہے۔یورپی طرز کے خوبصورت لباس میں وہ دونوں ملبوس ہیں اور ایک دوسرے کی بانہوں میں بانہیں ڈالے والٹز کی دھن پر تھرکتے ہوئے گا رہے ہیں۔

آوازیں،محمد رفیع اور گیتا دت۔

وجے:
ہم آپ کی آنکھوں میں اس دل کو بسا دیں تو
مینا:
ہم موند کے پلکوں کو اس دل کو سزا دیں تو
وجے:
ہم آپ کی آنکھوں میں اس دل کو بسا دیں تو
مینا:
ہم موند کے پلکوں کو اس دل کو سزا دیں تو
وجے:
ہم آپ کی آنکھوں میں اس دل کو بسا دیں تو

وجے:
اِن زلفوں میں گوندھیں گے ہم پھول محبت کے
مینا:
زلفوں کو جھٹک کر ہم یہ پھول گرا دیں تو
وجے:
اِن زلفوں میں گوندھیں گے ہم پھول محبت کے

Meena:
What if I were to shake them to the ground?

Zulfon ko jhatak kar hum ye phool gira den toh

Vijay:
What if my heart were to dwell in your eyes?

Hum aap ki aankhon mein is dil ko basa den toh

Vijay:
I will bring you into my dreams and tease you

Hum aap ko khwaabon mein la la ke sataayenge

Meena:
What if I were to rob your eyes of sleep?

Hum aap ki aankhon se neenden hi uda den toh

Vijay:
I will bring you into my dreams and tease you

Hum aap ko khwaabon mein la la ke sataayenge

Meena:
What if I were to rob your eyes of sleep?

Hum aap ki aankhon se neenden hi uda den toh

Vijay:
What if my heart were to dwell in your eyes?

Hum aap ki aankhon mein is dil ko basa den toh

Vijay:
I will lay my heart at your feet, swooning

Hum aap ke qadmon par gir jaayenge ghash kha kar

Meena:
What if I were to ignore you and walk away?

Is par bhi na hum apne aanchal ki hawa den toh

Vijay:
I will lay my heart at your feet, swooning

Hum aap ke qadmon par gir jaayenge ghash kha kar

Meena:
What if I were to ignore you and walk away?

Is par bhi na hum apne aanchal ki hawa den toh

Vijay:
What if my heart were to dwell in your eyes?

Hum aap ki aankhon mein is dil ko basa den toh

Meena:
What if I close my eyes and punish your heart?

Hum moond ke palkon ko is dil ko saza den toh

Vijay:
What if my heart were to dwell in your eyes?

Hum aap ki aankhon mein is dil ko basa den toh

The song ends. Meena climbs the grand staircase and vanishes in the mist. She is beyond Vijay's reach.

मीना:

ज़ुल्फ़ों को झटक कर हम ये फूल गिरा दें तो

विजय:

हम आपकी आँखों में इस दिल को बसा दें तो

विजय:

हम आपको ख़्वाबों में ला ला के सतायेंगे

मीना:

हम आपकी आँखों से नींदें ही उड़ा दें तो

विजय:

हम आपको ख़्वाबों में ला ला के सतायेंगे

मीना:

हम आपकी आँखों से नींदें ही उड़ा दें तो

विजय:

हम आपकी आँखों में इस दिल को बसा दें तो

विजय:

हम आपके क़दमों पर गिर जायेंगे ग़श खा कर

मीना:

इस पर भी ना हम अपने आँचल की हवा दें तो

विजय:

हम आपके क़दमों पर गिर जायेंगे ग़श खा कर

मीना:

इस पर भी ना हम अपने आँचल की हवा दें तो

विजय:

हम आपकी आँखों में इस दिल को बसा दें तो

मीना:

हम मूँद के पलकों को इस दिल को सज़ा दें तो

विजय:

हम आपकी आँखों में इस दिल को बसा दें तो

गीत ख़त्म होता है। मीना सीढ़ियों से ऊपर चली जाती है। धुंध में लिपटी वो विजय की आँखों से दूर हो जाती है।

مینا:

زلفوں کو جھٹک کر ہم یہ پھول گرا دیں تو

وجے:

ہم آپ کی آنکھوں میں اس دل کو بسا دیں تو

وجے:

ہم آپ کو خوابوں میں لا لا کے ستائیں گے

مینا:

ہم آپ کی آنکھوں سے نیندیں ہی اڑا دیں تو

وجے:

ہم آپ کو خوابوں میں لا لا کے ستائیں گے

مینا:

ہم آپ کی آنکھوں سے نیندیں ہی اڑا دیں تو

وجے:

ہم آپ کی آنکھوں میں اس دل کو بسا دیں تو

وجے:

ہم آپ کے قدموں پر گر جائیں گے غش کھا کر

مینا:

اس پر بھی نہ ہم اپنے آنچل کی ہوا دیں تو

وجے:

ہم آپ کے قدموں پر گر جائیں گے غش کھا کر

مینا:

اس پر بھی نہ ہم اپنے آنچل کی ہوا دیں تو

وجے:

ہم آپ کی آنکھوں میں اس دل کو بسا دیں تو

مینا:

ہم موند کے پلکوں کو اس دل کو سزا دیں تو

وجے:

ہم آپ کی آنکھوں میں اس دل کو بسا دیں تو

گیت ختم ہوتا ہے۔ مینا زینوں سے اوپر چلی جاتی ہے۔ دھند میں لپٹی وہ وجے کی دسترس سے دور ہو جاتی ہے۔

Reel Six

Vijay's reverie is over. He finds himself alone. He sees a letter on the bench. He reads it and is upset. The background music has become increasingly discordant. The flashback ends.

Dissolve to the reflection of Meena's face in the lift. Dialogue scene takes over.

Meena *(smiling awkwardly):*
How are you?

Kaise rahe ab tak?

Vijay:
Alive.

Zinda.

Meena:
I'd do anything to see you happy…

Tumhen khush dekhne ke liye main bahot kuchh…

Vijay *(interrupting her):*
Thank you. Don't worry. I have learnt how to be happy.

Shukriya. Fikr na karo. Main apni khushi aap haasil karna seekh gaya hoon.

Meena:
Has another girl been teaching you?

Ya kisi doosri ladki ne sikha diya?

Vijay *(with an ironic smile):*
Another girl? One was enough for a lifetime. I don't want such suffering again.

Doosri ladki? Ek hi bahot thi meri zindagi mein. Main vo dard dubaara nahin mol lena chaahta.

Meena:
You mean you've erased the heartache of your first love?

Yaani pehla dard bilkul mita chuke apne dil se?

ریل ۶

وجے کا خواب ٹوٹتا ہے۔وہ دیکھتا ہے کہ وہ نیچ پر تنہا پڑا ہے۔نیچ پر ایک خط رکھا ہوا ہے جسے پڑھ کر اُس کا مزاج بگڑ جاتا ہے۔وجے اُٹھ کر کیمرا کی طرف آتا ہوا دکھائی دیتا ہے۔بیک گراؤنڈ میں میوزک کی لے دم توڑ دیتی ہے۔فلیش بیک ختم ہوتا ہے۔

اگلا منظر مینا کی لفٹ میں شبیہ سے ہوتا ہوا مکالمے کے منظر پر آتا ہے۔

مینا (جھجکتے ہوئے):
کیسے رہے اب تک؟

وجے:
زندہ۔

مینا:
تمہیں خوش دیکھنے کے لیے میں بہت کچھ۔۔۔

وجے (اسے ٹوکتے ہوئے):
شکریہ۔ فکر نہ کرو۔ میں اپنی خوشی آپ حاصل کرنا سیکھ گیا ہوں۔

مینا:
یا کسی دوسری لڑکی نے سکھا دیا؟

وجے (طنزاً مسکراتے ہوئے):
دوسری لڑکی؟ ایک ہی بہت تھی میری زندگی میں۔ میں وہ درد دوبارہ نہیں مول لینا چاہتا۔

مینا:
یعنی پہلا درد بالکل مٹا چکے اپنے دل سے؟

रील ६

विजय की कल्पना टूटती है। वो देखता है कि वो उसी बेंच पर अकेला पड़ा है। बेंच पर एक चिट्ठी रखी हुई है जिसे पढ़ कर वह निराश हो जाता है। बैकग्राउँड संगीत की लय टूट जाती है। फ्लैशबैक ख़त्म होता है।

लिफ़्ट में खड़ी मीना के चेहरे से हटकर दृश्य बदलता है।

मीना (हिचकिचाते हुए):
कैसे रहे अब तक?

विजय:
ज़िंदा।

मीना:
तुम्हें ख़ुश देखने के लिए मैं बहुत कुछ...

विजय (टोकते हुए):
शुक्रिया। फ़िक्र ना करो। मैं अपनी ख़ुशी आप हासिल करना सीख गया हूँ।

मीना:
या किसी दूसरी लड़की ने सिखा दिया?

विजय (मुस्कुराते हुए कटाक्ष में):
दूसरी लड़की? एक ही बहुत थी मेरी ज़िन्दगी में। मैं वो दर्द दुबारा नहीं मोल लेना चाहता।

मीना:
यानी पहला दर्द बिलकुल मिटा चुके अपने दिल से?

Vijay (brusquely):
I should have.

Mitaana chaahiye tha.

The lift gates open loudly. The sound breaks the intimacy of their conversation. The crowded lift empties.[32]

Meena:
I completely forgot. I was going up.

Arey, main toh bhool hi gayi. Mujhe oopar jaana hai.

Vijay leaves. The gates close and the lift ascends with Meena.

Wipe. Night. Gulaab is alone at a table in the restaurant where she had met Vijay. A clock chimes in the distance. The restaurant is nearly empty.

Restaurant manager:
Lady, won't you let us close? Three hours you've waited — who for? Didn't he show up?

Ae baiji, hotel bandh karne dogi ya nahin? Teen ghante se kis ke liye jami ho? Aaya nahin koi?

Gulaab coldly stares at him. She goes over to the waiter and asks him gently.

Gulaab:
Mr. Vijay comes here often, doesn't he?

Sunn toh. Vijay babu yahaan aksar aate hain na?

Waiter:
Yes. But he hasn't for some days. Any message for him?

Haan. Lekin kayi dinon se nahin aaye. Koi sandesa hai unke liye?

As Gulaab leaves the restaurant, the owner calls out to her.

विजय (सख़्ती से):

मिटाना चाहिए था ।

लिफ़्ट का दरवाज़ा आवाज़ के साथ खुलता है और दोनों की बातों का सिलसिला टूट जाता है । लिफ़्ट से लोग बाहर निकल आते हैं ।

मीना:

अरे, मैं तो भूल ही गई। मुझे ऊपर जाना है ।

विजय लिफ़्ट से बाहर आ जाता है । लिफ़्ट मीना को लेकर ऊपर जाती है ।

अगला दृश्य । रात । गुलाब उस होटल के एक टेबल पर अकेली बैठी है जिस होटल में वो विजय से मिली थी । दूर से घड़ी का गजर सुनाई देता है । होटल खाली–सा हो चुका है ।

होटल मैनेजर:

ए बाईजी, होटल बंद करने दोगी या नहीं? तीन घंटे से किसके लिए जमी हो? आया नहीं कोई?

गुलाब उसे घूर कर देखती है । वो एक वेटर के पास जाकर उसे नर्मी से पूछती है ।

गुलाब:

सुन तो । विजय बाबू यहाँ अक्सर आते हैं ना?

वेटर:

हाँ । लेकिन कई दिनों से नहीं आए । कोई संदेशा है उनके लिए?

गुलाब जैसे ही होटल से निकलने लगती है, मैनेजर उसे छेड़ते हुए पूछता है ।

Restaurant manager:
Have you no one else? Why whisper sweetly to the waiter? I'm here, too.

Fade out.

Fade in. Day. Ghosh's office. Mr. Chatterjee is talking to his boss, the publisher Ghosh.

Chatterjee:
Have you found them? What do you think?

Ghosh:
They're all right. Vijay believes he writes poetry.

Chatterjee:
I see. I've read them. They're fine poems.

Ghosh:
Maybe they are.

Chatterjee:
Why not publish a few?

Ghosh:
Are you in your right mind?

Chatterjee:
Pardon?

Ghosh:
You should know that we only publish the work of famous poets in our magazine...
(unseen by either men, Vijay has entered the room)
...not the trash of novices. Fill the blank space with a soap advertisement.
(Chatterjee is leaving the room when Ghosh sees Vijay)
Yes, Vijay? Did you want something?

Maine kaha, vo chhokra hi bacha tha haule-haule baat karne ke liye? Hum bhi toh hain.

Theek se dhoond liya aap ne? Ye kaaghzaat kaise hain?

Hain kuchh. Vijay inhe apni nazmen kehte hain.

Oh, achha. Main padh chuka hoon. Badi achhi nazmen hain.

Hongien.

Toh inhin mein se ek-aadh nazm chhapwa dijiye na.

Hosh toh thikaane hain aap ke?

Ji?

Toh aap ko maaloom hona chaahiye ki hamaari magazine mein sirf mash'hoor shaayeron ki cheezen chhapti hain...

...kisi nau-sikhiye ki bakwaas nahin. Jaayiye, uss khaali jageh par kisi saabun ka ishtehaar daal dijiye.

Tum kuchh chaahte ho?

होटल मैनेजर:
मैंने कहा, वो छोकरा ही बचा था हौले-हौले बात करने के लिए? हम भी तो हैं।

दृश्य बदलता है।

अगला दृश्य। दिन। घोष के दफ़्तर में चैटर्जी अपने मालिक, घोष से बात कर रहे हैं।

चैटर्जी:
ठीक से ढूँढ लिया आपने? ये काग़ज़ात कैसे हैं?

घोष:
हैं कुछ। विजय इन्हें अपनी नज़्में कहते हैं।

चैटर्जी:
ओह, अच्छा। मैं पढ़ चुका हूँ। बड़ी अच्छी नज़्में हैं।

घोष:
होंगीं।

चैटर्जी:
इन्हीं में से एक-आध नज़्म छपवा दीजिए ना।

घोष:
होश तो ठिकाने हैं आपके?

चैटर्जी:
जी?

घोष:
तो आपको मालूम होना चाहिए कि हमारी मैगज़ीन में सिर्फ़ मशहूर शायरों की चीज़ें छपती हैं...
(विजय दाख़िल होता है, पर दोनों में से किसी की नज़र उस पर नहीं पड़ती)
...किसी नौसिखिए की बकवास नहीं। जाईए उस ख़ाली जगह पर किसी साबुन का इश्तहार डाल दीजिए।
(घोष की नज़र विजय पर तब पड़ती है जब चैटर्जी कमरे से बाहर जा रहे होते हैं)
यस विजय, तुम कुछ चाहते हो?

ریستوراں کا مینیجر :
میں نے کہا، وہ چھوکرا ہی بچا تھا ہولے ہولے بات کرنے کے لیے؟ ہم بھی تو ہیں۔

منظر بدلتا ہے۔

اگلا منظر۔ دن، چڑجی صاحب اپنے باس، پبلشر گھوش سے بات کر رہے ہیں۔ وہ گھوش کے آفس میں ہیں۔

چڑجی :
ٹھیک سے ڈھونڈ لیا آپ نے؟ یہ کاغذات کیسے ہیں؟

گھوش :
ہیں کچھ۔ وجے انھیں اپنی نظمیں کہتے ہیں۔

چڑجی :
اوہ، اچھا۔ میں پڑھ چکا ہوں۔ بڑی اچھی نظمیں ہیں۔

گھوش :
ہونگی۔

چڑجی :
تو انھیں میں سے ایک آدھ نظم چھپوا دیجیے نا۔

گھوش :
ہوش تو ٹھکانے ہیں آپ کے؟

چڑجی :
جی؟

گھوش :
تو آپ کو معلوم ہونا چاہیے کہ ہماری میگزین میں صرف مشہور شاعروں کی چیزیں چھپتی ہیں۔۔۔
(وجے داخل ہوتا ہے، دونوں ہی کی نظر اُس پر نہیں پڑتی)
۔۔۔کسی نوسکھیے کی بکواس نہیں۔ جائیے اُس خالی جگہ پر کسی صابن کا اشتہار ڈال دیجیے۔
(گھوش کی نظر اُس وقت پڑتی ہے جب چڑجی کمرے سے باہر جا رہے ہوتے ہیں)
یس وجے؟ تم کچھ چاہتے ہو؟

Vijay (walks over to Ghosh's desk and takes his file of poems):
Yes. This trash of a novice. May I take it away?

Ghosh (in a matter-of-fact tone):
Go ahead.
(stopping him leave)
Vijay!

Vijay:
Yes?

Ghosh (walking over to Vijay):
Are you free tomorrow evening?

Vijay:
Yes. Tell me.

Ghosh:
There's a party at my house. Come and lend a hand.

Vijay:
I'll be there.

Vijay leaves. The scene ends with a tracking shot to a close-up of Ghosh standing by the closed door of his office.

Cut. Night. Juhi and Sattar are walking in the park. The first part of the following scene is missing in some released film prints.

Sattar:
Can you see it, Juhi?

Ji haan. Ye nau-sikhiye ki bakwaas. Ye main le ja sakta hoon?

Haan.

Vijay!

Ji?

Tumhen kal shaam fursat hai?

Ji. Farmaayiye?

Mere ghar mein party hai. Tum bhi aa jaana haath bataane.

Haazir ho jaaunga.

Dekh rahi ho, Juhi?

وجے (گھوش کی میز تک جا کر اپنی نظموں کی فائل اُٹھا لیتا ہے):
جی ہاں۔ یہ نوسکھیے کی بکواس۔ یہ میں لے جا سکتا ہوں؟

گھوش (بلاجھجک):
ہاں۔
(جاتے ہوئے وجے کو روک دیتا ہے)
وجے!

وجے:
جی؟

گھوش (وجے کے پاس آتا ہے):
تمہیں کل شام فرصت ہے؟

وجے:
جی۔ فرمائیے؟

گھوش:
میرے گھر میں پارٹی ہے۔ تم بھی آ جانا ہاتھ بٹانے۔

وجے:
حاضر ہو جاؤں گا۔

وجے چلا جاتا ہے۔ گھوش بند دروازے سے لگا کھڑا ہے، منظر ختم ہوتا ہے۔

اگلا منظر۔ رات۔ جوہی اور ستار پارک میں گھوم رہے ہیں۔ اس منظر کا کچھ حصہ فلم کے دوسرے پرنٹس میں نہیں ہے۔

ستار:
دیکھ رہی ہو، جوہی؟

विजय (घोष की मेज़ के पास जाकर अपनी नज़्मों की फ़ाइल उठा लेता है):
जी हाँ। ये नौसिखिए की बकवास। ये मैं ले जा सकता हूँ?

घोष (बिना झिझक):
हाँ।
(जाते हुए विजय को रोकता है)
विजय!

विजय:
जी?

घोष (विजय के पास आकर):
तुम्हें कल शाम फ़ुरसत है?

विजय:
जी। फ़रमाइए?

घोष:
मेरे घर में पार्टी है। तुम भी आ जाना हाथ बँटाने।

विजय:
हाज़िर हो जाऊँगा।

विजय चला जाता है। घोष बंद दरवाज़े के पास खड़ा है। दृश्य खत्म होता है।

अगला दृश्य। रात। जूही और सत्तार बाग़ में टहल रहे हैं। इस दृश्य का कुछ हिस्सा फ़िल्म के कुछ प्रिन्ट में नहीं है।

सत्तार:
देख रही हो, जूही?

Juhi:
What?

Sattar:
What I see.

Juhi:
And what is that?

Sattar:
You can see it too, but don't want to recognise it.

Juhi:
You fool, all I can see is your face.

Sattar:
Keep looking. Is something making your heart uneasy?

Juhi:
Yes.

Sattar:
Let it get uneasy!

Juhi:
Confusion is making my heart uneasy.

Sattar *(making a movement with his hand to indicate a fluttering heart)*:
Confusion? Or is it something else?

Juhi:
No!

Sattar:
No?

Although the previous thirteen lines are missing from some film prints, there is no conspicuous break in the narrative in the prints

Kya?

Jo main dekh raha hoon.

Kya dekh raha hai?

Arey jo tu dekh kar bhi nahin dekh rahi.

Mooye, main tera thobda dekh rahi hoon.

Achha! Le dekh dekh dekh. Kuchh huwa dil mein?

Haan.

Hone de, hone de. Thoda aur hone de.

Teri shakal dekh ke dil mein uljhan ho rahi hai.

Uljhan ho rahi hai ya kuchh…

Ji nahin. Huh.

Nahin?

जूही:
क्या?

सत्तार:
जो मैं देख रहा हूँ।

जूही:
क्या देख रहा है?

सत्तार:
अरे जो तू देख कर भी नहीं देख रही।

जूही:
मुँए, मैं तेरा थोबड़ा देख रही हूँ।

सत्तार:
अच्छा! ले देख-देख-देख। कुछ हुआ दिल में?

जूही:
हाँ।

सत्तार:
होने दे, होने दे। थोड़ा और होने दे।

जूही:
तेरी शकल देख के दिल में उलझन हो रही है।

सत्तार (तड़पते हुए दिल की ओर हाथ से इशारा करता है):
उलझन हो रही है या कुछ...

जूही:
जी नहीं। हुँह।

सत्तार:
नहीं?

हालाँकि ये पहली तेरह लाईन फ़िल्म के कुछ प्रिन्ट में नहीं है फिर भी जिस प्रिन्ट में ये लाईनें नहीं हैं उसकी कहानी में कोई फ़र्क़ नहीं पड़ता। घोष के ऑफ़िस का दृश्य

جوہی:
کیا؟

ستار:
جو میں دیکھ رہا ہوں۔

جوہی:
کیا دیکھ رہا ہے؟

ستار:
ارے جو تُو دیکھ کر بھی نہیں دیکھ رہی۔

جوہی:
موئے، میں تیرا تھوبڑا دیکھ رہی ہوں۔

ستار:
اچھا! لے دیکھ دیکھ دیکھ۔ کچھ ہوا دل میں؟

جوہی:
ہاں۔

ستار:
ہونے دے، ہونے دے۔ تھوڑا اور ہونے دے۔

جوہی:
تیری شکل دیکھ کے دل میں اُلجھن ہو رہی ہے۔

ستار (ہاتھ کے اشارے سے تڑپتا ہوا دل بتاتا ہے):
اُلجھن ہو رہی ہے یا کچھ۔۔۔

جوہی:
جی نہیں۔ اُوں۔

ستار:
نہیں؟

حالآنکہ یہ لائنیں فلم کی کچھ پرنٹس میں نہیں ہیں پھر بھی جن پرنٹس میں یہ لائنیں نہیں ہیں اُن کے تسلسل میں کوئی فرق

where these lines are missing. Ghosh's office scene cuts straight to a shot of Juhi entering the frame and sitting on a park bench with Sattar following hot on her heels.

Sattar:
Juhi, be cross with me as much as you like. But have you ever thought who will care for you when you're old?

Juhi:
God will.

Sattar:
Don't talk of Him or a coconut will fall on your head and sort you out. If you don't want a bruised skull, listen to me.

Juhi:
If I listened to you, I'd starve to death. You can barely earn enough to buy two slices of bread, how can you feed me?

Sattar:
Feed you? You can have both slices. Just seeing you in my home will satisfy my hunger.

Juhi:
Really, Sattar?

Sattar:
Abdul Sattar.

Juhi:
Abdul Sattar, do you love me that much?

Sattar:
When do we go to the priest?

Juhi:
Stop it! You fool!

Juhi, tu abhi chaahe jitna bigad le mujh pe lekin kabhi ye bhi socha hai ki jab tu budhiya ho jaayegi toh tujhe kaun sambhalega?

Ooparwala.

Le. Naam matt le ooparwaale ka warna naariyal tapka kar khoopdi baraabar kar dega. Dekh, sar ki salaamati chaahti hai na toh meri baat maan le.

Teri baat maan loon toh bhooki mar jaaungi. Mushkil se toh do roti kama kar laata hai, mujhe kya khilaayega?

Tujhe? Tu donon roti kha lena. Mera pait toh tujhe mere ghar mein dekh kar hi bhar jaayega.

Sachchi, Sattar?

Abdul Sattar.

Abdul Sattar. Tu mujhe itna chaahta hai?

Kab chalti qaazi ke yahaan?

Chal hatt, mooye.

नहीं पड़ता। घोष के ऑफ़िस के मंज़र से बराहे-रास्त दूसरा मंज़र सामने आता है जिस में जूही के पीछे पीछे सत्तार लगा हुआ है।

बदलता है और बाग़ में एक बैंच पर जूही आकर बैठती है। सत्तार भी वहाँ पहुँच जाता है।

सत्तार:
जूही, तू अभी चाहे जितना बिगड़ ले मुझ पे लेकिन कभी ये भी सोचा है कि जब तू बुढ़िया हो जाएगी तो तुझे कौन सँभालेगा?

जूही:
ऊपरवाला।

सत्तार:
ले। नाम मत ले ऊपरवाले का वरना नारियल टपका कर खोपड़ी बराबर कर देगा। देख, सर की सलामती चाहती है ना तो मेरी बात मान ले।

जूही:
तेरी बात मान लूँ तो भूखी मर जाऊँगी। मुश्किल से तो दो रोटी कमा कर लाता है, मुझे क्या खिलाएगा?

सत्तार:
तुझे? तू दोनों रोटी खा लेना। मेरा पेट तो तुझे मेरे घर में देख कर ही भर जाएगा।

जूही:
सच्ची, सत्तार?

सत्तार:
अब्दुल सत्तार।

जूही:
अब्दुल सत्तार, तू मुझे इतना चाहता है?

सत्तार:
कब चलती क़ाज़ी के यहाँ?

जूही:
चल हट, मुँए।

Juhi leaves. Sattar resumes his dialogue with God.

Sattar:
Did You hear that? No? Nothing at all. No coconut today?

Suna, ooparwaale? Nahin bhai, kuchh nahin haan. Naariyal hai nahin?

Fade out.

Fade in. Night. Many guests have arrived for the party held at Mr. Ghosh's house.

Ghosh *(to a guest at the door):*
Why isn't your husband here?

Aap ke husband nahin aaye aaj?

Female guest:
He wasn't feeling well. He wanted me to take him to the hospital, but I put it off. How could I miss such a big party?

Unki tabiyat theek nahin thi. Keh rahe thay mujhe hospital le chalo lekin maine unko kal pe taal diya hai. Itni badi party bhala main kaise chhod sakti thi?

Ghosh *(smiling):*
Thank you. I appreciate your kindness.

Shukriya. Ye toh aap ki zarra-nawaazi hai.

Vijay enters the house. Meena is talking to a woman.

Meena:
Kamla, didn't you bring your son?

Kamla, Pappu ko saath nahin laayi?

Kamla:
No.

Nahin.

Meena *(looking up, surprised):*
Vijay? How did you find my address?

Vijay? Tumhen mera pata kaise maaloom huwa?

जूही चली जाती है। सत्तार की ऊपरवाले के साथ बातचीत जारी रहती है।

सत्तार:
सुना, ऊपरवाले? नहीं भाई, कुछ नहीं, हाँ। नारियल है नहीं।

दृश्य बदलता है।

अगला दृश्य। रात। घोष के घर पार्टी में बहुत से लोग मौजूद हैं।

घोष *(दरवाज़े पर खड़े होकर एक मेहमान महिला से):*
आपके हॅसबैन्ड नहीं आए आज?

मेहमान औरत:
उनकी तबियत ठीक नहीं थी। कह रहे थे मुझे हॉस्पिटल ले चलो। लेकिन मैंने उनको कल पे टाल दिया है। इतनी बड़ी पार्टी भला मैं कैसे छोड़ सकती थी?

घोष *(मुस्कुराते हुए):*
शुक्रिया। ये तो आपकी ज़र्रा-नवाज़ी है।

विजय दाख़िल होता है। मीना एक औरत से बातें कर रही है।

मीना:
कमला, पप्पू को साथ नहीं लाई?

कमला:
नहीं।

मीना *(विजय को देखकर हैरानी से):*
विजय? तुम्हें मेरा पता कैसे मालूम हुआ?

جو ہی چلی جاتی ہے۔ ستّار کا اوپر والے کے ساتھ مکالمہ جاری رہتا ہے۔

ستّار:
سنا، اوپر والے؟ نہیں بھائی، کچھ نہیں، ہاں۔ ناریل ہے نہیں۔

منظر بدلتا ہے۔

اگلا منظر۔ رات۔ گھوش کے گھر پارٹی پر بہت سے لوگ جمع ہوئے ہیں۔

گھوش (دروازے پر ایک مہمان خاتون سے):
آپ کے ہسبینڈ نہیں آئے؟

مہمان خاتون:
اُن کی طبیعت ٹھیک نہیں تھی۔ کہہ رہے تھے مجھے ہاسپٹل لے چلو۔ لیکن میں نے اُن کو کل پہ ٹال دیا ہے۔ اِتنی بڑی پارٹی بھلا میں کیسے چھوڑ سکتی تھی؟

گھوش (مسکراتے ہوئے):
شکریہ۔ یہ تو آپ کی ذرّہ نوازی ہے۔

وجے داخل ہوتا ہے۔ مینا ایک خاتون سے باتیں کر رہی ہے۔

مینا:
کملا، پپو، کو ساتھ نہیں لائیں؟

کملا:
نہیں۔

مینا (حیرت سے وجے کو آتا دیکھ کر):
وجے؟ تمہیں میرا پتا کیسے معلوم ہوا؟

Vijay:
Your address? Do you live here?

Tumhaara pata? Tum yahaan rehti ho?

Meena:
Yes. Let's step outside.

Haan. Chalo baahar chalen.

Vijay:
Mr. Ghosh asked me to come.

Mr...Mr. Ghosh ne mujhe yahaan bulaaya hai.

Meena:
Asked you? You mean you know him?

Tumhen? Yaani, tum unhen jaante ho?

Vijay:
I work for him. And you?

Main unka naukar hoon. Aur tum?

Meena:[33]
I am his...

Main...main unki...

Meena doesn't complete her sentence. On the other side of the room, Ghosh is talking to a guest.

Female guest *(to Ghosh):*
Who is the most talented poet here?

In tamaam shaayeron mein sab se achha shaayer kaun hai?

Ghosh:
All are good, but the man in the black jacket is considered...

Yun toh sabhi shaayer achhe hain. Lekin vo saaheb jo kaali sherwaani mein baithe huwe hain, duniya...

Ghosh stops in mid-sentence when he sees Meena talking to Vijay across the room.

Meena *(to Vijay):*
Don't say a word to him about us. Understand?

Dekho, unhen apni pichhli baaten bilkul nahin bataana. Samjhe?

Ghosh *(to a guest while observing Meena and Vijay):*
He's considered a god of poetry by the world. Excuse me. I'll be right back.

Duniya unhen khudaay-e-sukhan samajhti hai. Excuse me. Main abhi aaya.

Ghosh and his guests are now seated.

विजय:
तुम्हारा पता? तुम यहाँ रहती हो?

मीना:
हाँ। चलो बाहर चलें।

विजय:
मि...मि. घोष ने मुझे यहाँ बुलाया है।

मीना:
तुम्हें? यानी, तुम उन्हें जानते हो?

विजय:
मैं उनका नौकर हूँ। और तुम?

मीना:
मैं... मैं उनकी...

मीना की बात ख़त्म नहीं होती। कमरे के दूसरे कोने में घोष मेहमान से बात कर रहा है।

मेहमान औरत *(घोष से)*:
इन तमाम शायरों में सबसे अच्छा शायर कौन है?

घोष:
यूँ तो सभी शायर अच्छे हैं। लेकिन वो साहब जो काली शेरवानी में बैठे हुए हैं। दुनिया...

मीना को विजय से बात करता देख घोष खामोश हो जाता है।

मीना *(विजय से)*:
देखो, उन्हें अपनी पिछली बातें बिलकुल नहीं बताना। समझे?

घोष *(मीना और विजय की ओर देख कर मेहमान से)*:
दुनिया उन्हें ख़ुदा-ए-सुख़न समझती है। एक्सक्यूज़ मी। मैं अभी आया।

घोष और मेहमान बैठ जाते हैं।

وجے:
تمہارا پتا؟ تم یہاں رہتی ہو؟

مینا:
ہاں۔ چلو باہر چلیں۔

وجے:
مسٹر۔۔ مسٹر گھوش نے مجھے یہاں بلایا ہے۔

مینا:
تمہیں؟ یعنی، تم اُنھیں جانتے ہو؟

وجے:
میں اُن کا نوکر ہوں۔ اور تم؟

مینا:
میں ۔۔۔ میں اُن کی ۔۔۔

مینا کا جملہ مکمل نہیں ہوتا۔ کمرے کے دوسرے گوشے میں گھوش مہمان سے بات کر رہا ہے۔

مہمان خاتون (گھوش سے):
اِن تمام شاعروں میں سب سے اچھا شاعر کون ہے؟

گھوش:
یوں تو سبھی شاعر اچھے ہیں۔ لیکن وہ صاحب جو کالی شیروانی میں بیٹھے ہوئے ہیں۔ دنیا۔۔۔

مینا کو وجے سے بات کرتا دیکھ کر گھوش خاموش ہو جاتا ہے۔

مینا (وجے سے):
دیکھو، اُنھیں اپنی پچھلی باتیں بالکل نہیں بتانا۔ سمجھے؟

گھوش (مہمان خاتون سے۔ وہ مینا اور وجے کو دیکھے جا رہا ہے):
دنیا اُنھیں خدائے سخن سمجھتی ہے۔ ایکسکیوزمی۔ میں ابھی آیا۔

گھوش اور مہمان بیٹھ جاتے ہیں۔

Reel Seven

Unnamed poet (actor/dialogue writer Tanvir Farooqi):
I disagree, sir. Poetry that encourages the nation's progress is far better than poetry that hammers on about phony love.

Main nahin maanta, qibla. Apni shaayeri se quam-o-watan ko taraqqi dena khokhli mohabbat ke dhol peetne se kahin behtar hai.

Ghosh:
Gentlemen, for once, stop this tradition versus modernity argument. The drinks are here.

Arey saahebaan, chhodiye is naye-puraane ke qisse ko. Ah, lijiye. Jaam haazir hai.

Vijay enters with a tray laden with glasses. As he is putting the tray on the table, Meena gets up to help him.

Ghosh (to Meena):
Don't trouble yourself, dear. What are servants for? Vijay, why are you waiting? Serve the guests.

Naukaron ke hote huwe tum kyun takleef karti ho, dear? Vijay, sochte kya ho? Jaam do.

The poetry recital starts.

Unnamed poet:[34]
"What could I tell her of my sad story of love?
How would I say it?
Not a word escaped the lips
And tears welled in the eyes

"Roodaad-e-gham-e-ulfat unse hum kya kehte kyun-kar kehte
Ik harf na nikla honton se aur aankh mein aansu aa bhi gaye

The guests exclaim their appreciation. The poet continues.

"In the assembly of the ecstatic
In the gathering of the enlightened
They sat clasping the cup of wine
I quaffed the wine, I spilled drops, too."

"Uss mehfil-e-kaifo-masti mein uss anjuman-e-irfaani mein
Sab jaam-bakaf baithe hi rahe hum pi bhi gaye chhalka bhi gaye"

एक कवि *(कलाकार/संवाद लेखक तनवीर फ़ारूक़ी):*
मैं नहीं मानता, क़िबला। अपनी शायरी से क़ौम-ओ-वतन को तरक़्क़ी देना, खोखली मोहब्बत के ढोल पीटने से कहीं बेहतर है।

घोष:
अरे, साहेबान, छोड़िए इस नये-पुराने के क़िस्से को। आह! लीजिए, जाम हाज़िर है।

ट्रे में ग्लास रखे विजय आता है। टेबल पर वो ट्रे रखता है। मीना उसकी मदद के लिए उठना चाहती है।

घोष *(मीना से):*
नौकरों के होते हुए तुम क्यूँ तकलीफ़ करती हो, डियर? विजय, सोचते क्या हो? जाम दो।

महफ़िल शुरु होती है।

एक कवि:
"रूदादे-ग़मे-उलफ़त उनसे हम क्या कहते क्यों-कर कहते
इक हर्फ़ ना निकला होठों से और आँख में आँसू आ भी गए।

वाह-वाह की आवाज़ें सुनाई देती है।

उस महफ़िले-कैफ़ो-मस्ती में उस अन्जुमने-इरफ़ानी में
सब जाम-बकफ़ बैठे ही रहे हम पी भी गए छलका भी गए"

ایک شاعر (اداکارو مکالمہ نگار تنویر فاروقی):
میں نہیں مانتا، قبلہ۔ اپنی شاعری سے قوم و وطن کو ترقی دینا، کھوکھلی محبت کے ڈھول پیٹنے سے کہیں بہتر ہے۔

گھوش:
ارے، صاحبان، چھوڑیے اس نئے پرانے کے قصے کو۔ آہ! لیجیے، جام حاضر ہے۔

ٹرے میں گلاس رکھے وجے آتا ہے۔ ٹیبل پر وہ ٹرے رکھتا ہے۔ مینا اس کی مدد کے لیے اٹھنا چاہتی ہے۔

گھوش (مینا سے):
نوکروں کے ہوتے ہوئے تم کیوں تکلیف کرتی ہو، ڈیر؟ وجے، سوچتے کیا ہو؟ جام دو۔

شعرخوانی شروع ہوتی ہے۔

ایک شاعر:
"روداد غمِ الفت اُن سے ہم کیا کہتے کیوں کر کہتے
اک حرف نہ نکلا ہونٹوں سے اور آنکھ میں آنسو آ بھی گئے

واہ واہ کا شور بلند ہوتا ہے۔

اُس محفلِ کیف و مستی میں اُس انجمن عرفانی میں
سب جام بکف بیٹھے ہی رہے، ہم پی بھی گئے چھلکا بھی گئے

Poet laureate:
"The disquiet of my feelings came at last to my rescue
Perceiving my distressed state, she deigned to love me."

"Kaam aakhir jazba-e-be-ikhtiyaar aa hi gaya
Dil kuchh is soorat se tadpa unko pyar aa hi gaya"

A short lull follows. In the silence, Vijay recites a few lines (Hemant Kumar's voice).

Vijay:
"Who are the ones who love and are loved in return?"

"Jaane vo kaise log thay jin ke pyar ko pyar mila"

Guest (*turning to Ghosh*):
How wonderful, Mr. Ghosh. What an appreciative house! Even your servants are poets.

Bhai, bahot khoob, Ghosh babu. Bada sukhan-nawaaz hai ghar aap ka. Naukar-chaakar bhi shaayeri karte hain.

Meena (*getting up, disturbed*):
I'll see to the food.

Main ja kar khaane ka intezaam karti hoon.

Poet laureate:
Poetry is not the sole prerogative of the rich.
(*to Vijay*)
You were saying something, young man? Don't be silent. Pray continue.

Miyaan, shaayeri sirf daulat-mandon ki jaagir nahin.

Tum kuchh keh rahe thay, barkhur-daar? Chup kyun ho gaye? Kaho, kaho.

Encouraged by the grand old man of poetry, Vijay continues in song. The song is filmed in a series of tracking shots showing Vijay, Meena and Ghosh.[35]

Singer: Hemant Kumar

Who are the ones who love and are loved in return?
When I asked for flowers, I was given a garland of thorns
Who are the ones who love and are loved in return?

Jaane vo kaise log thay jin ke pyar ko pyar mila
Hum ne toh jab kaliyaan maangein kaanton ka haar mila
Jaane vo kaise log thay jin ke pyar ko pyar mila

महा कवि:

"काम आख़िर जज़्बाए-बे-इख़्तियार आ ही गया
दिल कुछ इस सूरत से तड़पा उनको प्यार आ ही गया"

वाह-वाह की आवाज़ें। ख़ामोशी छाने के बाद विजय कुछ लाईनें गाता है। (हेमंत कुमार की आवाज़)

विजय:

"जाने वो कैसे लोग थे जिनके प्यार को प्यार मिला।"

मेहमान *(मुड़ कर घोष से):*

भाई, बहुत ख़ूब, घोष बाबू। बड़ा सुख़न-नवाज़ है घर आपका। नौकर-चाकर भी शायरी करते हैं।

मीना *(परेशान-सी होकर खड़ी हो जाती है):*

मैं जा के खाने का इंतज़ाम करती हूँ।

महा कवि:

मियाँ, शायरी सिर्फ़ दौलत-मंदों की जागीर नहीं।
(विजय से)
तुम कुछ कह रहे थे बरख़ुरदार? चुप क्यूँ हो गए। कहो-कहो।

महा कवि की बात सुन कर विजय अपना गीत आगे बढ़ाता है। यह गीत विजय, मीना और घोष के ट्रैकिंग शॉट्स पर फ़िल्माया है।

गायक: हेमंत कुमार

जाने वो कैसे लोग थे जिनके प्यार को प्यार मिला
हमने तो जब कलियाँ माँगीं काँटों का हार मिला
जाने वो कैसे लोग थे जिनके प्यार को प्यार मिला

شاعرِ اعظم (کالی جیکٹ میں):

’’کام آخر جذبۂ بے اختیار آ ہی گیا
دل کچھ اس صورت سے تڑپا اُن کو پیار آ ہی گیا‘‘

داد و تحسین کی آوازیں بلند ہوتی ہیں۔ خاموشی چھانے کے بعد ہی وجے کچھ مصرعے پڑھتا ہے۔ ہیمنت کمار کی آواز۔

وجے:

’’جانے وہ کیسے لوگ تھے جن کے پیار کو پیار ملا۔‘‘

مہمان (مڑ کر گھوش سے):

بھئی، بہت خوب، گھوش بابو۔ بڑا سخن نواز ہے آپ کا۔ نوکر چاکر بھی شاعری کرتے ہیں۔

مینا (پریشان سی ہو کر کھڑی ہو جاتی ہے):

میں جا کے کھانے کا انتظام کرتی ہوں۔

شاعرِ اعظم:

میاں، شاعری صرف دولت مندوں کی جاگیر نہیں۔
(وجے سے)
تم کچھ کہہ رہے تھے برخوردار؟ چپ کیوں ہو گئے۔ کہو، کہو۔

بزرگ شاعر کی ہمت افزائی پر وجے گیت پیش کرتا ہے۔ وجے، مینا اور گھوش کے ٹریکنگ شاٹس پر یہ منظر مشتمل ہے۔

ہیمنت کمار کی آواز۔

جانے وہ کیسے لوگ تھے جن کے پیار کو پیار ملا
ہم نے تو جب کلیاں مانگیں کانٹوں کا ہار ملا
جانے وہ کیسے لوگ تھے جن کے پیار کو پیار ملا

Meena stands in a corner of the room. She is overcome with emotion.

When I searched for happiness
A forlorn, dusty path lay before me *(both lines repeated)*
When I sought songs of desire, I heard frozen sighs
Those who consoled me redoubled my heart's burdens
When I asked for flowers, I was given a garland of thorns
Who are the ones who love and are loved in return?

Ghosh intently watches Meena's reaction to Vijay's song.

Parted from me...
All companions parted, having shared fleeting moments
Who has the time to clasp the hand of an obsessed lover?
I have found even my shadow often weary of me
When I asked for flowers, I was given a garland of thorns
Who are the ones who love and are loved in return?

If this is called living, then I'll live somehow *(2)*
I'll not complain, seal my lips, swallow my tears
Why let sorrow worry me, familiar as it is?
When I asked for flowers, I was given a garland of thorns
Who are the ones who love and are loved in return?

A solitary guest shows appreciation of Vijay's song while the others look on with disdain.

Guest:
Wonderful! Excellent! Bravo...

The guests walk away.

A guest *(in the distance)*:
Oh yes, what were you saying?

Vijay stands in a corner of the room. Fade out.

Khushiyon ki manzil dhoondi toh gham ki gard mili *(2)*

Chaahat ke naghme chaahe toh aah-e-sard mili
Dil ke bojh ko doona kar gaya jo gham-khwaar mila
Hum ne toh jab kaliyaan maangein kaanton ka haar mila
Jaane vo kaise log thay jin ke pyar ko pyar mila

Bichhad gaya...bichhad gaya
Bichhad gaya har saathi de kar pal do pal ka saath
Kis ko fursat hai jo thaame deewaanon ka haath
Hum ko apna saaya tak aksar be-zaar mila
Hum ne toh jab kaliyaan maangein kaanton ka haar mila
Jaane vo kaise log thay jin ke pyar ko pyar mila

Is ko hi jeena kehte hain toh yunhi ji lenge *(2)*
Uff na karenge, lab seelenge, aansu peelenge
Gham se ab ghabraana kaisa gham sau baar mila
Hum ne toh jab kaliyaan maangein kaanton ka haar mila
Jaane vo kaise log thay jin ke pyar ko pyar mila

Bhai, waah waah. Bahot khoob. Bahot achhe. Subhaan...

Haan toh aap kya suna rahe thay?

कमरे के एक कोने में जज़्बात से भरी मीना खड़ी है।

ख़ुशियों की मंज़िल ढूँढी तो ग़म की गर्द मिली (२)
चाहत के नग़्में चाहे तो आहें-सर्द मिलीं
दिल के बोझ को दूना कर गया जो ग़म-ख़्वार मिला
हमने तो जब कलियाँ माँगीं कांटों का हार मिला
जाने वो कैसे लोग थे जिनके प्यार को प्यार मिला

विजय के गीत का असर मीना के चेहरे पर होते हुए घोष देख रहा है।

बिछड़ गया... बिछड़ गया
बिछड़ गया हर साथी देकर पल दो पल का साथ
किसको फुरसत है जो थामे दीवानों का हाथ
हमको अपना साया तक अक्सर बे-ज़ार मिला
हमने तो जब कलियाँ माँगीं कांटों का हार मिला
जाने वो कैसे लोग थे जिनके प्यार को प्यार मिला

इसको ही जीना कहते हैं तो यूँ ही जी लेंगे (२)
उफ़ ना करेंगे, लब सी लेंगे, आँसू पी लेंगे
ग़म से अब घबराना कैसा ग़म सौ बार मिला
हमने तो जब कलियाँ माँगीं कांटों का हार मिला
जाने वो कैसे लोग थे जिनके प्यार को प्यार मिला

एक ही मेहमान विजय की शायरी पसंद करता है जबकि दूसरों के चेहरों पर
ना-पसंदगी दिखाई देती है।

मेहमान:
भाई, वाह वाह। बहुत ख़ूब। बहुत अच्छे। सुभान...

बाक़ी मेहमान दूर हट जाते हैं।

दूसरा मेहमान (कुछ दूरी पर से):
हाँ तो आप क्या सुना रहे थे?

विजय कमरे के एक कोने में खड़ा है, दृश्य ख़त्म होता है।

Fade in. Ghosh's office. Meena enters to find Vijay leafing through a book.

Meena:
I've come to see you.

Main tumhin se milne aayi hoon.

Vijay *(under his breath):*
Here?

Yahaan?

Meena:
Mr. Ghosh has gone to the board meeting.

Haan, Mr. Ghosh board ki meeting mein gaye hain.

Vijay:
You shouldn't have come here.

Tumhen yahaan nahin aana chaahiye tha.

Meena:
I've been very troubled since the party, Vijay. I've given you many reasons for complaint, haven't I?

Uss party ke din se main bahot pareshan hoon, Vijay. Tumhen mujh se bahot shikaayat hai na?

Vijay:
No, Meena. I have no reason to complain against anyone.

Nahin, Meena. Mujhe kisi se koi shikaayat nahin.

Meena *(lying on a chaise longue):*
So why did you sing that heart-rending poem at the party? You revived my desires.

Toh phir uss din tum ne mujhe vo dard bhari nazm kyun sunaayi? Mere soye huwe jazbaat phir se jaag uthey.

Vijay:
Forget the past, Meena.

Phichhli baaten bhool jaao, Meena.

Meena:
I was trying to forget. I had remoulded my life. I had controlled my heart. Why have you come back into my life to unsettle it again?

Bhula toh rahi thi. Apni zindagi ko naye saanche mein dhaal liya tha maine. Dil ko samjha liya tha maine. Is dil ko phir se bechain karne ke liye dobaara kyun chale aaye meri zindagi mein?

Vijay:
When did I walk away from your life? You were the one who left me. That was your first mistake. Don't correct it now with another mistake, Meena.

Main tumhaari zindagi se gaya hi kab tha? Tum khud hi chali gayin thein meri zindagi se. Vo tumhaari pehli ghalati thi. Usay sudhaarne ke liye ab doosri ghalati na karo, Meena.

अगला मंज़र। घोष का दफ़्तर। विजय एक किताब के पन्ने उलट-पलट कर रहा है, मीना दाख़िल होती है।

मीना:
मैं तुम्हीं से मिलने आयी हूँ।

विजय (धीरे से):
यहाँ?

मीना:
हाँ, मि. घोष बोर्ड की मीटिंग में गए हैं।

विजय:
तुम्हें यहाँ नहीं आना चाहिए था।

मीना:
उस पार्टी के दिन से मैं बहुत परेशान हूँ, विजय। तुम्हें मुझसे बहुत शिक़ायत है ना?

विजय:
नहीं, मीना। मुझे किसी से कोई शिक़ायत नहीं।

मीना (दीवान पर लेटते हुए):
तो फिर उस दिन तुम ने मुझे वो दर्द भरी नज़्म क्यूँ सुनाई? मेरे सोये हुए जज़्बात फिर से जाग उठे।

विजय:
पिछली बातें भूल जाओ, मीना।

मीना:
भुला तो रही थी। अपनी ज़िंदगी को नये सांचे में ढाल लिया था मैंने। दिल को समझा लिया था मैंने। इस दिल को फिर से बेचैन करने के लिए दोबारा क्यूँ चले आए मेरी ज़िंदगी में?

विजय:
मैं तुम्हारी ज़िंदगी से गया ही कब था? तुम ख़ुद ही चली गयी थीं मेरी ज़िंदगी से। वो तुम्हारी पहली ग़लती थी। उसे सुधारने के लिए अब दूसरी ग़लती ना करो, मीना।

اگلامنظر۔گھوش کا آفس ۔ وجے ایک کتاب کی ورق گردانی کر رہا ہے۔ مینا داخل ہوتی ہے۔

مینا:
میں تمہیں سے ملنے آئی ہوں۔

وجے (زیرِ لب):
یہاں؟

مینا:
ہاں، مسٹرگھوش بورڈ کی میٹنگ میں گئے ہیں۔

وجے:
تمہیں یہاں نہیں آنا چاہیے تھا۔

مینا:
اُس پارٹی کے دن سے میں بہت پریشان ہوں، وجے۔ تمہیں مجھ سے بہت شکایت ہے نا؟

وجے:
نہیں، مینا۔ مجھے کسی سے کوئی شکایت نہیں۔

مینا (دیوان پر دراز ہوتے ہوئے):
تو پھر اُس دن تم نے مجھے وہ درد بھری نظم کیوں سنائی؟ میرے سوئے ہوئے جذبات پھر سے جاگ گئے۔

وجے:
پچھلی باتیں بھول جاؤ، مینا۔

مینا:
بھلا تو رہی تھی۔ اپنی زندگی کو نئے سانچے میں ڈھال لیا تھا میں نے۔ دل کو سمجھا لیا تھا میں نے۔ اِس دل کو پھر سے بے چین کرنے کے لیے دوبارہ کیوں چلے آئے میری زندگی میں۔

وجے:
میں تمہاری زندگی سے گیا ہی کب تھا؟ تم خود ہی چلی گئی تھیں میری زندگی سے۔ وہ تمہاری پہلی غلطی تھی۔ اُسے سدھارنے کے لیے اب دوسری غلطی نہ کرو، مینا۔

Meena *(standing up):*
I made no mistake. Besides love, every sensible woman needs the comfort of a home. She needs security and money. That's why I…

Vijay:
…married Mr. Ghosh. In other words, you sold your love in exchange of wealth.

Meena:
Don't accuse me wrongly. I loved you, but you were poor, and without work. Besides poetry and love, in life, there's hunger, too. When you couldn't feed yourself, how could you have married me and looked after me?

Vijay:
When did you ever give me the chance? When a man has responsibilities, he learns to shoulder them. Don't deceive yourself, Meena. You wanted to be rich. To live amidst high society. You wanted prestige and status. You have all that now, but it still isn't enough. You regret it all. You know why? Because you've always been selfish. You left me without caring how I would feel. And do you want to now snatch away your husband's happiness?
(he walks towards the door)
Life's real happiness is in making others happy. You never understood that — that's why you're unhappy.

Maine koi ghalati nahin ki. Har samajhdaar aurat ko zindagi mein pyar ke alaawa ghar-baar ki bhi zaroorat hoti hai. Thodi-bahot daulat ke sahaare ki bhi zaroorat hoti hai. Aur yahi cheezen paane ke liye maine…

…Mr. Ghosh se biyaah kiya. Yaani daulat ke liye tum ne apna pyar bech diya.

Ghalat ilzaam na do mujhe. Tum ne mera pyar paaya lekin tum ghareeb thay, berozgaar thay. Zindagi mein sirf shaayeri hi nahin, pyar hi nahin, bhook bhi hai. Jab tum khud apna pait nahin paal sakte thay uss haalat mein mujh se biyaah karke mera bhaar utha sakte thay tum?

Uss ka mauqa hi kab diya tum ne mujhe? Jab insaan ke sar par zimmedaariyaan aa jaati hain vo unhen uthaana bhi seekh jaata hai. Apne aap ko dhoka na do, Meena. Tum daulat chaahti thein. Oonchi society chaahti thein. Samaaji naam aur izzat chaahti thein. Aur aaj vo tamaam cheezen milne ke baad bhi tum bechain ho. Pachhta rahi ho. Jaanti ho kyun? Tum ne hamesha apna svarth dekha — is liye. Meri zindagi se jaate meri khushi ka khayaal nahin kiya. Aur aaj tum apne pati ki khushi chheenna chaahti ho?
Meena, zindagi ki asli khushi doosron ko khush rakh ke haasil ki jaati hai. Aur ye tum kabhi na samajh sakein, isi liye nakhush ho.

मीना (खड़े होते हुए):

मैंने कोई ग़लती नहीं की। हर समझदार औरत को ज़िंदगी में प्यार के अलावा घर-बार की भी ज़रूरत होती है। थोड़ी-बहुत दौलत के सहारे की भी ज़रूरत होती है। और यही चीज़ें पाने के लिए मैंने...

विजय:

...मि. घोष से ब्याह किया। यानी दौलत के लिए तुमने अपना प्यार बेच दिया।

मीना:

ग़लत इल्ज़ाम ना दो मुझे। तुमने मेरा प्यार पाया लेकिन तुम ग़रीब थे, बेरोज़गार थे। ज़िंदगी में सिर्फ़ शायरी ही नहीं, प्यार ही नहीं, भूख भी है। जब तुम ख़ुद अपना पेट नहीं पाल सकते थे, उस हालत में मुझसे ब्याह करके मेरा भार उठा सकते थे तुम?

विजय:

उसका मौक़ा ही कब दिया तुमने मुझे? जब इन्सान के सर पर ज़िम्मेदारियाँ आ जाती हैं वो उन्हें उठाना भी सीख जाता है। अपने आपको धोखा ना दो, मीना। तुम दौलत चाहती थीं। ऊँची सोसायटी चाहती थीं। समाजी नाम और इज़्ज़त चाहती थीं। और आज वो तमाम चीज़ें मिलने के बाद भी तुम बेचैन हो। पछता रही हो। जानती हो क्यूँ? तुमने हमेशा अपना स्वार्थ देखा – इस लिए। मेरी ज़िंदगी से जाते मेरी ख़ुशी का ख़याल नहीं किया। और आज, तुम अपने पति की ख़ुशी छीनना चाहती हो?
(वो दरवाज़े की ओर जाने लगता है)
मीना, ज़िंदगी की असली ख़ुशी दूसरों को ख़ुश रख के हासिल की जाती है। और ये तुम कभी ना समझ सकीं, इसी लिए नाख़ुश हो।

مینا(کھڑے ہوتے ہوئے):

میں نے کوئی غلطی نہیں کی۔ ہر سمجھدار عورت کو زندگی میں پیار کے علاوہ گھر بار کی ضرورت ہوتی ہے۔ تھوڑی بہت دولت کے سہارے کی بھی ضرورت ہوتی ہے۔اور یہی چیزیں پانے کے لیے میں نے۔۔۔

وج:

۔۔۔مسٹر گھوش سے بیاہ کیا۔ یعنی دولت کے لیے تم نے اپنا پیار بیچ دیا۔

مینا:

غلط الزام نہ دو مجھے۔تم نے میرا پیار پایا لیکن تم غریب تھے۔ بے روزگار تھے۔ زندگی میں صرف شاعری ہی نہیں، پیار ہی نہیں، بھوک بھی ہے۔ جب تم خود اپنا پیٹ نہیں پال سکتے تھے، اُس حالت میں مجھ سے بیاہ کر کے میرا بھار اُٹھا سکتے تھے تم؟

وج:

اُس کا موقع ہی کب دیا تم نے مجھے؟ جب انسان کے سر پر ذمے داریاں آ جاتی ہیں، وہ اُنھیں اُٹھانا بھی سیکھ جاتا ہے۔ اپنے آپ کو دھوکا نہ دو، مینا۔تم دولت چاہتی تھیں۔ اونچی سوسائٹی چاہتی تھیں۔سماجی نام اور عزت چاہتی تھیں۔ اور آج وہ تمام چیزیں ملنے کے بعد بھی تم بے چین ہو۔ پچھتا رہی ہو۔ جانتی ہو کیوں؟ تم نے ہمیشہ اپنا سوارتھ دیکھا۔۔۔اِس لیے۔ میری زندگی سے جاتے میری خوشی کا خیال نہیں کیا۔اور آج، تم اپنے پتی کی خوشی چھیننا چاہتی ہو؟
(وہ دروازے کی طرف جانے لگتا ہے)
مینا، زندگی کی اصلی خوشی دوسروں کو خوش رکھ کے حاصل کی جاتی ہے۔ اور یہ تم کبھی نہ سمجھ سکیں، اِس لیے نا خوش ہو۔

Vijay opens the door and finds Ghosh on the other side. He looks furious. Ghosh enters the office and closes the door behind him. Vijay overhears husband and wife arguing through the closed door. They are never seen in shot.

Ghosh:
Wonderful! My wife's no better than a streetwalker.

Bahot khoob! Meri biwi aur ek baazaari aurat mein koi farq nahin.

Meena:
Be sensible. Vijay and I hardly know each other.

Zara soch-samajh ke baaten karo. Sirf maamooli si jaan-pehchaan thi hum donon ki.

Ghosh *(angry):*
Stop making a fool of me! How long has this been going on?

Dhool matt jhonko meri aankhon mein. Ye silsila kab se chal raha hai?

Meena *(shouting):*
I assure you, we hardly know each other.

Main kehti hoon, maamooli se jaan-pehchaan thi hum donon ki.

Ghosh:
Nothing more?

Aur kuchh nahin?

Meena:
No.

Nahin.

Meena screams. It is unclear whether or not Ghosh has hit her.

Ghosh:
So you won't admit it? Let's see how upset you are when I sack your precious friend.

Tum yun na maanogi? Main abhi tumhaare chaheete ko naukri se nikaal deta hoon. Aur phir dekhta hoon ki tumhen is ka dard hota hai ki nahin.

Vijay moves closer to the door. Fade out.

Fade in. Title card: "INTERVAL."[36]

विजय दरवाजा खोलता है तो घोष को सामने ही खड़ा पाता है। उसके चेहरे पर गुस्सा नज़र आता है। वो कमरे में दाखिल होता है और कमरा बंद कर देता है। बंद दरवाज़े के पीछे से विजय को मियाँ-बीवी की तू-तू-मैं-मैं सुनाई दे रही है। इस दृश्य में वो नज़र नहीं आते।

घोष:
बहुत ख़ूब! मेरी बीवी और एक बाज़ारी औरत में कोई फ़र्क़ नहीं।

मीना:
ज़रा सोच-समझ के बातें करो। सिर्फ़ मामूली सी जान-पहचान थी हम दोनों की।

घोष (गुस्से से):
धूल मत झोंको मेरी आँखों में। ये सिलसिला कब से चल रहा है?

मीना (उँची आवाज़ में):
मैं कहती हूँ, मामूली सी जान-पहचान थी हम दोनों की।

घोष:
और कुछ नहीं?

मीना:
नहीं।

मीना चीख़ती है। साफ समझ नहीं आता की घोष ने उस पर हाथ उठाया है या नहीं।

घोष:
तुम यूँ न मानोगी। मैं अभी तुम्हारे चहीते को नौकरी से निकाल देता हूँ। और फिर देखता हूँ कि तुम्हें इसका दर्द होता है कि नहीं।

विजय बंद दरवाज़े के क़रीब आता है। दृश्य ख़त्म होता है।

अगला दृश्य। टाइटल कार्ड "इंटरवल"।

وجے دروازہ کھولتا ہے تو گھوش کو سامنے ہی کھڑا ہوتا ہے۔ اُس کے چہرے سے ظاہر ہو رہا ہے کہ وہ غصے میں ہے۔ وہ کمرے میں داخل ہوتا ہے اور اپنے پیچھے دروازہ بند کر لیتا ہے۔ بند دروازے کے پیچھے سے وجے کو میاں بیوی کی تو تو میں میں سنائی دے رہی ہے۔ اِس شاٹ میں وہ نظر نہیں آتے صرف اُن کی آوازیں سنائی دیتی ہیں۔

گھوش:
بہت خوب! میری بیوی اور ایک بازاری عورت میں کوئی فرق نہیں۔

مینا:
ذرا سوچ سمجھ کے باتیں کرو۔ صرف معمولی سی جان پہچان تھی ہم دونوں کی۔

گھوش (غصے سے):
دھول مت جھونکو میری آنکھوں میں۔ یہ سلسلہ کب سے چل رہا ہے؟

مینا (اونچی آواز میں):
میں کہتی ہوں، معمولی سی جان پہچان تھی ہم دونوں کی۔

گھوش:
اور کچھ نہیں؟

مینا:
نہیں۔

مینا کی چیخ سنائی دیتی ہے۔ صاف سمجھ نہیں آتا کہ گھوش نے اُس پر ہاتھ اُٹھایا ہے یا نہیں۔

گھوش:
تم یوں نہ مانو گی۔ میں ابھی تمہارے چہیتے کو نوکری سے نکال دیتا ہوں۔ اور پھر دیکھتا ہوں کہ تمہیں اِس کا درد ہوتا ہے کہ نہیں۔

وجے بند دروازے کے قریب آتا ہے۔ منظر ختم ہوتا ہے۔

اگلا منظر۔ ٹائٹل کارڈ۔ انٹرول۔

Reel Eight

Night. A car drives up a dark street near the now familiar park. Gulaab is pushed out of the car. She falls to the ground. She seems a little drunk. She gets up and comes to the car window.

Gulaab:
Give me my money.

Mere paise la.

Client *(off-screen):*
I earn my money the hard way. Be off!

Halaal ki kamaayi hai meri. Chal hatt.

Gulaab:
You rascal! Pay up.

Badmaash. Nikaal mere paise.

Client *(off-screen):*
Get lost! Constable!

Chal hatt. Hawaldaar!

A constable is heading towards the car. Gulaab sees him and walks swiftly away. He follows her. She runs through the winding alleys and in the darkness bumps into Vijay. She holds on to him as the constable approaches.

Gulaab:
Save me, do something.

Bachaayiye mujhe. Kisi bhi tarah bachaayiye.

Vijay:
You? What's the matter?

Tum? Kya baat hai?

Gulaab *(now recognising him):*
It's you?

Aap?

रील ८

रात। एक गाड़ी उसी जाने-पहचाने बाग़ के पास रुकती है। गुलाब को धक्का देकर गाड़ी से उतार दिया जाता है। वो ज़मीन पर गिर जाती है। वो कुछ नशे में भी है। वह कार की खिड़की के पास आती है।

गुलाब:
मेरे पैसे ला।

ग्राहक (ऑफ स्क्रीन):
हलाल की कमाई है मेरी। चल हट।

गुलाब:
बदमाश, निकाल मेरे पैसे।

ग्राहक (ऑफ स्क्रीन):
चल हट। हवलदार!

एक हवलदार कार की ओर आ रहा है। गुलाब उसे देख कर तेज़ी से दूसरी ओर निकल जाती है। वो उसके पीछे-पीछे चला आ रहा है। गलियों-गलियों में दौड़ती हुई वो अंधेरे में विजय से टकरा जाती है। हवलदार के डर से वो विजय से लिपट जाती है।

गुलाब:
बचाईए मुझे। किसी भी तरह बचाईए।

विजय:
तुम? क्या बात है?

गुलाब (उसे पहचानते हुए):
आप?

ریل ۸

اگلا منظر۔رات۔ایک گاڑی اُسی جانے پہچانے پارک کے پاس رکتی ہے۔گلاب کو دھکا دے کر گاڑی سے اُتار دیا جاتا ہے۔وہ زمین پر گر جاتی ہے۔وہ کچھ نشے میں بھی ہے۔کھڑکی کے پاس آ کر وہ کہتی ہے۔

گلاب:
میرے پیسے لا۔

گاہک (آف اسکرین):
حلال کی کمائی ہے میری۔چل ہٹ۔

گلاب:
بدمعاش۔نکال میرے پیسے۔

گاہک (آف اسکرین):
چل ہٹ۔حولدار!

ایک کنسٹبل کار کی طرف آ رہا ہے۔گلاب اُسے دیکھ کر تیزی سے دوسری طرف نکل جاتی ہے۔وہ اُس کے پیچھے پیچھے چلا آ رہا ہے۔گلیوں گلیوں وہ دوڑتی ہوئی اندھیرے میں وجے سے ٹکرا جاتی ہے۔کنسٹبل کے خوف سے وہ اُس سے چمٹی ہوئی ہے۔

گلاب:
بچائیے مجھے۔کسی بھی طرح بچائیے۔

وجے:
تم؟ کیا بات ہے؟

گلاب (اُسے پہچانتے ہوئے):
آپ؟

REEL 8   103

Constable (who has caught up with Gulaab):
Sir, has a girl run this way?

Babuji, is taraf ladki toh bhaag ke nahin aayi?

Vijay:
No.

Nahin toh.

Constable:
Who is this girl?

Ye ladki kaun hai?

Vijay:
She's my wife.[37]

Ye meri biwi hai.

Constable:
Sorry, sir. My mistake.

Maaf karna, babuji. Mujh se ghalati huwi.

The constable leaves. Vijay and Gulaab are alone.

Vijay:
What's your name?

Kya naam hai tumhaara?

Gulaab:
Gulaab.

Gulaab.

Vijay:
It's all clear now. You can go safely.

Ab koi khatra nahin. Tum itmenaan se ja sakti ho.

Vijay climbs the stairs of a house, which appears to be where his friend Shyam lives. Gulaab watches him. She hears a group of singers on the street.[38]

Geeta Dutt sings for the unnamed performer (Bengali actress Maya Dass)

O friends!
Enduring the torment of a long absence, Radha was weary
So one day she went to her enchanting Krishna and said:
Today, beloved, hold me in Your arms, my life will be fulfilled *(2)*

Sakhi ri
Birha ke dukhre seh-seh kar jab Radhe besudh ho li
Toh ik din apne manmohan se jaa kar yun boli
Aaj sajan mohe ang laga lo janam safal ho jaaye *(2)*

हवलदार (जो गुलाब के क़रीब आ चुका है):
बाबूजी, इस तरफ़ लड़की तो भाग के नहीं आई?

विजय:
नहीं तो।

हवलदार:
ये लड़की कौन है?

विजय:
ये मेरी बीवी है।

हवलदार:
माफ़ करना, बाबूजी। मुझसे ग़लती हुई।

विजय और गुलाब को छोड़ कर हवलदार चला जाता है।

विजय:
क्या नाम है तुम्हारा?

गुलाब:
गुलाब।

विजय:
अब कोई ख़तरा नहीं। तुम इतमीनान से जा सकती हो।

विजय एक मकान की सीढ़ियाँ चढ़ते हुए ऊपर जा रहा है जहाँ उसका दोस्त श्याम रहता है। गुलाब उसे जाता हुआ देख रही है। उसके कानों में गीत की आवाज़ पड़ती है।

गीता दत्त की आवाज़ (एक बंगाली कलाकार माया दास पर फ़िल्माया हुआ गीत)

सखी री
बिरहा के दुखरे सह-सह कर जब राधे बेसुध हो ली
तो एक दिन अपने मनमोहन से जा कर यूँ बोली
आज सजन मोहे अंग लगा लो जनम सफल हो जाए (२)

Ease the ache in my heart, cool the fire in my body
Today, beloved, hold me in Your arms, my life will be fulfilled

Gulaab climbs the flight of stairs to see Vijay making his way up to the roof terrace.

My hapless eyes have been sleepless for an age (2)
Without You, no place pleases me
I see no happiness ahead (2)
Sorrow follows me everywhere
Without You, the world is lonely
Beloved, the nectar of love
Beloved
Let the nectar of love overflow
So the world floods with feeling
Today, beloved, hold me in Your arms, my life will be fulfilled

Gulaab watches Vijay as he looks at the singers below. He does not see Gulaab behind him.

Make me Your own, make me Your own
Take me in Your arms, I have been born to serve You
Make me Your own
Take me in Your arms, I have been born to serve You
Slake the thirst in me, O beautiful Krishna
O beautiful Krishna, slake the thirst in me
O beautiful Krishna, thirst consumes me to the depths
Beloved, the nectar of love
Beloved
Let the nectar of love overflow
So the world floods with feeling

Hriday ki peeda, dehe ki agni, sab sheetal ho jaaye
Aaj sajan mohe ang laga lo janam safal ho jaaye

Kayi jugg se hain jaage moray nain abhaage (2)
Kahin jiya nahin laage bin toray
Sukh dikhe nahin aage (2)
Dukh peechhe-peechhe bhaage
Jugg soona-soona laage bin toray
Prem-sudha, moray saanwariya
Saanwariya
Prem-sudha itni barsa do
Jugg jal-thal ho jaaye
Aaj sajan mohe ang laga lo janam safal ho jaaye

Mohe apna bana lo, o mohe apna bana lo
Mori baanh pakad, main hoon janam-janam ki daasi
Mohe apna bana lo
Mori baanh pakad, main hoon janam-janam ki daasi
Mori pyaas bujha do manhar girdhar, pyaas bujha do
Manhar girdhar pyaas bujha do
Manhar girdhar, main hoon antar ghatt tak pyaasi
Prem-sudha, moray saanwariya
Saanwariya
Prem-sudha itni barsa do jugg jal-thal ho jaaye

हृदय की पीड़ा, देह की अग्नि, सब शीतल हो जाए
आज सजन मोहे अंग लगा लो जनम सफल हो जाए

गुलाब ऊपर जाती है, विजय छत की ओर सीढ़ियाँ चढ़कर जा रहा है।

कई जुग से हैं जागे मोरे नैन अभागे (२)
कहीं जिया नहीं लागे बिन तोरे
सुख दिखे नहीं आगे (२)
दुख पीछे-पीछे भागे
जग सूना-सूना लागे बिन तोरे
प्रेम-सुधा, मोरे साँवरिया
साँवरिया
प्रेम-सुधा इतनी बरसा दो
जग जल-थल हो जाए
आज सजन मोहे अंग लगा लो जनम सफल हो जाए

छत पर खड़े विजय को नीचे की ओर देखते हुए गुलाब देख रही है। विजय नीचे गाने वालों को देख रहा है। गुलाब पर उसकी नज़र नहीं पड़ती।

मोहे अपना बना लो, ओ मोहे अपना बना लो
मोरी बाँह पकड़, मैं हूँ जनम-जनम की दासी
मोहे अपना बना लो
मोरी बाँह पकड़, मैं हूँ जनम-जनम की दासी
मोरी प्यास बुझा दो मनहर गिरधर, प्यास बुझा दो
मनहर गिरधर प्यास बुझा दो
मनहर गिरधर, मैं हूँ अंतर घट तक प्यासी
प्रेम-सुधा, मोरे साँवरिया
साँवरिया
प्रेम-सुधा इतनी बरसा दो जग जल-थल हो जाए

Today, beloved, hold me in Your arms, my life will be fulfilled
Ease the ache in my heart, cool the fire in my body
Today, beloved, hold me in Your arms, my life will be fulfilled

Vijay does not know that Gulaab stands near him. She cannot bring herself to make him aware of her presence. At the end of the song, she turns and rushes away. Fade out.[39]

Aaj sajan mohe ang laga lo janam safal ho jaaye
Hriday ki peeda, dehe ki agni, sab sheetal ho jaaye
Aaj sajan mohe ang laga lo janam safal ho jaaye

Reel Nine

Fade in. Morning. Vijay gets up from the bench at the waterfront near the railway yard. He goes to a water pump but the tap is dry. Meena drives past in her chauffeur-driven convertible. The car stops. She gets out and looks at Vijay. He sees Meena but does not go to her. A train passes, obscuring Meena's view. She drives away. Wipe to a shot of Vijay at the waterfront. It is a stormy and windy day. He walks away. Fade out.[40]

Fade in. Gulaab, looking preoccupied, is sitting on a park bench.

Unnamed pimp:
Gulaabo, there's a millionaire in the car. Come with me.

Gulaabo, wahaan ek lakh-pati seth baitha hai motor mein. Chal aa.

Gulaab:
Go away. I'm not coming.

Tu ja yahaan se. Main nahin aaongi.

Unnamed pimp *(pulling her roughly)*:
Like hell you won't! I've promised him. Get up!

Hmm, aayegi kaise nahin? Main zabaan de chuka hoon. Chal uth.

आज सजन मोहे अंग लगा लो जनम सफल हो जाए
हृदय की पीड़ा, देह की अग्नि, सब शीतल हो जाए
आज सजन मोहे अंग लगा लो जनम सफल हो जाए

विजय को पता नहीं चलता कि गुलाब उसके क़रीब ही खड़ी है। गुलाब में इतनी हिम्मत नहीं कि वो विजय को छू कर अपनी मौजूदगी का एहसास दिला दे। गीत ख़त्म होते ही वो चली जाती है। दृश्य ख़त्म होता है।

रील ९

अगला दृश्य। सुबह। रेलवे यार्ड के पास, दरिया किनारे पर पड़ी बेंच पर सो रहे विजय की आँख खुलती है। सड़क के किनारे लगे एक पानी के नल के पास वो पानी पीने आता है लेकिन उसमें पानी नहीं होता। मीना अपनी कार में वहाँ से गुज़रती है जिसे ड्राइवर चला रहा है। कार रुकती है और वो बाहर आकर विजय को देखती है। विजय उसे देखता है पर वह उसकी तरफ़ नहीं जाता। उन दोनों के बीच रेलवे लाइन से एक ट्रेन गुज़रती है जिसकी वजह से विजय दिखाई नहीं देता। मीना अपनी कार में बैठ कर चली जाती है। अगला दृश्य। दरिया किनारे विजय खड़ा है। तूफ़ान के आसार नज़र आते हैं। विजय वहाँ से पलट आता है।

अगला दृश्य। गुलाब बाग़ में एक बेंच पर किसी सोच में डूबी हुई है।

दलाल:
गुलाबो, वहाँ एक लखपति सेठ बैठा है मोटर में। चल आ।

गुलाब:
तू जा यहाँ से। मैं नहीं आऊँगी।

दलाल (ज़बरदस्ती खींचते हुए):
हूँ, आएगी कैसे नहीं? मैं ज़बान दे चुका हूँ। चल उठ।

آج سجن موہے انگ لگا لو جنم سپھل ہو جائے
ردئے کی پیڑا دیہہ کی اگنی یہہ سب شیتل ہو جائے
آج سجن موہے انگ لگا لو جنم سپھل ہو جائے

وجے کو خبر نہیں کہ گلاب اُس کے قریب ہی کھڑی ہے۔ اُس میں اتنی ہمت نہیں کہ وہ اُسے چھو کر اپنی موجودگی کا احساس دلا دے۔ گیت ختم ہوتے ہی وہ چلی جاتی ہے۔ منظر بدلتا ہے۔

ریل 9

اگلا منظر۔صبح۔ریلوے یارڈ کے پاس ساحل کنارے پڑی بنچ پر وجے کی آنکھ کھلتی ہے جہاں وہ اکثر راتیں گزارا کرتا ہے۔ سڑک کنارے لگے نلکے پر وہ پانی پینے آتا ہے لیکن اُس میں پانی نہیں ہوتا۔ مینا اپنی کنورٹیبل کار میں وہاں سے گزرتی ہے جسے ڈرائیور چلا رہا ہے۔ کار رکتی ہے اور وہ وجے کی طرف دیکھتی ہے۔ وہ اُسے دیکھتا ہے لیکن اُس کی طرف نہیں جاتا۔ اُن دونوں کے بیچ سے ریلوے لائن سے ایک مال گاڑی گزرتی ہے جس کی آڑ میں وجے نظر نہیں آتا۔ مینا اپنی کار میں بیٹھ کر چلی جاتی ہے۔ اگلا منظر۔ ساحل پر وجے کھڑا ہے۔ طوفان کے آثار دکھائی دے رہے ہیں۔ وجے وہاں سے پلٹ آتا ہے۔

اگلا منظر۔گلاب پارک میں ایک بنچ پر کسی سوچ میں گم بیٹھی ہوئی ہے۔

دلال:
گلابو، وہاں ایک لکھ پتی سیٹھ بیٹھا ہے موٹر میں۔ چل آ۔

گلاب:
تُو جا یہاں سے۔ میں نہیں آؤنگی۔

دلال (جبراً کھینچتے ہوئے)
ہم، آئے گی کیسے نہیں؟ میں زبان دے چکا ہوں۔ چل اُٹھ۔

Gulaab:
Let go off my hand.

Chhod mera haath.

Gulaab walks off. The pimp follows her.

Unnamed pimp *(aggressively)*:
I'll show you. Come on.

Tu yun na maanegi. Chal idhar.

Sattar arrives and glares at the pimp. They make grunting sounds at each other. Sattar hits the pimp who falls to the ground. The pimp's cap falls off.

Sattar:
Pick up your cap! Sattar used his weak hand, or else your face would be soft as dough.
(the pimp leaves. Sattar and Gulaab sit on a bench)
Sit down. This park is my state. If anyone bullies you, just call me. I'll leave my clients and come running. Hey, where are you?

Abey topi utha. Ye toh Sattar bhai ka ulta haath pada hai. Seedha padta na toh moonh chapaati bana deta iska.

Baitho baitho. Ab baitho. Ye parak tere Sattar bhai ki state hai. Koi bhi chapad-ganju agar teen-paanch kare na, toh mujhe aawaaz de lena. Giraak chhod ke aaonga. Ein? Kahaan pahonch gayi hai, bhai?

Gulaab:
Did you say something, Sattar?

Tum ne kuchh kaha, Sattar bhai?

Sattar:
No! I didn't say a word. Who was that talking? I get it!
(looking up at the sky)
What do You say? Is she a goner?
(to Gulaab)
Who is he?

Nahin, nahin, main toh kuchh nahin bola. Kaun tha, kaun? Samajh gaya.

Kya khayaal hai? Gayi kaam se?

Kaun hai vo?

गुलाब:

छोड़ मेरा हाथ ।

गुलाब जाने लगती है। दलाल उसके पीछे पीछे ।

दलाल *(उसका हाथ खींचते हुए):*

तू यूँ ना मानेगी । चल इधर ।

सत्तार आता है और दलाल को घूरते हुए देखता है । दोनों एक-दूसरे को देख कर गुर्राते हैं । सत्तार दलाल को एक थप्पड़ लगा देता है । दलाल ज़मीन पर गिर जाता है । दलाल की टोपी उसके सर से गिर जाती है ।

सत्तार:

अबे, टोपी उठा । ये तो सत्तार भाई का उल्टा हाथ पड़ा है । सीधा पड़ता न तो मुँह चपाती बना देता इसका ।
(दलाल चला जाता है । सत्तार और गुलाब एक बेंच पर बैठ जाते हैं)
बैठो बैठो । अब बैठो । ये पारक तेरे सत्तार भाई की स्टेट है । कोई भी चपड़-गंजू अगर तीन-पाँच करे ना, तो मुझे आवाज़ दे देना । गिराक छोड़ के आऊँगा । एँ, कहाँ पहुँच गई है, भाई?

गुलाब:

तुमने कुछ कहा, सत्तार भाई?

सत्तार:

नहीं, नहीं, मैं तो कुछ नहीं बोला । कौन था, कौन? समझ गया ।
(आसमान की ओर देखते हुए)
क्या ख़याल है? गई काम से?
(गुलाब से)
कौन है वो?

گلاب:

چھوڑ میرا ہاتھ۔

گلاب جانے لگتی ہے۔ دلال اُس کے پیچھے پیچھے۔

دلال (اُس کا ہاتھ کھینچتے ہوئے):

تُو یوں نہ مانے گی۔ چل اِدھر۔

ستار آتا ہے اور دلال کو گھورتا ہے۔ دونوں ایک دوسرے کو دیکھ کر غراتے ہیں۔ ستار دلال کو ایک ہاتھ رسید کرتا ہے وہ زمین پر گر جاتا ہے۔ دلال کی ٹوپی اُس کے سر سے گر جاتی ہے۔

ستار:

اے، ٹوپی اُٹھا۔ یہ تو ستار بھائی کا اُلٹا ہاتھ پڑا ہے۔ سیدھا پڑتا نا تو منہ چپاتی بنا دیتا اُس کا۔
(دلال چلا جاتا ہے۔ ستار اور گلاب ایک بنچ پر بیٹھ جاتے ہیں)
بیٹھو بیٹھو۔ یہ پارک تیرے ستار بھائی کی اسٹیٹ ہے۔ کوئی بھی چپڑ گنجو اگر تین پانچ کرے نا، تو مجھے آواز دے لینا۔ گراک چھوڑ کے آؤنگا۔ ایں، کہاں پہنچ گئی ہے بھائی۔

گلاب:

تم نے کچھ کہا، ستار بھائی؟

ستار:

نہیں، نہیں، میں تو کچھ نہیں بولا۔ کون تھا، کون؟ سمجھ گیا۔
(آسمان کی طرف دیکھتے ہوئے)
کیا خیال ہے؟ گئی کام سے؟
(گلاب سے)
کون ہے وہ؟

Gulaab:
Whom do you mean?

Sattar:
If I knew, would I ask? Listen, Gulaabo. There's no genius in a postman reading a postcard. But remember, nothing escapes the eagle eyes of a masseur. Your faraway look, oblivious to the man sitting next to you, deaf to a word — sure signs that you're in love. In love…
(*Gulaab walks away*)
Slipping away without warning is another sign.
(*following her*)
Tell me the truth, who is he?

Gulaab:
A poet.

Sattar:
Excellent! I have a friend who is a poet too. What's your poet's name?

Gulaab:
Vijay.

Sattar:
Incredible! My friend's name is Vijay, too. I'll ask him who the hell this other Vijay is.

Gulaab:
Brother Sattar, maybe they're the same person?

Sattar:
No way! Aha! Maybe they are. Don't you worry. I'll ask him what's this mix-up.

Fade out.

Kaun?

Arey mujhe maaloom hota toh poochhta kaaye ko? Dekh, Gulaabo. Khat ka mazmoon bhaanp lete hain post kaarad dekh kar, aur maalish-waale qayaamat ki nazar rakhte hain. Ye nazar ka ek jagah jama rehna, pados mein baithe huwe aadmi ka na dikhna, aur kahi huwi baat ka na sunna, is baat ki nishaani hai ki tujhe ho gayi mohabbat re, mohab…

Arey khasak jaana bhi isi baat ki nishaani hai.

Sach sach bata, kaun hai vo?

Ek shaayer hai.

Arey waah. Apna ek yaar bhi shaayer hai. Kya naam hai tere shaayer ka?

Vijay.

Le, apne bhi yaar ka naam Vijay hai. Main uss se poochhunga ye doosra Vijay kahaan se aan tapka.

Sattar bhai, kahin vo donon ek hi toh nahin?

Arey nahin nahin. Aha! Ek bhi ho sakte hain. Tu fikr matt kar. Main uss se poochhunga ye kya ghapla hai.

गुलाब:
कौन?

सत्तार:
अरे मुझे मालूम होता तो पूछता काहे को? देख, गुलाबो, ख़त का मज़मून भाँप लेते हैं पोस्ट कारड देख कर, और मालिश-वाले क़यामत की नज़र रखते हैं। ये नज़र का एक जगह जमा रहना, पड़ोस में बैठे हुए आदमी का न दिखना, और कही हुई बात का न सुनना, इस बात की निशानी है कि तुझे हो गई मोहब्बत रे, मोहब...
(गुलाब उठकर दूसरी ओर चली जाती है)
अरे खसक जाना भी इसी बात की निशानी है।
(उसके पीछे-पीछे)
सच सच बता, कौन है वो?

गुलाब:
एक शायर है।

सत्तार:
अरे वाह। अपना एक यार भी शायर है। क्या नाम है तेरे शायर का?

गुलाब:
विजय।

सत्तार:
ले, अपने भी यार का नाम विजय है। मैं उस से पूछूँगा ये दूसरा विजय कहाँ से आन टपका।

गुलाब:
सत्तार भाई, कहीं वो दोनों एक ही तो नहीं?

सत्तार:
अरे नहीं-नहीं। अहाँ! एक भी हो सकते हैं। तू फ़िक्र मत कर। मैं उस से पूछूँगा ये क्या घपला है।

दृश्य ख़त्म होता है।

گلاب:
کون؟

ستار:
ارے مجھے معلوم ہوتا تو پوچھتا کائے کو؟ دیکھ، گلابو۔ خط کا مضمون بھانپ لیتے ہیں پوسٹ کارڈ دیکھ کر۔ اور مالش والے قیامت کی نظر رکھتے ہیں۔ یہ نظر کا ایک جگہ جما رہنا، پڑوس میں بیٹھے ہوئے آدمی کا نہ دکھنا، اور کہی ہوئی بات کا نہ سننا، اِس بات کی نشانی ہے کہ تجھے ہوگئی محبت رے، محبت۔۔۔۔
(گلاب اُٹھ کر چل دیتی ہے)
ارے کھسک جانا بھی اِس بات کی نشانی ہے۔
(اُس کے پیچھے پیچھے)
سچ سچ بتا، کون ہے وہ؟

گلاب:
ایک شاعر ہے۔

ستار:
ارے واہ۔ اپنا ایک یار بھی شاعر ہے۔ کیا نام ہے تیرے شاعر کا؟

گلاب:
وجے۔

ستار:
لے، اپنے بھی یار کا نام وجے ہے۔ میں اُس سے پوچھوں گا یہ دوسرا وجے کہاں سے آن ٹپکا۔

گلاب:
ستار بھائی، کہیں وہ دونوں ایک ہی تو نہیں؟

ستار:
ارے نہیں نہیں۔ آہا! ایک بھی ہوسکتے ہیں۔ تُو فکر مت کر۔ میں اُس سے پوچھوں گا یہ کیا گھپلا ہے۔

منظر بدلتا ہے۔

Reel Ten

Fade in. Vijay's two brothers are making their way down the steps to the river.

Vijay is sitting at the riverbank. He watches his brothers perform a ritual. Vijay approaches them when they are done.

Vijay:
Brothers, is everything all right? What brings you here?

Bhayya, sabb khairiyat toh hai na? Aap log yahaan kaise?

Middle brother:
What's it to you? Go! Carry on your loafing. As if you care who lives or dies!

Tumhen is say matlab? Jaao, ji bhar ke aawaara-gardi karo. Koi maray ya jiye tumhen is se kya?

Vijay:
Who has died? Whose last rites are you performing?

Kaun mar…? Kis ka kriya-karam karne aaye thay aap log?

Middle brother:
Mother's.

Ma ka.

Vijay:
Mother's? Brother…

Ma ka? Bhayya…

Middle brother:
Don't call me brother. We tolerated you because of her. Now she's dead, you're dead for us.

Bhayya matt kaho hamen. Usi ke damm se hamaara-tumhaara waasta tha. Vo mar gayi aur tum bhi mar gaye hamaare liye.

Vijay is grief-stricken. His mother's last words come back to him in an audio-flashback.[41]

रील १०

अगला दृश्य। विजय के दोनों भाई एक घाट के किनारे सीढ़ियों पर जाते हुए दिखाई देते हैं।

सीढ़ियों पर बैठा विजय उन्हें स्नान करते देख रहा है। उनके बाहर आते ही विजय उनके पास जाता है।

विजय:
भय्या, सब ख़ैरियत तो है ना? आप लोग यहाँ कैसे?

मंझला भाई:
तुम्हें इससे मतलब? जाओ, जी भर के आवारा-गर्दी करो। कोई मरे या जिए तुम्हें इससे क्या?

विजय:
कौन मर...! किसका क्रिया-कर्म करने आए थे आप लोग?

मंझला भाई:
माँ का।

विजय:
माँ का? भय्या...

मंझला भाई:
भय्या मत कहो हमें। उसी के दम से हमारा-तुम्हारा वास्ता था। वो मर गई और तुम भी मर गए हमारे लिए।

विजय का दिल दुःख से भर जाता है। माँ के कहे हुए शब्द उसके कानों में गूँज रहे हैं।

ریل ۱۰

اگلا منظر۔ وجے کے دونوں بھائی ایک گھاٹ کنارے دکھائی دیتے ہیں۔ سیڑھیوں پر بیٹھا وجے اُنھیں اشنان کرتا دیکھ رہا ہے۔

اُن کے فارغ ہوتے ہی وہ اُن کے پاس جاتا ہے۔

وجے:
بھیا، سب خیریت تو ہے نا؟ آپ لوگ یہاں کیسے؟

منجھلا بھائی:
تمھیں اِس سے مطلب؟ جاؤ، جی بھر کے آوارہ گردی کرو۔ کوئی مرے یا جیے تمھیں اِس سے کیا؟

وجے:
کون مر۔۔۔؟ کس کا کریا کرم کرنے آئے تھے آپ لوگ؟

منجھلا بھائی:
ماں کا۔

وجے:
ماں کا؟ بھیا۔۔۔

منجھلا بھائی:
بھیا مت کہو ہمیں۔ اُسی کے دم سے ہمارا تمہارا واسطہ تھا۔ وہ مر گئی اور تم بھی مر گئے ہمارے لیے۔

وجے کا دل دکھ کر رہ جاتا ہے۔ ماں کے کہے ہوئے پُرشفقت الفاظ اُس کے کانوں میں گونج رہے ہیں۔

Vijay's mother (voice-over):
Son. Where will you go on an empty stomach? Who will look after you, my sweet child? Take me with you. I won't stay in this house a minute longer. Not a minute longer, my...

Dissolve to a room where Chhammo (Shyam's girlfriend), Shyam and a male friend are playing cards and drinking.

Shyam's friend:
Let's see you dance, Chhammo. I'll play the drums for you.

Chhammo:
How can I dance? First ask your friend to join us.

Shyam (to Vijay):
Come on! Why don't you have a drink? I'd drink poison for her if she asked.

Shyam's friend:
Same here.

Chhammo:
He's shy. Come, sir, drink up. For my sake.

Shyam's friend:
He's a strange fellow. Is he a man or a mouse? He looks as if his grandmother has died.

Vijay grabs the whisky bottle and drinks all the contents.

Shyam's friend (laughing):
He's a beginner, but he finished it off in one go. What a tiger! When did you start drinking?

Beta, bhooka-pyaasa tu kahaan jaayega? Teri dekh-bhaal kaun karega, mere laal? Mujhe tu apne saath le chal. Main ab is ghar mein ek pal nahin rahoongi. Ek pal nahin rahoongi, mere...

Maine kaha, Chhammo, kuchh ho jaaye thumke. Taal main deta hoon.

Ho kya jaaye? Pehle apne dost ko toh mehfil mein shaamil karo.

Arey zaalim, ab toh pi le. Tumhaari qasam agar ye mujhe kahe toh zaher bhi pi jaaun.

Main bhi.

Sharmaate hain babuji. Aji huzoor, pi bhi lijiye na. Aap ko mere sar ki qasam.

Arey yaar, ajab aadmi hai. Aadmi hai ya paijaama? Aisa baitha hain jaise iski naani mar gayi ho.

Bhai, naya rangroot hai aur saari botal khalaas kar daali. Waah re mere mitti ke sher, jawaab nahin. Tum ne kab se peene ki shuru ki, bhai?

विजय की माँ *(आवाज़)*:

बेटा, भूखा-प्यासा तू कहाँ जाएगा? तेरी देख-भाल कौन करेगा, मेरे लाल? मुझे तू अपने साथ ले चल। मैं अब इस घर में एक पल नहीं रहूँगी। एक पल नहीं रहूँगी, मेरे...

अगला दृश्य। एक कमरे में छम्मो (श्याम की महबूबा), श्याम और उसका एक दोस्त ताश खेलते हुए शराब पी रहे हैं।

श्याम का दोस्त:

मैंने कहा, छम्मो, कुछ हो जाए तुमके। ताल मैं देता हूँ।

छम्मो:

हो क्या जाए? पहले अपने दोस्त को तो महफ़िल में शामिल करो।

श्याम *(विजय से)*:

अरे ज़ालिम, अब तो पी ले। तुम्हारी क़सम, अगर ये मुझे कहे तो ज़हर भी पी जाऊँ।

श्याम का दोस्त:

मैं भी।

छम्मो:

शरमाते हैं बाबूजी। अजी हुज़ूर, पी भी लीजिए ना। आपको मेरे सर की क़सम।

श्याम का दोस्त:

अरे यार, अजब आदमी है। आदमी है या पायजामा? ऐसा बैठा है जैसे इसकी नानी मर गई हो।

उदास विजय बोतल उठाकर मुँह से लगाता है और सारी व्हिस्की उतार जाता है।

श्याम का दोस्त *(कहकहा लगाकर)*:

भाई, नया रंगरूट है और सारी बोतल खलास कर डाली। वाह रे मेरे मिट्टी के शेर, जवाब नहीं। तुमने कब से पीने की शुरू की भाई?

وجے کی اماں (گونج):

بیٹا، بھوکا پیاسا تُو کہاں جائے گا؟ تیری دیکھ بھال کون کرے گا، میرے لال؟ مجھے تُو اپنے ساتھ لے چل۔ میں اب اس گھر میں ایک پل نہیں رہوں گی۔ ایک پل نہیں رہوں گی، میرے ۔۔۔۔

اگلا منظر۔ ایک کمرے میں چھمو، شیام کی محبوبہ، اور اُس کا ایک دوست تاش کھیلتے اور شراب پیتے دکھائی دیتے ہیں۔

شیام کا دوست:

میں نے کہا، چھمو، کچھ ہو جائے تھمکے۔ تال میں دیتا ہوں۔

چھمو:

ہو کیا جائے؟ پہلے اپنے دوست کو بھی تو محفل میں شامل کرو۔

شیام (وجے سے):

ارے ظالم، اب تو پی لے۔ تمہاری قسم اگر یہ مجھے کہے تو میں زہر بھی پی جاؤں۔

شیام کا دوست:

میں بھی۔

چھمو:

شرماتے ہیں بابوجی۔ اجی حضور، پی بھی لیجیے نا۔ آپ کو میرے سر کی قسم۔

شیام کا دوست:

ارے یار، عجب آدمی ہے۔ آدمی ہے یا پایاجامہ؟ ایسا بیٹھا ہے جیسے اس کی نانی مر گئی ہو۔

اُداس وجے نظر اُٹھا کر دیکھتا ہے اور منہ سے بوتل لگا کر ساری وہسکی اُتار جاتا ہے۔

شیام کا دوست (قہقہہ لگا کر):

بھئی، نیا رنگروٹ ہے اور ساری بوتل خلاص کر ڈالی۔ واہ رے میرے مٹی کے شیر، جواب نہیں۔ تم نے کب سے پینے کی شروع کی، بھئی؟

Vijay (reciting a poem, Mohammed Rafi's voice):[42]
"Sorrow became unbearable, in my anxiety I drank
This heart of mine was so helpless
Out of pity for it, I drank
The world has spurned me…"

"Gham is qadar badhe ki main ghabra ke pi gaya
Is dil ki be-basi pe taras kha ke pi gaya
Thukra raha tha mujh ko…"

Chhammo:
So, he's a poet, too?

Achha, toh ye shaayer bhi hain?

Shyam:
Didn't you know? He's composed over five hundred poems.

Shaayer! Arey tu dekhti nahin is ki toh paanch sau nazmen is ke sar ke peechhe padi hain.

Vijay (Mohammed Rafi's voice):
"The world has spurned me time and time again
Today I spurn the whole world and drank."(2)

"Thukra raha tha mujh ko badi der se jahaan
Main aaj sab jahaan ko thukra ke pi gaya" (2)

Dissolve to the dancer Bijli. Shyam, Vijay and other men are drinking in the brothel watching Bijli dance. Her baby is crying in a cot in the corner of the room. Vijay hears the baby's cries over the music and sees the anguished look on the dancer's face. Bijli wants to go to her child, but the brothel madam forces her to continue dancing. Overwhelmed with emotion at the dancer's plight, torn between earning her keep and tending to her sick child, Vijay's eyes fill with tears. Through his tears, he watches his friend Shyam stop Bijli.[43]

Shyam:
Bijli! Where are you going?

Bijli! Kahaan ja rahi thi, huh?

विजय *(एक नज़्म गुनगुनाते हुए, मोहम्मद रफ़ी की आवाज़):*

"ग़म इस क़दर बढे के मैं घबरा के पी गया

इस दिल की बे-बसी पे तरस खा के पी गया

ठुकरा रहा था मुझको…"

छम्मो:

अच्छा, तो ये शायर भी हैं?

श्याम:

शायर! अरे तू देखती नहीं इसकी तो पाँच सौ नज़्में इस के सर के पीछे पड़ी हैं।

विजय *(मोहम्मद रफ़ी की आवाज़):*

"ठुकरा रहा था मुझ को बड़ी देर से जहाँ

मैं आज सब जहान को ठुकरा के पी गया" (२)

अगला दृश्य। डान्सर बिजली। श्याम, विजय और दूसरे लोग कोठे पर बैठ कर बिजली का नाच देखते हुए शराब पी रहे हैं। कमरे के एक कोने में पड़े पालने में एक बच्चा रो रहा है। संगीत के साथ साथ बच्चे के रोने की आवाज़ भी विजय सुन रहा है, जिसकी वजह से बिजली को हो रही तकलीफ़ विजय देख रहा है। बिजली रुक कर अपने बच्चे को चुप कराना चाहती है लेकिन कोठे की मालकिन उसे नाचने पर मजबूर करती है। नाचती हुई बिजली अपने बीमार बच्चे को चुप भी कराना चाहती है और ज़िंदगी जीने के लिए पैसे भी कमाना चाहती है। उसकी ये कशमकश देख कर विजय की आँख में आँसू आ जाते हैं। अपनी आँसुओं से भरी आँखों से वो देखता है कि बिजली को श्याम नाचने पर मजबूर कर रहा है।

श्याम:

बिजली! कहाँ जा रही थी, हैं?

Bijli:
My child is ill.

Mera bachcha beemaar hai.

Shyam:
To hell with your child! We need you, too. Tend to us first then see to your child.
(handing her some rupee notes that she clutches)
Here. Start the music.

Bachche ko maar goli. Hum bhi toh beemaar hain tere. Pehle hamaara ilaaj karo. Baad mein bachche ko samajhna.

Ye le. Ustaadji, shuru ho jaao wahin se.

Vijay leaves. Cut. Outside the brothel where he has left his friends, Vijay, half-drunk, stumbles through the lanes of the red-light district. The music from the brothel fades away and Vijay's song, almost spoken as dialogue, takes over. The words of the poem appear as reactions to the scenes that Vijay witnesses.

Singer: Mohammed Rafi

These lanes…(hums)…these houses of pleasure
These lanes, these houses of auctioned pleasure
These ravaged caravans of life
Where are the guardians of dignity?
Where are they who claim to be proud of India?
Where are they? *(3)*

Ye kooche…ghar dil-kashi ke
Ye kooche ye neelaam-ghar dil-kashi ke
Ye lut'te huwe kaarwaan zindagi ke
Kahaan hain, kahaan hain muhaafiz khudi ke
Jinhen naaz hai Hind par vo kahaan hain
Kahaan hain, kahaan hain, kahaan hain

These twisting lanes, this infamous market
These anonymous men, this clinking of coins
This trading of chastity, this insistent haggling
Where are they who claim to be proud of India?
Where are they? *(3)*

Ye pur-pech galiyaan, ye bad-naam bazaar
Ye gum-naam raahi, ye sikkon ki jhankaar
Ye ismat ke sauday, ye saudon pe takraar
Jinhen naaz hai Hind par vo kahaan hain
Kahaan hain, kahaan hain, kahaan hain

These age-old, dreamless, fearful lanes
These crushed, pallid, half-open buds
This selling of sham celebrations
Where are they who claim to be proud of India?
Where are they? *(3)*

Ye sadiyon se be-khwab sehmi si galiyaan
Ye masli huwi adh-khili zard kaliyaan
Ye bikti huwi khokhli rang-raliyaan
Jinhen naaz hai Hind par vo kahaan hain
Kahaan hain, kahaan hain, kahaan hain

बिजली:

मेरा बच्चा बीमार है।

श्याम:

बच्चे को मार गोली। हम भी तो बीमार हैं तेरे। पहले हमारा इलाज करो। बाद में बच्चे को समझना।
(उसे कुछ रुपये थमाता है जो वो अपनी मुट्ठी में जकड़ लेती है)
ये ले। उस्ताद जी, शुरु हो जाओ वहीं से।

कट। कोठे के बाहर मदहोश विजय अपने दोस्तों को छोड़ कर रेड-लाइट डिस्ट्रिक्ट की गलियों में चल पड़ता है। बिजली का नाच और संगीत की आवाज़ कम हो जाती है और गीत के बोल धीरे-धीरे विजय के मुँह से निकलते हैं। ये गीत उन हालात को दर्शाता है जो विजय देख कर आया है।

गायक: मोहम्मद रफ़ी

ये कूचे... घर दिल-कशी के
ये कूचे ये नीलाम-घर दिल-कशी के
ये लुटते हुए कारवाँ ज़िंदगी के
कहाँ हैं, कहाँ हैं मुहाफ़िज़ ख़ुदी के
जिन्हें नाज़ है हिन्द पर वो कहाँ हैं
कहाँ हैं, कहाँ हैं, कहाँ हैं

ये पुर-पेच गलियाँ, ये बद-नाम बाज़ार
ये गुम-नाम राही, ये सिक्कों की झंकार
ये इसमत के सौदे, ये सौदों पे तकरार
जिन्हें नाज़ है हिन्द पर वो कहाँ हैं
कहाँ हैं, कहाँ हैं, कहाँ हैं

ये सदियों से बे-ख़्वाब सहमी-सी गलियाँ
ये मसली हुई अध-खिली ज़र्द कलियाँ
ये बिकती हुई खोखली रंग-रलियाँ
जिन्हें नाज़ है हिन्द पर वो कहाँ हैं
कहाँ हैं, कहाँ हैं, कहाँ हैं

بجلی:

میرا بچہ بیمار ہے۔

شیام:

بچے کو مار گولی۔ ہم بھی تو بیمار ہیں تیرے۔ پہلے ہمارا علاج کرو۔ بعد میں بچے کو سمجھنا۔
(بجلی کے ہاتھ میں کچھ روپے تھماتا ہے۔ بجلی اُنھیں مٹھی میں جکڑ لیتی ہے)
یہ لے۔ اُستاد جی، شروع ہو جاوٴ وہیں سے۔

اگلا منظر۔ کوٹھے کے باہر مدہوش وجے اپنے دوستوں کو چھوڑ کر لال بتی کی گلیوں میں چل پڑتا ہے۔ بجلی کا ناچ اور موسیقی کی آواز مدھم ہو جاتی ہے اور گیت کے بول ہولے ہولے وجے کے منہ سے نکلتے ہیں۔ یہ گیت اُن حالات کا منظرنامہ ہے جو ابھی وجے دیکھ کر آ رہا ہے۔

محمد رفیع کی آواز

یہ کوچے یہ...۔ گھر دل کشی کے
یہ کوچے یہ نیلام گھر دل کشی کے
یہ لٹتے ہوئے کارواں زندگی کے
کہاں ہیں، کہاں ہیں محافظ خودی کے
جنھیں ناز ہے ہند پر وہ کہاں ہیں
کہاں ہیں، کہاں ہیں، کہاں ہیں

یہ پُر پیچ گلیاں، یہ بدنام بازار
یہ گمنام راہی، یہ سکوں کی جھنکار
یہ عصمت کے سودے، یہ سودوں پہ تکرار
جنھیں ناز ہے ہند پر وہ کہاں ہیں
کہاں ہیں، کہاں ہیں، کہاں ہیں

یہ صدیوں سے بے خواب سہمی سی گلیاں
یہ مسلی ہوئی ادھ کھلی زرد کلیاں
یہ بکتی ہوئی کھوکھلی رنگ رلیاں
جنھیں ناز ہے ہند پر وہ کہاں ہیں
کہاں ہیں، کہاں ہیں، کہاں ہیں

Anklets chiming from latticed windows	Ye ujle dareechon mein paayal ki chhan-chhan
Tablas drumming over weary breaths	Thaki-haari saanson pe tablay ki dhan-dhan
(both lines repeated)	*(both lines repeated)*
These soulless rooms echo with coughing	Ye be-rooh kamron mein khaansi ki than-than
Where are they who claim to be proud of India?	Jinhen naaz hai Hind par vo kahaan hain
Where are they? *(3)*	Kahaan hain, kahaan hain, kahaan hain
These strings of flowers, these paan spittle stains	Ye phoolon ke gajre, ye peekon ke chheente
These shameless glances, these crude remarks	Ye be-baak nazren, ye gustaakh fiqre
These wilting bodies, these ailing faces	Ye dhalke badan aur ye beemaar chehre
Where are they who claim to be proud of India?	Jinhen naaz hai Hind par vo kahaan hain
Where are they? *(3)*	Kahaan hain, kahaan hain, kahaan hain

As Vijay staggers through the lanes of the red-light district, he passes old and young men, some look down in embarrassment.

Old men have passed through here, young men, too	Yahaan peer bhi aa chuke hain, jawaan bhi
Sturdy sons, fathers, too	Tanomand bete bhi, abba miyaan bhi
These are wives…	Ye biwi bhi hai…
These are wives and sisters and mothers, too	Ye biwi bhi hai aur bahen bhi hai, ma bhi
Where are they who claim to be proud of India?	Jinhen naaz hai Hind par vo kahaan hain
Where are they? *(3)*	Kahaan hain, kahaan hain, kahaan hain
This daughter of Eve seeks help	Madad chaahti hai ye Havva ki beti
The kin of Yashoda, the daughter of Radha	Yashoda ki ham-jins, Radha ki beti
(both lines repeated)	*(both lines repeated)*
The people of the Prophet, the daughter of Zulekha	Payambar ki ummat, Zulekha ki beti
Where are they who claim to be proud of India?	Jinhen naaz hai Hind par vo kahaan hain
Where are they? *(3)*	Kahaan hain, kahaan hain, kahaan hain

ये उजले दरीचों में पायल की छन-छन
थकी-हारी साँसों पे तबले की धन-धन
(दोनों पंक्तियाँ दोहराते हुए)
ये बे-रूह कमरों में खाँसी की ठन-ठन
जिन्हें नाज़ है हिन्द पर वो कहाँ हैं
कहाँ हैं, कहाँ हैं, कहाँ हैं

ये फूलों के गजरे, ये पीकों के छींटे
ये बे-बाक नज़रें, ये गुस्ताख़ फिक़रे
ये ढलके बदन और ये बीमार चेहरे
जिन्हें नाज़ है हिन्द पर वो कहाँ हैं
कहाँ हैं, कहाँ हैं, कहाँ हैं

रेड-लाइट डिस्ट्रिक्ट की गलियों से लड़खड़ाता हुआ विजय गुज़र रहा है। बूढ़े जवान आस-पास से गुज़र रहे हैं। कुछ की नज़रें शरमिंदगी से झुकी हुई हैं।

यहाँ पीर भी आ चुके हैं, जवाँ भी
तनोमंद बेटे भी, अब्बा मियाँ भी
ये बीवी भी है...
ये बीवी भी है और बहन भी है, माँ भी
जिन्हें नाज़ है हिन्द पर वो कहाँ हैं
कहाँ हैं, कहाँ हैं, कहाँ हैं

मदद चाहती है ये हव्वा की बेटी
यशोदा की हम-जिन्स, राधा की बेटी
(दोनों पंक्तियाँ दोहराते हुए)
पयंबर की उम्मत, ज़ुलेख़ा की बेटी
जिन्हें नाज़ है हिन्द पर वो कहाँ हैं
कहाँ हैं, कहाँ हैं, कहाँ हैं

یہ اُجلے دریچوں میں پائل کی چھن چھن
تھکی ہاری سانسوں پہ طبلے کی دھن دھن
(دونوں لائنیں دوہراتا ہے)
یہ بے روح کمروں میں کھانسی کی ٹھن ٹھن
جنھیں ناز ہے ہند پر وہ کہاں ہیں
کہاں ہیں، کہاں ہیں، کہاں ہیں

یہ پھولوں کے گجرے، یہ پیکوں کے چھینٹے
یہ بے باک نظریں، یہ گستاخ فقرے
یہ ڈھلکے بدن اور یہ بیمار چہرے
جنھیں ناز ہے ہند پر وہ کہاں ہیں
کہاں ہیں، کہاں ہیں، کہاں ہیں

لال بتی کی گلیوں سے وجے لڑکھڑاتا ہوا گزر رہا ہے۔ بوڑھے جوان آس پاس سے گزر رہے ہیں۔ کچھ کی نظریں شرمندگی سے جھکی ہوئی ہیں۔

یہاں پیر بھی آ چکے ہیں، جواں بھی
تنومند بیٹے بھی، ابا میاں بھی
یہ بیوی بھی ہے۔۔۔۔
یہ بیوی بھی ہے اور بہن بھی ہے، ماں بھی
جنھیں ناز ہے ہند پر وہ کہاں ہیں
کہاں ہیں، کہاں ہیں، کہاں ہیں

مدد چاہتی ہے یہ حوا کی بیٹی
یشودھا کی ہم جنس، رادھا کی بیٹی
(دونوں لائنیں دوہراتا ہے)
پیمبر کی اُمّت، زلیخا کی بیٹی
جنھیں ناز ہے ہند پر وہ کہاں ہیں
کہاں ہیں، کہاں ہیں، کہاں ہیں

Summon the leaders of this land
Show them these alleys, these lanes, this sight
Summon those who claim to be proud of India
Where are they who claim to be proud of India?
Where are they? *(3)*

Zara mulk ke reh-baraon ko bulaao
Ye kooche, ye galiyaan, ye manzar dikhaao
Jinhen naaz hai Hind par unko laao
Jinhen naaz hai Hind par vo kahaan hain
Kahaan hain, kahaan hain, kahaan hain

As the song ends, Vijay finds himself in a narrow lane of the red-light district where Gulaab lives.

Reel Eleven

Gulaab is leaving the house and sees Vijay outside her door. He is leaning against a pillar, drunk and half-asleep.

Gulaab:
Vijay?

Vijay babu.

Vijay:
Who is it? Oh, it's you, Gulaab.

Huh? Kaun? Oh, tum. Gulaab.

Gulaab:
Come with me.

Mere saath aao, Vijay babu.

Vijay:
Taking pity on me again? Today I'm not hungry, Gulaab. I have swallowed hunger in drink today. I've drunk a lot, swallowed the world's rebuffs and all the heartache. I have swallowed everything.
(she takes him into the courtyard of her house)
Where are you taking me?

Phir taras khaane aayi ho mujh pe? Aaj main bhooka nahin hoon, Gulaab. Aaj maine bhook ko sharaab mein dubo diya hai. Bahot pi hai maine. Zamaane ki jhidkiyaan pi gaya, saare gham pi gaya. Sab kuchh pi gaya.

Tum kahaan le ja rahi ho mujhe?

Gulaab:
Come to my house, you need to rest.
(they start climbing the many flights of stairs to Gulaab's room)
Leave when you feel better.

Andar chalo, Vijay babu. Mere ghar. Tumhen aaraam ki zaroorat hai.

Haalat sambhalne ke baad chale jaana.

ज़रा मुल्क़ के रहबरों को बुलाओ
ये कूचे, ये गलियाँ, ये मंज़र दिखाओ
जिन्हें नाज़ है हिन्द पर उनको लाओ
जिन्हें नाज़ है हिन्द पर वो कहाँ हैं
कहाँ हैं, कहाँ हैं, कहाँ हैं

गीत ख़त्म होते होते विजय गलियों में चलते-चलते गुलाब के घर तक पहुँच जाता है।

रील ११

घर से निकलती हुई गुलाब की नज़र विजय पर पड़ती है जो बाहर एक खंभे के सहारे मदहोश खड़ा है।

गुलाब:
विजय बाबू।

विजय:
हूँ? कौन? ओह, तुम, गुलाब।

गुलाब:
मेरे साथ आओ। विजय बाबू।

विजय:
फिर तरस खाने आई हो मुझ पे? आज मैं भूखा नहीं हूँ, गुलाब। आज मैंने भूख को शराब में डुबो दिया है। बहुत पी है मैंने। ज़माने की झिड़कियाँ पी गया, सारे ग़म पी गया। सब कुछ पी गया।
(गुलाब विजय को सहारा देकर अपने घर के आँगन में लाती है)
तुम कहाँ ले जा रही हो मुझे?

गुलाब:
अंदर चलो, विजय बाबू। मेरे घर। तुम्हें आराम की ज़रुरत है।
(कुछ सीढ़ियाँ चढ़ कर वे गुलाब के कमरे में आते हैं)
हालत संभलने के बाद चले जाना।

ذرا ملک کے رہبروں کو بلاؤ
یہ کوچے، یہ گلیاں، یہ منظر دکھاؤ
جنہیں ناز ہے ہند پر اُن کو لاؤ
جنہیں ناز ہے ہند پر وہ کہاں ہیں
کہاں ہیں، کہاں ہیں، کہاں ہیں

گیت ختم ہوتے ہوتے وجے غیرارادی طور پر لال بتی کی گلیوں سے گزرتا ہوا گلاب کے گھر تک پہنچ جاتا ہے۔

ریل ۱۱

گھر سے نکلتے ہوئے گلاب کی نظر وجے پر پڑتی ہے جو باہر ایک ستون سے ٹیک لگائے مدہوش کھڑا ہے۔

گلاب:
وجے بابو۔

وجے:
ہوں؟ کون؟ اوہ، تم، گلاب۔

گلاب:
میرے ساتھ آؤ، وجے بابو۔

وجے:
پھر ترس کھانے آئی ہو مجھ پہ؟ آج میں بھوکا نہیں ہوں، گلاب۔ آج میں نے بھوک کو شراب میں ڈبو دیا ہے۔ بہت پی ہے میں نے۔ زمانے کی جھڑکیاں پی گیا، سارے غم پی گیا۔ سب کچھ پی گیا۔
(اسے سہارا دے کر وہ اپنے گھر کے آنگن میں لاتی ہے)
تم کہاں لے جا رہی ہو مجھے؟

گلاب:
اندر چلو، وجے بابو۔ میرے گھر۔ تمہیں آرام کی ضرورت ہے۔
(کچھ زینے ٹیک کر کے وہ گلاب کے کمرے میں آتے ہیں)
حالت سنبھلنے کے بعد چلے جانا۔

Vijay:[44]
Leave when I feel better? I'll only feel better when I've left this world, Gulaab. It's all gone. I lost my job. I had my mother and now I've lost her. She's gone forever. So what am I doing here? Why am I alive, Gulaab?

Haalat sambhalne ke baad chala jaaun? Ab toh chale jaane ke baad hi ye haalat sambhlegi, Gulaab. Sab chale gaye. Naukri chali gayi. Ma thi vo bhi chali gayi. Hamesha ke liye chali gayi. Toh phir main yahaan kya kar raha hoon? Main kyun zinda hoon, Gulaab?

Gulaab:
Don't talk like that. The world needs you. The world needs your poetry.

Aisi baaten nahin karte, Vijay babu. Duniya ko tumhaari zaroorat hai, tumhaari shaayeri ki zaroorat hai.

Vijay:
The world needs no one. I tried so hard to have my poetry known by the world. But do you know how the world valued it? Waste paper sold for ten annas. My life is valued at ten annas, Gulaab. And you want me to live for those ten annas?

Duniya ko kisi ki zaroorat nahin. Hum ne apni shaayeri duniya tak ponhchaane ki kitni koshish ki, lekin jaanti ho us duniya ne us ka kya mol lagaaya? Raddi ke chandd tukde jo das aane mein beche gaye. Meri zindagi ka mol das aane hai, Gulaab. Aur tum chaahti ho ki main un das aanon ke liye zinda rahoon?

Gulaab:
Don't get disheartened, Vijay. There are many who are there for you. There's Meena.

Yun himmat na haaro, Vijay babu. Zindagi ke aur bhi toh sahaare hain. Meena bhi to hai.

Vijay:
Meena? How do you know her?

Meena? Tum usay kaise jaanti ho?

Gulaab:
Her name was on your file of poems. Who is Meena?

Tumhaari nazmon ke file par us ka naam padha tha. Kaun hai ye Meena?

विजय:

हालत संभलने के बाद चला जाऊँ? अब तो चले जाने के बाद ही ये हालत संभलेगी, गुलाब। सब चले गए। नौकरी चली गई। माँ थी वो भी चली गई। हमेशा के लिए चली गई। तो फिर मैं यहाँ क्या कर रहा हूँ। मैं क्यूँ ज़िंदा हूँ, गुलाब?

गुलाब:

ऐसी बातें नहीं करते, विजय बाबू। दुनिया को तुम्हारी ज़रूरत है, तुम्हारी शायरी की ज़रूरत है।

विजय:

दुनिया को किसी की ज़रूरत नहीं। हमने अपनी शायरी दुनिया तक पहुँचाने की कितनी कोशिश की लेकिन जानती हो दुनिया ने उसका क्या मोल लगाया? रद्दी के चंद टुकड़े जो दस आने में बेचे गए। मेरी ज़िन्दगी का मोल दस आने है, गुलाब। और तुम चाहती हो की मैं उन दस आनों के लिए ज़िंदा रहूँ?

गुलाब:

यूँ हिम्मत ना हारो, विजय बाबू। ज़िन्दगी के और भी तो सहारे हैं। मीना भी तो है।

विजय:

मीना? तुम उसे कैसे जानती हो?

गुलाब:

तुम्हारी नज़्मों की फ़ाइल पर उसका नाम पढ़ा था। कौन है ये मीना?

وجے:

حالت سنبھلنے کے بعد چلا جاؤں؟ اب تو چلے جانے کے بعد ہی حالت سنبھلے گی، گلاب۔ سب چلے گئے۔ گلاب۔ نوکری چلی گئی۔ ماں تھی وہ بھی چلی گئی۔ ہمیشہ کے لیے چلی گئی۔ تو پھر میں یہاں کیا کر رہا ہوں؟ میں کیوں زندہ ہوں، گلاب؟

گلاب:

ایسی باتیں نہیں کرتے، وجے بابو۔ دنیا کو تمہاری ضرورت ہے، تمہاری شاعری کی ضرورت ہے۔

وجے:

دنیا کو کسی کی ضرورت نہیں۔ ہم نے اپنی شاعری دنیا تک پہنچانے کی کتنی کوشش کی، لیکن جانتی ہو دنیا نے اُس کا کیا مول لگایا؟ ردّی کے چند ٹکڑے جو دس آنے میں بیچے گئے۔ میری زندگی کا مول دس آنے ہے، گلاب۔ اور تم چاہتی ہو کہ میں اُن دس آنوں کے لیے زندہ رہوں؟

گلاب:

یوں ہمت نہ ہارو، وجے بابو۔ زندگی کے اور بھی تو سہارے ہیں۔ مینا بھی تو ہے۔

وجے:

مینا؟ تم اُسے کیسے جانتی ہو؟

گلاب:

تمہاری نظموں کی فائل پر اُس کا نام پڑھا تھا۔ کون ہے یہ مینا؟

Vijay:
Meena? A high society and respectable woman who loves when it pleases her and sells that love in exchange of a comfortable life. But why are you so interested in her?

Gulaab:
Because you once were. That's why.

Vijay:
You mean you…no, Gulaab, no. Forget me. You'll get nothing from me but heartache. I've never made anyone happy…

Vijay collapses.

Gulaab:
Vijay! Juhi…

Dissolve to Gulaab's room later that night. She covers Vijay as he sleeps on her bed.

Dissolve. Vijay wakes some hours later. Gulaab is asleep near the door. Voices from the past torment him.

Vijay *(audio flashback, voice-over):*
You'll publish them in your magazine?

Vijay gets out of bed. The taunting voices continue.

Shaikh *(audio flashback, voice-over):*
Why should I publish them, mister? Have I lost my mind? Call that gibberish poetry?

Meena? Jagmagaati society ki ek shareef aurat jo apne shauq ke liye pyar karti hai aur apne aaraam ke liye pyar bechti hai. Lekin tum us mein itni dilchaspi kyun le rahi ho?

Tumhen kabhi us mein dilchaspi thi na? Isi liye.

Han? Ye tum mujh se…nahin, Gulaab, nahin, mujhe bhula do tum. Siwaaye dukh ke mujh se kuchh bhi nahin milega. Main aaj tak kisi ko sukhi nahin kar saka.

Vijay babu. Vijay babu. Juhi. Juhi!

Unhen apne risaale mein chhapiye na?

Kyun chhaapun, saaheb? Mera dimaagh kharaab huwa hai kya? Aap ki bakwaas koi shaayeri hai?

विजय:
मीना? जगमगाती सोसायटी की एक शरीफ़ औरत जो अपने शौक़ के लिए प्यार करती है और अपने आराम के लिए प्यार बेचती है। लेकिन तुम उसमें इतनी दिलचस्पी क्यूँ ले रही हो?

गुलाब:
तुम्हें कभी उसमें दिलचस्पी थी ना? इसी लिए।

विजय:
हैं? ये तुम मुझसे...नहीं, गुलाब, नहीं...मुझे भुला दो तुम। सिवाय दुःख के मुझसे कुछ नहीं मिलेगा। मैं आज तक किसी को सुखी नहीं कर सका।

विजय बेहोश हो जाता है।

गुलाब:
विजय बाबू, विजय बाबू! जूही, जूही!

अगला दृश्य। गुलाब का कमरा। रात का वक़्त। सोते हुए विजय को वो चद्दर ओढ़ाती है।

अगला दृश्य। कुछ देर बाद विजय की आँख खुलती है। गुलाब दरवाज़े से टेक लगाए सो रही है। विजय को पिछली यादें परेशान कर रही हैं।

विजय (आवाज़):
उन्हें अपने रिसाले में छापिए ना?

विजय बिस्तर से उठ जाता है। उसे गूंजें सुनाई दे रही है।

शेख़ (आवाज़):
क्यूँ छापूँ साहेब? मेरा दिमाग़ ख़राब हुआ है क्या? आपकी बकवास कोई शायरी है?

وجے:
مینا؟ جگمگاتی سوسائٹی کی ایک شریف عورت جو اپنے شوق کے لیے پیار کرتی ہے،اور اپنے آرام کے لیے پیار بیچتی ہے۔لیکن تم اُس میں اتنی دلچسپی کیوں لے رہی ہو؟

گلاب:
تمھیں کبھی اُس میں دلچسپی تھی نا؟ اسی لیے۔

وجے:
ہاں؟ یہ تم مجھ سے۔۔۔نہیں،گلاب،نہیں۔۔۔مجھے بھلا دو تم۔سوائے دکھ کے مجھ سے کچھ نہیں ملے گا۔میں آج تک کسی کو سکھی نہیں کر سکا۔

وجے بے ہوش ہو جاتا ہے۔

گلاب:
وجے بابو! وجے بابو! جوہی! جوہی!

اگلا منظر۔گلاب کا کمرہ۔رات کا وقت۔وجے کو وہ لحاف اُڑھاتی ہے جو سو رہا ہے۔

اگلا منظر۔کچھ دیر بعد وجے کی آنکھ کھلتی ہے۔گلاب دروازے سے ٹیک لگائے سو رہی ہے۔ماضی کی یادیں وجے کو پریشان کر رہی ہیں۔

وجے (بازگشت):
اُنھیں اپنے رسالے میں چھاپیے نا۔

وجے بستر سے اُٹھ جاتا ہے۔آوازیں گونج رہی ہیں۔

شیخ (بازگشت):
کیوں چھاپوں صاحب؟ میرا ماغ خراب ہوا ہے کیا؟ آپ کی بکواس کوئی شاعری ہے؟

Gulaab *(audio flashback, voice-over):*
The world needs you. The world needs your poetry.

Duniya ko tumhaari zaroorat hai. Tumhaari shaayeri ki zaroorat hai.

Ghosh *(audio flashback, voice-over):*
You should know that we only publish the work of famous poets, not the trash of novices.

Aap ko maaloom hona chaahiye ki hamaare yahaan sirf mash'hoor shaayeron ki cheezen chhapti hain, kisi nau-sikhiye ki bakwaas nahin.

Meena *(audio flashback, voice-over):*
When you couldn't feed yourself, how could you have married me and looked after me?

Jab tum khud apna pait nahin paal sakte thay, uss haalat mein mujh se biyaah kar ke mera bhaar utha sakte thay tum?

Middle brother *(audio flashback, voice-over):*
The responsibility of a father ended with father's death. It wasn't our wish that our parents produce such a good-for-nothing.

Mataji, baap ki jagah baap ki dum ke saath gayi. Ma-baap se hum ne toh nahin kaha tha ki aisi nikhattu aulaad paida karen.

A train whistle blows in the distance. Vijay writes a letter and puts it into his pocket. Gulaab is asleep. He looks at her and leaves.

Next scene. Vijay crosses a bridge where he sees a beggar shivering with cold. He takes off his jacket and gives it to the old man. He goes down the steps of the bridge and heads towards the railway yard. Wearing Vijay's jacket, the beggar follows him. Vijay is aware of the beggar but continues walking along the railway tracks. Vijay hears a train whistle and sees the light of the approaching train. He heads off in the direction of the oncoming train but walks away from the tracks. Still following Vijay, the aged beggar lets out a scream when his foot is caught in the track switch. Vijay runs back to save him but cannot free the old man. Pushing Vijay to safety, the beggar comes under the train. Fade out.[45]

गुलाब *(आवाज़):*

दुनिया को तुम्हारी ज़रूरत है । तुम्हारी शायरी की ज़रूरत है ।

घोष *(आवाज़):*

आपको मालूम होना चाहिए कि हमारे यहाँ सिर्फ़ मशहूर शायरों की चीज़ें छपती हैं, किसी नौसिखिए की बकवास नहीं ।

मीना *(आवाज़):*

जब तुम ख़ुद अपना पेट नहीं पाल सकते थे, उस हालत में मुझसे ब्याह कर के मेरा भार उठा सकते थे तुम?

मँझला भाई *(आवाज़):*

माताजी, बाप की जगह बाप के दम के साथ गई । माँ-बाप से हमने तो नहीं कहा था कि ऐसी निखट्टू औलाद पैदा करें ।

दूर से रेल की सीटी की आवाज़ सुनाई देती है । एक ख़त लिख कर विजय अपनी जेब में रखता है । सोती हुई गुलाब को पता नहीं चलता कि विजय चला गया ।

अगला दृश्य । रेल के पुल पर विजय को सर्दी से काँपता हुआ एक बूढ़ा फ़क़ीर दिखाई देता है । विजय अपना कोट उतार कर उसे दे देता है । पुल से उतर कर वो रेलवे यार्ड की ओर चला जा रहा है । विजय का कोट पहने बूढ़ा फ़क़ीर उसके पीछे-पीछे चला आ रहा है । विजय को एहसास है कि बूढ़ा फ़क़ीर उसके पीछे आ रहा है लेकिन वो रेल की पटरियों के किनारे चला जा रहा है । विजय सामने से आती हुई ट्रेन की ओर बढ़ा चला जा रहा है । कुछ सोच कर वो इरादा बदल देता है और मुड़ जाता है । विजय के पीछे आ रहे बूढ़े फ़क़ीर का पैर पटरियों में फँस जाता है और वो ज़ोर से चीखता है । विजय उसे बचाने के लिए दौड़ता है लेकिन उसका पैर बुरी तरह फँसा होता है । फ़क़ीर को एहसास होता है कि अब वो नहीं बचेगा तो वो विजय को धक्का देकर आती हुई ट्रेन से दूर कर देता है । बूढ़ा फ़क़ीर ट्रेन से टकरा जाता है । दृश्य बदलता है ।

گلاب (بازگشت):

دنیا کو تمہاری ضرورت ہے۔ تمہاری شاعری کی ضرورت ہے۔

گھوش (بازگشت):

آپ کو معلوم ہونا چاہیے کہ ہمارے یہاں صرف مشہور شاعروں کی چیزیں چھپتی ہیں کسی نو سکھیے کی بکواس نہیں۔

مینا (بازگشت):

جب تم خود اپنا پیٹ نہیں پال سکتے تھے اُس حالت میں مجھ سے بیاہ کر کے میرا بھار اُٹھا سکتے تھے تم۔

منجھلا بھائی (بازگشت):

ماتا جی، باپ کی جگہ باپ کے دم کے ساتھ گئی۔ ماں باپ سے تو نہیں ہم نے کہا تھا کہ ایسی نکھٹو اولاد پیدا کریں۔

ریل کی سیٹی دور سے سنائی دیتی ہے۔ ایک خط لکھ کر وجے اپنی جیب میں رکھتا ہے۔ سوتی ہوئی گلاب کو خبر نہیں کہ وہ چلا گیا۔

اگلا منظر۔ ایک پل پر وجے کو سردی میں ٹھٹھرتا ہوا ایک بوڑھا فقیر دکھائی دیتا ہے۔ وہ اپنا کوٹ اتار کر اُسے دے دیتا ہے۔ پل سے اُتر کر وہ ریلوے یارڈ کی طرف چلا جا رہا ہے۔ وہ کا کوٹ پہنے بوڑھا فقیر اُس کے پیچھے پیچھے چلا آ رہا ہے لیکن وہ ریل کی پٹریوں کے کنارے چلا جاتا رہتا ہے۔ وہ سامنے سے آتی ہوئی ٹرین کی طرف بڑھا جا رہا ہے۔ کچھ سوچ کر وہ ارادہ بدل دیتا ہے اور مڑ جاتا ہے۔ وہ کے پیچھے آتے ہوئے بوڑھے فقیر کا پیر پٹریوں میں پھنس جاتا ہے۔ وہ زور سے چیختا ہے۔ وہ اُسے بچانے کے لیے لپکتا ہے لیکن اُس کا پیر بری طرح پھنسا ہوا ہے۔ فقیر کو احساس ہوتا ہے کہ اب وہ نہیں بچ سکتا تو وہ وجے کو دھکا دے کر آتی ہوئی ٹرین کی زد سے دور دھکیل دیتا ہے۔ ٹرین بوڑھے فقیر سے ٹکراتی ہے۔ منظر بدلتا ہے۔

Reel Twelve

Fade in. A top shot. A teahouse where customers are seated. They are reading newspapers.

Man *(entering):*
Have you read about the poet's suicide?

Vo shaayer ki khudkushi ki khabar padhi tum ne?

Second man:
Sure! I knew him well. Who knows what problems the poor fellow was facing.

Arey bhai main toh usay jaanta bhi tha. Na jaane bechaare ki kya majboori thi.

Third man:
Hey boy! When are you serving the tea?

Chhokra, chai laata hai ki nahin?

Cut to Ghosh's house. Ghosh and Meena are having breakfast at a long dining table. Meena is reading Life *magazine and Ghosh has a newspaper in his hand.*

Ghosh *(reading aloud):*
"Tragic death of a young poet.
(Meena stops reading. Ghosh continues)
"A young man committed suicide by throwing himself in front of the Burdwan night train. His body was so badly mutilated that identifying him was impossible. A letter was found in his pocket. It contained a poem, his last message to the world. The poet's name was Vijay."
(Meena is crestfallen. Ghosh asks her casually)
Are you feeling all right, dear?

"Nau-jawaan shaayer ki dardnaak maut.

Raat Burdwan passenger ke neeche aa kar ek nau-jawaan ne khudkushi kar li. Laash is buri tarah se kat chuki thi ki shakl pehchaanna bhi namumkin ho gaya. Uss naujawaan ki jeb mein ek khat paaya gaya jis mein vo ek nazm apna aakhri paighaam ki soorat mein duniya ke liye chhod gaya. Shaayer ka naam Vijay tha."

Tumhaari tabiyat toh theek hai, dear?

अगला दृश्य । एक टी-हाउस में बहुत से लोग बैठे अख़बार पढ़ रहे हैं ।

एक आदमी (दाख़िल होते ही):
वो शायर की ख़ुदकुशी की ख़बर पढ़ी तुमने?

दूसरा आदमी:
अरे भाई मैं तो उसे जानता भी था । ना जाने बेचारे की क्या मजबूरी थी ।

तिसरा आदमी:
छोकरा, चाय लाता है कि नहीं?

अगला दृश्य । घोष का घर । घोष और मीना नाश्ते की मेज़ पर बैठे हुए हैं । मीना "लाइफ" मैगेज़ीन देख रही है । घोष अखबार पढ़ रहा है ।

घोष (उंची आवाज़ में पढ़ते हुए):
"नौ-जवान शायर की दर्दनाक मौत ।
(मीना संभलकर बैठ जाती है । घोष पढ़ रहा है)
रात बर्दवान पैसेन्जर के नीचे आकर एक नौजवान ने ख़ुदकुशी कर ली । लाश इस बुरी तरह से कट चुकी थी कि शक्ल पहचानना भी नामुमकिन हो गया । उस नौजवान की जेब में एक ख़त पाया गया जिस में वो एक नज़्म अपने आख़िरी पैग़ाम की सूरत में दुनिया के लिए छोड़ गया । शायर का नाम विजय था ।"
(मीना को सदमा पहुँचता है । घोष उसे पूछता है)
तुम्हारी तबियत तो ठीक है, डियर?

اگلا منظر۔ایک چائے خانے میں بہت سے لوگ بیٹھے اخبار پڑھ رہے ہیں۔

ایک آدمی (داخل ہوتا ہے):
وہ شاعر کی خودکشی کی خبر پڑھی تم نے؟

دوسرا آدمی:
ارے بھئی میں تو اُسے جانتا بھی تھا۔ نہ جانے بے چارے کی کیا مجبوری تھی۔

تیسرا آدمی:
چھوکرا، چائے لاتا ہے کہ نہیں؟

اگلا منظر۔گھوش کا متموّل گھر۔ گھوش اور مینا ناشتے کی میز پر بیٹھے ہوئے ہیں۔ مینا لائف میگزین کا ایک شمارہ دیکھ رہی ہے۔ گھوش اخبار پڑھ رہا ہے۔

گھوش (بہ آواز بلند):
''نوجوان شاعر کی دردناک موت۔
(مینا سنبھل کر بیٹھ جاتی ہے، گھوش پڑھ رہا ہے)
رات بردوان پینجر کے نیچے آ کر ایک نوجوان نے خودکشی کر لی۔ لاش اس بری طرح سے کٹ چکی تھی کہ شکل پہچاننا بھی ناممکن ہو گیا۔ اُس نوجوان کی جیب میں ایک خط پایا گیا۔ جس میں وہ ایک نظم اپنے آخری پیغام کی صورت میں دنیا کے لیے چھوڑ گیا۔ شاعر کا نام وجے تھا۔''
(مینا پر جیسے بجلی گر پڑتی ہے۔ گھوش پوچھتا ہے)
تمہاری طبیعت تو ٹھیک ہے، ڈیئر؟

Meena:
Hmm.

Hmm.

Meena picks up the copy of Life *magazine on the table and pretends to read. It obscures her face. The magazine has the cover image of Christ on the Cross.[46]*

Cut to Gulaab's room. Night. Hesitantly and almost furtively, she is applying marriage sindoor on her forehead. The sound of the wedding shehnai plays in the background. Sattar enters. He looks utterly devastated.[47]

Sattar:
Gulaabo.

Gulaabo.

Gulaab:
What's wrong, Sattar?

Kya baat hai, Sattar bhai?

He hands her a newspaper. She reads the article. The paper slips from her hand and she falls to the ground.

Dissolve. Night. Gulaab is sitting on her bed. It is windy night. She tries to catch the papers that fly around the room.

Dissolve. Day. The Modern Publishing House office. Gulaab is sitting near the door to Ghosh's room. The office boy sees Meena Ghosh arrive and greets her respectfully.

Office boy:
Morning, madam.

Salaam, memsaaheb.

Meena looks at Gulaab and sees a file on her lap marked "Parchhaiyyan" (Shadows). Meena knows at once that the file contains Vijay's poems.[48]

Meena *(to the office boy):*
Send her in.

Inhen andar bhej do.

Office boy:
Go in.

Jaao.

मीना:

हूँ।

मीना मैगेज़ीन उठाकर अपने चेहरे के सामने कर लेती है। लाइफ मैगेज़ीन के कवर पर क्रॉस पर टंगे इशु ख़्रीस्त की तसवीर है।

अगला दृश्य। गुलाब का कमरा। झिझकते और शरमाते हुए वो अपनी माँग में सिंदूर भर रही है। शहनाइयों की गूँज सुनाई दे रही है। चेहरे पर उदासी लिए सत्तार दाख़िल होता है।

सत्तार:

गुलाबो।

गुलाब:

क्या बात है, सत्तार भाई?

दरवाज़े के पास खड़ी गुलाब को वो अख़बार देता है। वो समाचार पर नज़र डालती है। अख़बार उसकी उंगलियों से फिसलता है और फ़र्श पर गिर जाता है।

अगला दृश्य। रात। गुलाब अपने बिस्तर पर बैठी है। तेज़ हवा चल रही है। चारों तरफ़ काग़ज़ात उड़ रहे हैं जिन्हें वो पकड़ने की कोशिश कर रही है।

अगला दृश्य। दिन। मॉडर्न पब्लिशिंग हाउस। घोष के कमरे के बाहर गुलाब बैठी है। मीना को देखकर ऑफ़िस बॉय सलाम करता है।

ऑफ़िस बॉय:

सलाम, मेमसाब।

गुलाब के हाथों में एक फ़ाइल, जिस पर, "परछाइयाँ" लिखा देख कर मीना समझ जाती है कि इसमें विजय की नज़्में हैं।

मीना (ऑफ़िस बॉय से):

इन्हें अंदर भेज दो।

ऑफ़िस बॉय (गुलाब से):

जाओ।

Meena enters the office, followed by Gulaab.

Meena *(coldly):*
Who are you?

Kaun hain aap?

Gulaab:
Gulaab.

Gulaab.

Meena:
From where?

Kahaan se aayi ho?

Gulaab:[49]
Sona…from Dharamtala.

Sona…Dharamtale se.

Meena:
Give me that file of poems.

Vo nazmon ki file do.

Gulaab:
So you know it contains poems? Then you'll know how beautiful they are. I've come to have them published.

Aap jaanti hain ye nazmon ki kaapi hai? Tabb toh aap ye bhi jaanti hongi ki kitni achhi nazmen hain. Main inhen chhapwaane aayi hoon.

Meena:
Did you come to show the poems to my husband? What's your price?

Toh ye nazmen tum mere pati ko dikhaane laayi thein? Iski kya qeemat logi?

Gulaab:
You will publish them, won't you?

Aap inhen chhapwaayengi na?

Meena:
I may publish them or I may not. Hurry up and tell me. What's your price?

Chhaapun ya na chhaapun, jaldi bataao. Inki qeemat kya logi?

Gulaab:
Price? I haven't come to sell them. I've brought them here to have them published.

Qeemat? Main inka sauda karne nahin aayi hoon. Inhen chhapwaane laayi hoon.

Meena realises that the young woman truly cares for Vijay. Her mood softens.

मीना के पीछे गुलाब ऑफ़िस में दाख़िल होती है।

मीना *(सख़्त अंदाज़ में)*:
कौन हैं आप?

गुलाब:
गुलाब।

मीना:
कहाँ से आयी हो?

गुलाब:
सोना... धरमतले से।

मीना:
वो नज़्मों की फ़ाइल दो।

गुलाब:
आप जानती हैं ये नज़्मों की कॉपी है? तब तो आप ये भी जानती होंगी कि कितनी अच्छी नज़्में हैं। मैं इन्हें छपवाने आयी हूँ।

मीना:
तो ये नज़्में तुम मेरे पति को दिखाने लायी थीं? इसकी क्या क़ीमत लोगी?

गुलाब:
आप इन्हें छपवायेंगी ना?

मीना:
छापूँ या ना छापूँ। जल्दी बताओ। इनकी क़ीमत क्या लोगी?

गुलाब:
क़ीमत? मैं इनका सौदा करने नहीं आयी हूँ। इन्हें छपवाने लायी हूँ।

गुलाब के चेहरे के हावभाव देख कर मीना समझ जाती है कि वो विजय को चाहती है। उसकी आवाज़ में थोड़ी नर्मी आ जाती है।

مینا کے پیچھے گلاب آفس میں داخل ہوتی ہے۔

مینا *(گلاب سے سرد لہجے میں)*:
کون ہیں آپ؟

گلاب:
گلاب۔

مینا:
کہاں سے آئی ہو؟

گلاب:
سونا۔۔۔دھرم تلے سے۔

مینا:
وہ نظموں کی فائل دو۔

گلاب:
آپ جانتی ہیں یہ نظموں کی کاپی ہے؟ تب تو آپ یہ بھی جانتی ہوںگی کہ کتنی اچھی نظمیں ہیں۔ میں انھیں چھپوانے آئی ہوں۔

مینا:
تو تم یہ نظمیں میرے پتی کو دکھانے لائی تھیں؟ اس کی کیا قیمت لوگی؟

گلاب:
آپ انہیں چھپوائیں گی نا؟

مینا:
چھاپوں یا نہ چھاپوں۔ جلدی بتاؤ۔ ان کی قیمت کیا لوگی؟

گلاب:
قیمت؟ میں ان کا سودا کرنے نہیں آئی ہوں۔ انہیں چھپوانے لائی ہوں۔

گلاب کے چہرے کے تاثرات دیکھ کر مینا سمجھ جاتی ہے کہ وہ وجے کو چاہتی ہے۔ اُس کے لہجے میں نرمی آ جاتی ہے۔

Meena:
These poems are very precious to you, aren't they? How did you know Vijay?

Gulaab:
By good fortune.

Meena:
What was your relationship with him?

Gulaab:
Relationship?

Meena *(roughly):*
I'd like to know how a decent man like him came to meet a respectable lady like you.

Gulaab:
By good fortune.

Meena:
You're prepared to sell anything for money, so why do you refuse to sell these poems?

Gulaab has understood that she is talking to Meena, who is indeed prepared to sell love for money, unlike the prostitute.

Gulaab:
Are you Meena?

Meena:
Listen. I have very little time. My husband will be here any minute. You will have to sell these poems to me before he comes.

Gulaab:
I won't sell them.

Meena:
I'll pay you 1,000 rupees.

Ye nazmen tumhen bahot pyari hain na? Tum Vijay ko kaise jaanti thein?

Saubhaagya se.

Uss se tumhaara kya rishta tha?

Rishta?

Main ye jaanna chaahti thi ki uss jaise bhale aadmi se aap jaisi shareef aurat ki jaan-pehchaan kaise huwi.

Saubhaagya se.

Daulat ke liye tum bahot kuchh bechti ho phir ye nazmen bechne se tumhen itna inkaar kyun?

Aap Meena hain na?

Dekho mere paas waqt bahot kam hai. Abhi abhi mere pati aa jaayenge. Uss se pehle tumhen ye nazmen bechni hi padengi.

Nahin bechoongi.

Main tumhen hazaar doongi.

मीना:
ये नज़्में तुम्हें बहुत प्यारी हैं ना? तुम विजय को कैसे जानती थीं?

गुलाब:
सौभाग्य से ।

मीना:
उससे तुम्हारा क्या रिश्ता था?

गुलाब:
रिश्ता?

मीना *(सख़्ती से):*
मैं ये जानना चाहती थी कि उस जैसे भले आदमी से आप जैसी शरीफ़ औरत की जान–पहचान कैसे हुई ।

गुलाब:
सौभाग्य से ।

मीना:
दौलत के लिए तुम बहुत कुछ बेचती हो तो फिर ये नज़्में बेचने से तुम्हें इतना इन्कार क्यूँ?

गुलाब समझ जाती है कि ये वही मीना है जो दौलत के लिए कुछ भी बेच सकती है । शायद यह बाज़ारी औरत भी ऐसा कभी न कर सके ।

गुलाब:
आप मीना हैं ना?

मीना:
देखो मेरे पास वक़्त बहुत कम है । अभी-अभी मेरे पति आ जाएँगे । उससे पहले तुम्हें ये नज़्में बेचनी ही पड़ेंगी ।

गुलाब:
नहीं बेचूँगी ।

मीना:
मैं तुम्हें हज़ार दूँगी ।

Gulaab:
I won't sell them.

Meena:
I'll give you 2,000.

Gulaab:
I won't sell them.

Meena:
3,000.

Gulaab:
Not even 30,000.

Ghosh (enters and sees the file of poems):
What's that?

Meena:
Nothing.

Ghosh:
Show me.
(he snatches the file from Meena's hand and reads)
"For Meena…whose memory lives in every word."

Meena leaves. Ghosh sits at his desk. Gulaab approaches him.

Gulaab:
I've brought them to have them published.

Nahin bechoongi.

Do hazaar doongi.

Main nahin bechoongi.

Teen hazaar doongi.

Tees hazaar bhi nahin.

Ye kya hai?

Kuchh nahin.

Dikhaao. Dikhaao.

"Meena ke naam. Jis ki yaad in nazmon ke har lafz mein basi huwi hai."

Main…main inhen chhapwaane ke liye laayi thi.

गुलाब:
नहीं बेचूँगी ।

मीना:
दो हज़ार दूँगी ।

गुलाब:
नहीं बेचूँगी ।

मीना:
तीन हज़ार दूँगी ।

गुलाब:
तीस हज़ार भी नहीं ।

घोष (दफ़्तर में दाख़िल होते हुए फ़ाइल देख लेता है):
ये क्या है?

मीना:
कुछ नहीं ।

घोष:
दिखाओ । दिखाओ ।
(मीना से फ़ाइल छीन कर पढ़ता है)
"मीना के नाम । जिसकी याद इन नज़्मों के हर लफ़्ज़ में बसी हुई है ।"

मीना चली जाती है । घोष कुर्सी पर बैठ जाता है । गुलाब उसके पास आती है ।

गुलाब:
मैं... मैं इन्हें छपवाने के लिए लायी थी ।

She opens a small cloth bundle and tips some cheap jewellery onto his desk.

Ghosh:
What's all this?

Ye sab kya hai?

Gulaab:
My life savings. I can't give more than this. It's very important to me that these poems are published. If you'll publish them, I'll be eternally grateful to you.

Meri zindagi ki saari poonji hai ye, inhen chhapwaane ki qeemat. Main is se ziyaada aur kuchh nahin de sakti. Inka chhapna mere liye bahot zaroori hai. Agar aap inhen chhaap den toh main umar bhar aap ka ehsaan maanungi.

Dissolve to a quick montage. Hundreds of copies of Vijay's book Parchhaiyyan (Shadows) roll off the press and are bought by enthusiastic readers. The montage ends with Gulaab standing in the corner of a bookshop. Vijay's college friend Shyam is among the angry crowd.

Customer *(to the bookshop attendant)*:
You're a fine bookseller! We want Vijay's book and you say you don't have it.

Publishing ka dhanda karte ho ya mazaaq? Humen Vijay babu ki kitaab chaahiye aur tum kehte ho ki nahin hai.

Shop attendant:
I did, but they're all sold out.

Amma! Thien. Khatm ho gayi.

Second customer:
The new edition only came out a few days ago — how can it be sold out that soon?

Kuchh din pehle hi toh naya edition nikla hai — itni jaldi khatm kaise ho gaya?

Third customer:
Why don't you say you're selling it "under the counter?"

Saaf kyun nahin kehte ki kitaab black se bechne ka iraada hai?

Fourth customer:
Have the third edition tomorrow. Or else we'll burn your shop! Understand?

Kal tak ki naya edition nahin chhaapa toh dukaan ko aag laga dega. Samjhe?

The crowd disperses. Shyam waits for a minute and then leaves the bookshop. Gulaab holds Vijay's book close to her heart. Her eyes fill with tears.

ستے زیورات ایک تھیلی سے نکال کر میز پر اُلٹ دیتی ہے۔

گھوش:
یہ سب کیا ہے؟

گلاب:
میری زندگی کی ساری پونجی ہے یہ، انھیں چھپوانے کی قیمت۔ میں اِس سے زیادہ اور کچھ نہیں دے سکتی۔ اِن کا چھپنا میرے لیے بہت ضروری ہے۔ اگر آپ اِنھیں چھاپ دیں تو میں عمر بھر آپ کا احسان مانوں گی۔

گلاب اور پرنٹنگ پریس کے ملے جلے مونتاج کا منظر۔ وجے کے شعری مجموعے، پرچھائیاں، کی سینکڑوں کاپیاں چھپ کر ہاتھوں ہاتھ بک جاتی ہیں۔ مونتاج کے آخر میں گلاب کتاب کی دکان کے ایک گوشے میں کھڑی ہے، لوگوں کا ہجوم غصے میں ہے، جس میں شیام بھی ہے۔

گاہک (دکاندار سے):
پبلشنگ کا دھندا کرتے ہو یا مذاق؟ ہمیں وجے بابو کی کتاب چاہیے اور تم کہتے ہو کہ نہیں ہے۔

دکاندار:
اماں، تھی۔ ختم ہو گئی۔

دوسرا گاہک:
کچھ دن پہلے ہی تو نیا ایڈیشن نکلا ہے۔۔۔ اِتنی جلدی ختم کیسے ہو گیا؟

تیسرا گاہک:
صاف کیوں نہیں کہتے کہ کتاب بلیک سے بیچنے کا ارادہ ہے۔

چوتھا گاہک:
کل تک کے نیا ایڈیشن نہیں چھاپا تو دکان کو آگ لگا دے گا۔ سمجھے؟

ہجوم چھٹ جاتا ہے۔ کچھ لمحے خاموش کھڑا رہ کر شیام بھی چلا جاتا ہے۔ ایک گوشے میں وجے کی کتاب کو سینے سے لگائے گلاب آنکھوں میں آنسو لیے کھڑی ہے۔

कुछ सस्ते-से ज़ेवरात भरी थैली मेज़ पर उलटती है।

घोष:
ये सब क्या है?

गुलाब:
मेरी ज़िन्दगी की सारी पूँजी है ये, इन्हें छपवाने की क़ीमत। मैं इससे ज़्यादा और कुछ नहीं दे सकती। इनका छपना मेरे लिए बहुत ज़रूरी है। अगर आप इन्हें छाप दें तो मैं उमर भर आपका एहसान मानूँगी।

गुलाब और प्रिंटिंग प्रेस के मोन्ताज का दृश्य। विजय की नज़्मों की किताब "परछाइयाँ" की सैंकड़ों कॉपियाँ छप कर हाथों-हाथ बिक जाती हैं। मोन्ताज के अंत में गुलाब किताब की दुकान में एक कोने में खड़ी है, लोगों की भीड़ गुस्से में हैं, जिसमें विजय का दोस्त श्याम भी है।

ग्राहक (दुकानदार से):
पब्लिशिंग का धंधा करते हो या मज़ाक? हमें विजय बाबू की किताब चाहिए और तुम कहते हो कि नहीं है।

दुकानदार:
अमाँ! थी। ख़त्म हो गई।

दूसरा ग्राहक:
कुछ दिन पहले ही तो नया एडिशन निकला है – इतनी जल्दी ख़त्म कैसे हो गया?

तीसरा ग्राहक:
साफ़ क्यूँ नहीं कहते कि किताब ब्लैक से बेचने का इरादा है।

चौथा ग्राहक:
कल तक की नया एडिशन नहीं छापा तो दुकान को आग लगा देगा। समझे?

भीड़ बिखरती है। कुछ समय तक ख़ामोश खड़ा रह कर श्याम भी चला जाता है। एक कोने में विजय की किताब को सीने से लगाए गुलाब आँखों में आँसू लिए खड़ी है।

Gulaab (to herself):
If only you could see all this with your own eyes.

Kaash ki aaj tum ye sab apni aankhon se dekh sakte.

Fade out.

Fade in. Day. A doctor enters a hospital ward.

Doctor (in English):
Good morning.

Nurse (in English):
Good morning, Doctor.

Doctor:
Have you established the identity of the patient in bed eight?

Kuchh pata chala? Bed number aanth ka patient kaun hai?

Nurse:[50]
We know nothing. He hasn't said a word since he was admitted. He just lies there quietly. See for yourself.

Abhi tak toh kuchh pata nahin chala. Jab se aaya hai kuchh bolta hi nahin. Gum-sum sa pada rehta hai. Dekhiye.

They walk over to Vijay.

Doctor:
Hello.
(Vijay's does not look at the doctor)
How are you today? Nurse, let me know at once if he says anything at all.

Kaisi tabiyat hai aaj? Sister, ye jab bhi kuchh baat karay mujhe fauran ittela kar dena.

Nurse (in English):
Yes, Doctor.

गुलाब *(मन ही मन विजय को याद करके)*:
काश कि आज तुम ये सब अपनी आँखों से देख सकते ।

दृश्य बदलता है ।

अगला दृश्य । दिन । अस्पताल के वार्ड में डॉक्टर आता है ।

डॉक्टर *(अंग्रेज़ी में)*:
गुड मॉर्निंग ।

नर्स *(अंग्रेज़ी में)*:
गुड मॉर्निंग, डॉक्टर ।

डॉक्टर:
कुछ पता चला! बेड नंबर आठ का पेशेन्ट कौन है?

नर्स:
अभी तक तो कुछ पता नहीं चला । जबसे आया है कुछ बोलता ही नहीं । गुम-सुम सा पड़ा रहता है । देखिए ।

वो विजय के पास आते हैं ।

डॉक्टर:
हैलो ।
(विजय डॉक्टर की ओर नहीं देखता)
कैसी तबियत है आज? सिस्टर, ये जब भी कुछ बात करें मुझे फ़ौरन इत्तला कर देना ।

नर्स *(अंग्रेज़ी में)*:
यस, डॉक्टर ।

گلاب (خودکلامی):
کاش کہ آج تم یہ سب اپنی آنکھوں سے دیکھ سکتے۔

منظر بدلتا ہے۔

اگلا منظر۔ دن۔ ہاسپٹل وارڈ میں ڈاکٹر آتا ہے۔

ڈاکٹر (انگریزی میں):
گڈ مارننگ۔

نرس (انگریزی میں):
گڈ مارننگ، ڈاکٹر۔

ڈاکٹر:
کچھ پتا چلا؟ بیڈ نمبر آٹھ کا پیشنٹ کون ہے؟

نرس:
ابھی تک تو کچھ پتا نہیں چلا۔ جب سے آیا ہے کچھ بولتا ہی نہیں۔ گم سم سا پڑا رہتا ہے۔ دیکھیے۔

وہ اُس کے پاس آتے ہیں۔

ڈاکٹر:
ہیلو۔
(وہ ڈاکٹر کی طرف نہیں دیکھتا)
کیسی طبیعت ہے آج؟ سسٹر، یہ جب بھی کچھ بات کرے، مجھے فوراً اطلاع کر دینا۔

نرس (انگریزی میں):
ییس، ڈاکٹر۔

The scene ends with a tracking shot to Vijay's expressionless face. Cut to Ghosh's office. Shyam arrives, twirling a cane in his hand.

Ghosh (*irritated tone*):
I tell you. I can't pay more than 5,000. Yes, the poems are by Vijay, but the price is too high.

Shyam:
Mr. Ghosh, let's talk business. Must you cream off all the profit and leave me with nothing?

Ghosh:
Then name a sensible price. But show some respect.

Shyam:
Sir, can treasures ever be sold? You know these are Vijay's poems — unpublished and his last. I'll take fifty-fifty.

Ghosh (*partly in English*):
Impossible. I can't pay that much.

Shyam:
Nice to have met you. Good day.

Ghosh:
Wait. You're an odd fellow. Never mind. My last offer: twenty-five per cent. Now you may go if you want.

Shyam:
Very well. I wouldn't want you to think Shyam isn't open to reason. Here. Let's shake hands.

Ghosh reluctantly extends his hand.

Ghosh (*in English, under his breath*):
Scoundrel.

Main kehta hoon ki inke ziyada se ziyada paanch hazaar de sakta hoon. Ye Vijay ki nazmen sahi lekin qeemat bhi toh kuchh kam nahin.

Ghosh babu, kuchh len-den ki baaten kijiye. Malaayi-maalayi toh aap chatt kar jaayen aur tal-chhat hamaare liye?

Toh phir aap farmaayiye ki aap kitne mein bechenge lekin zara tameez se.

Huzoor, bhala kuber ka khazana bhi bika hai kahin? Ye jaan lijiye ki ye Vijay ki nazmen hain, uski achhooti nazmen hain aur aakhri nazmen hain. Munaafe mein aadha hissa loonga.

Impossible. Itna bada hissa main nahin de sakta.

Tabb aap se mil kar badi khushi huwi. Aadaab arz hai.

Thairiye. Ajeeb aadmi hain aap. Khair. Aakhri baar sunn lijiye, munaafe ka chauthaayi hissa doonga. Ab agar aap chaahen toh ja sakte hain.

Chaliye, aap bhi kya sochenge ki Shyam se ek hi toh tuk ki baat kahi aur vo bhi khaali gayi. Ye lijiye. Aur laayiye haath.

विजय के स्थिर बने चेहरे पर मंज़र बदलता है। अगला दृश्य। घोष का दफ़्तर। श्याम उससे मिलने आया है। छड़ी को हाथ में घुमाते हुए वो कह रहा है।

घोष (कुछ परेशानी में):
मैं कहता हूँ कि इनके ज़्यादा से ज़्यादा पाँच हज़ार दे सकता हूँ। ये विजय की नज़्में सही लेकिन क़ीमत भी तो कुछ कम नहीं।

श्याम:
घोष बाबू, कुछ लेन−देन की बातें कीजिए। मलाई−मलाई तो आप चट कर जाएँ और तल−छट हमारे लिए।

घोष:
तो फिर आप फ़रमाईए कि आप कितने में बेचेंगे लेकिन ज़रा तमीज़ से।

श्याम:
हुज़ूर, भला कुबेर का ख़ज़ाना भी बिका है कहीं? ये जान लीजिए कि ये विजय की नज़्में हैं। उसकी अछूती नज़्में हैं और आख़िरी नज़्में हैं। मुनाफ़े में आधा हिस्सा लूँगा।

घोष (कुछ अंग्रेज़ी में):
इम्पॉसिबल। इतना बड़ा हिस्सा मैं नहीं दे सकता।

श्याम:
तब आपसे मिल कर बड़ी ख़ुशी हुई। आदाब अर्ज़ है।

घोष:
ठहरिए। अजीब आदमी हैं आप। ख़ैर। आख़िरी बार सुन लीजिए, मुनाफ़े का चौथाई हिस्सा दूँगा। अब अगर आप चाहें तो जा सकते हैं।

श्याम:
चलिए, आप भी क्या सोचेंगे कि श्याम से एक ही तो तुक की बात कही, और वो भी ख़ाली गई। ये लीजिए। और लाईए हाथ।

झिझकते हुए वो श्याम से हाथ मिलाता है।

घोष (अंग्रेज़ी में, हल्की−सी आवाज़ में):
स्काउंड्रल।

Reel Thirteen

Fade in. Night. The hospital ward. Sitting near Vijay, who is sleeping, a nurse reads a poem aloud. Hearing her voice, Vijay wakes up.

Nurse:[51]
"The shadows of thought and dream stir

I am adorning your hair with flowers
Your eyes lower, full of feeling
I do not know what I will say today
My lips are parched. My voice is hesitant
The shadows of thought and dream stir

I am holding your soft arms in an embrace
My lips cast a shadow on your lips
You are sure we will never be parted now
Though I feel we may be one, but still strangers
(Vijay gets out of his bed and rushes to the nurse)
The shadows of thought and dream stir"

Vijay *(taking the book from the nurse):*
Shadows?

Nurse *(running out of the ward):*
Doctor. Doctor.

The doctor and nurse come running back.

Vijay *(looking through the book):*
My poems. Everyone of them. This is my book.

Doctor:
Of course! This is your book. But what's your name?

Vijay:
My name? I'm Vijay. Look. I wrote this book.

"Khayaal-o-khwab ki parchhaayiyaan ubharti hain

Main phool taank raha hoon tumhaare joode mein
Tumhaari aankh massarrat se jhukti jaati hai
Na-jaane aaj main kya baat kehne waala hoon
Zabaan khushk hai aawaaz rukti jaati hai
Khayaal-o-khwab ki parchhaayiyaan ubharti hain

"Mere galay mein tumhaari gudaaz baanhen hain
Tumhaare honton pe mere labon ke saaye hain
Tumhen yaqeen ki hum ab kabhi na bichhdenge
Mujhe gumaan ki hum mil ke bhi paraaye hain

"Khayaal-o-khwab ki parchhaayiyaan ubharti hain"

Parchhaayiyaan?

Meri nazmen. Sab ki sab meri nazmen. Ye meri kitaab hai.

Ji haan, ji haan, aap hi ki kitaab hai, lekin aap ka naam kya hai?

Mera naam? Main Vijay hoon. Ye dekhiye. Ye kitaab meri likhi huwi hai.

अगला दृश्य। रात। हॉस्पिटल का कमरा। एक नर्स नज़्म पढ़ रही है। वो विजय के क़रीब बैठी है जो सो रहा है। नर्स की आवाज़ सुनकर वो उठ जाता है।

नर्स:
"ख़याल-ओ-ख़्वाब की परछाइयाँ उभरती हैं

मैं फूल टाँक रहा हूँ तुम्हारे जूड़े में
तुम्हारी आँख मसर्रत से झुकती जाती है
ना-जाने आज मैं क्या बात कहने वाला हूँ
ज़बान खुश्क है, आवाज़ रुकती जाती है
ख़याल-ओ-ख़्वाब की परछाइयाँ उभरती हैं

मेरे गले में तुम्हारी गुदाज़ बाँहें हैं
तुम्हारे होठों पे मेरे लबों के साये हैं
तुम्हें यक़ीन कि हम अब कभी ना बिछड़ेंगे
मुझे गुमान कि हम मिल के भी पराये हैं
(बिस्तर से उठकर विजय नर्स की तरफ़ तेज़ी से आगे बढ़ता है)
ख़याल-ओ-ख़्वाब की परछाइयाँ उभरती हैं"

विजय (नर्स के हाथ से किताब झपटता है):
परछाइयाँ?

नर्स (वार्ड से बाहर भागती हुई):
डॉक्टर। डॉक्टर।

डॉक्टर और नर्स तेज़ी से अंदर आते हैं।

विजय (किताब देखते हुए):
मेरी नज़्में। सब की सब मेरी नज़्में। ये मेरी किताब है।

डॉक्टर:
जी हाँ। जी हाँ। आप ही की किताब है। लेकिन आपका नाम क्या है?

विजय:
मेरा नाम? मैं विजय हूँ। ये देखिए। ये किताब मेरी लिखी हुई है।

اگلا منظر۔رات۔ہاسپٹل وارڈ۔ایک نرس بلند آواز میں ایک نظم پڑھ رہی ہے۔وہ وجے کے قریب بیٹھی ہے جوسو رہا ہے۔نرس کی آواز سن کر وہ اٹھ جاتا ہے۔

نرس:
''خیال و خواب کی پرچھائیاں اُبھرتی ہیں

میں پھول ٹانک رہا ہوں تمہارے جوڑے میں
تمہاری آنکھ مسرت سے جھکتی جاتی ہے
نہ جانے آج میں کیا بات کہنے والا ہوں
زبان خشک ہے، آواز رکتی جاتی ہے
خیال و خواب کی پرچھائیاں اُبھرتی ہیں

مرے گلے میں تمہاری گداز بانہیں ہیں
تمہارے ہونٹوں پہ میرے لبوں کے سائے ہیں
تمہیں یقین کہ ہم اب کبھی نہ بچھڑیں گے
مجھے گمان کہ ہم مل کے بھی پرائے ہیں
(بستر سے اُٹھ کر وجے نرس کی طرف لپکتا ہے)
خیال و خواب کی پرچھائیاں اُبھرتی ہیں''

وجے (نرس کے ہاتھ سے کتاب جھپٹتے ہوئے):
''پرچھائیاں؟''

نرس (باہر کی جانب لپکتی ہے):
ڈاکٹر، ڈاکٹر۔

ڈاکٹر اور نرس تیزی سے اندر آتے ہیں۔

وجے (کتاب کے ورق اُلٹتے ہوئے):
میری نظمیں۔ سب کی سب میری نظمیں ہیں۔ یہ میری کتاب ہے۔

ڈاکٹر:
جی ہاں، جی ہاں۔ آپ ہی کی کتاب ہے۔ لیکن آپ کا نام کیا ہے؟

وجے:
میرا نام؟ میں وجے ہوں۔ یہ دیکھیے۔ یہ کتاب میری لکھی ہوئی ہے۔

Doctor:
The Vijay who wrote it died a long time ago. Think carefully. What is your name?

Aji saaheb, jis Vijay ne ye kitaab likhi hai vo na-jaane kab ka mar chuka hai. Achhi tarah se yaad kijiye. Kya naam hai aap ka?

Vijay:
Why don't you believe me? I am Vijay.
(agitated)
I told you. I am Vijay.
(he looks at the doctors and nurses, realising they do not believe him. The ward boys restrain him as he struggles)
Why have you kept me here? Let me go. Let me go!

Aap log mujh par yaqeen kyun nahin karte? Main Vijay hoon.

Maine aap se kaha na main Vijay hoon.

Mujhe yahaan kyun rakh chhoda hai? Jaane do mujhe. Jaane do.

Second doctor:
Doctor, I think he's lost his mind.

Doctor, mera khayaal hai ki bichare ka dimaagh kuchh…

Doctor:
Telephone Doctor Sen at once.

Hmm. Doctor Sen ko fauran telephone karo.

Dissolve to Ghosh's office. Vijay's two brothers arrive.

Middle brother *(in English):*
Sir, sir.

Elder brother *(in English):*
Sir, please, sir.

Ghosh *(turns to look at them with disdain):*
Yes? So you are Vijay's brothers?

Yes? Oh, toh aap log Vijay ke bhai hain?

डॉक्टर:

अजी साहब, जिस विजय ने ये किताब लिखी है वो ना-जाने कब का मर चुका है । अच्छी तरह से याद कीजिए। क्या नाम है आपका?

विजय:

आप लोग मुझ पर यक़ीन क्यूँ नहीं करते? मैं विजय हूँ।

(झुंझलाते हुए)

मैंने आपसे कहा ना मैं विजय हूँ।

(वो डॉक्टर और नर्सों की ओर देखता है। वॉर्डबॉय उसे पकड़ लेता है)

मुझे यहाँ क्यूँ रख छोड़ा है? जाने दो मुझे। जाने दो ।

दूसरा डॉक्टर:

डॉक्टर, मेरा ख़याल है कि बेचारे का दिमाग़ कुछ...

डॉक्टर:

हूँ, डॉक्टर सेन को फ़ौरन टेलीफ़ोन करो।

दृश्य बदलता है। घोष का दफ़्तर। विजय के दोनों भाई वहाँ आए हैं।

मंझला भाई *(अंग्रेजी में)*:

सर, सर।

बड़ा भाई *(अंग्रेजी में)*:

सर, प्लीज़, सर।

घोष *(एक किताब पढ़ते हुए उन दोनों की तरफ़ घूमता है)*:

यस? ओह, तो आप लोग विजय के भाई हैं?

ڈاکٹر:

اجی صاحب، جس وجے نے یہ کتاب لکھی ہے وہ نہ جانے کب کا مر چکا ہے۔ اچھی طرح سے یاد کیجیے۔ کیا نام ہے آپ کا؟

وجے:

آپ لوگ مجھ پر یقین کیوں نہیں کرتے؟ میں وجے ہوں۔

(جھنجھلا کر)

میں نے آپ سے کہا نا میں وجے ہوں۔

(اسے احساس ہوتا ہے کہ ہاسپٹل اسٹاف اُس کی باتوں پہ یقین نہیں کر رہا)

مجھے یہاں کیوں رکھ چھوڑا ہے؟ جانے دو مجھے۔ جانے دو۔

دوسرا ڈاکٹر:

ڈاکٹر، میرا خیال ہے کہ بچارے کا دماغ کچھ۔۔۔

ڈاکٹر:

ہوں۔ ڈاکٹر سین کو فوراً ٹیلیفون کرو۔

منظر بدل کر گھوش کا آفس۔ وجے کے دونوں بھائی سودے بازی کے لیے آئے ہیں۔

منجھلا بھائی (انگریزی میں):

سر، سر۔

بڑا بھائی (انگریزی میں):

سر، پلیز، سر۔

گھوش (ایک کتاب پڑھتے ہوئے اُن دونوں کی طرف گھومتا ہے):

یس؟ اوہ، تو آپ لوگ وجے کے بھائی ہیں؟

Middle brother:
We are indeed. His older brothers.

Ji haan. Hum donon Vijay se bade hain.

Elder brother:
And I am the eldest of the three.

Aur main is se bhi bada hoon.

Ghosh:
What do you want?

Aap logon ko mujh se kuchh kaam hai?

Elder brother (to his brother):
You speak.

Tu bol.

Middle brother:
You tell him, brother.

Tumhin bata do na, bhayya.

Elder brother:
Shall I?

Main bataaun?

Middle brother:
Yes.

Hmm.

Elder brother:
All right. No, you speak.

Achha. Nahin, nahin, tu bata.

Ghosh (impatient):
I asked you what you want.

Maine poochha ki aap logon ko mujh se kuchh kaam hai.

Elder brother:
Well, the thing is…I educated Vijay and fed him and brought him up. Showered affection on him and made him capable of making a name for himself.

Ji. Baat kuchh yun hai ki maine Vijay ko padhaaya, likhaaya, khilaaya, pilaaya. Bade pyar se rakkha usay is qaabil banaaya ki vo naam paida kar sakay.

Middle brother (grinning):
So did I.

Maine bhi.

Ghosh:
I don't have time to waste. Get to the point.

Mere paas waqt kam hai. Matlab ki baat karo.

मंझला भाई:

जी हाँ। हम दोनों विजय से बड़े हैं।

बड़ा भाई:

और मैं इससे भी बड़ा हूँ।

घोष:

आप लोगों को मुझसे कुछ काम है?

बड़ा भाई (मंझले भाई से):

तू बोल।

मंझला भाई:

तुम ही बता दो ना, भय्या।

बड़ा भाई:

मैं बताऊँ?

मंझला भाई:

हाँ।

बड़ा भाई:

अच्छा। नहीं, नहीं। तू बता।

घोष (बेसब्री से):

मैंने पूछा कि आप लोगों को मुझसे कुछ काम है।

बड़ा भाई:

जी, बात कुछ यूँ कि मैंने विजय को पढ़ाया, लिखाया, खिलाया, पिलाया। बड़े प्यार से रक्खा उसे, इस क़ाबिल बनाया कि वो नाम पैदा कर सके।

मंझला भाई (मुस्कुराते हुए):

मैंने भी।

घोष:

मेरे पास वक़्त कम है। मतलब की बात करो।

Middle brother *(still grinning)*:
The point is…we're here to collect some money from you.

Matlab ki baat toh ye hai ki hum log aap ke paas se kuchh rupiya vasool karne ke liye aaye thay.

Ghosh *(partly in English)*:
What nonsense! Are you in your right mind?

What nonsense! Aap logon ka dimaagh toh theek hai?

Middle brother:
You see…we are the rightful heirs to all his property.

Ji…vo…Vijay ke baad uski har cheez ke waaris hum hi log hain.

Elder brother:
Including his songs and poems.

Uske geeton aur nazmon ke bhi.

Middle brother:
And we have a legal right to the money you're making from his work.

Aur un geeton aur nazmon se jo faayeda aap logon ko ho raha hai vo qaanoonan hum logon ko hona chaahiye.

Elder brother:
We don't want all the profit. But we won't object to getting a small share.

Hum poora munaafa toh nahin maangte. Uss mein se thoda-bahot bhi mil jaaye toh hamen koi etraaz nahin.

Ghosh:
I don't know you. Nor did I get the poems from you. So, you won't get a single penny. Understand?

Main aap logon ko nahin jaanta. Aur na hi vo nazmen mujhe aap logon se mili hain. Is liye aap ko ek paayi bhi nahin mil sakti. Samjhay?

Fade out.

Fade in. Vijay is locked in a room with bars on the windows. The room is more like a prison cell than a mental asylum ward.[52] Distressed patients pace the room. Vijay covers his ears, trying to block out the crazy screaming around him. Doctor Sen, Ghosh and Shyam enter the corridor of the mental asylum. They look at Vijay from afar.

Doctor Sen:
Come. There he is.

Aayiye, aayiye. Vo raha.

मंझला भाई (*मुस्कुराते हुए*):

मतलब की बात तो ये है कि हम लोग आपके पास से कुछ रुपिया वसूल करने के लिए आए थे।

घोष (*कुछ अंग्रेज़ी में*):

व्हॉट नॉनसेन्स! आप लोगों का दिमाग़ तो ठीक है?

मंझला भाई:

जी... वो... विजय के बाद उसकी हर चीज़ के वारिस हम ही लोग हैं।

बड़ा भाई:

उसके गीतों और नज़्मों के भी।

मंझला भाई:

और उन गीतों और नज़्मों से जो फ़ायदा आप लोगों को हो रहा है वो क़ानूनन हम लोगों को होना चाहिए।

बड़ा भाई:

हम पूरा मुनाफ़ा तो नहीं माँगते। उस में से थोड़ा-बहुत भी मिल जाए तो हमें कोई ऐतराज़ नहीं।

घोष:

मैं आप लोगों को नहीं जानता। और ना ही वो नज़्में मुझे आप लोगों से मिली हैं। इस लिए आपको एक पाई भी नहीं मिल सकती। समझे?

अगल दृश्य।

विजय एक कमरे में है जिसकी खिड़कियों और दरवाज़े पर सलाखें लगी हुई हैं, पागलखाने से ज़्यादा वो जेल का कमरा नज़र आता है। कमरे में शोर मचाते हुए मरीज़ घूम रहे हैं। विजय शोर से बचने के लिए अपने कानों पर हथेलियाँ रखकर बैठा है। गलियारे में डॉक्टर सेन, घोष और श्याम दाख़िल होते हैं। वो लोग दूर से विजय को देख रहे हैं।

डॉक्टर सेन:

आईए, आईए। वो रहा।

Shyam (to Ghosh):
No. It isn't Vijay.

Nahin. Vo Vijay nahin hai.

Seeing Shyam and Ghosh, Vijay runs to the bars of the ward.

Vijay (shouts):
Shyam!

Shyam!

Ghosh (to the doctor):
That's right. He isn't Vijay.

Ji haan. Ye Vijay nahin.

Vijay realises that both men have disowned him. He is devastated.[53]
Fade out.

Fade in. Day. Ghosh's office. Vijay's two brothers arrive.

Ghosh:
So you want a share in the profit?

Hmm. Toh aap logon ko munaafe mein hissa chaahiye?

Brothers (grinning and in unison):
Yes.

Ji.

Ghosh:
But the rightful claimant is Vijay — and he's alive.

Lekin munaafe ka asli haq-daar Vijay — zinda hai.

Elder brother:
What?

Ein?

Middle brother:
Vijay?

Vijay?

श्याम *(घोष से)*:

नहीं। वो विजय नहीं है।

श्याम और घोष को देखकर विजय सलाखों वाले दरवाज़े की ओर बढ़ता है।

विजय *(चिल्लाकर)*:

श्याम!

घोष *(डॉक्टर से)*:

जी हाँ। ये विजय नहीं।

विजय को एहसास हो जाता है कि दोनों ने उसे पहचानने से इन्कार कर दिया है। उसे सदमा पहुँचता है। दृश्य बदलता है।

अगला दृश्य। दिन। घोष का दफ़्तर। विजय के दोनों भाई वहाँ मौजूद हैं।

घोष:

हूँ। तो आप लोगों को मुनाफ़े में हिस्सा चाहिए?

दोनों भाई *(मुस्कुराते हुए एक ही आवाज़ में)*:

जी।

घोष:

लेकिन मुनाफ़े का असली हक़दार विजय – ज़िंदा है।

बड़ा भाई:

एँ?

मंझला भाई:

विजय?

شیام (گھوش سے):

نہیں۔ وہ وجے نہیں ہے۔

شیام اور گھوش کو دیکھ کر وجے جالی دار دروازے کی طرف لپکتا ہے۔

وجے (بلند آواز سے):

شیام!

گھوش (ڈاکٹر سے):

جی ہاں۔ یہ وجے نہیں۔

وجے کو احساس ہوتا ہے کہ دونوں نے اُسے پہچاننے سے انکار کر دیا ہے۔ اُسے صدمہ پہنچتا ہے۔ منظر بدلتا ہے۔

اگلا منظر۔ دن۔ گھوش کا آفس۔ وجے کے دونوں بھائی موجود ہیں۔

گھوش:

ہوں۔ تو آپ لوگوں کو منافع میں حصہ چاہیے؟

دونوں بھائی (مسکراتے ہوئے ایک آواز میں):

جی۔

گھوش:

لیکن منافع کا اصلی حقدار وجے ۔۔۔ زندہ ہے۔

بڑا بھائی:

ایں؟

منجھلا بھائی:

وجے؟

Ghosh:
Vijay is alive.

Middle brother:
Vijay is alive?
(taken aback, the brothers sit down)
No. You must be joking.

Ghosh:
I am not a man who jokes. However, you can get a share of the profit. Two percent — on condition that you refuse to identify Vijay.

They smile at each other. The smarter of the brothers stops the other from speaking and turns to Ghosh.

Middle brother:
What do you mean? Why shouldn't we identify our brother?

Elder brother:
You think we're so nasty?

Middle brother:
You think we're so low?

Elder brother:
Refuse to identify our brother for a mere two per cent?

Middle brother *(grinning):*
At least make it sixteen.

Ghosh *(partly in English):*
You scoundrels. Very well.

Middle brother:
Mr. Ghosh is a real gentleman, brother.

Vijay zinda hai.

Vijay? Zinda hai?

Nahin nahin. Aap mazaaq kar rahe hain.

Main mazaaq nahin jaanta. Lekin baharhaal, aap logon ko munaafe mein kuchh hissa mil sakta hai. Yaani rupay mein do paise. Lekin vo bhi sirf ek shart par — ki aap ko Vijay ko pehchaanne se inkaar karna padega.

Kya baat kar rahe hain aap? Kya hum apne sagay bhai ko nahin pehchaanen?

Kya hum itne kameene hain?

Kya aap ne hum ko zaleel samjha hai kya?

Ki do paise ke liye hum apne bhai ko na pehchaanen?

Kam-se-kam ek aana toh kar dijiye.

You scoundrels. Achha, achha.

Borda, Ghosh babu khoob bhaalo maanush. *(in Bangla)*

घोष:

विजय ज़िंदा है।

मंझला भाई:

विजय? ज़िंदा है?

(परेशान होकर दोनों बैठ जाते हैं)

नहीं–नहीं। आप मज़ाक कर रहे हैं।

घोष:

मैं मज़ाक नहीं जानता। लेकिन बहरहाल, आप लोगों को मुनाफ़े में कुछ हिस्सा मिल सकता है। यानी रुपये में दो पैसे। लेकिन वो भी सिर्फ़ एक शर्त पर – कि आपको विजय को पहचानने से इन्कार करना पड़ेगा।

एक–दूसरे को देखकर मुस्कुराते हैं। दोनों में से ज़्यादा चालाक दूसरे को बोलने से रोकते हुए।

मंझला भाई *(घोष से)*:

क्या बात कर रहे हैं आप? क्या हम अपने सगे भाई को नहीं पहचानें?

बड़ा भाई:

क्या हम इतने कमीने हैं?

मंझला भाई:

क्या आपने हमको ज़लील समझा है क्या?

बड़ा भाई:

कि दो पैसे के लिए हम अपने भाई को ना पहचानें?

मंझला भाई *(हँसते हुए)*:

कम–से–कम एक आना तो कर दीजिए।

घोष *(कुछ अंग्रेज़ी में)*:

यू स्काउंड्रल्स। अच्छा, अच्छा।

मंझला भाई *(कुछ बंगला में)*:

बोरदा, घोष बाबू ख़ूब भालो मानुष।

گھوش:

وہ زندہ ہے۔

منجھلا بھائی:

وہ زندہ ہے؟

(حیرت زدہ ہوکر دونوں بیٹھ جاتے ہیں)

نہیں نہیں۔ آپ مذاق کر رہے ہیں۔

گھوش:

میں مذاق نہیں جانتا۔ لیکن بہرحال، آپ لوگوں کو منافع میں کچھ حصہ مل سکتا ہے۔ یعنی روپے میں دو پیسے۔ لیکن وہ بھی صرف ایک شرط پر۔۔۔ کہ آپ کو وجے کو پہچاننے سے انکار کرنا پڑے گا۔

دونوں بھائی ایک دوسرے کو دیکھ کر مسکراتے ہیں۔ دونوں میں سے زیادہ چالاک دوسرے کو بولنے سے روکتے ہوئے۔

منجھلا بھائی (گھوش سے):

کیا بات کر رہے ہیں آپ؟ کیا ہم اپنے سگے بھائی کو نہیں پہچانیں گے؟

بڑا بھائی:

کیا ہم اتنے کمینے ہیں؟

منجھلا بھائی:

کیا آپ نے ہمیں کوئی ذلیل سمجھا ہے کیا؟

بڑا بھائی:

کہ دو پیسے کے لیے ہم اپنے بھائی کو نہ پہچانیں؟

منجھلا بھائی (ہنستے ہوئے):

کم سے کم ایک آنہ تو کر دیجیے۔

گھوش (کچھ انگریزی میں):

یو اسکاؤنڈرلز۔ اچھا، اچھا۔

منجھلا بھائی (بنگلہ میں):

بورڈا، گھوش بابو خوب بھالو مانش۔

Reel Fourteen

Fade in. Morning. Abdul Sattar is walking on the road near the mental asylum garden.

Sattar:
Massage! Oil massage! *(3)*   Maalish. Tel maalish. Champi. *(3)*

Vijay sees Sattar through the bars of the barrier and stops him.

Vijay:
Sattar.   Sattar.

Sattar is terrified to see Vijay. He rubs his eyes thinking he has just seen a ghost. Squealing with fear, Sattar walks away.

Sattar:
A ghost!   Bhoot!
(closing his eyes, he repeats a chant)
O sweet Lord, Performer of miracles, make it vanish! *(3)*   Jalle-jalaal tu, saaheb-e-kamaal tu, aayi bala ko taal tu. *(3)*
(looking behind him and seeing no one there, he smiles with relief)
Gone!   Tal gayi…

Vijay grabs hold of Sattar through the bars.

Vijay:
Sattar.   Sattar.

Sattar:
Let go of my neck! This neck doesn't belong to me.   Gala chhod bhayi. Gala Sattar ka nahin hai.

रील १४

अगला दृश्य । सुबह । पागलख़ाने के क़रीब से अब्दुल सत्तार गुज़र रहा है ।

सत्तार:
मालिश । तेल मालिश । चंपी (३)

जाली के पीछे खड़ा विजय सत्तार को देखता है और उसे रोकता है ।

विजय:
सत्तार ।

विजय को देखकर सत्तार की बोलती बंद हो जाती है । वो आँखें मल कर उसे देखता है । उसे लगता है कि ये विजय का भूत है । डर से काँपता हुआ आगे भागता है ।

सत्तार:
भूत!
(आँखें बंद कर के मंत्र पढ़ रहा है)
जल्ले-जलाल तू, साहेब-ए-कमाल तू, आई बला को टाल तू (३)
(पलट कर देखता है तो किसी को न पाकर मुस्कुराता है)
टल गई...

लेकिन विजय जाली के पीछे से हाथ निकालकर उसे पकड़ लेता है ।

विजय:
सत्तार ।

सत्तार:
गला छोड़ भाई । गला सत्तार का नहीं ।

ریل ۱۴

اگلا منظر۔ صبح۔ پاگل خانے کے قریب سے عبدالستار گزر رہا ہے۔

ستار:
مالش۔ تیل مالش۔ چمپی (۳)

جالی کے پیچھے سے ستار کو وجے دیکھ کر روکتا ہے۔

وجے:
ستار۔

وجے کو دیکھ کر ستار کی گھگی بندھ جاتی ہے۔ وہ آنکھیں مل کر اُسے دیکھتا ہے۔ اُسے یقین ہو جاتا ہے کہ یہ وجے کا بھوت ہے۔ وہاں سے وہ فرار ہو جانا چاہتا ہے۔

ستار:
بھوت!
(وہ آنکھ بند کر کے ورد کرنے لگتا ہے)
جلہ جلالہٗ، صاحب کمال تٗو، آئی بلا کو ٹال تٗو۔(۳)
(پلٹ کر دیکھتا ہے تو کسی کونہ پاکر مسکراتا ہے)
ٹل گئی۔

لیکن وجے سلاخوں کے پیچھے سے ہاتھ ڈال کر اُس کا گلا پکڑ لیتا ہے۔

وجے:
ستار۔

ستار:
گلا چھوڑ بھائی، گلا ستار کا نہیں ہے۔

REEL 14   161

Vijay:
Sattar, it's me, Vijay.

Sattar, main hoon, Vijay.

Sattar:
Vijay? You? Aren't you dead yet?
(touching him)
He really is alive.

Vijay? Tu, tu, tu...tu mara nahin abhi tak?

Ye toh vaaqayi zinda hai.

Vijay:
Sattar, they're holding me here against my will.

Sattar, mujhe zabardasti bandh kar rakkha hai yahaan.

Sattar:
Really?

Achha?

Vijay:
Get me out somehow.

Kisi tarah nikalo mujhe yahaan se.

Sattar clicks his finger and heads to the entrance of the garden. He catches the guard's attention.[54]

Guard (curtly):
What do you want?

Kya chaahiye?

Sattar:
To whirl my hands on your head. Only if you let me. Massage!
Take your cap off. Oil massage!

Ji. Aap ke sar pe haath phiraana chaahta hoon. Ijaazat ho toh.
Maalish...
Topi pakadiye na. Champi.

Sattar sings while massaging the hapless guard's head.

Singer: Mohammed Rafi

If your head is reeling or your heart is sinking
Come to me, my friend, no point fretting
(Sattar gestures to Vijay to go)
No point fretting

Sar jo tera chakraaye ya dil dooba jaaye
Aaja pyare paas hamaare kaahe ghabraaye

Kaahe ghabraaye

(line spoken)
"Massage! Oil massage!"

"Maalish. Tel maalish."

विजय:

सत्तार, मैं हूँ, विजय।

सत्तार:

विजय? तू, तू, तू... तू मरा नहीं अभी तक?

(उसे छूते हुए)

ये तो वाक़ई ज़िंदा है।

विजय:

सत्तार, मुझे ज़बरदस्ती बाँध कर रक्खा है यहाँ।

सत्तार:

अच्छा?

विजय:

किसी तरह निकालो मुझे।

चुटकी बजाता हुआ सत्तार दरवाज़े की ओर जाता है। किसी तरह वह चौकीदार का ध्यान अपनी ओर करता है।

चौकीदार *(सख़्ती से)*:

क्या चाहिए?

सत्तार:

जी। आपके सर पे हाथ फिराना चाहता हूँ। इजाज़त हो तो? मालिश...
टोपी पकड़िये ना। चंपी...

चौकीदार का सर सहलाते हुए सत्तार गाता है।

गायक: मोहम्मद रफ़ी

सर जो तेरा चकराए या दिल डूबा जाए
आजा प्यारे पास हमारे काहे घबराए
(विजय को निकल जाने का इशारा करता है)
काहे घबराए

(पंक्ति बोलता है)
"मालिश। तेल मालिश।"

وجے:

ستار، میں ہوں، وجے۔

ستار:

وجے؟ تُو ، تُو ، تُو ۔۔ تُو مرا نہیں ابھی تک؟
(اُسے چھوتے ہوئے)
یہ تو واقعی زندہ ہے۔

وجے:

ستار، مجھے زبردستی بند کر رکھا ہے یہاں۔

ستار:

اچھا؟

وجے:

کسی طرح نکالو مجھے یہاں سے۔

اُنگلیاں چٹخا تا ہوا ستار گیٹ کی طرف جاتا ہے۔ دربان کو اپنی طرف کسی طرح متوجہ کرتا ہے۔

دربان (سختی سے):

کیا چاہیے؟

ستار:

جی۔ آپ کے سر پہ ہاتھ پھرانا چاہتا ہوں، اجازت ہو تو؟ مالش۔۔۔
ٹوپی پکڑیے نا۔ چمپی۔

دربان کا سر سہلاتے ہوئے ستار گاتا ہے۔

محمد رفیع کی آواز

سر جو تیرا چکرائے یا دل ڈوبا جائے
آ جا پیارے پاس ہمارے کاہے گھبرائے
(وجے کو نکل جانے کا اشارہ کرتا ہے)
کاہے گھبرائے

(صدا لگاتا ہے)
"مالش۔ تیل مالش۔"

If your head is reeling or your heart is sinking
(Vijay sneaks out of the gate while Sattar continues singing)
Come to me, my friend, no point fretting
No point fretting

Dissolve to Vijay's house. There is a padlock on the door. His two brothers arrive.

Vijay:
Brother.
(the brothers shrug their shoulders. Ignoring Vijay, they enter the house. He follows them into the courtyard)
Don't you recognise me? I'm Vijay, your brother. Why don't you say something? Don't you want to recognise me, either?

Elder brother *(to a shocked Vijay)*:
Are you mad? Vijay died a long time ago.

Middle brother:
Who invited you here? Have you no shame pretending to be our brother? Like hell, you are. Now get out of here. Hurry up! Out.

Vijay is pushed out of the door. Dissolve to Vijay getting onto a crowded bus.

Male passenger:
Gopu, where to?

Gopu:
To the Town Hall — they're going to commemorate Vijay's death anniversary. Will you come?

Male passenger:
Of course I will. Vijay was a great poet and a friend too.

Second passenger:
So you knew Vijay?

Sar jo tera chakraaye ya dil dooba jaaye

Aaja pyare paas hamaare kaahe ghabraaye
Kaahe ghabraaye

Bhayya. Bhayya.

Bhayya! Aap ne mujhe nahin pehchaana? Main Vijay hoon. Aap ka bhai. Aap chup kyun hain? Kya aap bhi nahin pehchaanna chaahte?

Paagal toh nahin ho gaye ho? Vijay toh kab ka mar chuka hai.

Maan na maan main tera mehmaan. Hamaara bhai bante tumhen sharam nahin aati? Tum hamaare kahaan se bhai ho? Chalo. Niklo. Niklo yahaan se. Jaldi niklo.

Gopu-da, kidhar?

Town Hall ja raha hoon. Swargwasi Vijay babu ki barsi manaayi ja rahi hai na. Chaloge saath mein?

Chalunga kaise nahin? Vijay babu itne bade shaayer toh thay hi, saath hi apne dost bhi thay.

O mahashay, Vijay babu ko jaante thay aap?

सर जो तेरा चकराए या दिल डूबा जाए
(विजय दरवाज़े से बाहर निकल जाता है। सत्तार का गाना जारी है)
आजा प्यारे पास हमारे काहे घबराए
काहे घबराए

दृश्य बदलकर विजय का घर नज़र आता है। दरवाज़े पर ताला लगा हुआ है। दोनों भाई आते हैं।

विजय:
भय्या। भय्या।
(अनजान बनते हुए दोनों भाई एक दूसरे को देखते हैं। दरवाज़ा खोल कर वो घर में दाख़िल होते हैं। विजय उनके पीछे-पीछे आँगन में आ जाता है)
भय्या! आपने मुझे नहीं पहचाना? मैं विजय हूँ। आपका भाई। आप चुप क्यूँ हैं। क्या आप भी नहीं पहचानना चाहते?

बड़ा भाई *(अचंभे में पड़े विजय से)*:
पागल तो नहीं हो गए हो? विजय तो कब का मर चुका है।

मंझला भाई:
मान ना मान मैं तेरा मेहमान। हमारा भाई बनते तुम्हें शरम नहीं आती? तुम हमारे कहाँ से भाई हो? चलो। निकलो। निकलो यहाँ से। जल्दी निकलो।

विजय का भाई उसे दरवाज़े से बाहर धकेल देता है। दृश्य बदलता है। विजय एक भीड़ से भरी बस में है।

यात्री:
गोपू-दा, किधर?

गोपू:
टाउन हॉल जा रहा हूँ। स्वर्गवासी विजय बाबू की बरसी मनाई जा रही है ना। चलोगे साथ में?

यात्री:
चलूँगा कैसे नहीं? विजय बाबू इतने बड़े शायर तो थे ही, साथ ही अपने दोस्त भी थे।

दूसरा यात्री:
ओ महाशय। विजय बाबू को जानते थे आप?

سر جو تیرا چکرائے یا دل ڈوبا جائے
(وجے گیٹ سے نکل جاتا ہے، ستار کا گانا جاری ہے)
آجا پیارے پاس ہمارے کاہے گھبرائے
کاہے گھبرائے

منظر بدل کر وجے کا گھر۔ دروازے پر تالا لگا ہوا ہے۔ اُس کے دونوں بھائی آتے ہیں۔

وجے:
بھیا۔ بھیا۔
(انجان بنتے ہوئے دونوں بھائی ایک دوسرے کو دیکھتے ہیں۔ دروازہ کھول کر وہ گھر میں داخل ہوتے ہیں وجے کے پیچھے پیچھے آنگن میں آجاتا ہے)
بھیا! آپ نے مجھے نہیں پہچانا؟ میں وجے ہوں۔ آپ کا بھائی۔ آپ چپ کیوں ہیں؟ کیا آپ بھی نہیں پہچاننا چاہتے؟

بڑا بھائی (حیرت زدہ وجے سے):
پاگل تو نہیں ہوگئے ہو؟ وجے تو کب کا مر چکا ہے۔

منجھلا بھائی:
مان نہ مان میں ترا مہمان۔ ہمارا بھائی بنتے تمہیں شرم نہیں آتی؟ تم ہمارے کہاں سے بھائی ہو؟ چلو۔ نکلو۔ نکلو یہاں سے۔ جلدی نکلو۔

وجے کا بھائی اُسے دروازے کے باہر دھکا دیتا ہے۔
منظر بدل کر ایک پُرہجوم بس میں وجے۔

ایک آدمی:
گوپو دا، کدھر؟

گوپو:
ٹاؤن ہال جا رہا ہوں۔ سورگواسی وجے بابو کی برسی منائی جارہی ہے نا۔ چلوگے ساتھ میں؟

آدمی:
چلوں گا کیسے نہیں؟ وجے بابو اتنے بڑے شاعر تو تھے ہی ساتھ ہی اپنے دوست بھی تھے۔

دوسرا آدمی:
او، مہاشے۔ وجے بابو کو جانتے تھے آپ؟

Male passenger:
Yes.

Ji haan.

Vijay overhears the men talking. He does not know the man who is claiming to be a friend.[55]

Gopu:
Come over here.

Toh phir yahin aa jao na.

Male passenger *(pushing Vijay out of the way):*
Just coming, Hey mister, don't block the way. Move aside.

Aata hoon. Ae mahashay, rasta roke kya khade ho? Hato na aage se.

Gopu:
Vijay was such a fine poet.

Bada hi achha shaayer tha Vijay.

Male passenger:
And a gem of a man. He often used to ask me for help.
(on a shot of Vijay listening to the man who is lying through his teeth)
If I hadn't helped him, he would've died six months sooner.

Arey heera aadmi tha, Gopu-da. Aksar mere paas madad maangne aaya karta tha.

Main na hota toh chhe mahine pehle hi mar gaya hota.

Gopu:
Died? How?

Mar gaya hota? Vo kaise?

Male passenger:
Of starvation.

Bhook se.

Gopu:
Is that right?

Oho, ho. Aise kya?

Male passenger *(getting off the bus):*
We're here. Hurry, or else we won't get a seat.

Arey jaldi karo. Town Hall aa gaya. Nahin toh jageh nahi milegi.

Cut from the bus interior to the Town Hall steps. Scores of people are entering the imposing building. Vijay pushes his way through the crowd and enters the hall. A large audience is gathered. Ghosh is standing at the stage mike. Much of his speech is over shots of Vijay at the doorway.

पहला यात्री:
जी हाँ।

विजय के कानों में लोगों की आवाज़ें पड़ती हैं। उसे नहीं पता कि उसके दोस्त होने का दावा करने वाले हैं कौन।

गोपू:
तो फिर यहीं आ जाओ ना।

यात्री *(विजय को धक्का देकर हटाते हुए):*
आता हूँ। ए महाशय, रास्ता रोके क्या खड़े हो? हटो ना आगे से।

गोपू:
बड़ा ही अच्छा शायर था विजय।

यात्री:
अरे हीरा आदमी था, गोपू-दा। अक्सर मेरे पास मदद माँगने आया करता था।
(विजय उस आदमी को सफेद झूठ बोलते हुए सुन रहा है)
मैं ना होता तो छह महीने पहले ही मर गया होता।

गोपू:
मर गया होता? वो कैसे?

यात्री:
भूख से।

गोपू:
ओहो, हो। ऐसे क्या?

यात्री *(बस से उतरते हुए):*
अरे जल्दी करो। टाउन हॉल आ गया। नहीं तो जगह नहीं मिलेगी।

बस का दृश्य बदलता है और टाउन हॉल की सीढ़ियाँ दिखाई देती हैं। लोगों की भीड़ इस शानदार इमारत में दाखिल हो रही है। भीड़ में से रास्ता बनाता हुआ विजय भी उस इमारत में दाखिल होता है। अंदर काफी मात्रा में भीड़ दिखाई देती है। घोष माईक पर कुछ कह रहा है, पर ज़्यादातर डायलॉग में विजय का चेहरा दिखता है, जो राहदारी में खड़ा है।

Ghosh:

Friends! As you know we are gathered to commemorate poet laureate Vijay's death. Last year, on this sad day, the world's great poet was taken from us in that terrible moment. I would have given my fortune and my life, if it were possible to save Vijay. But that was not to be. Why? Because of you all. It is said that Vijay took his own life, but in fact you killed him. If only Vijay were alive today, he would see the world that let him starve is now ready to weigh him in gold and silver. The world in which he was unknown is ready to crown him the king of their hearts, crown him with glory.
(over shot of Vijay at the doorway. He is in silhouette)
Rescue him from the clutches of poverty and give him a kingdom that he would rule.

Vijay answers in song, cut between tracking shots and close-up shots of Vijay, Ghosh, the Urdu publisher Shaikh, Gulaab, Juhi, Meena and Shyam.[56]

Singer: Mohammed Rafi

This world of palaces, of thrones, of crowns
This world of division, enemy of man
(both lines repeated)
This world of blind custom, hungry for wealth
Would I care if such a world were mine? *(2)*

Saahebaan! Aap log toh jaante hain ki shaayer-e-aazam Vijay marhoom ki barsi manaane hum log yahaan jama huwe hain. Pichhle saal isi din vo manhoos ghadi aayi thi jis ne duniya se itna bada shaayer chheen liya tha. Agar ho sakta toh main apni saari daulat luta kar bhi, khud mit kar bhi, Vijay ko bacha leta. Lekin aisa na ho saka. Kyun? Aap logon ki vajah se. Kehne ko toh duniya kehti hai ke Vijay ne apni jaan li, lekin dar-asal aap logon ne uski jaan li hai. Kaash aaj Vijay marhoom zinda hote toh vo dekh lete ki jis samaaj ne unhen bhooka maara, aaj wahi samaaj unhen heere aur jawahraat mein tolne ke liye tayyaar hai. Jis duniya mein vo gum-naam rahe, aaj wahi duniya unhen apne dilon ke takht pe bithaana chaahti hai. Unhen shohrat ka taaj pehnaana chaahti hai.

Unhen ghareebi aur muflisi ki galiyon se nikaal kar mehlon mein raj dilaana chaahti hai.

Ye mehlon, ye takhton, ye taajon ki duniya
Ye insaan ke dushman samaajon ki duniya
(both lines repeated)
Ye daulat ke bhooke rivaajon ki duniya
Ye duniya agar mil bhi jaaye toh kya hai *(2)*

घोष:

साहेबान! आप लोग तो जानते हैं कि शायर-ए-आज़म विजय मरहूम की बरसी मनाने हम लोग यहाँ जमा हुए हैं। पिछले साल इसी दिन वो मनहूस घड़ी आयी थी जिस ने दुनिया से इतना बड़ा शायर छीन लिया था। अगर हो सकता तो मैं अपनी सारी दौलत लुटा कर भी, ख़ुद मिट कर भी, विजय को बचा लेता। लेकिन ऐसा ना हो सका। क्यूँ? आप लोगों की वजह से। कहने को तो दुनिया कहती है कि विजय ने अपनी जान ली, लेकिन दर-असल आप लोगों ने उसकी जान ली है। काश आज विजय मरहूम ज़िंदा होते तो वो देख लेते कि जिस समाज ने उन्हें भूखा मारा, आज वही समाज उन्हें हीरे और जवाहरात में तोलने के लिए तैयार है। जिस दुनिया में वो गुमनाम रहे, आज वही दुनिया उन्हें अपने दिलों के तख़्त पे बिठाना चाहती है। उन्हें शोहरत का ताज पहनाना चाहती है।

(दरवाज़े की चौखट पर विजय का साया नज़र आ रहा है)

उन्हें ग़रीबी और मुफ़लिसी की गलियों से निकालकर महलों में राज दिलाना चाहती है।

विजय शायरी में जवाब देता है। गीत के बोलों पर विजय और भीड़ में से चेहरे नज़र आते हैं, जिन में घोष, उर्दू प्रकाशक शेख़, गुलाब, जूही, मीना और श्याम भी नज़र आ रहे हैं।

गायक: मोहम्मद रफ़ी

ये महलों, ये तख़्तों, ये ताजों की दुनिया
ये इन्साँ के दुश्मन समाजों की दुनिया
(दोनों पंक्तियाँ दोहराता है)
ये दौलत के भूखे रिवाजों की दुनिया
ये दुनिया अगर मिल भी जाए तो क्या है (२)

گھوش:

صاحبان! آپ لوگ تو جانتے ہیں کہ شاعرِ اعظم وجے مرحوم کی برسی منانے ہم لوگ یہاں جمع ہوئے ہیں۔ پچھلے سال اسی دن وہ منحوس گھڑی آئی تھی جس نے دنیا سے اتنا بڑا شاعر چھین لیا تھا۔ اگر ہوسکتا تو میں اپنی ساری دولت لٹا کر بھی، خود مٹ کر بھی، وجے کو بچالیتا۔ لیکن ایسا نہ ہوسکا۔ کیوں؟ آپ لوگوں کی وجہ سے۔ کہنے کو تو دنیا کہتی ہے کہ وجے نے اپنی جان لی۔ لیکن دراصل آپ لوگوں نے اُس کی جان لی ہے۔ جس سماج نے اُنھیں بھوکا مارا، آج وہی سماج اُنھیں ہیرے اور جواہرات میں تولنے کے لیے تیار ہے۔ جس دنیا میں وہ گمنام رہے آج وہی دنیا اُنھیں اپنے دلوں کے تخت پہ بٹھانا چاہتی ہے۔ اُنھیں شہرت کا تاج پہنانا چاہتی ہے۔

(دروازے کی چوکھٹ میں وجے کا سایہ نظر آرہا ہے)

اُنھیں غربی اور مفلسی کی گلیوں سے نکال کر محلوں میں راج دلانا چاہتی ہے۔

وجے شاعری میں جواب دیتا ہے۔ گیت کے بول پر وجے اور سامعین کے چہرے نظر آتے ہیں۔ جن میں گھوش، اُردو پبلشر شیخ، گلاب، جوہی، مینا اور شیام بھی نظر آ رہے ہیں۔

محمد رفیع کی آواز۔

یہ محلوں، یہ تختوں، یہ تاجوں کی دنیا
یہ انساں کے دشمن سماجوں کی دنیا
(دونوں لائنیں دہراتا ہے)
یہ دولت کے بھوکے رواجوں کی دنیا
یہ دنیا اگر مل بھی جائے تو کیا ہے (۲)

Bodies wounded, souls thirsting
Confusion in eyes, despondency in hearts
Is this a world or a place of bewilderment?
Would I care if such a world were mine? (2)

Hearing his song, Gulaab is the only one who is overwhelmed with happiness to see him alive.

Here a man's life is a plaything
Here live worshippers of the dead
Here life has no value, death comes cheaper
Would I care if such a world were mine? (2)

Youth strays into crime
Young bodies are adorned for the marketplace
Here love is another name for trade
Would I care if such a world were mine? (2)

This world where man counts for nothing
Loyalty and friendship count for nothing
(both lines are repeated, as Ghosh orders his henchmen to throw Vijay out)
Where love has no importance
Would I care if such a world were mine? (2)

Ghosh's henchmen drag Vijay towards the exit

Burn it, blow this world away
Burn it! (2)
Burn it, blow this world away

Har ik jism ghaayal, har ik rooh pyaasi
Nigaahon mein uljhan, dilon mein udaasi
Ye duniya hai ya aalam-e-bad-hawaasi
Ye duniya agar mil bhi jaaye toh kya hai (2)

Yahaan ik khilauna hai insaan ki hasti
Ye basti hai murda-paraston ki basti
Yahaan par toh jivan se hai maut sasti
Ye duniya agar mil bhi jaaye toh kya hai (2)

Jawaani bhatakti hai badkaar ban kar
Jawaan jism sajte hain baazaar ban kar
Yahaan pyar hota hai biyopaar ban kar
Ye duniya agar mil bhi jaaye toh kya hai (2)

Ye duniya jahaan aadmi kuchh nahin hai
Wafa kuchh nahin, dosti kuchh nahin hai
(both lines repeated)
Jahaan pyar ki qadr hi kuchh nahin hai
Ye duniya agar mil bhi jaaye toh kya hai (2)

Jala do ise phoonk daalo ye duniya
Jala do, jala do
Jala do ise phoonk daalo ye duniya

हर इक जिस्म घायल, हर इक रूह प्यासी

निगाहों में उलझन, दिलों में उदासी

ये दुनिया है या आलमे-बद-हवासी

ये दुनिया अगर मिल भी जाए तो क्या है (२)

गुलाब ही एक व्यक्ति है जो विजय को गाता देख बेहद खुश होती है कि वो
ज़िंदा है।

यहाँ इक खिलौना है इन्साँ की हस्ती

ये बस्ती है मुर्दा-परस्तों की बस्ती

यहाँ पर तो जीवन से है मौत सस्ती

ये दुनिया अगर मिल भी जाए तो क्या है (२)

जवानी भटकती है बदकार बन कर

जवाँ जिस्म सजते हैं बाज़ार बन कर

यहाँ प्यार होता है ब्योपार बन कर

ये दुनिया अगर मिल भी जाए तो क्या है (२)

ये दुनिया जहाँ आदमी कुछ नहीं है

वफ़ा कुछ नहीं, दोस्ती कुछ नहीं है

(दोनों पंक्तियों के दोहराते वक़्त घोष का चेहरा दिखाई देता है, जो अपने गुंडों से कह रहा है कि
विजय को उठवाकर बाहर फेंक दो)

जहाँ प्यार की क़द्र ही कुछ नहीं है

ये दुनिया अगर मिल भी जाए तो क्या है (२)

घोष के गुंडे विजय को पकड़ कर बाहर की तरफ खींच रहे हैं।

जला दो इसे फूँक डालो ये दुनिया

जला दो, जला दो

जला दो इसे फूँक डालो ये दुनिया

Take this world away from my sight
Take charge of this world, it's all yours
Would I care if such a world were mine?

Mere saamne se hata lo ye duniya
Tumhaari hai tum hi sambhaalo ye duniya
Ye duniya agar mil bhi jaaye toh kya hai

Shyam switches the lights off at the mains and the hall is plunged into darkness.

Reel Fifteen

A stampede follows. In the violent pushing and shoving, Vijay is freed from the grip of Ghosh's henchmen. The publisher Shaikh is among the crowd and is looking desperately for Vijay. He finally manages to find him and embraces Vijay as though he were meeting an old friend. Meanwhile Gulaab struggles to escape. In the pandemonium, she is pushed to the ground and trampled underfoot. Juhi manages to take the injured Gulaab to safety.

Fade out.

Fade in. Night. Shyam has come to Ghosh's house.

Ghosh *(angry):*
Why are you sitting here? Go and stop his brothers! Give them ten thousand, twenty thousand — anything they want, but they mustn't identify Vijay.

Baithe kya ho? Jaao unn bhaaiyon ko roko. Das hazaar, bees hazaar, jitna bhi unko chaahiye unko do lekin unko Vijay ke pehchaanne se roko.

Shyam:[57]
Mr. Ghosh, even if you were the ten-headed demon, you cannot stop Vijay from being identified now. How many will you silence?

Agar aap ke dus sar bhi hon, Ghosh babu, toh bhi aap Vijay ko naqli saabit nahin kar sakte. Kis-kis ka moonh bandh karenge aap?

Ghosh *(unseen, Meena is watching them):*
I'll spend money like water. I'll buy everyone. But I don't want it proved that he's the real Vijay. Or else our name will be mud. We'll be finished.

Main daulat paani ki tarah baha doonga. Har shakhs ko khareed loonga lekin ye saabit nahin hona chaahiye ki ye Vijay asli Vijay hai — warna hamaari izzat mitti mein mil jaayegi. Hum kahin ke nahin rahenge.

मेरे सामने से हटा लो ये दुनिया

तुम्हारी है तुम ही संभालो ये दुनिया

ये दुनिया अगर मिल भी जाए तो क्या है

श्याम हॉल के अंदर की बिजली काट देता है और अंधेरा छा जाता है ।

रील १५

अंधेरे के कारण हॉल में भगदड़ मच जाती है । विजय गुंडों के हाथों से छूट जाता है । उर्दू प्रकाशक शेख इस हड़बड़ी में विजय को ढूंढ रहा है । अन्त में उसे विजय मिल जाता है और वो किसी पुराने दोस्त की तरह उसे गले लगा लेता है । इस बीच गुलाब इस भगदड़ से निकलने की कोशिश कर रही है । उसे लोग ज़मीन पर गिरा देते हैं । जूही उसकी मदद के लिए आती है और ज़ख़्मी गुलाब को उठा कर बाहर ले जाती है ।

दृश्य बदलता है ।

अगला दृश्य । रात । घोष का मकान । श्याम उससे मिलने आया है ।

घोष (गुस्से में):
बैठे क्या हो? जाओ उन भाईयों को रोको । दस हज़ार, बीस हज़ार, जितना भी उनको चाहिए उनको दो, लेकिन उनको विजय के पहचानने से रोको ।

श्याम:
अगर आपके दस सर भी हों, घोष बाबू, तो भी आप विजय को नकली साबित नहीं कर सकते । किस-किस का मुँह बंद करेंगे आप?

घोष (मीना उन्हें छुपकर देख रही है):
मैं दौलत पानी की तरह बहा दूँगा । हर शख़्स को ख़रीद लूँगा । लेकिन ये साबित नहीं होना चाहिए कि ये विजय असली विजय है – वरना हमारी इज़्ज़त मिट्टी में मिल जाएगी । हम कहीं के नहीं रहेंगे ।

میرے سامنے سے ہٹا لو یہ دنیا

تمہاری ہے تم ہی سنبھالو یہ دنیا

یہ دنیا اگر مل بھی جائے تو کیا ہے

شیام ہال کی بجلی کاٹ دیتا ہے اور اندھیرا چھا جاتا ہے ۔

ریل ۱۵

اندھیرے ہال میں وجے غنڈوں کے ہاتھوں سے چھوٹ جاتا ہے ۔ اس بھگدڑ میں وجے غنڈوں کے ہاتھوں سے چھوٹ جاتا ہے ۔ اردو پبلشر شیخ اس افراتفری میں وجے کو تلاش کر رہا ہے ۔ آخرکار اسے وجے مل جاتا ہے اور وہ کسی پرانے دوست کی طرح اسے گلے سے لگا لیتا ہے ۔ ۔ ۔ اس دوران گلاب بھگدڑ سے نکلنے کی کوشش کر رہی ہے ۔ اسے لوگ زمین پر گرا دیتے ہیں ۔ جوہی اس کی مدد کے لیے آتی ہے ۔ زخمی گلاب کو اٹھا کر لوگ باہر لے جاتے ہیں ۔ منظر بدلتا ہے ۔

اگلا منظر ۔

رات ۔ گھوش کا مکان ۔ شیام اس سے ملنے آیا ہے ۔

گھوش (غصے میں):
بیٹھے کیا ہو؟ جاؤ ان بھائیوں کو روکو ۔ دس ہزار، بیس ہزار جتنا بھی ان کو چاہیے ان کو دو ۔ لیکن ان کو وجے کے پہچاننے سے روکو ۔

شیام:
اگر آپ کے دس سر بھی ہوں، گھوش بابو، تو بھی آپ وجے کو نقلی ثابت نہیں کر سکتے ۔ کس کس کا منہ بند کریں گے آپ؟

گھوش (مینا انہیں چھپ کر دیکھ رہی ہے):
میں دولت پانی کی طرح بہا دوں گا ۔ ہر شخص کو خرید لوں گا ۔ لیکن یہ ثابت نہیں ہونا چاہیے کہ یہ وجے اصلی وجے ہے ۔ ۔ ۔ ورنہ ہماری عزت مٹی میں مل جائے گی ۔ ہم کہیں کے نہیں رہیں گے ۔

Shyam:
Save yourself, sir. I know how to turn things in my favour in no time at all.

Ghosh:
Meaning? Oh, so you think you'll get away with it so easily? Don't forget you disowned him at the mental asylum. You bore witness against him.

Meena's expression turns to shock.

Shyam:
I see which way the wind is blowing. I followed you when it was in my interest, now I'll ally Vijay to better interest.

Ghosh (in English):
You scoundrel. Get out!

Shyam:
Good day to you, sir.

Ghosh (in English):
I said get out.

As Shyam is leaving, his hat slips off his head and lands near the door. He does not return to pick it up, but slowly drags his hat out with his cane. Dissolve to Shaikh's office. Shyam enters.

Visitor (off-screen):
Well, Shaikh saaheb, have you won the lottery?

Shaikh:
Not yet! But I have my hands on the king of fame. Vijay is in my clutches. I'll earn millions by publishing his poems.

Aap apni khair maanayiye, huzoor. Banda toh apna kaam yun bana lega.

Tumhaara matlab? Oh, tum samajhte ho ki tum aasaani se apni jaan chhuda sakte ho? Par ye na bhoolo ki tum ne bhi paagalkhaane mein uske khilaaf bayaan diya tha.

Hawa ka rukh dekh ke baat karte hain apan. Jab aap ka palla bhaari tha toh aap ke saath thay, ab Vijay ka palla bhaari hai toh uske saath jaayenge.

Aadaab arz hai. Aadaab arz hai.

Kyun, Shaikh saaheb, satta bazar mein koi number lag gaya hai kya?

Abey nahin! Shohrat ke baazaar ka baadshaah haath aa gaya hai. Vijay meri mutthi mein hai. Uski nazmen chhaapunga aur laakhon kamaaunga.

श्याम:
आप अपनी ख़ैर मनाईये, हुज़ूर। बंदा तो अपना काम यूँ बना लेगा।

घोष:
तुम्हारा मतलब? ओह, तुम समझते हो कि तुम आसानी से अपनी जान छुड़ा सकते हो। पर ये ना भूलो कि तुम ने भी पागलख़ाने में उसके ख़िलाफ़ बयान दिया था।

उनकी बातें सुन कर मीना को सदमा पहुँचता है।

श्याम:
हवा का रुख़ देख के बात करते हैं अपन। जब आपका पल्ला भारी था तो आपके साथ थे, अब विजय का पल्ला भारी है तो उसके साथ जाएँगे।

घोष *(अंग्रेज़ी में):*
यू स्क्राउंड्रल। गेट आउट!

श्याम:
आदाब अर्ज़ है। आदाब अर्ज़ है।

घोष *(अंग्रेज़ी में):*
आय सेड गेट आउट।

श्याम जाने लगता है तब उसकी टोपी दरवाज़े की चौखट पर गिर जाती है। वो बाहर से ही अपनी छड़ी से टोपी को खींच लेता है। दृश्य बदलता है और शेख़ का दफ़्तर दिखाई देता है। श्याम दाख़िल होता है।

मुलाक़ाती *(ऑफ़ स्क्रीन):*
क्यूँ, शेख़ साहब, सट्टा बाज़ार में कोई नंबर लग गया है क्या?

शेख़:
अबे नहीं! शोहरत के बाज़ार का बादशाह हाथ आ गया है। विजय मेरी मुट्ठी में है। उसकी नज़्में छापूँगा और लाखों कमाऊँगा।

شیام:
آپ اپنی خیر منائیے، حضور۔ بندہ تو اپنا کام یوں بنا لے گا۔

گھوش:
تمہارا مطلب؟ اوہ، تم سمجھتے ہو کہ تم آسانی سے اپنی جان چھڑا سکتے ہو۔ پر یہ نہ بھولو کہ تم نے بھی پاگل خانے میں اُس کے خلاف بیان دیا تھا۔

اُن کی کہانی سن کر مینا کو صدمہ پہنچتا ہے۔

شیام:
ہوا کا رخ دیکھ کے بات کرتے ہیں اپن۔ جب آپ کا پلّہ بھاری تھا تو آپ کے ساتھ تھے۔ اب وجے کا پلّہ بھاری ہے تو اُس کے ساتھ جائیں گے۔

گھوش (انگریزی میں):
یو اسکاؤنڈرل۔ گیٹ آؤٹ!

شیام:
آداب عرض ہے۔ آداب عرض ہے۔

گھوش (انگریزی میں):
آئی سیڈ گیٹ آؤٹ۔

شیام جانے لگتا ہے تو اُس کی ٹوپی دروازے کی چوکھٹ پر گر جاتی ہے۔ وہ باہر ہی سے اپنی چھڑی سے ٹوپی کو کھینچ لیتا ہے۔ منظر بدل کر شیخ کا آفس دکھائی دیتا ہے۔ شیام داخل ہوتا ہے۔

ایک آدمی (آف اسکرین):
کیوں، شیخ صاحب، سٹّے بازار میں کوئی نمبر لگ گیا ہے کیا؟

شیخ:
ابے نہیں! شہرت کے بازار کا بادشاہ ہاتھ آ گیا ہے۔ وجے میری مٹھی میں ہے۔ اُس کی نظمیں چھاپوں گا اور لاکھوں کماؤں گا۔

Shyam:
Excellent! I admire you, Shaikhji. You have found a veritable gold mine, but do you think you can mine it all alone? You'll have to share it with me.

Bahot achhe. Bahot achhe. Bhai, maan gaye, Shaikhji. Khoob murgha phaansa hai aap ne, lekin kya aap usay akele hazam kar sakenge? Uh huh. Baant ke khaana hoga.

Shaikh (to his staff):
You idiots! What are you gawping at? Get out of here. Go on! Be off!

Ein? Kambakhto! Huqqe jaisa moonh phailaaye tum log kya dekhte ho? Jaao bhaago yahaan se, jaao.

(to his assistant Khairati)
Well, are you going?

Jaata hai ki nahin? Jao.

(to Shyam)
Young man, you are a most arrogant type. To whom have I the honour?

Janaab, nihaayat hi be-hooda qism ke insaan hain aap. Aap ki taareef?

Shyam:
No honour is high enough for me. I can identify Vijay, if I so choose. And if I don't, I can have him locked away in a mental asylum.

Jitni bhi ki jaaye kam hai. Chaahun toh aap ke murghe ko pehchaan kar Vijay bana doon, aur chaahun toh usay na pehchaan kar paagalkhaane ka ticket katwa doon.

Shaikh:
Of course! Your father is the head of state, so you can commit anyone you want to the mental asylum. If you don't identify him, do you think his brothers won't?

Aji haan, aap ke baba ka raj hai? Jise chaahen paagalkhaane bhijwa den? Aap na pehchaanege usay toh kya uske bhai bhi na pehchaanege?

Vijay's brothers step forward.

Middle brother:
Why shouldn't we recognise him?

Kyun na pehchaanege?

Elder brother:
Of course we will.

Zaroor pehchaanege.

Middle brother:
He's my brother, after all.

Aakhir bhai jo thehre.

Elder brother:
So what if he did not care about us?

Uss ne bhale hi hamaari parwaah na ki ho.

Middle brother:
So what if others have profited from his work?

Uski nazmon se bhale hi doosron ko faayeda huwa ho.

श्याम:

बहुत अच्छे। बहुत अच्छे। भाई, मान गए, शेख़जी। ख़ूब मुर्ग़ा फाँसा है आपने, लेकिन क्या आप उसे अकेले हज़म कर सकेंगे? ऊँ हूँ। बाँट के खाना होगा।

शेख़ (अपने आदमियों से):

ऐं? कमबख़्तो! हुक्के जैसा मुँह फैलाए तुम लोग क्या देखते हो? जाओ भागो यहाँ से, जाओ। भागो।

(अपने सहायक ख़ैराती से)

जाता है कि नहीं? जाओ।

(श्याम से)

जनाब, निहायत ही बेहूदा क़िस्म के इन्सान हैं आप। आपकी तारीफ़?

श्याम:

जितनी भी की जाए कम है। चाहूँ तो आपके मुर्ग़े को पहचान कर विजय बना दूँ, और चाहूँ तो उसे ना पहचान कर पागलख़ाने का टिकट कटवा दूँ।

शेख़:

अजी हाँ, आपके बाबा का राज है? जिसे चाहें पागलख़ाने भिजवा दें। आप ना पहचानेंगे उसे तो क्या उसके भाई भी ना पहचानेंगे?

विजय के दोनों भाई सामने आते हैं।

मंझला भाई:

क्यूँ ना पहचानेंगे?

बड़ा भाई:

ज़रूर पहचानेंगे।

मंझला भाई:

आख़िर भाई जो ठहरे।

बड़ा भाई:

उसने भले ही हमारी परवाह ना की हो।

मंझला भाई:

उसकी नज़्मों से भले ही दूसरों को फ़ायदा हुआ हो।

شیام:

بہت اچھے۔ بہت اچھے۔ بھئی، مان گئے، شیخ جی۔ خوب مرغا پھانسا ہے آپ نے، لیکن کیا آپ اُسے اکیلے ہضم کر سکیں گے؟ اوہوں۔ بانٹ کے کھانا ہوگا۔

شیخ (اپنے اسٹاف سے):

ایں؟ کمجنو! حقے جیسا منہ پھیلائے تم لوگ کیا دیکھتے ہو؟ جاؤ بھاگو یہاں سے، جاؤ۔ بھاگو۔

(اپنے اسسٹنٹ خیراتی سے)

جاتا ہے کہ نہیں۔ جاؤ۔

(شیام سے)

جناب، نہایت ہی بیہودہ قسم کے انسان ہیں آپ۔ آپ کی تعریف؟

شیام:

جتنی بھی کی جائے کم ہے۔ چاہوں تو آپ کے مرغے کو پہچان کر وجے بنا دوں، اور چاہوں تو اُسے نہ پہچان کر پاگل خانے کا ٹکٹ کٹوا دوں۔

شیخ:

اجی ہاں، آپ کے بابا کا راج ہے؟ جسے چاہیں پاگل خانے بھجوا دیں۔ آپ نہ پہچانیں گے اُسے تو کیا اُس کے بھائی بھی نہ پہچانیں گے؟

وجے کے بھائی سامنے آتے ہیں۔

منجھلا بھائی:

کیوں نہ پہچانیں گے؟

بڑا بھائی:

ضرور پہچانیں گے۔

منجھلا بھائی:

آخر بھائی جو ٹھہرے۔

بڑا بھائی:

اُس نے بھلے ہی ہماری پرواہ نہ کی ہو۔

منجھلا بھائی:

اُس کی نظموں سے بھلے ہی دوسروں کو فائدہ ہوا ہو۔

Elder brother:
He is our blood, isn't he?

Phir bhi hamaara hi khoon hai na?

Middle brother:
So why shouldn't we identify him?

Phir kyun nahin pehchaanege?

Shaikh:
Well done! That answers this joker once and for all. Hear that, mister? Brothers will always be brothers.

Shaabaash! Moonh todd jawaab diya hai aap ne is maskhare ko. Dekha, miyaan? Bhai phir bhi bhai hain.

Elder brother:
That's right. I spent 5,000 on his education.

Ji. Uski likhaayi-padhaayi par paanch hazaar rupay kharch kiye hain.

Middle brother:
4,000 to feed him.

Khilaayi-pilaayi par chaar hazaar.

Elder brother:
If we had loaned that at interest we would have 15,000 now.

Ye nau hazaar rupiya biyaaj par dete toh pandrah hazaar rupay khade karte.

Middle brother:
Will you pay 15,000 rupees to have him identified?

Usay pehchaanne ki qeemat pandrah hazaar doge?

Shaikh:
What? Fifteen thousand?

Ji? Pandrah hazaar?

Middle brother:
Yes. Fifteen thousand.

Ji. Pandrah hazaar.

Shaikh (wiping the sweat off his brow):
Gentlemen, you have your precious brother back, what more could you want?

Saahebaan, aap logon ko jeeta-jaagta anmol bhai mil raha hai, aur aap logon ko kya chaahiye?

बड़ा भाई:

फिर भी हमारा ही ख़ून है ना?

मंझला भाई:

फिर क्यूँ नहीं पहचानेंगे?

शेख़:

शाबाश! मुँह तोड़ जवाब दिया है आपने इस मसख़रे को। देखा मियाँ? भाई फिर भी भाई हैं।

बड़ा भाई:

जी। उसकी लिखाई-पढ़ाई पर पाँच हज़ार रुपये ख़र्च किए हैं।

मंझला भाई:

खिलाई-पिलाई पर चार हज़ार।

बड़ा भाई:

ये नौ हज़ार रुपिये ब्याज पर देते तो पंद्रह हज़ार रुपये खड़े करते।

मंझला भाई:

उसे पहचानने की क़ीमत पंद्रह हज़ार दोगे?

शेख़:

जी? पंद्रह हज़ार?

मंझला भाई:

जी। पंद्रह हज़ार।

शेख़ (अपने माथे से पसीना पोंछते हुए):

साहेबान, आप लोगों को जीता-जागता अनमोल भाई मिल रहा है और आप लोगों को क्या चाहिए?

Middle brother:
Old man, we don't want a brother, we want money. Money.

Bhai miyaan, hamen bhai-waai nahin, rupiya chaahiye, rupiya.

Elder brother:
We can't marinate him, can we?

Uss bhai ka achaar daalenge kya?

Vijay's brothers, Shaikh and Shyam are horrified to see Vijay is listening to their conversation. The middle brother feigns delight.

Middle brother:
Vijay, my brother!

Vijay! Vijay, mera bhai.

Dissolve to a short montage showing newspapers roll off the press. Shaikh and Vijay's brothers are ecstatic.

Dissolve to a packed auditorium in the Town Hall. Vijay stands at the stage mike.

Audience member (*aggressively*):
Is he Vijay? What proof do you have?

Ye Vijay hai? Iska kya saboot hai aap ke paas?

Sattar:
What rubbish! Sit down! Soon you'll say I'm not Sattar. Just listen to their nonsense.

Le. Abey baith ja jageh pe. Kal ko toh tu bolega hum Sattar bhai nahin hai. Sunn toh inki baat.

Second audience member:
Why should we accept he is Vijay?

Hum kaise maanen ki ye Vijay hai?

Third audience member:
If he is Vijay, then who came under the train and was mutilated beyond recognition?

Agar ye Vijay hai toh vo kaun tha jo rail ke neeche aa kar kat gaya?

Elder brother (*stepping forward. He has a triumphant expression*):
We prove it. We are Vijay's brothers.

Saboot hum hain. Hum Vijay ke bhai hain.

Middle brother:
Everyone in the neighbourhood knows we're Vijay's brothers. And we say he is Vijay.

Sara muhalla jaanta hai Vijay hamaara bhai hai. Aur hum kehte hain yahi Vijay hai.

मंझला भाई:
भाई मियाँ, हमें भाई-वाई नहीं रुपिया चाहिए। रुपिया।

बड़ा भाई:
उस भाई का अचार डालेंगे क्या?

विजय के भाई, शेख़ और श्याम यह देखकर परेशान हो जाते हैं कि विजय उनकी सारी बातें सुन रहा है। मंझला भाई झूठी ख़ुशी जताते हुए।

मंझला भाई:
विजय! विजय, मेरा भाई।

मोन्ताज। अख़बार की कॉपियाँ निकल रही हैं। शेख़ और विजय के भाई ख़ुश हैं।

अगला दृश्य। टाउन हॉल लोगों से भरा है। विजय स्टेज पर माईक के सामने खड़ा है।

एक श्रोता *(उत्तेजित होकर):*
ये विजय है? इसका क्या सबूत है आपके पास?

सत्तार:
ले। अबे बैठ जा जगह पे। कल को तो तू बोलेगा हम सत्तार भाई नहीं है। सुन तो इनकी बात।

दूसरा श्रोता:
हम कैसे मानें कि ये विजय है?

तीसरा श्रोता:
अगर ये विजय है तो वो कौन था जो रेल के नीचे आकर कट गया?

बड़ा भाई *(दावे के साथ खड़ा होकर):*
सबूत हम हैं। हम विजय के भाई हैं।

मंझला भाई:
सारा मोहल्ला जानता है विजय हमारा भाई है। और हम कहते हैं यही विजय है।

منجھلا بھائی:
بھائی میاں، ہمیں بھائی وائی نہیں، روپیہ چاہیے۔ روپیہ۔

بڑا بھائی:
اُس بھائی کا اچار ڈالیں گے کیا؟

وجے کے بھائی، شیخ اور شیام یہ دیکھ کر پریشان ہو جاتے ہیں کہ وجے نے اُن کی باتیں بھی سن لی ہیں۔ منجھلا بھائی مکاری سے کہتا ہے۔

منجھلا بھائی:
وجے! وجے، میرا بھائی۔

مونتاج۔ اخبار کی کاپیاں نکل رہی ہیں۔ شیخ اور وجے کے بھائی خوش نظر آرہے ہیں۔

اگلا منظر۔ ٹاؤن ہال لوگوں سے کھچا کھچ بھرا ہوا ہے۔ اسٹیج پر وجے مائک کے سامنے کھڑا ہے۔

پہلا آدمی (ڈپٹ کے):
یہ وجے ہے؟ اس کا کیا ثبوت ہے آپ کے پاس؟

ستار:
لے۔ ابے بیٹھ جا جگہ پہ۔ کل کو تو بولے گا ہم ستار بھائی نہیں ہے۔ سن تو ان کی بات۔

دوسرا آدمی:
ہم کیسے مانیں کہ یہ وجے ہے؟

تیسرا آدمی:
اگر یہ وجے ہے تو وہ کون تھا جو ریل کے نیچے آکر کٹ گیا؟

بڑا بھائی (دعوے کے ساتھ کھڑا ہوکر):
ثبوت ہم ہیں۔ ہم وجے کے بھائی ہیں۔

منجھلا بھائی:
سارا محلّہ جانتا ہے وجے ہمارا بھائی ہے۔ اور ہم کہتے ہیں یہی وجے ہے۔

As Vijay's brothers, Shyam and Shaikh declare that the man who stands before them is none other than Vijay, two verses from the song "Ye duniya agar mil bhi jaaye"(Would I care if such a world were mine?) underscore the scene. Vijay looks incredulously at his false friends.

Shyam:
I prove it. I confirm he is Vijay, my boyhood friend.

Saboot main bhi hoon. Vijay mere bachpan ka dost tha aur main kehta hoon ki yahi Vijay hai.

Shaikh:
The poet laureate Vijay!

Shaayer-e-aazam Vijay!

Crowd:
Long live!

Zindabad.

The crowd's enthusiastic cries are drowned in the background song.

Singer: Mohammed Rafi

Here life has no value, death comes cheaper
Would I care if such a world were mine? *(2)*

Yahaan par toh jivan se hai maut sasti
Ye duniya agar mil bhi jaaye toh kya hai *(2)*

Vijay stares at the crowd. Meena is delighted that Vijay is famous at last.

Vijay *(at the mike)*:
Gentlemen!

Saahebaan!

A man in the audience silences the noisy crowd.

विजय के भाई, श्याम और शेख़ इस बात को साबित कर रहे हैं कि उनके सामने जो इन्सान खड़ा है वो विजय ही है। बैकग्राउँड में "ये दुनिया अगर मिल भी जाए" के दो शेर गूंज रहे हैं। विजय अचंभे से उन सबको देख रहा है।

श्याम:
सबूत मैं भी हूँ। विजय मेरे बचपन का दोस्त था और मैं कहता हूँ कि यही विजय है।

शेख़:
शायर-ए-आज़म विजय!

भीड़:
ज़िंदाबाद।

बैकग्राउँड में गूंजने वाला गीत भीड़ की आवाज़ में गुम हो जाता है।

गायक: मोहम्मद रफ़ी

यहाँ पर तो जीवन से है मौत सस्ती
ये दुनिया अगर मिल भी जाए तो क्या है (२)

विजय भीड़ को देखे जा रहा है। मीना यह देखकर मुस्कुराती है कि आख़िर विजय को शोहरत मिल ही गई।

विजय (माईक पर):
साहेबान!

भीड़ में अब भी शोर मचा है। एक आदमी भीड़ को शांत कराता है।

وجے کے بھائی، شیام اور شیخ اس بات کو ثابت کر رہے ہیں کہ اُن کے سامنے کھڑا ایسی شخص وجے ہے، بیک گراؤنڈ میں ''یہ دنیا اگر مل بھی جائے'' کے دو شعر گونج رہے ہیں۔ وجے حیرت سے ان لوگوں کو تک رہا ہے۔

شیام:
ثبوت میں بھی ہوں۔ وجے میرے بچپن کا دوست تھا اور میں کہتا ہوں کہ یہی وجے ہے۔

شیخ:
شاعرِ اعظم، وجے!

مجمع:
زندہ باد۔

بیک گراؤنڈ میں گونجنے والا گیت ہجوم کے شور پر غالب آ جاتا ہے۔

محمد رفیع کی آواز۔

یہاں پر تو جیون سے ہے موت سستی
یہ دنیا اگر مل بھی جائے تو کیا ہے (2)

وجے، ہجوم کو دیکھے جا رہا ہے۔ مینا یہ دیکھ کر مسکراتی ہے کہ آخر وجے کو شہرت مل ہی گئی۔

وجے (مائک پر):
صاحبان!

ہجوم اب بھی شور مچائے جا رہا ہے۔ ایک آدمی اُنھیں خاموش کرواتا ہے۔

Audience member:
Be quiet. Vijay wishes to say a few words. Quiet!

Chup ho jayiye. Vijay babu kuchh farma rehe hain. Chup ho jayiye.

Vijay:
Friends! The Vijay you are ready to accept with open arms… the Vijay for whom you shout slogans…I am not that Vijay.

Saahebaan! Jis Vijay ko aaj aap haathon-haath lene ke liye tayyaar hain, jis Vijay ke naam pe aap zindabad ke naare laga rahe hain — main vo Vijay nahin hoon.

Crowd (many stand up):
What?

Kya?

Both brothers (in unison):
Vijay!

Vijay!

Vijay (firmly):
I'm not Vijay.

Main Vijay nahin hoon.

Audience member:
If you aren't Vijay, why have you been deceiving us?

Tum Vijay nahin ho toh abhi tak hamen dhoke mein kyun rakkha?

Second audience member:
Brothers! I always said he was an imposter.

Bhaaiyo! Main pehle hi kehta tha ye koi dhongi hai.

Third audience member:
A publicity-seeker.

Muft ki publicity chaahta hai.

Crowd (shouting):
Hit him!

Maaro isay!

एक श्रोता:

चुप हो जाईए। विजय बाबू कुछ फ़रमा रहे हैं। चुप हो जाईए।

विजय:

साहेबान! जिस विजय को आज आप हाथों-हाथ लेने के लिए तैयार हैं, जिस विजय
के नाम पे आप ज़िंदाबाद के नारे लगा रहे हैं – मैं वो विजय नहीं हूँ।

भीड़ *(कुछ लोग खड़े होकर)*:

क्या?

दोनों भाई *(एक साथ)*:

विजय!

विजय *(दृढ़ता से)*:

मैं विजय नहीं हूँ।

एक श्रोता:

तुम विजय नहीं तो अभी तक हमें धोखे में क्यूँ रखा?

दूसरा श्रोता:

भाईयों! मैं पहले ही कहता था ये कोई ढोंगी है।

तीसरा श्रोता:

मुफ़्त की पब्लिसिटी चाहता है।

भीड़ *(चीख़ते हुए)*:

मारो इसे!

Vijay is stunned to see the audience have so quickly turned against him.[58] Pandemonium breaks out. A group of angry men surge towards the stage and soon Vijay's admiring fans turn into a lynch mob. They attack Vijay, tear his clothes and push him around violently. Sattar fights his way onto the stage to save Vijay. Background song.

Singer: Mohammed Rafi

Burn it, blow this world away Burn it! (2) Burn it, blow this world away Take this world away from my sight Take charge of this world, it's all yours	Jala do ise phoonk daalo ye duniya Jala do, jala do Jala do ise phoonk daalo ye duniya Mere saamne se hata lo ye duniya Tumhaari hai tum hi sambhaalo ye duniya

Sattar frees Vijay from the angry mob and pushes him into a library in the Town Hall. Sattar starts punching the men around him. Meena, who has seen Vijay led to safety, elbows her way through the crowd and enters the library. She closes the door behind her.

Reel Sixteen

Vijay stands in the doorway at the far corner of the room. His clothes are torn and his hair is dishevelled.[59]

Meena:

Vijay! Have you gone mad? What have you done? Go and stop them! There's still time. Tell them you are Vijay. *(Vijay comes forward. He is in silhouette)* What's stopping you? They all came here for you. Why don't you explain to them?	Vijay! Paagal ho gaye ho kya? Ye tum ne kya kiya? Jaao, roko unn logon ko. Ab bhi waqt hai, unn se kaho ki tum hi Vijay ho. Soch kya rahe ho? Vo sab tumhaare liye aaye thay. Tum ja ke unhen samjhaate kyun nahin?

विजय यह देखकर हैरान हो जाता है कि पलभर में यह भीड़ क्या से क्या हो गई। भीड़ में से कुछ लोग कुर्सियाँ तोड़ रहे हैं। हर तरफ़ हड़बड़ी मच जाती है। विजय को चाहने वाले लोग गुस्से में स्टेज पर चढ़ जाते हैं। वो विजय के कपड़े फाड़ देते हैं और उसे ज़ोर से धक्का देते हैं। इस हड़बड़ी में विजय को बचाने सत्तार स्टेज पर आता है। बैकग्राउँड में गीत के बोल गूँज रहे हैं।

गायक: मोहम्मद रफ़ी

जला दो इसे फूँक डालो ये दुनिया
जला दो, जला दो
जला दो इसे फूँक डालो ये दुनिया
मेरे सामने से हटा लो ये दुनिया
तुम्हारी है तुम ही संभालो ये दुनिया

विजय को बचाकर सत्तार उसे टाउन हॉल के पुस्तकालय के एक कमरे में लाता है। सत्तार आसपास के लोगों से हाथापाई किए जा रहा है। विजय को सुरक्षित देखकर मीना कोहनियों से रास्ता बनाती हुई कमरे में दाख़िल होती है और दरवाज़ा बंद कर लेती है।

रील १६

विजय कमरे के दूसरे छोर पर खड़ा है। उसके कपड़े फटे हुए और बाल बिखरे हुए हैं।

मीना:
विजय! पागल हो गए हो क्या? ये तुमने क्या किया? जाओ, रोको उन लोगों को। अब भी वक़्त है, उनसे कहो कि तुम ही विजय हो।
(विजय आगे बढ़ता है। उसकी पीठ पर रोशनी के कारण उसका बड़ा साया दिखाई देता है)
सोच क्या रहे हो? वो सब तुम्हारे लिए आये थे। तुम जा के उन्हें समझाते क्यूँ नहीं?

وجے یہ دیکھ کر حیران کھڑا ہے کہ پل بھر میں یہی ہجوم کیا سے کیا ہو گیا۔ ہجوم کرسیاں توڑ رہا ہے۔ ہر طرف افراتفری ہے۔ وجے کی محبت کا دم بھرنے والا ہجوم غصے میں اسٹیج پر چڑھ جاتا ہے۔ وہ وجے کے کپڑے پھاڑ دیتے ہیں اور اُسے زور دار دھکا دیتے ہیں۔ اس ہڑبونگ میں وجے کو بچانے کے لیے ستار اسٹیج پر آتا ہے۔ بیک گراؤنڈ میں گیت کے بول گونج رہے ہیں۔

محمد رفیع کی آواز

جلا دو اسے پھونک ڈالو یہ دنیا
جلا دو، جلا دو
جلا دو اسے پھونک ڈالو یہ دنیا
مرے سامنے سے ہٹا لو یہ دنیا
تمہاری ہے تم ہی سنبھالو یہ دنیا

وجے کو بچا کر ستار ٹاؤن ہال کی لائبریری کے ایک کمرے میں لے آتا ہے۔ ستار آس پاس بھرے ہوئے لوگوں سے ہاتھاپائی کیے جا رہا ہے۔ وجے کو محفوظ دیکھ کر مینا کہنیوں سے راستہ بناتی ہوئی کمرے میں آتی ہے اور دروازہ بند کر لیتی ہے۔

ریل ۱۶

وجے کمرے کے دوسرے سرے پر کھڑا ہے۔ اُس کے کپڑے پھٹے ہوئے اور بال بکھرے ہوئے ہیں۔

مینا:
وجے! پاگل ہو گئے ہو کیا؟ یہ تم نے کیا کیا؟ جاؤ، روکو اُن لوگوں کو۔ اب بھی وقت ہے، اُن سے کہو کہ تم ہی وجے ہو۔
(وجے آگے بڑھتا ہے۔ اُس کی پشت پر روشنی ہے جس سے آگے اُس کا دراز سایہ دکھائی دے رہا ہے)
سوچ کیا رہے ہو؟ وہ سب تمہارے لیے آئے تھے۔ تم جا کے اُنہیں سمجھاتے کیوں نہیں؟

Vijay:
I am not that Vijay. He died a long time ago.

Meena:
A long time ago? What are you saying? Be sensible, Vijay. Shaikh, your brothers, your friends — they all say you are the same Vijay.

Vijay:
Friends? They're not my friends. They are friends of wealth. They refused to identify me. But now…never mind…

Meena:
To take revenge on a few false friends, why turn against yourself, Vijay? Why are you refusing fame and fortune? If you must, then be rid of your brothers, Shaikhji and the friends against whom you have reason to complain.

Vijay:
I have nothing against them. I have nothing against anyone. But I have reason to complain against a world that snatches humanity from a human being. That makes — for self-interest — a brother a stranger, a friend an enemy. I complain against a culture that worships the dead and tramples the living. Where crying for the suffering of others is considered cowardly. Where humility is considered a weakness. In such an atmosphere I shall never find peace, Meena. I shall never find peace. That is why I am going far away. Far away…

A top shot. As Vijay walks towards the door, the lights slowly dim and papers fly in the air filling the room like falling leaves.

Cut. A window is blown open by the wind. Through a corridor with billowing curtains, a tracking shot leads to Gulaab's room. The door opens to reveal Gulaab lying on a bed and Juhi sitting on a chair by her side. Gulaab suddenly sits up. She hears the windows rattling.

Main vo Vijay nahin hoon. Vo toh kab ka mar chuka.

Mar chuka? Kya keh rahe ho tum? Hosh mein aao, Vijay. Tumhaare bhai, Shaikhji, tumhaara dost, sab kehte hain ki tum wahi Vijay ho.

Dost? Ye log mere dost nahin. Ye sab daulat ke dost hain. Kal tak jo mujhe pehchaanne se inkaar kar rahe thay, vo aaj…khair…

Unn teen-chaar logon se badla lene ke liye tum apne aap se bair nahin kar sakte, Vijay. Daulat, naam-o-shohrat ko is tarah kyun thukra rahe ho? Agar thukraana hi hai toh unn bhaaiyon ko thukraao, Shaikhji aur uss dost ko thukraao jin se tumhen shikaayat hai.

Mujhe unse koi shikaayat nahin. Mujhe kisi insaan se koi shikaayat nahin. Mujhe shikaayat hai samaaj ke uss dhaanche se jo insaan se uski insaaniyat chheen leta hai. Matlab ke liye apne bhai ko begaana banaata hai, dost ko dushman banaata hai. Mujhe shikaayat hai uss tehzeeb se, uss sanskriti se jahaan murdon ko pooja jaata hai aur zinda insaan ko pairon talay raunda jaata hai. Jahaan kisi ke dukh-dard par do aanson bahaana buzdili samjha jaata hai. Jhuk ke milna ek kamzori samjha jaata hai. Aise maahaul mein mujhe kabhi shaanti nahin milegi, Meena. Kabhi shaanti nahin milegi. Isi liye main door ja raha hoon. Door…

विजय:

मैं वो विजय नहीं हूँ। वो तो कब का मर चुका।

मीना:

मर चुका? क्या कह रहे हो तुम? होश में आओ। विजय तुम्हारे भाई, शेख़जी, तुम्हारा दोस्त, सब कहते हैं कि तुम वही विजय हो।

विजय:

दोस्त? ये लोग मेरे दोस्त नहीं। ये सब दौलत के दोस्त हैं। कल तक जो मुझे पहचानने से इन्कार कर रहे थे वो आज...ख़ैर...

मीना:

उन तीन-चार लोगों से बदला लेने के लिए तुम अपने आप से बैर नहीं कर सकते, विजय। दौलत, नाम-ओ-शोहरत को इस तरह क्यूँ ठुकरा रहे हो? अगर ठुकराना ही है तो उन भाईओं को ठुकराओ, शेख़जी और उस दोस्त को ठुकराओ जिनसे तुम्हें शिक़ायत है।

विजय:

मुझे उनसे कोई शिक़ायत नहीं। मुझे किसी इन्सान से कोई शिक़ायत नहीं। मुझे शिक़ायत है समाज के उस ढाँचे से जो इन्सान से उसकी इन्सानियत छीन लेता है। मतलब के लिए अपने भाई को बेगाना बनाता है। दोस्त को दुश्मन बनाता है। मुझे शिक़ायत है उस तहज़ीब से, उस संस्कृति से जहाँ मुर्दों को पूजा जाता है और ज़िंदा इन्सान को पैरों तले रौंदा जाता है। जहाँ किसी के दु:ख-दर्द पर दो आँसू बहाना बुज़दिली समझा जाता है। झुक के मिलना एक कमज़ोरी समझा जाता है। ऐसे माहौल में मुझे कभी शांति नहीं मिलेगी, मीना। कभी शांति नहीं मिलेगी। इसी लिए मैं दूर जा रहा हूँ। दूर...

टॉप शॉट। जैसे ही विजय दरवाज़े की तरफ़ बढ़ता है, रोशनी कम होने लगती है और कमरे में हर तरफ़ टूटे पत्तों की तरह काग़ज़ उड़ने लगते हैं।

अगला दृश्य। हवा के ज़ोर से खिड़की खुल जाती है। राहदारी में उड़ते हुए पर्दे के दृश्य के बाद गुलाब का कमरा दिखाई देता है। हवा से दरवाज़ा खुलता है तो बिस्तर पर लेटी हुई बीमार गुलाब के पास जूही बैठी नज़र आती है। गुलाब अचानक से बिस्तर पर बैठ जाती है। हवा की वजह से खिड़कियों का शोर सुनाई देता है।

وج:

میں وہ وجے نہیں ہوں۔ وہ تو کب کا مر چکا۔

مینا:

مر چکا؟ کیا کہہ رہے ہو تم؟ ہوش میں آؤ، وجے۔ تمہارے بھائی، شیخ جی، تمہارا دوست، سب کہتے ہیں کہ تم وہی وجے ہو۔

وج:

دوست؟ یہ لوگ میرے دوست نہیں۔ یہ سب دولت کے دوست ہیں۔ کل تک جو مجھے پہچاننے سے انکار کر رہے تھے وہ آج۔۔۔خیر۔۔۔

مینا:

اُن تین چار لوگوں سے بدلہ لینے کے لیے تم اپنے آپ سے بیر نہیں کر سکتے، وجے۔ دولت، نام و شہرت کو اِس طرح کیوں ٹھکرا رہے ہو؟ اگر ٹھکرانا ہی ہے تو اُن بھائیوں کو ٹھکراؤ، شیخ جی اور اُس دوست کو ٹھکراؤ جن سے تمہیں شکایت ہے۔

وج:

مجھے اُن سے کوئی شکایت نہیں۔ مجھے کسی انسان سے کوئی شکایت نہیں۔ مجھے شکایت ہے سماج کے اُس ڈھانچے سے جو انسان سے اُس کی انسانیت چھین لیتا ہے۔ مطلب کے لیے اپنے بھائی کو بیگانہ بناتا ہے، دوست کو دشمن بناتا ہے۔ مجھے شکایت ہے اُس تہذیب سے، اُس سنسکرتی سے جہاں مردوں کو پوجا جاتا ہے۔ جہاں کسی کے دکھ درد پر دو آنسو بہانا بزدلی سمجھا جاتا ہے۔ جھک کے ملنا ایک کمزوری سمجھا جاتا ہے۔ ایسے ماحول میں مجھے کبھی شانتی نہیں ملے گی، مینا۔ کبھی شانتی نہیں ملے گی۔ اسی لیے میں دور جا رہا ہوں۔ دور۔۔۔

ٹاپ شاٹ۔ جیسے ہی وجے دروازے کی طرف بڑھتا ہے روشنی مدھم ہونے لگتی ہے اور کمرے میں ہر طرف ٹوٹے پتوں کی طرح کاغذ اڑنے لگتے ہیں۔

اگلا منظر۔ ہوا کے زور سے کھڑکی کھل جاتی ہے۔ راہداری میں اڑتے ہوئے پردوں سے ہوتا ہوا منظر گلاب کا کمرہ دکھا دیتا ہے۔ ہوا سے دروازہ کھلتا ہے تو بستر پر لیٹی ہوئی بیمار گلاب کے سرہانے جوہی بیٹھی نظر آتی ہے۔ گلاب اٹھ کر بستر پر بیٹھ جاتی ہے۔ ہوا سے کھڑکیوں کا شور سنائی دے رہا ہے۔

Gulaab:
Juhi, someone called me.

Juhi! Kisi ne mujhe pukaara.

Juhi:
No one called, Gulaabo. Go to sleep.

Kisi ne nahin, Gulaabo. So ja.

Juhi closes the window. All of a sudden, Gulaab gets up and heads towards the door. Juhi stops her.

Juhi:
Gulaabo, where are you going? You have a high fever.

Gulaabo, is tarah kahaan ja rahi hai? Dekh toh kitna bukhaar hai tujhe.

Gulaab:
Someone called me. Let me go, Juhi. Let me go.

Kisi ne pukaara mujhe. Mujhe jaane de, Juhi, mujhe jaane de.

Gulaab runs down the stairs. The staircase is half-lit. The wind blows fiercely. Leaves fly about. From a landing, Gulaab sees Vijay at her courtyard door. Overwhelmed with emotion, she smiles. The background music is an instrumental version of the song "Aaj sajan mohe ang laga lo janam safal ho jaye" (Today, beloved, hold me in Your arms, my life will be fulfilled). Gulaab runs down the stairs and makes her way towards Vijay who is waiting for her. She falls into his arms.[60]

Vijay:
I am going far away, Gulaab.

Main door ja raha hoon, Gulaab.

Gulaab:
Where to?

Kahaan?

गुलाब:

जूही! किसीने मुझे पुकारा ।

जूही:

किसीने नहीं, गुलाबो । सो जा ।

जूही खिड़की बंद करने जाती है । गुलाब बिस्तर से उठ कर दरवाज़े की ओर जाती है । जूही उसे रोकती है ।

जूही:

गुलाबो, इस तरह कहाँ जा रही है? देख तो कितना बुख़ार है तुझे ।

गुलाब:

किसीने पुकारा मुझे । मुझे जाने दे, जूही, मुझे जाने दे ।

गुलाब दौड़ती हुई सीढ़ियाँ उतरती है । सीढ़ियों पर हल्की-सी रोशनी है । तेज़ हवा चल रही है, पत्ते उड़ रहे हैं । सीढ़ियों के ऊपरी हिस्से पर खड़ी गुलाब देखती है कि विजय उसके आँगन के दरवाज़े पर खड़ा है । भावनाओं में बहती हुई वो मुस्करा रही है । "आज सजन मोहे अंग लगा लो" की धुन सुनाई दे रही है । गुलाब तेज़ी से दौड़ती हुई सीढ़ियाँ उतरती है और विजय के क़रीब आकर उसकी बाँहों में समा जाती है ।

विजय:

मैं दूर जा रहा हूँ, गुलाब ।

गुलाब:

कहाँ?

گلاب:
جوہی! کسی نے مجھے پکارا۔

جوہی:
کسی نے نہیں، گلاب۔ سوجا۔

جوہی کھڑکی کی بند کرنے جاتی ہے اور گلاب بستر سے اُٹھ کر دروازے کی طرف جاتی ہے۔ جوہی اُسے روکتی ہے۔

جوہی:
گلابو، اس طرح کہاں جا رہی ہے؟ دیکھ تو کتنا بخار ہے تجھے۔

گلاب:
کسی نے پکارا مجھے۔ مجھے جانے دے، جوہی، مجھے جانے دے۔

گلاب دوڑتی ہوئی زینے اترتی ہے۔ زینوں پر مدھم سی روشنی ہے۔ آندھی جیسی ہوا چل رہی ہے، پتے اُڑ رہے ہیں۔ زینے کے اوپری حصے سے گلاب دیکھتی ہے وجے اُس کے آنگن کے دروازے پر کھڑا ہوا ہے۔ جذبات سے مغلوب ہوکر وہ مسکراتی ہے۔ "آج سجن موہے انگ لگا لو" کی دھن سنائی دے رہی ہے۔ گلاب تیزی سے دوڑتی ہوئی زینے اُتر کر منتظر وجے کی بانہوں میں سما جاتی ہے۔

وجے:
میں دور جا رہا ہوں، گلاب۔

گلاب:
کہاں؟

Vijay:
To a place from where I shall not have to go any further.

Jahaan se mujhe phir door na jaana pade.

Gulaab (sadly):
Is that all you came to say?

Bas yahi kehne aaye thay?

Vijay:
Will you come with me?

Saath chalogi?

Gulaab looks at Vijay with eyes filled with longing. She hugs Vijay and hand in hand they walk away into the distance.[61]

The End

विजय:
जहाँ से मुझे फिर दूर ना जाना पड़े ।

गुलाब *(उदास होकर)*:
बस यही कहने आए थे?

विजय:
साथ चलोगी?

गुलाब अरमान भरी लगाव से विजय की ओर देखती है और उसे गले से लगा लेती है । और एक-दूसरे का हाथ थामे वो दूर जाते दिखाई देते हैं ।

وجے:
جہاں سے مجھے پھر دور نہ جانا پڑے۔

گلاب (مایوسی سے):
بس یہی کہنے آئے تھے؟

وجے:
ساتھ چلوگی؟

گلاب ارمان بھری نظروں سے وجے کو دیکھتی ہے۔ وہ وجے کو گلے سے لگا لیتی ہے اور ایک دوسرے کی بانہہ تھامے وہ دور جاتے دکھائی دیتے ہیں۔

Film Credits: Order of credits as they appear on the screen. Year of release: 1957.

S.D. BURMAN: *Music*

SAHIR: *Lyrics*

ABRAR ALVI: *Dialogue*

V.K. MURTHY: *Photography*

[Wipes are used as transitions between the title cards]

IN THE FOND MEMORY
OF
LATE SHRI GYAN MUKHERJEE

*Guru Dutt Films
Private Ltd*
Present

PYAASA

प्यासा (in Hindi)
پياسا (in Urdu)

Starring

Mala Sinha

Guru Dutt

Waheeda Rehman

Rehman

and
Johnny Walker

Supported by
Kum Kum
Leela Misra

with
Shyam
Mehmood
Radheshyam
Tun Tun
Maya Dass
Moni Chatterji
Ashita
Neel Kamal
Mohan Sandow and
Rajendar

Dialogues
Abrar Alvi

Lyrics
Sahir Ludhianvi

Photography
V.K. Murthy
W.I.C.A

Editing
Y.G. Chawhan

Art Direction
Biren Naag

Dances
Surya Kumar

Songs Recorded by
Mukul Bose

Playback Artistes
Geeta Dutt
Mohd. Rafi
Hemant Kumar

Stills
Kamat (Foto Flash)
Publicity
Press Agents

Costumes Designed by
Bhanu Mati
Make-up
Babu Rao

Production Manager
G.L. Kashmiri

Asst. Directors
Niranjan
Shyam

Assistants
Camera Moses, Prabhakar
Editing Shinde
Music Suhrit Kar
Make-up Jayant
Costumes Ramlal

Produced at
Kardar Studios Ltd.
RECORDED ON RCA SOUND SYSTEM
Records on
H.M.V.

Processed at
Famous Cine Labs.
MAHALAXMI
Processing
G.R. Narveker

Production Incharge
S. Guru Swamy

Music
S.D. Burman

Produced & Directed
by
Guru Dutt

Technical Information
Number of reels: 16
Total footage: 13,698 feet
Duration of 35mm print: 2 hrs 19 mins

Y.G. CHAWHAN: *Editing*

BHANU MATI: *Costumes*

S. GURU SWAMY: *Production*

BABU RAO: *Make-up*

Commentary Nasreen Munni Kabir

Reel I (pp. 2–16)

1. When Guru Dutt (GD) came to make *Pyaasa*, he dedicated his most personal work to director Gyan Mukherjee, who died in Calcutta on 13 November 1956, some months before the film's release on 22 February 1957 at Minerva Cinema, Bombay. A framed photograph of this master director was said to have hung on the wall of GD's office years after Mukherjee had passed away.

Younger brother Atmaram once commented on GD's relationship with Mukherjee: "After Gurudutt left Prabhat in 1947, India got its independence and then there was Partition. Films suffered a big setback during this time and my brother was without work for about a year. He managed to become Gyanji's assistant and had very great regard for him. He was the intellectual mind behind the hits of Bombay Talkies." (Atmaram, interview by NMK, 1983.)

Prior to working with Gyan Mukherjee (*Sangram*, 1950), GD assisted four other directors: V. Bedekar (*Lakhrani*, 1945, also appearing in a minor role and working as choreographer); P.L. Santoshi (*Hum ek hain*, 1946; also choreographer); A. Banerjee (*Mohan*, 1947); and Amiya Chakravorty (*Girls' School*, 1949).

2. Despite the fact that *Pyaasa* was loosely based on a story written by GD sometime in 1947/48 and titled "Kash-ma-kash," no story or screenplay credit features in the opening titles.

The story is written in GD's own hand (page one of thirty-two pages is missing) on fine letter-headed paper of Pramukh Films. It is unclear how GD was connected to Pramukh Films, a company untraceable and probably now defunct. These rare documents, preserved by his second son Arun Dutt, provide a fascinating insight into the story elements that GD discarded and those he retained in the final film. Selected pages of "Kash-ma-kash" have been reproduced in the book's Introduction.

Characters developed from story to film
    Shree (on whom Vijay is based)
    Rani (Gulaab)
    Ramesh (Shyam)
    Shambu (Ghosh)
    Sushama (Meena)
    Vijay's cruel brothers are identical in both versions.

Shree's doting mother dies in the story as she does in the film. Abdul Sattar, publisher Shaikh, Pushpa and Juhi do not feature in the story.

It is interesting to note that the publisher (later called Ghosh) was initially named "Patel." The name has a strike through it and is replaced by "Shambu." GD's first name choice probably alluded to the powerful film critic of the time, Baburao Patel and his wife Sushila Rani, whose name also has a strike through it and is replaced by "Sushama" on whom Meena is modelled. GD was said to have had an uneasy relationship with Baburao Patel whose reviews of GD's films were appallingly negative. Patel's review of *Pyaasa* was downright personal and aggressive and had for caption: "*Pyaasa* brings confusion to the screen. Guru Dutt's vain attempt to look intelligent." (*Filmindia*, April 1957.)

Plot differences and similarities
Like Vijay in *Pyaasa*, the hero Shree is a struggling poet in the story. He befriends Rani, a young prostitute, and the circumstances in which they first meet are a close match to the film. Rani's song (a poem by Shree) draws him to her. As the story develops, Shree loses all hope of ever being recognised for his poetry, and decides to commit suicide. Instead of the aged beggar falling under the train, a thief attacks the poet and is accidentally killed. Shree does not end up in hospital like Vijay, but is persuaded by the deceitful Ramesh to pretend to have died, and so take advantage of the sympathy that news of his suicide will provoke. Ramesh and Sushama publish Shree's poems and they are an overnight sensation. Despite the acclaim for his work, Shree, now living in disguise, becomes increasingly disillusioned. The ending of the story and film are almost identical. Shree rejects fame and riches and walks away from the adoring crowd. He goes to Rani to tell her that he is going far away but does not ask her to come with him. GD's however ends his story with the line: "She follows him."

"Kash-ma-kash" has no romantic relationship between Shree and Sushama. The Vijay and Meena love angle was probably added to heighten Vijay's sense of rejection, thereby adding to the emotional impact of his situation. Another major difference in the story is the significance given to the scoundrel Ramesh. By reducing Ramesh's importance (the individual as villain), GD accentuates in the film, the villainy of a faceless society. It is also clear that Sahir's poetry (that GD later came to know) gave the film its political edge, which the story lacked.

3. When casting for *Pyaasa*, GD had initially wanted Nargis to play Gulaab and Madhubala to play Meena. It is uncertain whether these excellent actresses declined, or if GD himself decided to give the roles instead to newcomers Mala Sinha and Waheeda Rehman. In the article "Wanted New Faces," GD expressed the need for Indian cinema to encourage a larger pool of acting talent, which traditionally depended (and still depends) on a handful of actors: "The industry should adopt the Hollywood system. In Hollywood the major studios have stars under long-term contract and loan them out to producers who want them for their pictures. It is fatal for a new star to sign contracts indiscriminately. The result of his action is the exact opposite of what he expects…today there is a growing class of independent producers who are so well established that they can afford to take on new talent. But they don't. Because everyone else expects somebody else to take the risk." (*Filmfare*, 30 August 1957.)

It is widely known that GD approached Dilip Kumar to play the lead role of Vijay. This most brilliant actor declined, believing that the character was too close in temperament to the eponymous hero, Devdas, that he had brought to life on screen in 1955 under Bimal Roy's direction. Assistants working on *Pyaasa* have however insisted that Dilip Kumar just did not show up on the first day of the shoot and so GD decided to play Vijay instead.

His underplayed performance and brooding presence add to the blurring between GD and *Pyaasa*'s Vijay, especially given GD's melancholic personality. Any other actor in the role of Vijay would have undoubtedly diminished the sense of doomed tragedy that permeates the film.

4. Although Bengal was not a centre for Urdu poetry, its impressive literary and cinematic life was reason enough for GD to situate the film in Calcutta. It was the city of his childhood and held great nostalgia for him. He lived in Calcutta between the ages of five and seventeen and, encouraged by his maternal uncle B.B. Benegal, GD's early dreams of becoming a dancer and learning about photography began there. His uncle was also instrumental in getting GD a scholarship to train as a dancer at Uday Shankar's India Cultural Centre in Almora. GD's fine understanding of song and dance, and choreographed camera movements benefitted hugely from his work with Uday Shankar.

During the Calcutta release of *Mr & Mrs 55*, in a letter to Geeta Dutt (dated 7 May 1955), and scrawled in English on the Grand Hotel paper, GD described his feelings for the city: "Today Bengali 'Devdas' is running [he probably meant the P.C. Barua version] and I am going to see it. When I come to Cal, I feel so sad. It reminds me of the past — the childhood days, the struggle here…I had been to uncle's [B.B. Benegal] place and last night, I dined though I couldn't eat anything. Please come soon. With love & kisses to self and Baba [son Tarun]. Your husband, Guru Dutt." (Nasreen Munni Kabir, *Yours Guru Dutt: Intimate Letters of a Great Indian Filmmaker*, Roli Books, Delhi, 2005, p. 91.)

5. The opening poem sets the tone for *Pyaasa*. The use of voice-over and close-ups instantly establish Vijay's perspective on the world. As each line is recited, his facial expressions change from peaceful to happy, from concern to defeat. Sahir Ludhianvi's verse also expresses Vijay's feelings of inadequacy in returning to Nature its inherent purity and innocence.

> *Main doon bhi toh kya doon tumhen ae shokh nazaaro*
> *Le-de ke mere paas kuchh aansu hain kuchh aahen*
>
> What can I give to you, O splendid Nature?
> All I have is a few tears, a few sighs.

6. Rajendar, who often played Muslim characters, and did so to perfection, plays the publisher Shaikh. Known as a junior artist or character actor, he also appeared in GD's *Aar Paar* (1954).

7. In this scene, Shaikh implies that Vijay knows nothing of romantic poetry and hence could not have read Mir and Momin.

A key eighteenth-century poet of the Delhi School of the Urdu *ghazal*, Mir Taqi Mir (1715–1810) was considered to have shaped Urdu itself and is remembered for his melancholic verse. He was called "Khudaay-e-sukhan" (God of Poetry). Equally eminent was Momin Khan Momin (1800–1851), a contemporary of Mirza Ghalib and Zauq.

8. Vijay suggests his own leftist leanings by speaking of the famous revolutionary poets, Josh and Faiz. Noted Urdu poet Josh Malihabadi (1894–1982) wrote passionately in favour of India's independence from the British Raj and was known as "Shaayar-e-inquilaab" (Poet of the Revolution). He migrated to Pakistan in 1958, believing that the position of Urdu had weakened substantially in independent India.

An affirmed Marxist, Faiz Ahmed Faiz (1911–1984) was a very influential and respected Pakistani poet and a key member of the Marxist-oriented Progressive Writers' Association (PWA), an important literary group, which had great influence on Urdu literature in the thirties and forties.

Also an active PWA member, Sahir Ludhianvi once commented that Faiz, Majaaz, Josh, Iqbal and journalist/poet Gopal Mittal influenced his writing more than other poets. He also credits Mittal for giving him the first book on socialism that he read. *Pyaasa*'s socialist ideas are strongly expressed through some of Sahir's songs (particularly "Jinhen naaz hai"), whereas GD's politics seemed to lean towards humanitarianism rather than socialism. GD's point of view is articulated in the film through an underlying and somewhat uncomplicated desire for a new India, post-British Raj, that rejects corruption and stands for equality.

9.   The young boy who runs after Vijay in the market calling him "Uncle" does not resurface in the film. It is likely that the boy is supposed to be Vijay's nephew.

10.   GD paints a dark portrait of the family. His elder brothers are shown as cruel and money-grabbing. On the other hand, Vijay's mother loves him unconditionally. She is the embodiment of a selfless and nurturing mother. Vijay finds another nurturing mother-figure in Gulaab, who feeds him (restaurant scene), protects and consoles him. She is ultimately responsible for getting his poems published and bringing him fame.

The absent father is an important aspect of Vijay's personality. Unlike many films in which, if a protagonist's father/mother has died, a garlanded portrait of the deceased parent hangs on a wall, Vijay's father remains faceless. Like many fatherless heroes of Indian cinema, Vijay must shape his world, defining the values and codes of morality by which he will live. The 1970s hero written by Salim-Javed and played by Amitabh Bachchan — frequently named "Vijay" — is largely shaped by his fatherless status and driven by his desire to take the absent father's place as protector of his mother. But unlike the Salim-Javed hero, GD's Vijay is unable to protect or provide for his helpless mother.

It is also interesting to note that neither the Vijay of *Pyaasa* nor the Vijay of the 1970s has a surname. Perhaps this was deliberate in order to steer clear from identifying the character as belonging to a particular caste, which surnames would suggest.

11.   In 1943, when director Gyan Mukherjee made *Kismet*, Mehmood was persuaded by his father Mumtaz Ali (actor and dance director at Bombay Talkies) to play the role of young Ashok Kumar. Early in his career, Mehmood did many odd jobs, including teaching Meena Kumari how to play table tennis (and subsequently marrying her sister Madhu). He got to know GD when working for the director of *Kismet*: "I was Gyan Mukherjee's driver. He treated me like a son. Guru Dutt was his chief assistant in those days and he always had a camera hung around his neck. He used to keep on taking photographs. After that time, I did not see him. One day Guru Dutt happened to see some rushes in which I appeared and asked me to play his elder brother in *Pyaasa*. I told him: 'But I'm younger than you!'" (Nasreen Munni Kabir, *Guru Dutt: A Life in Cinema*, Oxford University Press, Delhi, new edition, 2005, p. 124.)

A brilliant comedian and director, Mehmood acted in over 300 films and is still loved for his unforgettable performances in *Padosan* (1968) and *Bombay to Goa* (1972). He died on 23 July 2004, aged seventy-one.

Mehmood and GD's family became closely linked. His younger sister, Minoo Mumtaz, worked on Guru Dutt's subsequent films and Mehmood's nephew, Naushad, is married to Nina, GD's only daughter. Nina is a singer in her own right and has recently released her first album titled *Pal*.

Reel 2 (pp. 16–30)

12.   GD shot a few reels of *Pyaasa* but was dissatisfied with the results. So he scrapped these and started all over again. The early footage had Johnny Walker in the role of Shyam. Believing that audiences would not accept Johnny Walker in a negative role, GD recast his assistant Shyam Kapoor to play the deceitful Shyam, which he does admirably well. In this scene when we first meet Shyam, he boasts of bearing false witness for money. He will have no qualms in doing the same when his friend Vijay is in trouble.

13.   On a visit to Hyderabad, GD was invited to see the Telugu film, *Rojulu Marayi* (released on 14 April 1955), directed by Tapi Chanaki, and was impressed by the dance/song performance of the lovely nineteen-year old Waheeda Rehman. The song "Eruvaka sagaroo rannoo chinnananna" (the song clip can be viewed on *Youtube*) is mostly filmed in wide and long-duration shots, but the young actress's sparkling eyes and excellent dancing attract immediate attention.

Born on 14 May 1936 into a traditional Muslim family from Tamil Nadu, Waheeda Rehman trained in classical dance and wanted to work in Hindi films. When they met, GD's first question to her was whether she spoke Urdu. On learning that she spoke the language well, he offered her a contract in his film company, Guru Dutt Films Pvt. Ltd.

Waheeda Rehman's first Hindi release was *C.I.D.* (1956), directed by GD's assistant and friend, Raj Khosla, and produced by GD. She was among the early actresses to introduce a modern, natural approach to acting, moving away from the high-pitched melodramatic style of the time. Her delicate and soft presence light up many scenes in *Pyaasa*. She is absolutely wonderful in the film. In the only song that Waheeda Rehman lip-synchs ("Jaane kya tu ne kahi"), her dazzling beauty eclipses the hero who follows her and becomes barely visible in the half-light — so characteristic of GD's/Murthy's lighting. Gulaab's smile and air of innocence seductively mesmerise the camera and audience.

The off-screen relationship between GD and Waheeda Rehman has been subject to much speculation. Even in the current era of reveal-all journalism, she has refused to discuss her personal life. When they met in 1955, GD was already married to the amazingly gifted playback singer Geeta Dutt and they had a son, Tarun. Their second son, Arun, was born in 1956, during the making of *Pyaasa*. Despite GD's strong feelings for this fine actress, which are evident in the kind of roles he gave her, and in the transparently emotional scenes they shared on screen (particularly in *Kaagaz ke Phool*), GD chose not to leave his wife to whom he was deeply attached. By the time *Sahib Bibi aur Ghulam* was released in 1962, GD and Waheeda Rehman had drifted apart.

Atmaram believed that close relationships hardly mattered to GD: "He felt no responsibility towards the family or society. He wouldn't attend family functions. It was very difficult for Geeta. He worked round the clock and sometimes he would just drive off to Lonavala straight from the studio without telling anyone. I don't think Guru Dutt was meant for a normal married sort of life. But he was tied by tradition. At times he was open and friendly, and at other times he would go into his shell and be available to no one." (Atmaram, interview by NMK, 1986.)

14. The couplet "Phir na kijiye meri gustaakh nigaahi ka gila" that introduces Gulaab (first seen back to camera) is extracted from Sahir's nine-stanza poem "Kisi ko udaas dekh kar" featured in his collection

Talkhiyaan (1943). Giving context to the poem, scriptwriter Suraj Sanim wrote: "The college campus buzzed again — this time with the love stories of Sahir and Birender [also known as "Ishar"] Kaur. Sahir's poem 'Kisi ko udaas dekh kar' was a tribute to this romance...the college principal came to know of these secret rendezvous and Birender [and Sahir] was expelled from college. Once more it seemed as if Sahir would not be able to smile again but before long, his attentions were rivetted elsewhere." (Sanim, *Filmfare*, 16–31 August 1985.)

Suhail Akhtar, who has transcribed the Urdu dialogue and songs in this book, has noted the first and last stanzas of the nine-stanza poem "Kisi ko udaas dekh kar" as below.

> First stanza
> *Tumhen udaas si paata hoon main kayi din se*
> *Na jaane kaun se sadme utha rahi ho tum*
> *Vo shokhiyaan, vo tabassum, vo qehqahe na rahe*
> *Har ek cheez ko hasrat se dekhti ho tum*
> *Chhupa-chhupa ke khamoshi mein apni bechaini*
> *Khud apne raaz ki tash'heer ban gayi ho tum*
>
>
> I find you sad and listless for days now
> I wonder what traumas you face
> That joy, that smile, that laughter have gone
> You look upon everything with longing
> Though silently you hide your unease
> Your face veils your secret sorrow
>
> Last stanza
> *Gali-gali mein ye bikte huwe jawaan chehre*
> *Haseen aankhon mein afsurdagi si chhaayi huwi*
> *Ye jangg aur ye mere vatan ke shokh jawaan*
> *Khareedi jaati hain uth'ti jawaaniyaan jin ki*
> *Ye baat-baat pe qaanoon-o-zaabte ki giraft*
> *Ye zillaten, ye ghulaami, ye daur-e-majboori*
> *Ye gham bahot hain meri zindagi mitaane ko*
> *Udaas reh ke mere dil ko aur ranj na do*
> *Phir na kijiye meri gustaakh nigaahi ka gila*
> *Dekhiye aap ne phir pyar se dekha mujh ko*

These young faces sold in every lane
Sorrow is cast over beautiful eyes
These pleasing youths of my country, youths of wars
Whose youth is bought and sold as they come of age
At every step law is enforced
These humiliations, this slavery, these times of constraint
Many are the sorrows to erase my life
Do not sadden my already heavy heart
Do not complain if I look at you with impunity
There! You looked at me again with such longing.

Recurrent themes and imagery run through much of Sahir's poems. A few lines in the last stanza of "Kisi ko udaas dekh kar" take another form in *Pyaasa*'s song "Ye duniya agar mil bhi jaaye."

Jawaani bhatakti hai badkaar ban kar
Jawaan jism sajte hain baazaar ban kar

Youth strays into crime
Young bodies are adorned for the marketplace.

Sahir later expanded the couplet "Phir na kijiye meri gustaakh nigaahi ka gila" into a duet for *Phir Subah Hogi* (1958). Directed by Ramesh Saigal, the film is loosely based on Dostoyevsky's *Crime and Punishment*. Beautifully composed by Khayyam and sung by Mukesh and Asha Bhonsle for Raj Kapoor and Mala Sinha, the song verses develop the theme of the couplet.

15. GD's excellent staging has key encounters between Vijay and Gulaab as they make their way up a flight of stairs. Filming a long conversation on stairs is especially effective in creating choreographed camera movements. GD cleverly manages to avoid a lengthy shot-reverse-shot sequence in which similar encounters could be filmed. One of the things that set GD apart is how he always presented his story in visual language.

The staircase also becomes an important space for their meeting and parting — a socially neutral space as people from all walks of life cross one another, and so representing an impartial space for the meeting of poet and prostitute. The only song that speaks of Gulaab's feelings for Vijay ("Aaj sajan…") is structured around a staircase as well.

At the end of the film, Gulaab is seen running down the many flights from her room to find Vijay waiting at her door.

16. *Mother India*, another important film for the fine actress and dancer Kum Kum, was released in 1957, the same year as *Pyaasa*. She has retired from films and lives in Mumbai. Her last release was *Ek kunwari ek kunwara* (1973). She is lovely as Juhi and is terrific in her scenes with Johnny Walker.

Pyaasa has in fact three love stories running through it, involving Meena and Vijay, Gulaab and Vijay (forming a love triangle), and Abdul Sattar and Juhi. Outside of providing comic relief to the story, Johnny Walker was nearly always shown as a romantic character, looking for love.

Reel 3 (pp. 32–46)

17. Away from the usual practice of filming in studios, GD shot extensively on the streets of Calcutta, including this scene filmed on the city's famous Park Street. Renowned film critic Iqbal Masud quotes Shyam Benegal (GD's cousin) on the choice of *Pyaasa*'s location: "Calcutta is one of the most important elements in Guru Dutt's work. Calcutta, not merely as a physical city but the concept of it. One can write about the Calcuttas of Ray, Ghatak and Mrinal Sen. Each has distinct lineaments, separate flavours. They may not have much to do with the real Calcutta. But they exist as entities in their own right. So does Guru Dutt's Calcutta." (Masud, *The Telegraph,* "Calcutta, Romanticism and Guru Dutt," 13 July 1986.)

18. GD uses a musical theme for the main protagonists. The haunting mouth organ tune was composed and played by R.D. Burman and is identified with Meena. S.D. Burman's young son, Rahul Dev, who was seventeen at the time, assisted his father on *Pyaasa*. He composed (un-credited) the rhythmic calypso number "Sar jo tera chakraaye."

On working with GD, R.D. Burman said: "He was whimsical. He used to like a person in the morning and after he had drunk the whole evening, he'd ask them to leave, telling them he didn't like them. Mehmood had joined the industry and played a small role in *Pyaasa*; he heard the songs we had recorded for *Raaz* and asked Guru Dutt if he wasn't going to make the film [GD finally shelved *Raaz*], then he should allow him to use the songs in *Chhote Nawab* [1961], Mehmood's first film as producer, which became my first film too." (Burman, interview by NMK, 1993.)

R.D. Burman's rich musical legacy continues to hold great sway over the current generation of composers and music lovers. This first-rate composer died on 4 January 1994, aged fifty-four.

19. Born into a Nepalese-Christian family in Calcutta in 1936, Mala Sinha appeared in many Bengali films before moving to Bombay where she met Geeta Dutt, who helped her to find work in Hindi cinema. It is likely that she might have recommended Mala Sinha for the role of Meena, but this is unconfirmed.

Mala Sinha was also a singer on *All India Radio*, but chose not to sing in her films. Two years after *Pyaasa's* release, she played the lead in Yash Chopra's debut film *Dhool ka Phool* (1959), and following that success, Mala Sinha became a prominent star of the 1950s and '60s. Largely underrated, her interpretation of the negative and dishonest Meena brings complexity to a flawed character.

20. Born into a Punjabi family, Uma Devi enjoyed a brief but successful career as a playback singer. Among her famous songs is Naushad's "Afsaana likh rahi hoon dil-e-beqaraar ka" in *Dard* (1947). She was one of Naushad's regular singers till she got married and decided to stop singing. He always believed that Uma Devi was a natural comedienne and so persuaded her to act in *Babul* (1954) with Dilip Kumar, Munawar Sultana and Nargis. Uma Devi's performance stood out and audiences took a shine to her. Adopting the screen name, Tun Tun (her character's name in *Babul*), she enjoyed a successful career as comedienne.

In the 1987 article "Funny Lady," she recalled that once GD had explained the scene to her, he gave her total freedom to improvise: "In fact he would say: 'You just keep talking. I'll edit later.'" (Payal Singh, *The Illustrated Weekly of India,* 19 April 1987.) Credited in *Pyaasa* as Uma Devi, the wonderful Tun Tun passed away on 24 November 2003.

21. This merry duet (which appears to be reduced in length) might well have been inspired by celebrated Ghulam Haider's trend-setting song "Saawan ke nazaare," from the 1941 *Khazanchi* by D.N. Pancholi. The song has the hero and heroine in *Khazanchi* sing a duet, followed by a group of friends, as they cycle through the countryside.

While courting Meena at college, Vijay appears well off, playing badminton, going on picnics and enjoying an apparently comfortable middle-class lifestyle. Vijay's college years are in sharp contrast to

his later life. It is unclear how his circumstances changed so drastically. The outcome of the love story between Meena and Vijay unravels in the second flashback.

22. The gifted actor Tulsi Chakraborty appears here in a cameo role (un-credited in the film titles). His association with the best of Bengali cinema and his work with Satyajit Ray must have prompted GD to persuade this exceptional actor to be part of *Pyaasa*. His presence gives an immediate authenticity to GD's Calcutta.

The film was shot in synchronous sound and as a result most of the filming took place at nights when the city had quietened down.

No location stills of *Pyaasa* are traceable today. While shooting the film in Calcutta, GD wrote two letters to Geeta, who was in Bombay, pregnant with Arun, their second son. He provides a little detail of the shooting in his letter dated 23 May 1956: "Since I wrote to you last I have finished a lot of work — I have finished the sad song [unclear to which song he is referring] — half of Waheeda's song [this may be "Jaane kyatu ne kahi"] and scenes etc. There is little work left over but the night shooting goes very slow because of the generators and lights etc, but the result is good...now all the work that remains is mine alone. So don't think I am having a very happy time here. Our daily work schedule is both in the day and night." (NMK, *op. cit.,* 2005, pp. 104–7.)

GD's second letter was written three days later on 26 May 1956, their third wedding anniversary: "I am really sorry we could not spend this anniversary together. I tried my best to finish all work but it was of no use as the sun was never there. I have done almost all work except for a few bits here and there which I hope to finish as soon as possible...believe it or not I am sick of this place and want to go back to B'bay. Excepting for work — I haven't been to see a picture even. Only today I am thinking of seeing *Pather Panchali* again as the whole unit has been invited [It is unclear whether Ray invited GD personally or whether it was the film's distributor]. (NMK, *ibid.,* pp. 109–12.)

23. This is a beautiful exchange by Abrar Alvi in which Gulaab poignantly describes to a silent Vijay how badly streetwalkers are treated and exploited. Many aspects of Gulaab's character were based on a prostitute that Alvi had known and who was called Gulaabo: "It was something I can never forget the way she fed me. And I translated it directly from my life into *Pyaasa*. I think she found me different

because I was the first man to treat her like a human being, to talk to her." (Sathya Saran, *Ten Years with Guru Dutt, Abrar Alvi's Journey*, Penguin Books India, 2008, p. 49.)

GD's story "Kash-ma-kash," written in 1948/49, some years before he met Abrar Alvi, also indicates that GD had a similar character in mind in the young prostitute Rani.

Reel 4 (pp. 46–60)

24. Almost thirty minutes into the film, sublime comic relief arrives in the shape of the masseur, Abdul Sattar (Johnny Walker). And what an introduction he has! The only three sympathetic characters are in fact introduced not speaking dialogue: Vijay appears underscored by a poem; Gulaab enters the story reciting a couplet," and Abdul Sattar instantly wins our hearts through the song "Sar jo tera chakraaye."

Few Indian directors can match GD's art in song picturisation and this is one of his most uplifting examples. The song does not stop the story-telling, while every moment is brightly choreographed, either through the sharp editing of Johnny Walker's amazing face in close-up or shots of the masseur's hands whirling around a client's head in time to the rhythms of a calypso.

The careers of GD and Johnny Walker were linked from the very start. During the making of *Baazi*, GD first met Johnny Walker, whose real name was Badruddin Jamaluddin Qazi. He came to Bombay from Indore, and when his father lost his job as a textile worker, Qazi's large family had to struggle to get by. It was Balraj Sahni, the screenplay writer of *Baazi*, who discovered this comic genius. Qazi was working as a bus conductor when Sahni asked him to audition for GD. Playing a drunk, the young man was so convincing that GD gave him a bit role in *Baazi* and the screen name "Johnny Walker," inspired by the famous Scotch whisky (spelt as "Johnnie" Walker).

From 1951, this outstanding comedian became a key member of the GD team. They were close friends, going on hunting and fishing expeditions together. On the sets of *Mr & Mrs 55*, Johnny Walker fell in love with his co-star Noor (actress Shakila's sister), and later they married. Acting in over 300 films, he remains one of India's best-loved comedians. He was among the few stars who had a film, *Johnny Walker*, named after him which was released in 1957, the same year as *Pyaasa*. He died on 29 July 2003, aged eighty.

25. In this humorous song (sung to perfection by Mohammed Rafi), Sahir does not depart from the action and vocabulary of head massaging, using words like "ganj" (baldness) and "khushki" (dandruff), but subtly gives the modest masseur (or common man) political sway too:

> *Naukar ho ya maalik, leader ho ya public*
> *Apne aage sabhi jhuke hain kya raaja kya sainik*

> Be you a servant, be you a master
> Be you a leader, or among the led
> King or soldier, to me all bow their head.

Sahir Ludhianvi believed a good tune was essential for the popularity of the film lyric. When talking about the basic needs of a film song, he said: "In song writing, the writer must keep in mind the fact that film is a mass medium. The song writer should use simple language and he must express even complex emotions and feelings in an easily understandable manner…" In the same article, Sahir added that he was far from happy "with the common practice of Indian music directors of composing the music first and then requiring the lyric-writer to tailor words for the music. This method of song writing is not conducive to the lyricist doing justice to the story and its different situations." (Ludhianvi, "Poet of Two Worlds," *Filmfare*, 26 January 1962.)

26. One of the key changes to *Pyaasa's* story was the addition of comedy through Johnny Walker's scenes, as recalled by S. Guruswamy: "I believe GD liked *Pyaasa* the most among his films. No doubt he made some changes in it. Some portions were edited out, others added. The comedy factor was planted. When you see the film, you will realise the comedy works as a block within the story. He added this to give some sort of relief. It wasn't there to start off with. Whenever Johnny would come on the set, the whole mood changed. Murthy used to get annoyed because he had to concentrate on the lighting etc. And Guru Dutt would say: 'Murthy, let Johnny do what he wants. Why are you shouting?'" (Guruswamy, interview by NMK, 1983.)

27. As evident in this scene, Abrar Alvi wrote great dialogue for both serious and light moments. Comedy in Hindi films was not very subtle and tended towards buffoonery till the end of the 1950s. Alvi was among the first writers to use repartees and witticisms. His dialogue in

Mr & Mrs 55, based on his play *Modern Marriage*, has many scintillating examples of his subtle and clever approach to comedy.

28. Moving away from the clichéd use in Hindi films of flashback shots that remind audiences of the hero's past, GD evoked days gone by through audio flashbacks. This sophisticated device allows us to enter Vijay's memories through the song Vijay and Meena sang in earlier carefree times.

This was not the first time GD had used this technique. The heroine (played by Geeta Bali) in *Jaal* (1952) walking alone on the beach is reminded of her absent lover through the song he once sang ("Ye raat ye chaandni phir kahaan"). Moved by his memory, she sings: "Chaandni raatein pyar ki baatein." Though Lata Mangeshkar did not often sing for GD, her rendition of this *Jaal* song is sublime.

Reel 5 (pp. 62–72)

29. The poem recited at the college reunion extracts three couplets from Sahir's *ghazal* featured in his book *Talkhiyaan* (1943).

The additional couplet, noted below, was written specifically for the film and is the last couplet recited by Vijay. The repeated way in which poems and songs are introduced in the narratives of GD's films, Vijay's poem too is an answer to a question asked in dialogue (for further information see commentary, no. 56):

Man in audience:
"Ji janaab, khushi ke mauqe pe kya bedili ka raag chheda huwa hai? Koi khushi ka geet sunaayiye."

Why such a sad song on this happy occasion, sir? Recite a happy song.

Vijay:
Hum ghamzada hain laayen kahaan se khushi ke geet
Denge vahi jo paayenge is zindagi se hum

Afflicted by grief, how do I find a song of joy?
I can only return to this life what it has given to me.

Sahir's original six-couplet *ghazal*:

Tang aa chuke hain kash-ma-kash-e-zindagi se hum
Thukra na den jahaan ko kahin bedili se hum

Maayusi-e-ma'aal-e-mohabbat na poochhiye
Apnon se pesh aaye hain begaangi se hum
(not in the film)

Lo aaj hum ne tod diya rishtay-e-ummeed
Lo ab kabhi gila na karenge kisi se hum
(the last couplet recited by Vijay at the college reunion)

Ubhrenge ek baar abhi dil ke valvale
Go dab gaye hain baar-e-ghum-e-zindagi se hum
(simplified as: *Maana ke dab gayen hain ghum-e-zindagi se hum*)

Gar zindagi mein mil gaye phir ittefaaq se
Poochhenge apna haal teri bebasi se hum
(not in the film)

Allah re fareb-e-mashiyyat ki aaj tak
Duniya ke zulm sehte rahe khaamoshi se hum
(not in the film)

I am weary of the struggles of life
The weariness of my heart may spurn the world

Do not ask what grief and disappointment love brings
We now meet loved ones as strangers

There! Today I break all ties with hope
There! Never shall I voice a complaint again

Desires of the heart will stir once again
I confess that I have been crushed by life's sorrows

By chance if we were to meet again
I shall know my condition by your helplessness

The illusion of God's will still reigns
In silence we endure all tyranny.

A year later, Sahir made "Tang aa chuke hain…" into a beautiful song for *Light House* (1958), directed by G.P. Sippy, starring Ashok Kumar and Nutan. The music was composed by N. Datta and sung by Asha Bhonsle for Nutan.

30. Rehman was born on 23 June 1923. Two years older than GD and of Afghan descent, Rehman started his career as assistant director to V. Bedekar in 1944 at Prabhat Studios in Pune. There he met GD and Dev Anand and the three young men became firm friends. Rehman's first acting role was in *Hum ek hain* (1946), in which he played the Muslim character and Dev Anand played the Hindu. Rehman was a popular actor whose career started in the 1940s. In GD's movies, he usually played the second lead and his refined and suave performance added great dignity to those roles. Rehman's soft-toned voice, and first-rate dialogue delivery in Urdu is unrivalled. He is exceptional as the cynical Ghosh, adding the right measure of irony and scorn. At the end of his career, Rehman was said to have fallen on hard times. He died of cancer on 6 November 1979.

31. The second flashback shows the outcome of the Vijay and Meena romance. Vijay is unaware that Meena wants to tell him she is about to marry another man. He is lost in the music that drifts from the nearby dance floor where some young couples dance a waltz. The melody sets off his imagination. Vijay sees Meena descend a grand staircase dressed in an elegant European dress. Her forehead is adorned with twinkling stars, and the moon shines brightly on the horizon.

This is the only lavish set in *Pyaasa* and aptly establishes the atmosphere for the romantic duet "Hum aap ki aankhon mein." Engulfed by wisps of mist, the backdrop creates a romantic mood, sharply contrasted by the dismissal and rejection of love expressed in Meena's song words. At the end of the duet, Vijay longingly watches Meena as she disappears into the fantasy space from where she came. The melody turns melancholic and Vijay wakes from his reverie. He turns to see a letter on the bench where Meena sat. When Vijay reads the letter, we can guess by his expression that Meena has left him. The scene ends with the background music turning discordant. Their relationship has literally ended on a sour note.

Set designer Biren Naug (spelt as Naag in the film's credits) perfectly contrasts the realistic sets and locations of *Pyaasa* with this otherworldly place. It is likely that the duet's inspiration came from the gifted set designer M.R. Achrekar's dream sequence in *Awaara* (1951), directed by Raj Kapoor. In that exquisite film, the three-part dream represents transformation for the hero — he turns away from a life of crime. By having Vijay drift from waking state to active fantasy, GD departs from the typical Hindi film dream sequence in which we see the hero fall asleep, followed by the unfolding of a dream. It is clear that GD had great admiration for M.R. Achrekar and it was he who designed the sets in *Kaagaz ke Phool* (1959), *Chaudhvin ka Chand* (1960), and *Sahib Bibi aur Ghulam* (1962).

Reel 6 (pp. 74–88)

32. The use of the lift as setting for this scene is ingenious. Standing in a corner of the lift, Meena and Vijay are trapped in a capsule of time and space, not unlike the very nature of their relationship. GD creates the illusion that they are alone, cut off from reality. Vijay looks at Meena's reflection on the lift's glass panel and her smiling face takes us to the past through a flashback leading to the duet "Hum aap ki aankhon mein."

When the flashback ends they speak to one another, full of emotion. The camera pulls back to reveal they are not alone. The lift fills with people. Vijay steps out as Meena says: "I completely forgot. I was going up." This line subtly suggests she had abandoned Vijay for upward social mobility. The metal gates close violently on her as she stands behind what now look like the bars of a self-made prison.

Mala Sinha once described working on *Pyaasa* to Dinesh Raheja: "I was in awe of Guru Dutt. If he asked me to report on the sets at nine, I would be there with full make-up on at six! But he was never overbearing, in fact he gave me full freedom to enact my scenes. The most challenging scene in the film was the unspoken-conflict lift scene where Guru Dutt and I come face-to-face for the first time since I ditched him for the rich man not realising that he is there seeking the help of my publisher husband. Guru Dutt's only instruction to me was to feel the emotions — which I did." (Raheja, "Trip down memory lane," *Screen Weekly*, 13 March 2007.)

33. There is fabulous consistency in the characterisation of Meena. Even though years have passed, she is still the same dishonest kind of person. Here again, she does not admit to Vijay that she is now publisher Ghosh's wife.

Reel 7 (pp. 90–100)

34. The unnamed poet in this scene (wearing a waistcoat) is modelled on the famous Urdu poet Asrarul Haq Majaaz. The recited couplet features in Majaaz's collection of poems *Aahang*. Javed Akhtar's maternal uncle, Majaaz was a famous poet and PWA member. He was also a close friend of Sahir's.

The grand old man of poetry seen here recites a couplet by Jigar Muradabadi from his poetry collection *Aatish-e-Gul*. (Research by Suhail Akhtar, October 2010.)

35. It was the usual practice in the 1950s to have the same playback singer sing all the songs of a film hero in a given film. But S.D. Burman decided that Hemant Kumar would sing "Jaane vo kaise" instead of Mohammed Rafi who sang Vijay's other songs. Hemant Kumar's voice is so perfectly suited to the song, adding irony and pathos to its melancholic mood.

An active member of IPTA, Hemant Kumar was celebrated for his interpretation of Rabindra Sangeet (Rabindranath Tagore's songs). He collaborated with Salil Choudhury on many popular Bengali non-film songs. His first Hindi hit was the memorable "Ye raat ye chaandni phir kahaan," composed by S.D. Burman and written by Sahir for GD's *Jaal* (1952). Hemant Kumar was not only an outstanding singer but also composed great music for Bengali and Hindi films, including the award-winning *Nagin* (1954) and *Sahib Bibi aur Ghulam* (1962). He died on 26 September 1989 in Calcutta.

36. S. Guruswamy's description of the way GD approached this scene is very telling of his obsessive desire to get things right: "We were shooting this scene in Kardar Studios in Bombay. It was a lengthy dialogue scene between Guru Dutt and Mala Sinha that takes place in Ghosh's office. It was a very difficult scene and Guru Dutt wanted to do large portions of the dialogue in an extended shot. He kept at it till take number 78 and then said: 'It's not working. Pack up.' The next morning we went back on set. The first take was okayed. That's how he used to work." (Guruswamy, interview by NMK, 21 October 1986.)

Another excellent example of GD's staging is having the argument between Ghosh and Meena take place behind closed doors. Visually GD stresses the fact that the love affair between Meena and Vijay remains hidden. At no point does Meena, in this scene or elsewhere, confess to Ghosh she was ever involved with Vijay. If Meena had told her husband, his actions towards Vijay could have been interpreted as acts of revenge. Meena's silence keeps the clichéd avenging husband out of the story. Doubt rather than certainty ignites Ghosh's hostility and jealousy towards the poet.

Reel 8 (pp. 102–8)

37. Vijay's intuitive compassion for the plight of others is most obvious in this scene. He saves Gulaab by telling the constable she is his wife. The young prostitute is taken aback that a man whom she regards so highly could ignore their social differences and speak of her as a wife. This exchange is a prelude to the next scene in which a *bhakti geet* (devotional song) speaks of the love between Radha and Krishna.

38. The narrative shifts from Vijay's to Gulaab's point of view and the song "Aaj sajan mohe ang laga lo" works like voice-over. The first lines suggest that Gulaab's desires need no longer be contained and she can now declare her love for him:

> *Birha ke dukhre seh-seh kar jab Radhe besudh ho li*
> *Toh ik din apne manmohan se jaa kar yun boli*
> *Aaj sajan mohe ang laga lo janam safal ho jaaye*

> Enduring the torment of a long absence, Radha was weary
> So one day she went to her enchanting Krishna and said:
> Today, beloved, hold me in Your arms, my life will be fulfilled.

Still uncertain that she has a right to his love, Gulaab says nothing to Vijay and rushes away at the end of the song.

An additional verse, featured in the original 1957 film booklet (appearing as a second verse), might never have been filmed or deleted during the edit. The missing lines are:

Kiye laakh jatan morey mann ki tapan
Morey tann ki jalan nahin jaaye
Kaisi laagi ye lagan kaisi jaagi ye agan
Jiya dheer dharan nahin paaye...prem sudha morey saanwariya...

I have tried countless times but the flames in my heart...
The flames in my heart could never be put out
What is this obsession? What is this fire?
My heart can find no peace. The nectar of love, beloved...

As noted, again GD crucially uses the staircase for this important encounter between Vijay and Gulaab. The stairs symbolically lead to and away from the social worlds to which they belong and represent a yearning for a higher spiritual plane. V.K. Murthy's mood lighting and Geeta Dutt's sublime singing add to this scene.

39. Many have commented on this devotional song, including Meenakshi Mukherjee who observed: "It is performed on screen by a Bengali Vaishnavi in *kirtan* style perhaps because the eroticism of the lyric could be permissible only in the context of Radha's love for Krishna." (Mukherjee, "*Pyaasa* in the new Millennium," undated article.)

Iqbal Masud also perceptively wrote: "A brilliant substitute [for eroticism] is the sequence where Waheeda climbs the staircase to meet Guru Dutt and her physical longing is magnificently orchestrated in the *bhakti geet* — 'Aaj sajan mohe ang lago lo.' The camera cuts brilliantly between the staircase and the *bhakti* singers to sublimate the eroticism. The flute, the spare music, the words evoke very precisely the religious-erotic ecstasy. I think that sequence is unmatched in our cinema." (Masud, "The Legend of Guru Dutt," *The Illustrated Weekly of India*, 27 November 1983.)

Following the publication of Masud's article, a telling comment by Fahmida Riaz from Delhi in a letter to the Editor is a reminder that even in the mid-1980s, the reappraisal of GD's work had not yet fully taken place. Riaz writes: "The piece on Guru Dutt was a pleasant surprise. Any writer of a lesser stature would have squirmed at the idea of taking up an artist not 'officially' highbrow." (Letters to the Editor, *The Illustrated Weekly of India*, 12 February 1984.)

Reel 9 (pp. 108–12)

40. GD's introverted personality finds its most stirring expression in the film's wordless scenes. He creates deeply emotional moments without resorting to the usual verbosity associated with much of Hindi cinema. The expression in his eyes, particularly in close-up, has an arresting and soft quality — this is also said of James Dean whose expressive eyes do not reveal the fact he was near-sighted. Guru Dutt was also near-sighted and off-screen always wore thick glasses.

In an interview, GD explained where he had gone wrong in the financial disaster that was *Kaagaz ke Phool*: "It was good in patches. It was too slow and it went over the heads of audiences. *Pyaasa* was thematically the most satisfying." The journalist interviewing GD insightfully added: "Never impolite, Guru could chill a tentative move to friendship with monosyllabic responses or absent-minded nods. Exchange of words to him apparently is no light matter — they are an act of commitment. But once he thaws, he can be very friendly. When warming up to any subject, he talks in a soft, low voice, looking at the world through spectacled eyes, introspective and mildly quizzical, smoking almost continuously and occasionally helping himself to chew out of a little silver *paan-daan* [betel leaf box]. He can joke at himself, 'I was bad at mathematics. I still am.'" (Unidentified author and article, *Filmfare, c.* 1962.)

Raj Khosla also remarked on GD's introverted personality and said: "The closer I tried to get to him, the further he shrank. And since I was his assistant, I decided to keep my distance. He didn't like that either. If I suffixed his name with a 'ji,' it annoyed him because he wanted to be loved more than respected...he was a very ambitious man...he aspired to make a great film, a different film and he wanted to be the best filmmaker. He always wanted things in absolute terms. Be it acclaim or success. He would settle for nothing less." (Khosla, "Memories" as told to Sushama Shelly, *Filmfare*, 16–31 December 1987.)

Reel 10 (pp. 114–24)

41. The death of Vijay's mother is a great blow to him. It severs his ties with his family and sense of belonging. In an audio flashback, her words

return to remind him of his failure in saving her from her bleak life. Losing his job, all hope of recognition and the absence of his mother's nurturing love triggers a chain of events that leads to Vijay heading off to the railway tracks contemplating suicide. His silhouetted figure walking away from the river where his mother's last rites have been performed starts a descent into a dark emotional tunnel.

Girish Karnad once described Guru Dutt as the "Hamlet of Indian Cinema." Celebrated theatre actress Alaknanda Samarth also believes there is a lot of Hamlet in GD: "Whether we realise it or not, Hamlet has affected the world imaginary. Not only artists but subliminally everyone has been affected, such is the power of the 'new self' Shakespeare gave birth to. The most deeply moral debate on suicide is of course the soliloquy 'To be or not to be' (Act III, Scene I, Line 56). This to me is very much in Guru Dutt's psychic universe. Another soliloquy says: 'How weary, stale, flat, and unprofitable seem to me all the uses of this world.' *Hamlet* is Shakespeare's investigation of theatre itself — the phony, corrupt styles of acting, the declaiming, which Hamlet deplores. He urges that theatre be radicalised, made less melodramatic. Does this not resonate with Guru Dutt's anger at the world, especially as expressed through Sahir's poetry?" (Samarth, interview by NMK, October 2010.)

42. This poem was written especially for the film. In despair, Vijay takes to drink. But even in his drunken state, he cannot ignore the desperate situation of Bijli, the dancer who is forced to entertain her male clients and continue dancing though her ailing child cries for her attention. By the end of the scene, Vijay's eyes fill with tears as he sees Bijli's grim life.

GD is expert at enhancing the impact of a song by making the preceding scene emotionally strong. We see Bijli's story made universal in "Jinhen naaz hai Hind par," and in that song/poem we see the universal story of all exploited women. GD's eldest son, Tarun Dutt, once said: "To miss a song in my father's film is to miss a scene." (Dutt, interview by NMK, 1985.)

43. Commenting on "Jinhen naaz hai Hind par," in his article "Songs of Injustice," Carlo Coppola wrote: "It is specifically in this use of political and social comment, then, that Sahir adds further substance to his film songs, which already display a superb lyricism and vitality of imagery. For Sahir, the film song is something more than a mere vehicle with which to embellish a love scene. It is for him a medium through which to call — with subtlety and discretion — the attention of tens of millions who will view the film, to the wrongs and injustices which society has inflicted on its members." (Coppola, *Cinema Vision, The Golden Age of Hindi Film Music*, Vol. 2, No. II, Edited by Siddharth Kak and Rani Burra, 1983.)

Marvellously photographed in *film noir* style, the song has virtually no musical accompaniment and reproduces the mood of a poetry recital. By inserting humming into the first line, the poem is presented as though the poet were composing it extempore.

> Ye kooche ye...ghar dilkashi ke
> These lanes...(hums)...these houses of pleasure.

The original poem "Chakle" (Brothels) on which this song is based has ten stanzas (the film only uses eight of these with some minor word changes) and was published in Sahir's collection of poems *Talkhiyaan* (1943). The missing stanzas are:

Fifth stanza
Ye goonje huwe qehqahe raaston par
Ye chaaron taraf bheed si khidkiyon par
Ye aawaaze khinchte huwe aanchalon par
Sana khwaan-e-taqdees-e-mashriq kahaan hain

This laughter echoing on streets
This crowd gathered under windows
These crude remarks hurled at veiled bodies
Where are they who sing praise of the East?

Seventh stanza
Ye bhooki nigaahen haseenon ki jaanib
Ye badhte huwe haath seenon ki jaanib
Lapakte huwe paaon zeenon ki jaanib
Sana khwaan-e-taqdees-e-mashriq kahaan hain

These eyes lusting after beauties
These hands groping breasts
These bounding feet climbing stairs
Where are they who sing praise of the East?

Sahir changed the first line "Sana khwaan-e-taqdees-e-mashriq kahaan hain" to "Jinhen naaz hai Hind par vo kahaan hain" in order to simplify the Persianised language of the original and so not alienate audiences.

Mohammed Rafi's excellent singing in *Pyaasa* won him his first National Award.

Reel 11 (pp. 124–30)

44. Vijay's questions show GD's deep fears that the value of an artist is judged only by commercial success. The dialogue suggests GD's doubts whether he will be recognised for his work in cinema. This idea seemed to plague him and in an article titled "Cash and Classics," strongly identifying with past writers, poets and artists whose work had limited recognition in their lifetime, he wrote: "Coming to recent times, unbearable frustration curtailed the life of Miss Amrita Sher-Gil, one of India's greatest artists, at the age of 29, in 1944 [she actually died in 1941]. Shortly before her untimely death she wrote: 'I am starving for appreciation. I am literally famished. My work is understood less and less as time passes.' Indeed posthumous acclaim has been the tragic fate of many creators of classics." (Guru Dutt, *Celluloid*, 1963.)

Starting with *Pyaasa*, made when he was thirty-two, the themes in GD's later films point to a growing disenchantment with life that might have contributed to his committing suicide seven years later. Recalling his own words, posthumous acclaim has also been GD's tragic fate.

Paradoxically, GD's fears, expressed in his article "Cash and Classics" seems unfounded. During his lifetime, his peers, audiences and many film critics showed great appreciation for his work. With the exception of *Kaagaz ke Phool*, his films were largely successful at the box-office, yet his success was perceived by him as failure. GD's complex mind and "disturbances," as described once by his sister Lalitha Lajmi, never allowed the admiration to make much of a difference. A perfectionist by nature, GD was easily disillusioned. Like Vijay of *Pyaasa*, he sought the impossible in wanting what he could not attain.

45. It is important to note that Vijay, intending to kill himself, walks away at the last minute from the railway tracks. This may suggest that GD at that point in his life did not entirely believe in suicide, except possibly as a later option.

Reel 12 (pp. 132–46)

46. In his excellent essay, French film critic Henri Micciollo commented on how surprised he was to find repeated Christian imagery in *Pyaasa*. (Micciollo, "Guru Dutt," *Anthologie du Cinéma, L'Avant-Scène*, Tome IX, Paris, 1976.) Reminiscent of the breakfast setting in Orson Welles' *Magnificent Ambersons*, this scene has the most obvious reference to Christ. Still concealing her true feelings about Vijay from her husband, and, on hearing Vijay has committed suicide, Meena pretends to read an issue of *Life* with the cover image of Christ on the Cross. She hides her face with the magazine to conceal her emotions from her probing husband, but more importantly, by using the image of Christ to coincide with the announcement of Vijay's death, GD suggests the idea of ultimate sacrifice and martyrdom.

GD was said to have been interested in all religions, including Christianity, and though many might assume that the magazine was a fabricated prop for this scene, in reality it is a genuine issue unearthed thanks to the intelligently organised *Life* Magazine Archives on the Net. The *Life* that Meena reads was not a regular issue but a "Special Issue on Christianity," costing 35 cents and dated 26 December 1955, and was most likely to have been GD's personal copy.

It may not be preposterous to imagine that GD saw the magazine some months before the start of *Pyaasa*'s filming (April/May 1956), and it gave him the idea of alluding to Christ in *Pyaasa*. These allusions do not feature in his original story "Kash-ma-kash." By using the image of Christ's crucifixion when Vijay's death is announced, GD draws parallels. However Vijay's assumed suicide is a personal act of redemption — not a sacrifice of his life in the name of all humanity.

In an audience held on 26 October 1988 titled "The Redemptive Value of Christ's Sacrifice," Pope John Paul II sheds light on the larger meaning of Christ's sacrifice: "It meant that He gave His life 'in the name of' and in substitution for all humanity, to free all from sin. This substitution excludes any participation whatsoever in sin on the part of the Redeemer. He was absolutely innocent and holy... precisely because 'He committed no sin' (I Peter, 2:22), He could take upon Himself that which is the effect of sin, namely, suffering and death, giving to the sacrifice of His life a real value and a perfect redemptive meaning."

Audiences and film critics have noted GD's references to Christ in the film. He stands Christ-like in both songs "Jaane vo kaise" and more noticeably in "Ye duniya agar mil bhi jaaye." The words of this song correspond in essence to Christ's question: "For what shall it profit a man, if he shall gain the whole world and lose his own soul?" (*The Gospel According to Mark*, 8:36). And finally as noted, the image of Christ is again evoked in the library scene at the end of the film and shows Vijay lit in a circle of light (halo-like) as he tells Meena that he has no reason to complain against anyone, but squarely blames society for lacking compassion. The world as he sees it is not a place for him. He will seek peace and redeem his soul by distancing himself from it. Here all allusions to Christ end. Vijay's departure from the world is a purely personal decision and is neither one of sacrifice nor martyrdom.

47.   In the quiet privacy of her room, Gulaab tentatively applies *sindoor* (vermilion, a mark of marriage) to her forehead. This scene is underscored by a wedding *shehnai*. She has in spirit married the poet. Sattar, who brings news of Vijay's death, breaks this secret union. The parallels between Gulaab and Chandramukhi of *Devdas* are most evident here. Both women, once prostitutes and available to all men, decide to devote their lives to one man who is out of their reach. They are seen to sacrifice the material world in pursuit of unattainable love.

The prostitute with the golden heart is an adored character of Hindi cinema. Some months after *Pyaasa*'s release, the well-known director Satyen Bose shared his take on why Chandramukhi (of *Devdas*) and Gulaab have enduring appeal: "In both films the hero undergoes a self-imposed suffering because he is unsuccessful in love. Another important feature of these two pictures is the selfless love and solace the hero gets from another woman who sacrifices everything for him. This serves to relieve the tragic gloom with the bright flame of human sympathy and devotion. The filmgoer who identifies with the hero, and every filmgoer does, feels that in such cases he too will get such comfort and solace. (Bose, "What is the magic formula for box-office success?" *Filmfare*, 21 June 1957.)

48.   Written on the file that Gulaab carries in her hand is the word "Parchhaiyaan" (Shadows). The title instantly recalls, for a perceptive audience, Sahir's famous anti-war poem. GD introduces hence an element of the real into the fictive life of his character.

49.   Gulaab starts by telling Meena that she has come from "Sona..." but then changes her mind mid-sentence and says: "Dharamtala." She is trying to conceal from Meena that she is from Sonagachi, the red-light district. Meena however guesses that Gulaab is a prostitute.

Sonagachi (translated as the Golden Tree) is Calcutta's main red-light district — now said to be one of Asia's largest. It has allegedly over ten thousand sex workers who live and work in several hundred multi-storey brothels set in innumerable narrow lanes. His son, Arun Dutt, remembers being told that his father tried to film "Jinhen naaz hai Hind par" on location, but it became impossible to control the crowd. Set designer Biren Naug then photographed the area and used these photographs as reference for the building of the song's set.

Dharamtala is the neighbourhood where GD spent much of his youth at his uncle B.B. Benegal's home. Dharamtala Street has been renamed Lenin Sarani and that is where B.B. Benegal lived till he passed away on 25 January 1987.

At the end of this moving scene, Gulaab gives Ghosh all her worldly possessions, consisting of some jewellery and trinkets, to have Vijay's poetry published. S. Guruswamy recalled that Gulaab's gesture of sacrifice was added during the shoot: "When Gulaab gives Ghosh her jewellery — it was a new addition to the scene. It wasn't originally thought of and gave a new dimension to her character. It is finally Gulaab who makes the publishing of Vijay's work possible." (Guruswamy, interview by NMK, 21 October 1986.)

50.   A popular narrative twist in Hindi films comes from the hero losing his memory. It is unclear whether Vijay has in fact lost his memory or whether he is suffering from shock at the trauma of witnessing the death of the aged beggar.

Reel 13 (pp. 148–58)

51. In this scene, GD makes a second direct reference to Sahir. The verses read by the nurse (unidentified voice) are extracts from Sahir's long anti-war poem titled *Parchhaiyaan*. The verses used in the film are taken from the poem's middle section. Faiz Ahmed Faiz's "Mujh se pehli si mohabbat mere mehboob na maang" (Do not ask for the love I once gave you, my beloved) was said to have influenced Sahir's original poem.

Describing this work, Sahir once said: "*Parchhaiyan* is my first long poem and is inspired by the current international peace movement. I believe that every new generation, inheriting the world from its elders, should make it a better and more beautiful place for future generations. This poem is a literary attempt to propagate peace."

52. GD's depiction of a mental asylum is not subtle and has all the clichés of Hindi cinema, which usually portrays mentally ill patients in a grossly exaggerated and uninformed way. In *Pyaasa*, GD too sees the mental asylum as a living hell.

On the night before GD died (10 October 1964), Abrar Alvi, who was working on the dialogue of *Baharen Phir Bhi Aayengi*, recalled the conversation they had: "Guru Dutt had started drinking very early that evening. I was busy writing. He sat down and talked of many things, some crazy things too. He talked of a friend who was in an asylum and who had written to him. Guru Dutt said: 'You can't tell by reading his letter that he is crazy. Sometimes I think I'll go insane.' I said: 'What are you saying, why would you go mad?' He was very, very disturbed. I was with him until I a.m. He didn't open up. And if I had known he was going to do that mad thing, I would never have left him. He sat with me at the dining table, but didn't eat. Finally he said: 'Abrar, if you don't mind, I'd like to retire.'" (Kabir, *op. cit.*, 2005, pp. 201–2.)

53. The last straw for Vijay is when Ghosh and Shyam disown him. This scene alludes to the Denial of Christ, an allusion reinforced by the underscoring of a church organ. In utter anguish, Vijay cries out Shyam's name. But Shyam is unmoved. The stunned expression on Vijay's face suggests a deeper realisation. No one will save him in a world without compassion and hope. If he is to be saved, he must save himself.

When Vijay finally escapes from the asylum, with the help of Abdul Sattar, and discovers that his blood brothers also disown him,

his demeanour undergoes a profound change. From this point on, Vijay slowly withdraws into himself and barely speaks. He no longer yearns for acceptance from the outside, having understood the world for what it is. Vijay words come from an inner truth when he tells his admirers in the crowded auditorium:

> "Jis Vijay ko aaj aap haathon-haath lene ke liye tayyaar hain… jis Vijay ke naam pe aap zindaabaad ke naare laga rahe hain…main vo Vijay nahin hoon."
>
> The Vijay you are ready to open your arms to…the Vijay for whom you shout slogans…I am not that Vijay.

Indeed in spirit he is no longer that Vijay. The transformation that began in the mental asylum also takes an outer physical form. His crumpled jacket and worn trousers have been shed like old skin. The look of a homeless drifter now finds a spiritual home/identity in traditional clothes. Only once before his transformation did we see him in non-Western attire — at Ghosh's party when he tries to mingle with other poets. Since his escape from the mental asylum, Vijay consistently wears traditional Indian clothes: a *kurta*, *dhoti* and shawl. His transformation is complete. He may reject the world but in a sense he has found himself.

Reel 14 (pp. 160–72)

54. This most uplifting scene moves from comedy to valiant action. Sattar proves that he is the fearless hero of the film. Here he saves Vijay through song and guile, and later in the auditorium, fights the lynching mob to rescue his friend again.

55. GD's dark view of human behaviour never lets up. He shows how blatantly people lie for self-aggrandisement. Posthumous fame is fame nevertheless. The dishonest are even freer now, since the artist has died, to claim credit for his life and talent, and to grab a share of the artist's belated acclaim.

56. The gifted Urdu poet and lyricist Majrooh Sultanpuri insightfully analysed how GD brought about a song in the story: "Guru Dutt looked for two things in a song: the lyrics of a song should not have any opening music, and secondly, the song must not be dull. If a song has

a long introductory tune that leads to the first line, the audience think to themselves: 'Let's sit back, here comes a song.' But Guru Dutt would cut straight from dialogue to the first line of the song. In this way, he made the song work as a direct extension of dialogue." (Kabir, *op.cit.*, 2005, pp. 84–5.) Using the same technique, Ghosh's speech leads to the song:

"Kaash aaj Vijay marhoom zinda hote toh vo dekh lete ki jis samaaj ne unhen bhooka maara, aaj wahi samaaj unhen heere aur jawaahraat mein tolne ke liye tayyaar hai. Jis duniya mein vo gumnaam rahe, aaj wahi duniya unhen apne dilon ke takht pe bithaana chaahti hai. Unhen shohrat ka taaj pehnaana chaahti hai. Unhen ghareebi aur muflisi ki galiyon se nikaal kar mehlon mein raaj dilaana chaahti hai."

If only Vijay were alive today, he would see the world that let him starve is now ready to weigh him in gold and silver. The world in which he was unknown is ready to crown him the king of their hearts, crown him with glory. Rescue him from the clutches of poverty and give him a kingdom that he would rule.

A brief moment of silence follows Ghosh's phony declarations. Vijay is barely visible in the half-lit doorway of the auditorium. From afar, a few strains of music are heard; Rafi's unmatched voice is soft yet firm. In close-up, Vijay, quiet and solemn, stands as the music rises and spreads his arms like Christ on the Cross. Vijay has won the world only to spurn it.

Ye mehlon, ye takhton, ye taajon ki duniya
Ye insaan ke dushman samaajon ki duniya
Ye daulat ke bhooke rivaajon ki duniya
Ye duniya agar mil bhi jaaye toh kya hai

This world of palaces, of thrones, of crowns
This world of divisions, enemy of man
This world of blind custom, hungry for wealth
Would I care if such a world were mine?

Reel 15 (pp. 172–86)

57. Unlike the repeated allusions in Indian cinema to Hindu mythology, this is the first and only mention of a character from the Ramayana when Shyam suggests that even if Ghosh were as powerful as the ten-headed demon (Ravana), he could not stop Vijay from returning to life — a resurrection of sorts.

58. The suspicion that public adoration is fickle is borne out in the lives of Vijay in *Pyaasa* and Suresh Sinha in *Kaagaz ke Phool*. Both films show how easily gushing admirers can change into a violent mob. GD never seemed to trust how his work would be received. Like many gifted but insecure artists, he wanted success and expected failure. "The première show was on in the cinema hall. We were pacing up and down outside. When the film was over, all the greats of Indian cinema came out. Everyone had a different opinion of the film. Some said: 'Guru Dutt's acting was good,' while others said the dialogue was good. The only person who said *Pyaasa* would work was Ismat Chugtai, Shahid Lateef's wife. She said: 'Guru, it's going to click.' It was a writer who predicted its great success." (Guruswamy, interview by NMK, 21 October 1986.)

Reel 16 (pp. 186–92)

59. As noted, allusions to Christ resurface in this scene, enhanced by organ music. Vijay enters the room, his head is encircled by light. His words are essentially a reworking of "Ye duniya agar mil bhi jaaye" (Would I care if such a world were mine?), but do not have the song's rage and frustration. Though Vijay decries the cruelty of the world, he insists that society, and not individuals, is to blame. He has repeated the same idea ("I have no reason to complain against anyone") in earlier scenes to both Gulaab and Meena. Vijay now seeks peace of mind. The last shot (a top shot) shows Vijay leaving, as the room fills with papers floating in the air like autumn leaves.

According to GD's brother, Devi Dutt, who worked on *Pyaasa*, this scene was intended to be the film's ending. But later GD added a further sequence in which Vijay comes to take Gulaab away with him. This was added because film distributors felt the original was too heavy and for the movie to succeed a "happier" ending was needed.

The fact GD relented shows that he wanted to appeal to audiences and was not averse to listening to the advice of others.

60. Another striking example of GD's visual mastery. The wind blows through Gulaab's room, making the windows rattle and so wake her. She is lying in bed, having been injured in the auditorium stampede. She sits up, knowing that Vijay is calling her. She rushes out of her room and runs down the stairs. She smiles as she sees Vijay standing at her door. Her face is sublimely serene. Gulaab's life has at last been fulfilled as he asks her to come away with him. The instrumental version of "Aaj sajan mohe ang laga lo janam safal ho jaaye" (Today, beloved, hold me in Your arms, my life will be fulfilled) appropriately underscores the scene.

Pyaasa is among the few, if not the only Hindi film, in which we see the hero making a new life with a prostitute. Typically the hero or the prostitute dies so they can never be together. It is also unclear whether Gulaab is a Muslim, as many Hindu prostitutes were known to take Muslim names. If Gulaab was intended to be a Muslim, then GD makes nothing of the union between a Hindu and a Muslim unlike other films in which this becomes the central drama.

The marvellous poet/lyricist Kaifi Azmi speaking on GD's deeply secular views, once remarked: "He often said of himself: 'I am not a single entity from head to toe. I am part Muslim, part Christian and part Hindu. I wear a *sherwaani*. And I think in one language and speak in another. Ours is a composite culture.' This thinking was integrated in him and he would preach that in his films. The connection with what was going on in the country during the 1950s and Guru Dutt's films was manifest in broad terms." (Azmi, interview by NMK, 1986.)

61. Abrar Alvi recalled how upset he was with *Pyaasa*'s ending: "I believed that Vijay should not leave, that he should stay and fight the system. I told him: 'Wherever Vijay goes, he will find the same society, the same values, the same system.' But I was overruled by Guru Dutt.

So I wrote the scene in which Vijay comes to Gulaab and tells her to come with him to a place from where he will not need to go further. I asked Guru Dutt: 'Where does such a place exist in this world?' But he put his foot down saying: 'I like it. It's sunset, they walk away into the distance, hand in hand. It will be emotionally satisfying to the audience.'" (Kabir, *op.cit.*, 2005, p. 136.)

In *Pyaasa*, Vijay's renunciation of the world shows GD's unconscious desire to walk away from life. His achievements and the possibility of creating still better films did not alleviate his deep anxieties. Perhaps his death can be understood through Sahir's words:

Tang aa chuke hain kash-ma-kash-e-zindagi se hum
Thukra na den jahaan ko kahin bedili se hum

I am weary of the struggles of life
The weariness of my heart may spurn the world.

There is much more that can, and will, be documented on Guru Dutt's life and work. The tragedy of his early death has undoubtedly augmented his mystique and reputation as a gifted filmmaker. Although the internal demons that often engulfed him were to lead to his suicide, his works have immortalised him. *Pyaasa*, so central to Guru Dutt's legacy, has at last found its place among the classics of world cinema.

— *Commentary edited by Shameem Kabir and Dipa Chaudhuri*

Bibliography

Banerjee, Shampa, "Guru Dutt," *Profiles: Five Filmmakers from India*, Festival of India, 1985–86.

Chatterjee, Partha, "Remembering Guru Dutt," *Cinemaya* 13, 1991.

Cooper, Darius, *In Black and White: Hollywood and the Melodrama of Guru Dutt*, Seagull Books, Calcutta, 2005.

Coppola, Carlo, "The Legendary Ludhianvi," *Cinema Vision, The Golden Age of Hindi Film Music*, Vol. 2, No. 11, Edited by Siddharth Kak and Rani Burra, 1983.)

Creekmur, Corey, "Pyaasa/Thirst," *The Cinema of India* (ed. Lalitha Gopalan), Wallflower Press, London, 2009.

Doraiswamy, Rashmi, *Guru Dutt: The Legends of Indian Cinema*, Wisdom Tree, New Delhi, 2008.

Filmfare, Special Issue on Guru Dutt, *"Khuda, Maut aur Ghulam"* (God, Death and Servant), 30 October 1964.

Hasan, Saif Hyder, *One Yesterday*, Rupa and Co, New Delhi, 2004.

Kabir, Nasreen Munni, *Guru Dutt: A Life in Cinema*, Oxford University Press, New Delhi, 1996, new edition 2005.

——— (presented by), *Yours Guru Dutt: Intimate Letters of a Great Indian Filmmaker*, Lustre Press/Roli Books, New Delhi, 2008.

———, *Hindi cinema ka ek kavi* [Hindi translation], Prabhat Prakashan, 2010.

Khopkar, Arun, *Guru Dutt: Teen Anki Shokantika* [Marathi], Granthali, Mumbai, 1985.

Levich, Jacob, "Shooting Star," *Film Comment*, September–October 2009.

Masud, Iqbal, "The Legend of Guru Dutt," *The Illustrated Weekly of India*, 27 November – 3 December 1983.

Micciollo, Henri, "Guru Dutt" [French], *Anthologie du Cinéma, L'Avant-Scène*, Tome IX, Paris, 1976.

Mir, Raza & Mir, Ali Husain, *Anthems of Resistance: A Celebration of Progressive Urdu Poetry*, India Ink/Roli Books, New Delhi, 2006.

Mujawar, Isak, *Guru Dutt: Ek Asanta Kalabanta* [Marathi], Srividya Prakasana, Pune, 1985.

Padukone, Vasanthi, "My Son Guru Dutt," *Imprint*, April 1979.

Pithodiya, Jayant, *Guru Dutt ki Parchhaiyan* [Gujarati and Hindi], Pithodiya Jayant, 2000

Rangoonwalla, Firoze, *Guru Dutt 1925–1965: A Monograph*, National Film Archive of India, Poona, 1973.

Saran, Sathya, *Ten Years with Guru Dutt: Abrar Alvi's Journey*, Penguin Books India, New Delhi, 2008.

Screen, Special Issue on Guru Dutt, 13 October 1989.